Frances Fyfield is ~~~~~~~~~~~~~ used to huge success in many of her novels. She lives in London and in Deal, by the sea which is her passion. She has won several awards, including the CWA/Duncan Lawrie Gold Dagger and the CWA Silver Dagger.

FRANCES FYFIELD OMNIBUS

Half Light

Let's Dance

Frances Fyfield

sphere

SPHERE

This omnibus edition first published in Great Britain in 2009 by Sphere

Previously published separately:
Half Light first published in Great Britain in 1992 by Hamish Hamilton
Paperback edition published by Time Warner Paperbacks in 2005
Reprinted by Sphere in 2007
Copyright © Frances Hegarty 1992
Let's Dance first published in Great Britain in 1995 by Viking
Paperback edition published by Sphere in 2006
Copyright © Frances Fyfield 1995

A CIP catalogue record for this book
is available from the British Library.

ISBN 978-0-7515-4152-6

Printed and bound in Great Britain by
Clays Ltd, St Ives plc

Sphere
An imprint of
Little, Brown Book Group
100 Victoria Embankment
London EC4Y 0DY

An Hachette UK Company
www.hachette.co.uk

www.littlebrown.co.uk

Half Light

To Barbie Boxhall, a friend indeed

CHAPTER ONE

Running up the hill to the station, late for the afternoon train, late for life, she had seen an old man with a stick walking ahead and had stopped to avoid him. He had been identical to a stranger putting flowers on a grave in the cemetery, and both times the sight filled her with fear and fury, made her wilt, wounded with memory. After that, she had sat too long by the graveside, distracted by the monuments of chipped angels and worn sandstone, the new stones of vibrant white, the flowers and shrubs, new or faded. She was not mourning: she was assuaging a constant sense of guilt and loss, aware that it was not quite the same sensation. Flowers took a long time to die when left in the air. It was the only place for miles where she could see colours.

Her father had dictated this letter, she was sure of it; his vitriol was infectious. She could feel the pink paper crumpled in her pocket, the reminder of the address they never ever put on letters since they moved and the thousand and one recriminations which would have followed if ever she had dared to knock on their door. Father would have come towards her leaning on his stick and, never after all these years meeting her eyes, mumbling accusations until her willpower fell away with her coat. She had satisfied the insatiable appetite of guilt by taking flowers to her mother's grave. Standing there in front of a new, crude white and gold headstone which reminded her of a bathroom fitting, she could feel similar waves of disapproval rising like heat, drowning her own anguish in their blind lack of understanding.

It was the grey, utilitarian mess of the landscape above all, but she no longer knew if this judgement was the selective nature of her own eyes which made it seem so dead. The bus from the graveyard into town took her past some rare fields of glowing yellow stubble, blinding in the light, but she could not take unmitigated pleasure in that. She could look at a field in a state of beauty and know it would change with the same unreliability of people, but a painting of the same thing could make her shout for joy.

After art, nature. Never the other way round. Green fields and wide skies were better in oil paint, more easily controlled, invoked no loneliness. Which could not be said for the station, unmanned after the truculent man selling tickets left at four. A dearth of trains to take her into lovely, filthy, metropolitan anonymity. Empty feelings and empty stations, no sense of belonging. If you do not belong when you are a child, you will never belong.

2

He never touched me, father, only you. I have tried, mother, father, sister, brother, to gain some sort of acceptance, but you haunt me, even in solitude, with all your bitter hopelessness.

Standing alone on the station platform, one line extending each way round a curve, she felt uncomfortably conspicuous, shook herself beneath the dark purple coat, gave way to annoyance to hide creeping alarm. The time of year, she told herself: this time of year, far more unsettling than any mere time of month. The British change their clocks, trick time by an hour, and suddenly afternoon melts into inky black by the time they all go home. In the hour's wait for this train to London, the sky had ceased to comfort. She had been denied her preoccupation of looking up at rain-filled clouds scudding across the sun, the same preoccupation which made her see colour even in shadows: shadows were made of colours.

Feeling the ticket to freedom along with the letter in her pocket, pink-papered, the last accusation of the many which had followed her down the years to confirm her status as an alien, she had watched the sky change. Still inside a welter of confusion because she always forgot to change the clock, and had spent the Sunday before working with no one to remind her, a state of affairs most devoutly to be wished. Days like this were idyllic until that sense of outrage intervened as the precious light suddenly seeped away by late afternoon. The sky altered then into an angel's sky, like the one first seen beyond the roof of this station. Clouds battling with half-hearted sunshine, the one fighting the other into submission, the sun seen as a spotlight fading away, like a lamp removed from behind a muslin curtain. An early darkness, pale, then dramatically black as the gusty rain began to fall. Attempting to conjure shapes and light from the dead foliage in the hanging baskets left for next spring, she found nothing, no solace for the eye: the single bulb burning in the foyer seen across the tracks surrounded by a haze. The rain was uneven, spitting off the roof and slapping the stone of the platform, like a sharp, unexpected punishment.

They were not footsteps. She had not heard footsteps: for a moment, she panicked and turned her face to the wall. The platform north and the platform south were connected by a tunnel, dimly lit and grimly clean, unlike the city to which she was so anxious to return. She fastened her eyes on the aperture which would soon produce a head if the steps were real. Rain disorientated sound. The hazy bulb opposite swung slightly, as if disturbed by another presence and she realized then she was mistaken about the placing of these disembodied feet: man, woman or child passing beneath that bulb towards the tunnel would have registered; she would have seen him or her, even a cat. Silence, a slap of rain, a finger of wind lifting the heavy fabric of her long skirt, teasing the hem which drooped behind. The steps were closer. A shuffling in the alcove of a locked waiting room obscured by one of the pillars supporting the roof she had admired in the last of the sunlight, a figure hidden there or beyond the building, where the ground sloped away and a dustbin lay on one side. The

4

steps (no, they were not steps, please do not be foolish) might have come from behind the door. She thought of her father, lurking. It serves you right, daughter, it serves you right.

She was not brave, merely stoic, concentrated on the hazy light beyond. Fear like this, a sense of danger repeated so often now, was time-consuming, energy-consuming, a creator of anger and other sensations she simply could not afford. Like love and flattery, she thought illogically: all redundant nonsense. You walk towards blind footsteps: you do not ignore them. Or so you do if you know where they are or what they may want, or why they haunt you. No one need harm you; no one hates you; you have cleared all your debts, owe nothing, not even the flowers on your mother's grave. So she did walk, slowly and noisily towards the end of the platform, passed the alcove door of the waiting room, an empty space with 'Out of Order' on the door, paused stupidly, the fear suddenly acute, like a pain ignored, her own steps paralysed. The same fear as yesterday, as last week, an extension of that same dread whenever the door bell rang. Father coming home, her turn now.

What made her falter to a halt, cough bravery for the sake of sound, was that tiny tip of reflected light protruding from the corner of the wall, catching in a pinpoint the hazy bulb which served all humanity on both platforms of a small northern station which had forgotten the imminence of winter. The metal, the reflected thing, silver or gold (she tried to describe the colour even as she gazed), quickly withdrawn, but in that split second, looking like a giant needle pressed into black cloth, hidden. She retreated, again noisily, as far as the empty doorway, pressed herself into it, watched the rain and pretended she had not seen. There was life down there; life and shuffling steps, but life required courage. When she made herself turn to face the infinitesimal sound from that dark hiding place, muffled by the wind and rain, there was no needle, no wicked blade and then, with exquisite relief, she felt the vibrations of the distant train, large, bright, packed, sliding towards the curve beyond the platform with all the efficiency and power of a long, stiff snake.

Trains no longer crash into stations, she realized, a comparative stranger to trains: they creep heavily and expire in reluctant standstill. She moved to the edge as the sound grew louder, watching the rain which glistened on the last six inches of platform uncovered by the roof, clasping her bag with knuckles already white. Three steps, four steps to the door from which no one alighted, her hand extending to touch it wishing for that cold touch of metal which gave entry into a blast of smoky warmth. And then a great black, rustling shape, thrust against her face, flapping round her shoulders, wet, suffocating, filthy. She pushed away frantically as she screamed, hitting out with her bag and one fist as the muffling cloak dragged down her body in curious intimacy, embracing her arms, pressing through the coat, circling her neck, then tugging at the dropping hem, viciously insistent, clutching. She kicked and flailed with her arms, and spat, turned full circle, her mouth full of grit, felt her hand on the door, wrenching it open, staggering inside

6

while the train paused, breathing politely, ignoring such embarrassment. Her skirt hem snagged on the step: she threw the bag first, clutched great swatches of coat and skirt in one hand and leapt after, holding the door in the other hand to slam shut, crash. Turned back to look at the platform, breathing with the engine, go go, go on, move.

As the train drew breath, ready to move, she wanted to laugh, stuck her knuckle into her mouth to preserve that stupid shriek of sound. Dancing across the place where she had stood was a wind-blown, torn, dirty, wet, black piece of plastic, moving like a whirling dervish, taunted by fury. A rubbish sack escaped, doomed to an existence pushed through wind tunnels, driven by trains, made live by winds. Nothing. No footsteps, no life, nothing. She could feel the blood flow back from her feet, wanted to sink where she stood. What a fool. A flushed idiot, dusting herself down busily, avoiding the curious stares of a carriage half full of people travelling from one city to the next, wondering if she dare sit down amongst them, loving the sight of all those faces and rustling newspapers, books, crumbs, dismembered sandwiches which had come with the train so far. All that noise, that glorious, disgusting noise. She moved to join it, embarrassed, a quiet woman who dismissed fantasies. Seating herself, folding her coat around her, she missed the other door clunking shut two carriages down, level with the end of the platform. Someone sat, smiled at the disapproval of passengers, while she sat, ignoring their glances, still with her knuckle in her mouth.

Late. Trains from the North, wherever that was, were often

late, he'd been told, and this was a very bad idea. All the same, Francis was stunned when he saw her, had not expected her to be so predictable, since one of her enduring fascinations was a consistent failure to do what other people did, such as catching the train she had said she would catch. Equally unpredictable was her pleasure, or not, to see him. He had no idea about that: he had come like a pupil with a crush to carry teacher's bag and he knew he was taking the risk of her saying not today, thank you, young man. Which was why he hesitated, did not come forward with his diffident greeting when he saw her striding through the barrier, swinging her big bag to correspond with her long walk and, for all that assurance, that frowning, preoccupied busyness of hers, looking curiously vulnerable. And colourful. A proficient young woman returning from a visit to her family. He tried to recall what she had said about them; he had asked often with only half an ear to the answers which were slow in coming. Oh, they're fine, a bit like all families, I suppose. She never supplied detail and he never pursued the quest since families other than his own were the stuff of boring anecdotes and he did not really want to know. He actually assumed they were all the same, only remembered her describing something which brought to mind a cottage with roses round the door, wind-blown, no doubt to go with the North. It took his breath away under the bright lights of St Pancras to see the array of her: she would approve when he confessed his noticing of that eccentric purple coat, the many-shaded carpet bag, the vibrant shiny black, or was it grey, of her dancer's shoes, so unsuitable for a jaunt into the mud of the country. Damn the country, she had said. They must take my feet as they are: I haven't got any others.

How coy, to stand back, half admiring, half irritated, slightly put off by the very briskness of her he had noticed before. He watched, biding for his moment of risky surprise. Hallo, darling, I thought I'd come and meet you, do you mind, racing off the train like that, was the visit so awful. I thought you were looking forward to it . . . Did you walk through all the carriages just so you could get off first, nearest the barrier? You must have known I was here. While he rehearsed the words and moved forwards, she suddenly began to run. Looking neither left, right nor behind herself, running across the concourse where people waited and examined the departure board against their watches, she shrugged them aside in a headlong rush down the stairs into the Underground, swinging the bag as if it weighed nothing, a sprite in flight so fast and so amazing he watched without moving. He had never visualized her, so consistently serene, so tranquil, so absorbed, to be capable of such swiftness, which somehow lent her the elegance she often lacked. She flowed with her eccentric coat, drooping hems and magnificent hair, her mouth only slightly parted with the effort. There was an athlete in that Junoësque frame, running like a boy.

Francis sighed, tapped his feet, pulled a face, always performing, ready to make himself laugh. This had been meant as a surprise. Perhaps she had seen him out of the corner of one of those great, curious eyes, seen and avoided, but he liked to think not: the running was instinctive, an unknown quantity, like so many of her instincts,

9

but the suspicion remained. What a waste of time, coming all this way to meet a woman like that. What an effort to be so shaken and stirred like a souring cocktail.

Irritation gave way to inertia. He stood where he was and watched the rest of the passengers emerge, while yet more passengers stood round the barrier, impatient for the late train to breathe again. Families, inter-city commuters mainly: the end of light made one forget how early it really was, the ebb tide of the day, neither evening nor afternoon. She had probably forgotten the changing of the clocks. He was beginning, just beginning to wonder why he bothered with the kind of person who forgot clothes and people, lived by the patterns and demands of neither, rooted in an impossibly private world.

Francis watched the last person clear of the barrier. At the time he noticed, with a small, distracted touch of pity, a man limping far behind the straggling queue, carrying a furled umbrella.

Later, he forgot.

CHAPTER TWO

Francis Thurloe knew he had earned the reputation of being a likeable young man. He knew that because he was always popular and had been brought up to honour politeness, to be aware of his privileges and not to abuse his own education of which humility had been part. Entry into any form of society he chose was further massaged by a fine, fair face and a long lean body which somehow suggested competence, a man who was good at playing the game, whatever the team. He was a kind person, he supposed, only slightly lazy and spoiled by the ease of a successful life and the ability to claim immediate attention. A relatively smooth passage made him ignorant of how others lived, but he told himself he was tolerant, gave respect wherever it was due to things he did not understand. He honestly did try to understand, but he was not always aware of his own insensitivities, while his role as a barrister enforced his impression of himself as worldly-wise: he forgot he acquired his knowledge second hand, like his pictures, from beyond a screen, like his ancestors. There were ancestors, after a fashion; a long line of professional men and quiescent, patrician wives; he was bred to charm, stability and the kind of privilege marred only by minor scandals, and he was currently relishing his freedom before continuing a well-established line. Indecision was foreign to him: Elisabeth rendered him indecisive, which he disliked, but then he had been wilfully ensnared into that alien world of hers by the desire for some uncertainty, some other interest but self-perpetuating success. Unattached at thirty-two, he felt, wearily, that he had run the gamut of human experience: it had been a kind of boredom which led him into the whole new suspense of possessions. He had been looking for a new passion.

Elisabeth Young, he had been told by Annie Macalpine, renovated, restored, cleaned, mended and otherwise gave solace to oil paintings, and it was oil paintings, preferably conventional, figurative, glowing, story-telling canvases, which had formed the new passion. About Elisabeth, he was less sure: she defied possession, but he was interested, like a speculative purchaser unsure about his investment, the way he had always been with his relationships, scouring the ground, giving up quickly if the going ever got rough and waiting without impatience for the one who would ensure a lifetime's effortless fidelity. Besides, the sentimental streak in Francis, normally well under the control of his pragmatism, made him believe that any meeting between the sexes in the pure context of a painting had to be romantic, although there was precious little romance in

12

first standing in that bare, strange flat of hers. Francis's normal assurance had deserted him. If the thing he had delivered had been alive, he could not have been more nervous and protective. His mouth was dry, and his fluent speech stilted.

'You do enjoy what you do, don't you?' he asked, the voice emerging slightly high. 'You enjoy the suspense.'

She had frowned, as if any words were an irritating interruption to the concentration devoted to what was held in her hands. Large hands, he noticed. Rather intimidating, like the rest of her. She was looking at the surface of the thing she held, traced with one finger a pale discoloration which resembled a layer of watered milk, frowned again while he stood by as anxious as the patient's relative waiting for a verdict and talking to hide the pain. Elisabeth's reply was brusque, equally free from emotion's visible, weakening signs. Or it may have been they were teasing each other.

'Enjoy this? Yes, or I wouldn't do it, I suppose. I trained as a chemist, but chemistry seems far too good for chemists, if you see what I mean. Although that's what I was supposed to be. Professional with a capital P. Well. Nothing too serious here. Only a surface bloom, I think. Just varnish.'

'Oh.' Francis felt stupid and he treasured his dignity. 'Why does varnish "bloom", as you call it? Looks more like a fading to me. I thought all the paint might have perished underneath. I was worried. Why "bloom"?'

'Because it grows. All clear surfaces bloom, even glass. Sometimes prettily in an odd kind of way, a sort of delicate

13

cloudiness. Trapped moisture, or something. The reasons don't matter. Some varnishes are better than others.'

'So the patient is curable?'

'Oh yes.' She smiled at him, which was enough for the moment to distract his fading anxiety, although there was a hint of impatience in her. 'You could deal with this yourself, probably. As long as the varnish isn't cracked, easy.'

'Thank you, I'd rather pay you.'

'As you like. All I have to do is rub it all over carefully with light oil, then take that off, every last bit, and revarnish. The time will be in the drying, as usual. Like that one,' she added nonchalantly, nodding her head towards an easel which stood in the corner of her living room. He started towards it in pleasure. 'Oh I do love this.'

'Well, you can't have it. I wish it was mine but it isn't.'

'Oh.'

She was so abrupt, so complete, so short in her explanations, it took away his sang-froid. This was only a painting, he told himself: only an object, paid for with money, but such an object, in common with every painting he bought, invested with energy and part of himself, more powerful than a credit card.

'Would you like some tea? A drink, perhaps?'

He had sat back into the armchair in her living room, the only room to which anyone on similar errands was ever given access. Later, he extended the range, but never saw where she worked. The armchair groaned ominously as if in despair for the automatic way he looked at his watch and nodded, yes, tea, please, already thinking of his next appointment, not saying what he thought in failing to

14

announce a distinct, and he thought, presumptuous, preference for alcohol. Elisabeth Young was so modest in her requests for payment, so businesslike even in her eccentricity, drinking her wine would be less than generous. A very private person, Elisabeth Young. Friendly and, come to think of it, beautiful but as closed as a country shop on Sundays. All her remarks were gruff.

'I bet I know where you got this blooming thing. That place in Marylebone. I thought I'd seen it before and I'm glad you ignored the bloom. I hope you're one of those people who'd buy a painting straight from a leper colony, if you liked it enough, and never mind the name. Oh dear, what a disease.'

'Leprosy?'

'No. Being led along by the eye.'

In a few, very short words, he had been approved as a fellow enthusiast and felt absurdly flattered; he did not ask for a more specific endorsement, but looked down into the tea instead and noticed the rich rusty colour. Burnt sienna or raw umber, she would have said: no such thing as a simple colour. Only a girl from outside the south of England would make tea like this, so strong he imagined that if he let go of the spoon, the shaft would stand up by itself. She drank hers with the thirst of a workman.

'What on earth do you do when you have to spend hours on a canvas you loathe?'

'Oh, I don't mind. As long as someone loves it. I just get on. I don't judge. That's not what I'm paid for.'

Elisabeth had risen as she spoke, not as a gesture of

dismissal, but because of the restless twitch of her limbs which always accompanied some kind of lie. The tea tasted of the past and for this man, at least, the most seductive in her own array of perfumes was linseed oil. She pulled down the long sleeves of her smock, smiled, her arms crossed.

'I know where you can get more of this artist,' she said casually, knowing the merest suggestion of the hunt would make him salivate with the old collector's excitement which was tantamount to the pursuit of love. 'He was a portrait painter, not well known, died about 1950 . . . I know some-one who has some.'

The looking and the seeing were enough for her, she had said; let him buy. He simply believed her, followed her directions to out-of-the-way places and purchased avidly what she could not afford. He did not see any oddity in this: they both had a fatal attraction to pictures which were flawed, as if the damage made them more irresistible; they had evolved a system of mutual benefit. She mended and restored what he had acquired, and after that he had the final ownership. Perfectly fine. Another servant, another master and for both of them, after a short probation, another lover.

He had left abruptly, that first time. Back to his com-plete life. Look at me, she said to herself; will one of you, preferably you, just look at me. With my accent and my shovellike hands and my strong tea, will one of you look at me. I know I am bad-mannered: I know I am your servant, you the master class, but will you please look at me. She observed him into the street, permitted herself no more

16

than that, imprinted on her mind the colour of his coat, his hair and his car, wiped her hands on the end of her smock and did not see him looking back.

Look at me.

Francis sat in his flat, comforted by all those glowing canvases on the wall. Thirty-five paintings he had now, ten found by Elisabeth. The numbers were important, gave solidity to his life. Look at me, Elisabeth. You never look at anything but paintings: you are mesmerized by colours. Look at me. I know you need nothing and no one, but look at me. She had run away at the station, but then she always ran from a crowd, her distaste for life as obvious as her hatred for mediocrity. He would go and see her, not tonight, tomorrow. But, for a likeable, popular young man, there was too much in her of the objective perfectionist, too much self-control, too little of the ebullient affection he craved with embarrassing hunger. He did not want an affair which was complicated and he felt he deserved rather more adoration, the kind he had always had from everyone else. That was his birthright.

Elisabeth Young shifted her position and, in doing so, felt the beginning of a draught creeping down her back. The radiator was cold and the window, with a limited view over a scrubby front garden, fitted badly, one of the endless tasks jostling for the price of repair. She stretched her legs, which were long, curved and pale in the light from the street outside. The arms which reached from her sleeves were equally pale; she noticed the slenderness of her own wrist in an absent fashion, sipped her drink and then

17

quickly replaced her hands over her head. The door bell was still ringing.

It had rung, on and off, for a long time, more often on than off. Possibly Francis, with his recent persistency, possibly Annie, possibly another man, but probably Francis. It did not matter who it was: there was nothing on offer. She had an entryphone: she could have picked up the receiver and said, Why don't you just go away? Don't you know the time? But somehow she did not quite have the energy. Even at one remove, such an exchange had all the makings of a confrontation. He would say, Let me in; where have you been? and she would simply let him in, all flushed from the cold and as angry as a bite. She knew she would, which was why she was sitting under the kitchen table with her back against the radiator, her long legs stretched all over the floor, refusing evacuation but waiting for a bomb.

It might not be Francis: it could be the man with the stick. Slumped on the cusp of drunkenness, she took a stock of her surroundings. This is my home and the floor is sticky. That cooker is a disgrace because I do not care for cookers. Why did I buy this table? Shaped like a half moon, unable to resist heat and always wanting a polish. It was pretty and cheap, for why, and I can never afford anything which is not the latter. Nothing changes: my empire is junk. This room, my kitchen, is always so dark.

The door to her flat was carelessly ajar. The door shut did not increase safety, since it was not an immediate invasion from close neighbours in the building she feared: no one came down the stairs to her basement without invitation, except Enid; they would not dare since she had so

18

emphatically shut them out. There were several other apartments, all mercifully private apart from the plumbing, otherwise sound-proofed by age, nothing in common but a series of stairs to each of three floors, lit by pressing the time switch on each landing and everyone dead again as soon as the light went out on their own closed doors. The bell rang once more, a sound as imperative as screaming. The cat from another of the dwellings, locked out from the garden and used to taking refuge here, suddenly appeared, tail waving, a mix of cupboard love and suspicion, ready for welcome.

'Shhhh,' Elisabeth said. 'Shhhh. He might hear you.' Who? Alarmed to find a voice at eye level, the cat raised its tail to ninety degrees. The whiskers tickled one of the large human feet, noted a discarded shoe on the floor and stiffened in indignation. You never really liked me, Elisabeth thought: nobody does and I don't give a shit. What a cat you are. She wondered what the cat, a handsome animal named Brutus, would do in the absence of food or fuss normally provided on demand. The cat turned, tail resembling a flagpole, picked a route for the open door with rear end contemptuously exposed. Et tu, Brute. The door bell rang again. Elisabeth, still immobile beneath the kitchen table with the glass of indifferent white wine in hand, knew she was ludicrous. Began to laugh, a small sound which became uproarious. He might not be able to get a taxi home; he might be drunk and about to drive. He might be someone ringing the wrong door bell: he might be the footsteps incarnate. She laughed in desperation because the floor needed cleaning and she was afraid and because he

19

would not leave, if it was a he, incapable of taking the hint. Unlike the cat. So helpless in a man to lean on a door bell in the otherwise silent state of being on heat, attracted to some sort of spoor.

Elisabeth Young was opulent as well as tall; equipped with wide hips unfashionably at odds with a small waist and a generous bosom. She found it difficult to acquire clothes which fitted at any points on her whole, well-endowed anatomy, which curved before and swung behind in curious flexibility. It was a body which the life class of several art schools had loved to draw for those gracious but definite lines, but she saw herself as unbearably heavy instead of light, fluid as a dancer, if ample; unaware of the way she proceeded across the room in a series of exquisitely moving parts, only unenviable to the female eye for never resembling a boy, while to the male combining titillation and ferocity. She had a sharp tongue and a sharper intelligence, far-seeing eyes of troubled brown, which did not, for all their size, look as if they forgave much, especially intruders. Which was where the contrast lay. They forgave everything in the end. Her mouth was both full and severe: malice was rarely spoken although the ears had heard plenty of filth. She had no apparent vices except unremitting reserve, impatience, abruptness and intolerance, but responded as well to the cry of a cat or a baby in the street. In the event, sitting there in the half dark to avoid detection, she had no cats, no babies, no authority, no money, the doubtful benefit of thirty eventful years, considerable skills, dirt beneath her fingernails and madness in her heart. She could summon neither the indignation nor the majesty of the neighbour's cat and she could never ever sustain an argument. She had never acquired the arts of confrontation. Sitting still, she knew she was a failure, which she did not mind, but she resented being bothered, disliked being poor and was made miserable by the lack of light.

'Excuse *me*, and what do you think you're doing, then?'

There was one apartment on the ground floor between Elisabeth and the street door, two above that in a twilight zone of largely rented property. The bells of each apartment could not disturb anyone for whom the signal was not intended unless they happened to be paying close attention. Enid Daley, who had risen from her bed to wipe an irritating smear of something from her dressing-table mirror, a souvenir from the assassination of insects which had occupied most of her afternoon, gave close attention constantly. Although the sounds which invaded one flat from another were minimal, she could identify them all. Her head was in the grip of two dozen small clamps, constructions of wire and rubber around which strands of her thin salt-and-pepper hair were twisted into place, the whole kept firm by a red scarf. Tomorrow, curls would explode after vigorous brushing, a vision well worth the nightly torture to which years had inured her. Vanity would normally forbid Enid to parade in this state of preparation, but vanity was weaker than curiosity. 'Excuse me!' she muttered, repeating the lines to stoke the anger. 'What exactly do you think you're doing?' She opened the door of her apartment with the silence of long practice and tiptoed down the passage to the front door. Progress was slowed by the high-heeled mules she wore, one of which always caught in the fringed rug in the hall. The rug was old, worn, gracefully faded by sunlight, and had been supplied by that girl downstairs to catch the mess she made when she came and went. Enid tripped on this rug every single time she made the identical journey, pursed her lips but did not swear. Everyone else liked this covering: she planned the accidental spilling of acid or the introduction of an incontinent horse into the hall and allowed the rug to drive malice into her soul. It was dirty. So was the girl who owned it.

Enid flung open the front door without putting on the light, a deliberate movement to give herself the advantage of surprise over whoever it was standing there with his hand hovering over the array of bells. Listening indoors to the sound of him, she had imagined more than one scenario: she might yell at him, this last of Miss Young's broken hearts, then invite him in for the comfort of her company. Equally, she could imagine her own shrill indignation making him cower and yelp like a kicked dog. Either episode would carry enormous satisfaction, but when the door was open there was no one in sight. On the other side of the road, a car's headlights illuminated the car in front and as her eyes detected this, Enid felt a great wash of fury like a hot flush. Unable to contemplate the vision of any one of Elisabeth's men without this kind of sensation, she crooked her finger towards the car, beckoning imperiously, but the occupant was reversing into a space, stared back with puzzled insolence. Not the man who had been chewing the door bell, then, another. Enid knew she had been fooled into looking the lunatic and the shame made her hotter. She had beckoned the wrong person to her light.

Turning on her heel, she forgot the rug and stumbled. In the unlit hall her hand flailed for support on the walls, her mouth sealed over her teeth but still she fell, one knee hitting the skirting board with a sharp crack, the other thudding into the burning fabric of the wine-coloured rug. She broke the fall by her hand on the table which was for letters delivered daily, rarely for her, and she knew as she rose that all this, the falling, the rising, it being midnight, the misplaced curler which dug into her scalp, was Elisabeth's fault. She had heard them, down in the lobby, another time, Elisabeth and a man, talking about her. Dislike and envy had percolated into a poisonous mixture. Elisabeth had all the options, including the right to intolerance: Enid had none.

Inside her own kitchen, still trembling, she wrote a note she would never send.

'Dear Liz' – the handwriting sloped backwards, more so at this hour – 'I hope you don't mind, but someone called for you quite late!!! Do you think you could tell them to stop ringing the bell and then going away!!! Thought you would like to know. Love, Enid.'

People were always calling for Elisabeth, who never knew her luck. Spoiled, she was. Enid never told lies, only ever told the truth, but truth was a large canvas from which she selected and discarded. Such as admissions about Liz downstairs being a nice girl who responded so well to a thoughtful neighbour. Such a lovely calm girl: generous, kind, considerate, even-tempered and popular with the opposite sex. Who made an apparently effortless living and did not have to get up in the morning. Listening to the faint sound of bath water running out in the drain below her window, Enid had never known quite such a degree of hatred in her life.

Outside, the man whose face Enid had seen none too clearly, walked back to his car, satisfied. He opened the door and put inside what he had carried. There was a sharp click of metal against metal, a glint of silver quickly hidden as he hauled himself clumsily inside, following his umbrella to sit at the wheel, tranquil. No hurry, Thomas, boy, no hurry, now. Almost one a.m., that dead hour of night, and a number of things more clearly established. He had known very well where she lived (a shabby house with a shabbier interior, he imagined), and he knew equally well her habit of not answering the door. Perhaps there was a cat who could see in the dark, and there was certainly a contemptible piranha of a neighbour who could not. Also a willingness, quite deplorable in a woman of her age, he thought, to travel alone and ignore whatever followed her: she would dismiss some fears as puerile fantasies while exaggerating the rest. He suspected, simply from the way in which she tended to walk, often hunched, that she found herself ugly. The habits of self-abnegation always made a person less aware of what others thought, rendered them vulnerable. Thomas knew all about that, he and his sister Maria, who, like himself, walked hunched even when she did not need to. But Elisabeth was so beautiful, so completely unaware of it, like the women in his portraits.

Thomas's encyclopaedia was almost complete, the trap almost ready to spring, although he did not begin to think of it as a trap, more as a privilege. He had compiled his references laboriously, from the first to the last; knew her skills, hard-honed if eccentric, impeccable. He knew it from the best of sources. A little more isolation first, a little more reminding of poverty's impotence . . . a little more fear, and then she would come to him. Violence towards objects was detestable, but necessary. She was too wary to come willingly, but look at how she lived in the comparative darkness of a basement, hurting her eyes.

Cars did not count. They had no intrinsic worth. The one in the next street, round the corner (three derelict houses and two more for sale, the avenue reeking with indifference), was very old indeed, suffering rust gallantly. Thomas stopped to check the number, reluctant to do what he must towards something so innocuous. All cars were ugly. Everyone asleep, the old car conveniently far from the nearest sleeper. She must have parked here deliberately next to a lamp post, as if the thing needed light in order to survive. How soft she was really, soft as butter under the knife.

He reversed carefully, with all the deliberation of a man who drove his adapted car less than once a month (and then only at night or on Sundays), until the heavy Mercedes was facing the flank of the rusty little Fiat. Then he drove forward, slowly but definitely, his own engine whirring in protest, but the sound of impact surprisingly small. He reversed again and hit again, enjoying the sensation a little more this time but not increasing the speed, doubting the need to beware of the neighbours: they all believed in each for his own, the most popular of all beliefs, he had found. The solid front of the Mercedes ground into the fragile body of the Fiat. The Fiat groaned and stirred: he withdrew at that point because he did not want a wreck, merely a dramatic disability, revved once more, felt through the vibrating body the offside wing buckle against the force. The twisted metal resembled a smile when he got out to examine, a leer of final protest, the smile of subjection. Only a metal machine. To be sure of his vandalism, first looking up and down the deserted road, he took the jack from the Fiat's open boot and flung it against the back window. There was a crunching sound as the window crazed into an opaque design, like frost on glass. Risky, that. Then he crept into his own driving seat and purred away with scarcely a mark on his car and none on his soul, which had undergone a kind of cleansing.

Swinging from the mirror of his car was a small picture tied to a brilliant blue St Christopher medal by a cheap, pink ribbon. A present from Maria, a crude good luck emblem presented on a birthday, ugly in his eyes as she was superbly ugly, so manifestly imperfect she did not count, although he knew she had her own version of beauty which included this picture and its attendant piece of glitter. Showing a saint who was made into a legend, purely by such effigies as these. Christopher, the Canaanite, a huge and ugly man who had served the devil first and then dedicated his prodigious strength to God,

26

carried Christ across the water and now brought luck to travellers.

Thomas slewed the car, tore down the medal with violence and hurled it from the window. Then felt guilty. His sister's gift. A sort of bribery which verged on love, he supposed. He wondered what she was doing, angry for having to wonder, turned his ludicrous car past Elisabeth's house, where no lights showed.

Downstairs in the same house, the cat whose owners had gone away finally recognized the futility of howling distress, a method of gaining attention which Elisabeth could have told it was bound to fail. Aiming to exact prompt obedience to its needs in the future, the cat coughed and deposited her anguished disgust on the fringed rug in the hall.

Maria clambered into bed in her basement flat which seemed to consist of no space at all. Not enough to swing a cat or for her to turn without knocking something over, which was one reason why there was so little to knock. There was a tiny kitchenette, screened from her bedsitting room by a piece of floral curtain which Thomas had thrown out long since, another room for lavatory and basin. In her bedsit room was a comfortable bed, also his once, a chair from the same source, but all the pictures were her own. Down to Westminster Cathedral once or twice a week for replenishments, and she knew all about art, reckoning her knowledge was far superior to his, although the passion shared made her tolerate him better than she might. There was the Virgin Mother, the

Madonna with Child, St Bernadette surrounded by an aura of unearthly light, with a blue robe and roses at her feet, each holy picture replaced when the touch of her fingertips dirtied the surface. Art was wonderful: it was her religion, and for that reason alone she understood Thomas. Maria would have liked other people to see. Thomas visited rarely, never lingered: he might learn a thing or two about what made paintings inspirational, but the need was not urgent. These were hers and this was her only home, stamped thus as her own although it depended completely on him. She did not mind her relative poverty and, not usually, her ugliness. There were no mirrors, no reminders in this home, a womb lined with holy colours, no luxuries. She whistled and wheezed to the tune of a hymn, rubbed her body with cold water, never looking down at it, making her ablutions deliberately rough. The proper treatment for a body was mortification, but the soul needed art.

CHAPTER THREE

'People shouldn't complain of being poor, Annie said, apropos of nothing. 'Being poor means having nothing to steal, which is nothing to envy. Someone whipped some of my stock yesterday. Three gilt frames. Bastards.'

'Nothing much, I hope.'

'No. You've done this beautifully, Liz. Sorry, Elisabeth. Beautiful. Wouldn't know it was the same canvas.' Elisabeth detested that shortening of her name. Call her Liz and she glared; call her Lizzie and she practically spat. No, not spat: that was far too violent a reaction for Liz. I wish I knew you better, Annie was thinking. But then again, perhaps not.

'Yes, I have. Done it beautifully, I mean.'

'I don't know how you manage. You can't even see where the tear was. No bump, even.'

'Bandage,' said Elisabeth with a hint of pride. 'Patch it with gauze instead of canvas. I get it from medical suppliers, pull together all the threads in the tear, face the back with bandage. Then it never shows through.'

'Well, I don't know,' Annie repeated. 'Medical suppliers, you do shop in strange places. Is there anything you can't mend? I mean, that picture looked as if it had been kicked for a hundred years.'

'Fire,' Elisabeth murmured. 'You can't make them recover from fire. If you want to kill oil paint, burn it, acid or flame, similar effect.'

'Fancy that.' Annie's mind already running on to the selling of the picture, the profit after Elisabeth's bill: she had become so used to this constant calculation, the mechanics of trade, that she almost forgot to look at the pictures themselves. She was bored with the complexities and sometimes wished she was selling handkerchiefs. Not like Elisabeth: hers was not merely a living but an ongoing love affair more consistent than anything Annie had ever encountered. Until death do us part, me and my paint box, Annie thought wryly, uncomfortable with such intensity. She didn't much care for people who lived for art and they certainly weren't the best customers. Annie was preparing to haggle, the exercise of second nature. A graceful haggle since she was fond of Elisabeth, equally fond of her friend's habit of undercharging from modesty, but still a haggle with the merest undertone of guilt.

'I shan't get much for this, you know. It might be good, but it isn't signed. Why do so many good artists forget to sign? Anyway, it's Mrs Ballantyre's and she's only paying three hundred.'

'Uh-oh . . .'

'Don't knock her, Liz – Elisabeth. She's a good customer.'

'More money than sense. Comes in here with her Gucci bag and says, Hmm, I'll have that and that and ye-e-es, I think so, like someone in church, all whispers and reverence, as if she was buying icons. Taps her little trotters, snaps her little jaws and signs her little cheques. No smiles, no joy. People with her money should be singing and dancing, wild with excitement, but she never buys anything just because she likes it. She'd kill herself rather than buy anything anonymous, always knows the artist, always for investment, like buying by numbers.'

'Now, now,' Annie remonstrated, surprised at such vehemence. 'Don't like to see you standing in judgement. Have a coffee. Envy makes your eyes crossed.'

'I am envious. I'm riddled with it.'

'Listen, if you owned half the things you mend, it wouldn't make any difference.'

'Yes it would. I'd be able to work on pictures I like. I'd be able to buy what I wanted to save. I'd be able to afford light, a better studio.'

'Oh, I thought you meant you could buy a swimming pool. All you want is work. You must be mad. All right then, I'll get us some coffee. Watch the shop.'

Life at Annie's stall in the basement of the Antiques Centre was one long nibble, especially when business was bad; coffee, tea, Coke in summer, pastries, chocolate, cigarettes in between, no deference to health. This floor was empty of customers, floodlit but unprofitable early in the day. The coffee shop was on the third floor: Annie's high heels clicked away into the distance on the uneven floor-boards, her cigarette smoke floating back, her eyes looking ahead, ignoring the stalls as she went. Seen it all before. So had Elisabeth, but in ten years' watching, never learned the indifference of the woman who was at least the equivalent of a friend. As much as anyone was. Unfailingly, Elisabeth found the Antiques Centre a church to her spirit, the way a born housewife might find a supermarket, taking half an hour for each aisle, which was why Annie was so quick to volunteer for the coffee. Our Lizzie looked at everything *en route*, looked and touched in the same way Annie herself could not get across the room at a party because she knew so many people and always stopped for each. Elisabeth would stand transfixed by the colours of a Paisley shawl, mesmerized apparently by the sheen of mahogany or walnut on a veneered music box, smiling at the vivid blues of Venetian glass. Delivering back to Annie a picture she had restored was only an excuse. Going for coffee was only an excuse to renew acquaintance with old friends, spotlit, the presence of paintings, tapestries, bronze, brass, vases, silks, china, pottery and porcelain, cloaks, scarves and shawls, violins and fans, the only panacea she needed. Objects, shapes, sizes and colours brought all the sensations of peace. As long as such things existed and were treasured, life was not mad and all was more or less tolerable with her world. There was no such stability in people.

He saw her from the other end of the aisle in the basement of an uncomfortable warehouse, far from the subdued galleries of the West End; watched her and knew exactly why

32

she was there. She had come for the work and the colour, so distracted she might simply forget to tell the other woman about anything new or distressing in her life, supposing she had noticed: her secretive habits such that the troubling of anyone else with her own woes would be anathema. Even *in extremis*, she was not a person who knew how to scream for help; a useful attribute, that. Instead, she removed herself from whatever it was tormented her, stood as she was now, examining the three new pictures Annie was giving her to restore. Thomas marvelled at her from where he stood, but he did not speak. Naïve paintings, he noticed: American, once fresh portraits of wide open faces painted in poor materials and now vividly aged by cracking, with no shadows beyond those solemn heads. Shadows are multicoloured; naïve paintings have no shadows: the naïve artist does not understand shadows, paints, like a child, a vision of what he thinks he sees, not what is there. Elisabeth had cleansed the shadows out of her life, deleted them for ever. Not this shadow: never this one. Look at me, he wanted to say. Look at me, damn you, but he did not want her to look. If she did, she would only turn away and dismiss him. In that piercing light, created from dozens of spotlights illuminating stalls where one or two owners were polishing their silver the better to reflect the curves, Elisabeth knew no fear. Despite the footsteps so close to her ears, a sound diffused by murmuring voices, approaching, then receding, her broad back impervious as long as she clutched the painting, examined and held like a shield. A three-cornered step, one two click, one two click, like a man with a stick who did not need a stick but carried it for affectation, an Edwardian gentleman who placed little weight on his prop. Edwardian, the era for decorative painting, ladies in fine frocks. Concentrate. One two click, fainter now: she still could not turn towards that sound, heard here for the first time, as familiar as dusk or dawn: one two click, sounding on the pavement beyond her house, in the station two days before, inside and outside of everything she did. Fainter and fainter, another sound superimposed. Annie's high heels clattering back, progress announced with loud greetings to left and right, such an audible perambulation as the other faded away. You shouldn't live alone, Annie told her, she who liked a crowded life. Too much space: space means shadows.

'You naffed off a buyer, then?' Annie said. 'You look sick.' Elisabeth took a cup of scalding liquid, beigey brown coffee slopping and scalding her fingers. Pink, pudgy fingers, swollen: the dermatitis caused by chemicals was back for a while. Never mind. A little dribbled on the olive green of the cardigan she wore, edged with violet ribbon: the belt matched, olive and violet striped, the whole effect a neat patchwork. She drank, burning her mouth. The footsteps became part of a compendium of memory, dreaded and resisted, ignored and absorbed in unequal proportion. It was the first time she had heard them here: fear made her unnaturally calm and objective. There was no point telling Annie because Annie would not listen. No one did.

'I don't know what I can do with these,' Elisabeth said, pointing at the naïve paintings. 'I can't get them back to what they were.' The faces reminded her of an undertaker's

34

work, another kind of artistry not so different from her own, turning dead flesh into serenity with the help of scientific *maquillage*. She was trembling.

'Never mind,' said Annie, comfortably. 'You'll think of something. If you don't, it doesn't matter. Paint them over, if you like. Who'd know? Not the buyer.'

'I'd know.'

'You purist. Don't complain about being poor, then.'

'All right,' said Elisabeth. 'I won't.'

'Got a lot of work coming in? As well as mine? Only I could do with these in a hurry.'

'I might have an awful lot.' She hesitated, as if about to confess. 'A dealer, at least I think a dealer, phoned about a contract to restore the paintings in his flat. In fact,' she rushed on with a level of concern in her voice which Annie chose to ignore, 'he's phoned several times, keeps leaving messages, impressive address. Should I go?'

'What do you mean, should you go? For Christ's sake, beats me how you stay in business at all. Too honest, Elisabeth, too honest. A man, you said. What do you think he's going to do, rape you?' Annie's cursory glance at Elisabeth's vivid colours and generous size spoke loud her own opinion that Liz was the last person a modern rapist might consider. Annie herself was built like a stick.

'I was wondering if you'd come with me. To look it over, I mean?' She did not add, I am frightened of footsteps: I would go almost anywhere for a safe haven, but I do not want to go into strange territory alone.

'Is he selling anything, this dealer?'

'No, he says not, the paintings are his own.'

35

'Sorry then, no. Why don't you ask your friend Francis? How's that going, by the way?'

'Goes fine, I suppose. He's too busy, I don't like to ask . . .'

'Well, so am I busy,' said Annie sharply, stung by the notion that her time was less precious.

'All right, all right, I'm sure it's genuine.'

'Course it is. If it's work you want, you get along there, double quick.'

It was a lie, about Annie being busy, and Elisabeth knew it was a lie. Enough of a lie to hurt and she no more knew a way of bouncing back from a hurt than she knew how to make demands. Suddenly, the quiet house of a stranger seemed preferable to what she knew.

'Business is business,' said Annie. Elisabeth fell silent. The footsteps were coming back, purely imaginary, echoing. He had come so close, but never touched.

'How about a hundred on account?' Annie said lightly. 'For the work, I mean. I know I owe you more, but trade's not good. You know that.'

'What? Oh, yes, I suppose so.'

The pain of the lies, the casual insolence towards a skilled friend, continued silently, like a toothache. Annie the bargainer was picking up cake crumbs from her desk with the ball of one finger decorated with shredded nail varnish, this shrewd Annie, not meeting her eyes, replacing the friendly Annie with the ease of a chameleon changing colour, a natural instinct for survival where money was concerned.

'And, of course, I want you to do these three, like I

said.' Cunning: the offer of work was always seductive; money promised better than nothing. 'That OK, then?'

'What? Oh yes, of course.'

Elisabeth's hallmark, Annie recognized with irritation, this bloody humility. Always let you get away with it; always took money on account; too humble by half, couldn't bargain her way out of a paper bag. Why hadn't she learned, like everyone else, how to confront the world? But she wasn't even going to try, simply accepted a bum deal. Liz could never bargain for her own price. Thank God you aren't a tart, Annie thought with a tiny hint of malice: you'd be dead by now. Annie breathed on the end of her cigarette, which acted as a *digestif* for her cake, watched the tip glow under her breath. Business was business.

'Can't say I like these naïve paintings much,' said Elisabeth mildly, preparing to move.

'Other people do. I suppose you'd like to restore a bloody Gainsborough?'

'No, I don't want anything priceless. I want something brilliant but unrecognized.'

'Well, maybe your posh contact with the posh address has got one waiting for you. Not damaged by fire. Get back to your answerphone. See you.'

Annie watched Elisabeth depart, kicked a frame into a corner. Small flakes of gold leaf showered from where her foot had landed. Annie scooped them up, muttering, looked at the glittering dust in her hands and wiped them on her skirt. Costly stuff, temper. Elisabeth's fault for her incessant, calm goodwill, an attribute Annie did not share. Annie was uncomfortably aware that although she and

Elisabeth acted as friends, she had, in one mean sense, cheated the other for at least three years.

Thomas put down the phone, unplugged it for removal to his bedroom. He had left two messages: any more would be redundant, until, perhaps, she had found her car. The telephone was by his leather wing armchair, a high-backed chair in which he could almost conceal his small self, facing the other, identical chair on the far side of an elegant fireplace. The apartment, top floor on the corner of the block, had two living rooms. A night room and a day room, he called them. One faced north, one south and that was the room with the turret and the high windows. Both had the same wooden floors and the same chairs, the same dimensions and thick rugs. This room in which the fireplace formed a focus was vast and faced north, the walls cream, the paintings many. Three hot Tuscan landscapes compared themselves with the grey sky which was all he could see over the rooftops on the other side of the back road. The other room, across the corridor, had cream walls and no pictures hanging. It had been extended into the turret and thus boasted high windows on one wall and low windows with a view on to the road below on the adjacent wall, light from two sources. Far too light for him to sit in there by day.

'I don't suppose you'd think of moving? To somewhere smaller, where you might make friends? Really, you are ridiculous. Oh God, I didn't mean that. Not ridiculous as in, Ridiculous. I mean your situation. You're so incredibly stubborn. You pursue a perfection you will never find.'

'No, I don't think of moving. I have plans. This is my inheritance, all this space, and I have plans.' Thomas looked at his feet. Well shod in slip-on shoes, one slipping off. He bent to tidy himself, smiling. Thomas had realized from frequent glances in the mirror that one of his afflictions was the inability to conceal a look of amusement. Or any facial expression. His smiles were far from subtle, all expressions exaggerated, forehead never quite in repose, except when Thomas ceased to struggle with speech when his whole face lapsed into something unfathomably sad, bitter or grim, depending on the angle of his smoked-glass spectacles, worn to rakish effect. This was equally uncomfortable for the uninitiated: it was almost preferable to make him talk, not that his speech was poetry in sound, either. He often consulted a photograph to wonder at how much and how dramatically his appearance had changed, aware that it had never been memorable in the first place and now bore no resemblance to the younger man. He looked far older than he was.

'Of course. You meant what you said. You have that tendency, admirable in you. I am quite ridiculous in all respects. Perfectly ridiculous.'

The words, hesitating and then rushed, emerged before a small bark of laughter and a smile of such width it consumed discomfort. He looked back towards his shoes and the saffron rug which had slid into ripples beneath his feet.

'Self-deception: an art form,' Thomas said suddenly and apologetically. He was able to speak with clarity although the words were like shots from an ancient gun; he could not always control their speed or emphasis. He always knew exactly what he was saying and was able to correct.

'I meant, I should have to develop self-deception into an art form to make myself believe I was anything but ridiculous. If you see what I mean.' He grunted and waved a hand in vague explanation, grinning again, that boyish grin which belied his physical condition, a condition more appropriate to ripe old age. Thomas had been forty-two when he had suffered the stroke: the other accidents were earlier. He was now forty-eight, a parcel of gross and bitter irritation, a real hair shirt of a man to himself, charming to others.

'You're looking well, Tom: healthy and fit.' Thomas spoke in a high voice heralded by an arc of spittle as he leant forward to the chair opposite across the empty fireplace.

'What absolute rubbish you talk. Would you like a gin? The room's ready, any time you like. The room's been ready for a long time. I simply want you to restore perfection to my life. In return, I shall give you a perfect life, perfect opportunities and you will understand this bargain, won't you? People rarely understand the gift horse, you see. They expect it to bite. You'll understand, though. You were always highly receptive.'

At his feet the dog stirred. An ugly dog, black and white with a grey muzzle, the colour mimicking the mottle of Thomas's own hair, where the grey blonde was artfully streaked with black. The door opened to a timid knock. Maria came in with his coffee, glanced as she often did towards the pictures, checking for changes, smiling but not quite approving. He smiled back automatically as she left. Dear Maria: she liked only the icons. Those contrived images which were part of his inheritance too, the few remaining relegated to the hall because he did not enjoy them; living in shadow, they were, long since.

The chair opposite Thomas was empty.

Elisabeth left the rug at the dry-cleaners on the way home. The smell of it, inelegant even before the pungent deposits of the cat, which Enid had displayed that morning with ill-concealed triumph, afflicted several nostrils on the Underground train and allowed Elisabeth, who never cared much for such sensitivities, inured as she was to strange smells, the privilege of space. She knew she was only requesting the express cleaning of the rug in an unstated desire to infuriate Enid. Enid with her constant notes, her pernicious cleanliness, nosiness, open-door policy, the unofficial concierge of the house who trapped them all as they came indoors and expected nothing back in exchange but tea and company, entry into all their apartments for gossip. Which was too high a price, far too high. No one else minded paying it when they were there, but Elisabeth did not share the view of Enid as godsent and made that clear. She never let Enid past her portals, and Enid was bitterly hurt, encouraged herself in the impression that the highly coloured Miss Young, whom she judged as being half her age, with twice her opportunities, serenely free of tragedy, was a person who never opened her door to anyone who was not a man. The fact that Enid was both wounded and envious did not impinge on Elisabeth, who

41

simply considered her domineering, a power-hungry old woman who deserved no more than please and thank-you. Enid considered Elisabeth a walking indictment of everything she was not: free, beautiful, loved; one from whom she had begged affection only to be slapped in the soul. Sharply. Misunderstanding had grown to virulent dislike, unhinging now into something more because of the corrosive effect of Enid's loneliness. On Sundays the loneliness drove Enid mad. She was not herself on the Sabbath.

Elisabeth stopped on the corner, decided to postpone checking her car. It would be a waste of precious daylight and the ambivalence, and occasionally snobbery, with which she regarded her small store of possessions depressed her. She hesitated, dazzled by the leaves beginning to fall in a green and gold litter which would soon become a carpet. There were times when she wished she could paint instead of labouring so assiduously to present what others had done, but that was no more than a passing thought. Then, without her knowing whether the sound was fact or fanciful, she heard the footsteps again, one two click, one two click, slowly, the sound muffled as the stick touched on the cushion of leaves. Without looking round, Elisabeth ran to the door of the house.

Pattering up the street with two large bags of groceries and her mind divided equally between a new home perm to save on the nightly ritual, and the grocer who had tried to cheat her out of two pence, Enid saw the door of her shared house open and close. As soon as the door slammed, a sound she recognized as the product of Elisabeth's carelessness and contempt, another figure came from the opposite direction, crossing the man who had followed Elisabeth up the street, twenty yards distant like an Indian servant. Really. Enid watched the taller figure bounding up the steps. One of the young men: delivery man, customer, friend, foe or relative, Enid did not distinguish. Elisabeth had more visitors a month than herself in six. Enid, the abandoned one who drove herself out of doors each day to work in a job she had loathed for years, while Elisabeth need not. She stiffened and readjusted her shopping. If that rug was back in the hallway, she might well scream. Politely, bitterly, Enid paused until the door was once again closed. No one ever waited for her. The one consolation she knew in that tide of deferential, viciously curious dislike, was the fact that Elisabeth's visitors might also fall on the rug in the hall. So would Enid's son and daughter if they ever visited, but that was another, long forgotten story.

'You're very trusting, Lizzie. How did you know it was me? What happened to the rug in the hall?'

'I saw you from the window. Your feet, anyway. The rug's at the cleaners.'

'I see,' said Francis, disbelieving, but cheerful. 'You weren't expecting anyone else, then?' This last with the merest touch of jealousy.

'Nope. I was going to do some work.'

'What? As well as wait in hope for me? Too dark for your kind of work, isn't it? Especially in here? Why on

43

earth do you live in a basement? Thought you might like a drink instead. Fine Rioja.' He had been trying to educate her palate, which seemed geared to quantity rather than quality. 'Come on, Lizzie, you look as white as a sheet.' Work was the only occupation which defined her life, the only thing which would distract her sufficiently now to quell the fear. Elisabeth did not begin to explain that it was perfectly possible to work all night, dark or not, provided she used the lights in her studio room. The daylight bulbs, clever neon tubes to simulate morning, swamping the canvas with a chilly glow like a bright dawn, also used for cold colours. Or the warm lights, tungsten, for earth colours, illuminating each tone of flesh and soil. Possible to work like this, but not comfortable for long: she had come to crave natural daylight more than she craved food. Francis enjoyed the end product of her labours, without any real curiosity about how anything was actually done: mercifully never interfered. There were four rooms in this small rented apartment which he had needed to see in their three-month affair: the living room, the bedroom, the kitchen the better to find a corkscrew, and the bathroom, in that order. He cavorted in front of her, danced back with a glass, presented it full with an elaborate flourish. He was a mimic, a raconteur, a natural cheerer, waiting his chance to tell the tales of his days and make her laugh. Francis tried to make people laugh: it was one of his talents.

'What's the matter, Lizzie?' he repeated. 'How was yesterday?'

'Oh, fine.' She seemed mesmerized by his constant activity, his presumption of welcome, his determination, his simply being there. All energy and optimism: she could hear it in his step, remembered instead the other footsteps, one two click, one two click, hounding from the distance of her imagination, all the way up the street, still in her ears like the buzzing of tinnitus.

'Good,' he said comfortably, making himself at home on the leather wing chair which Elisabeth seemed to supply solely for guests, battered, festooned with fine spots of white emulsion paint; nothing in here was unflawed. 'So you had an easy day, then.'

She sat, wearily, the eyes straying to the naïve paintings she had propped against the wall of the living room, detesting those innocent faces, wishing she were alone, but grateful to be otherwise. How unreliable was this need for company, an unstable addiction. Francis was the last of a succession, the man she loved with a quiet desperation because he so loved life. She envied him nothing, rejoiced in his uncomplicated enthusiasm. She loved his body, too, which gave and received with such abandon and then slept its sound, uncluttered sleep like an athlete after a race. She loved him for his look of surprise on waking, the artless anticipation of another day, the sheer youthfulness of him which seemed to have died in her own soul but fell from his like a blessing. But she endeavoured, successfully with her disciplined mind, not to need him, because he clearly did not need her. She was not fit for this golden boy, who loved her back, but only as a bee might relish a flower. He was like all the others, come to take honey, because she could be relied upon never to criticize, always to encourage, rarely to refuse, succumbing to an endless desire to

45

please which was not the same thing as a graceful welcome. She should work, subdue this longing.

'I wish I were like you. You never worry,' was all she said. He does not need me, I must not need him, was what she thought.

'Of course I do!' He was indignant. 'Of course I have to worry about work, I never know from one day to the next, shows how little you know . . .' He paused, aware, with a strictish regard for truth, that this was not entirely accurate; he might not have known exactly what he would have to do, but employment was guaranteed. 'Well,' he continued, defensively, 'you don't have to worry, either, do you? You're a qualified scientist, and if you're stuck on your beam ends, wouldn't your parents help?'

Elisabeth shot him a look of withering scorn, quickly translated into a half smile. That look of contempt for his ilk, no explanation ever forthcoming; an accusation of his lack of knowledge of the real world. He resented the element of condescension. She had a father, hadn't she? Families like theirs were always supportive, however complicated.

'Oh, come on, Liz; you don't have to live on the breadline. You could teach, or become a famous fraudster, make a fortune. The choice is yours.'

'Please don't call me Liz, and yes, I do. Need to live like this. Where I come from, you got beaten for stealing, thrashed for cheating.'

'It all depends on whether you get caught.'

He sat beside her, put his arm round her without response or resistance, kissed her neck. She smiled, felt

46

warm, but did not move. Her eyes had gone back to the staring canvases which awaited removal to the scene of work where Francis never went, nor herself, either, if there were someone else on the premises: her secret studio, her preserve, her room with insufficient light. She was one long tunnel of closed doors, Francis thought, suddenly vile-tempered, full of his own news, remembering her running away at the station, wanting one-hundred-per-cent attention and realizing in the same awful moment of knowledge that she might not have given him that, ever. Even in bed: it was the same in bed. She let you take her; she would lie with you; she was kind and attentive and affectionate, stroked your back, responded in a passionate, pliantly animal and silent way: you would leave semen traces on her sheets and not a fingerprint on her soul. In the early regions of Saturday evening he could already imagine Sunday morning, when this woman would make him coffee, and then, ever so politely, hang round him until he left. Never push or a shove; never a word to say, I wish you would leave, or I wish you would not leave; never anything which might provoke argument. Simply Elisabeth returning to her own private self, needing you to be gone so she could resume exactly where she had left off with a sigh of relief.

'You don't really want me here, do you, Liz?'

'I love to see you,' she was saying, avoiding his eyes as Annie the bargainer had avoided hers. Thinking of footsteps, she knew she could not tell him and risk his contempt; risk the rejection which might follow such needing. Better stay silent.

'No, you don't love to see me,' he said, working himself into righteous anger. 'You don't at all. Sitting here, and going to bed with you is like snuggling up to some nice soft cushion. Which you knock back into shape as soon as my bum has left it. You do everything to please; you never say no, but you never say yes, either.' Elisabeth began to shake.

'Don't get angry,' she pleaded. 'What is it? What do you want me to do? Kneel?' Francis paused but only briefly. It was not him who was under attack for being a lazy, incurious lover; it was her, for being so diffident, deliberately leaving him ignorant. He did not treat her with public generosity or regard her as a major commitment: so far, she was too eccentric. Nor could he describe himself as a man in love, only a man wanting to be loved, choking on the huge but subtle insult of not being indispensable, being welcomed because he was there, no other reason. Anger returned in full force. He sat with his arms crossed, a man unloved, ready to shout.

'I'll tell you what you are, Elisabeth. You're a cold fish, pretending to be a warm fish. You look like the Venus de Milo in the flesh, but you've already lost an arm. You couldn't give a shit. And I suppose I might be one of many. It's all an act with you. No wonder you could never keep a man. They'd just give up. They'd go out and get an inflatable rubber doll.'

She was cringing slightly, enough to let him know he was hitting some raw nerve, and the pleasure of the stroke encouraged him. He was sick of the passivity of calm Elisabeth who never lost her cool or lost track of anything: he wanted to see what she did in the limelight of his retaliation. Gentleness, avoiding conflict, was part of the problem and the sharp suspicion that he, too, might have been the disposable man who was drawn from a closet whenever he should happen to open the door, his ego inflated and then put tidily away. The vision was insupportable: he got up in a state of delighted disgust.

'Cold fish, Elisabeth. Oh, you're wonderfully warm on the skin, but the rest of you's an emotional frost. What happened to you? Come on, why?'

'Could it be something to do with you? Why accuse me? You never asked, you know. You never really asked. Please don't –'

'Talk to you like this?' he finished for her on a whining chant, remembering not her but some other woman who had nagged him for his ambivalence. Elisabeth never whined. 'Mustn't talk to Lizzie in any way which might get a reaction? Oh, no, no, no. Why should I bother?'

Francis was on his feet by now and the last outrage he could perceive was the fact that she still looked away from him, into the corner where stood three musty canvases, the smell of which had assaulted him as soon as he had reached the room, not a smell he would otherwise have minded, but one which was offensive in a place where his body was supposed to be welcome. Oil paintings, absorbent, taking in the smell of where they had been. She sat very still: the limits of her ability to respond even to insults and challenges were quickly exhausted. There was no point. In all the acuteness which dizzied him this evening, Francis knew that however much she shrank, she was already planning what she would do when he left, wanting no more than an end to this confrontation, and, what was more, he could envisage the same scene enacted by a dozen different men of the past or future. He crossed the room to the three stacked canvases, kicked the first savagely on the stretcher side, forgetting all his respect for the art of paint. All three fell with a crash, bringing her to her feet with a whimper of pain, over to his side in one ungainly stride to lift her arm and slap his face. Not a hard slap; it faltered in the execution, stroked the side of his lips, her open palm apologizing for the action even as it was made. They were both embarrassed.

'I'm sorry,' she said. 'Sorry, sorry, sorry. I didn't mean to do that. Only these were damaged already. They deserve better.'

'I'm sorry, too,' he mumbled. 'I probably deserved that.' His voice became mocking. 'Not for what I said, but how I said it. And kicking your precious, defenceless babies.' He pushed his hand through his hair, frustrated more by her apology: she was mutely insisting he should have the last word. 'All I can say to you is that you'd better get rich, or get safe. You'd better start acquiring a few creature comforts against your old age, because there won't be anyone to share it. You'd never let anyone share anything about you. We rent space off you, that's all. You like things, love things, better than people.'

'That's my problem,' she said, without indignation.

'Yes,' he said. 'So it is.'

*

50

In the aftermath of his departure, Elisabeth was tempted to tilt the wine bottle to her mouth and drain the last drop. Then found she was holding a glass still half full, her knuckles crunched round the stem, clutching so hard with her labourer's hand that the stem broke and blood oozed, gently at first, from a cut in the soft crook of her thumb. Life, what a colourful life. She cleaned the cut in the bathroom, feeling the sting in a delayed reaction of pain, noticing the faint pink colour of the water, swirling and dancing before flowing away. There were words pumping through her head and out through the gash in her hand. He never touched me, I tell you; it doesn't matter: he never touched me. Don't hit him: he never touched me. Men do not like to be touched, except on the skin.

Slowly, Elisabeth carried the damaged canvases into her studio, her hand swathed with the same gauze she used for torn canvas. She would not, could not cry, discipline forbade it, made her keep moving instead. This was the largest room in her empire, the room other people never saw. It was at the end, inadequately supplied with daylight for a studio, but immune from Enid's eavesdropping or spying, Elisabeth's sanctuary. The place where she kept her soul, her possessions and her work, all equally inviolate. Motley possessions. Most bizarre was a large wooden pig by the door, carved from rosewood, fashioned while the wood was fresh from the tree, unseasoned, and cleft down the back in one curving fissure which did not reach the grinning snout. Deep into the slit she had stuffed those letters she did not want to see but could not discard, the pink paper hidden in the rose-pink wood. The pig was designed to act as a small door stop, although the door was never left open and its purpose was redundant. She relied on the smooth belly of it to brush her calf in passing, always warm. Then there were heads of soapstone, three, looking like conspirators, all damaged slightly, oiled like the pig to harden the stone. They stood on an ornate Victorian table, black wood inlaid with brass and walnut on four ornate legs which formed a delicate pedestal, each leg in need of repair. Cluttered round the room were more than a hundred jugs, china and pottery, some brilliantly glazed, some duller, definite colours. Banked in the spaces left were a couple of dozen damaged paintings, hung in tattered beauty, a blazing mass of shades, the collection of a pittance. There was nothing perfect except the solid easel, made of beech and a vital tool of trade which could tilt, bow, grow or shrink, holding a small oil painting restored from sagging decrepitude. Elisabeth drew forward her tungsten light, which made all the earth colours spring into being with its extra eye.

The light showed nuances of colour applied with the precise touch of a rigger's brush, delineating a room of splendid self-sufficiency; a large Victorian room, perfect for a studio with its two sets of windows, where a man and a woman sat on facing leather chairs, a rug at their feet. The room was bare, apart from a magnificent fire and a set of drawers in chestnut, each drawer cross-banded in a wood as light as apple. The honey-coloured boards of the floor were scrubbed, a warm and spartan comfort, and from the far windows came a misty colour which might have been sea. The man wore a rich brown suit, and the woman a full dress of rose silk and a merino shawl of creamy softness. The rug at their feet was saffron, red, blue, fringed.

The colours in the painting were not merely reds and greens, browns and blues, nor the skin tones merely pink. She could recite the names of the pigments like a litany. Not merely white, but flake white, best for covering and potentially poisonous. Never merely red, but cadmium light for peachier shades, Mars red and alizarin. Ultramarine, the best of blues, most precious in the palette, made from lapis lazuli. No simple yellow, but viridian, Naples yellow, raw sienna. Nothing called purple, but manganese violet and cobalt. From the simplest selection of pigment someone wove the complicated magic which ruled her existence, often mixing ruin in with his choices. Succumbing to this dominion had been wise: the fascination of it was entirely reliable.

Pigment and mixtures. The spotting on the bandage was already turning duller red to brown. Did hearts really break and did blood spill out like spilt wine? It felt so. She wondered idly how one would mix the paint to make the true, ever-changing colour of blood, which seemed to have drained from all her limbs and left her dark skin the colour of parchment.

She did not weep for Francis. The cut was simply a punishment for the blow, the defection inevitable. There was nothing else she deserved. There was only herself, the way it had always been. There was nothing left now but a spreading bruise of hurt, and her eyes for the work and the colours, a conduit for other versions of beauty.

CHAPTER FOUR

Elisabeth stayed the night in the studio because she felt safe in there and because it faced the garden at the back. Should footsteps echo through her sleep, she would be able to tell herself they were dreams. No sound penetrated into the garden other than the distant drone of cars. She had opened the window to dispel the trace of chemical fumes, the lingering remnants of the products which made her hands scalding pink whenever she forgot the gloves. Poisons. Before oils, painters had used the gifts of the earth: tempera was composed of pigment and egg, casein made of milk solids, glaze and varnish made of honey, ingredients reminiscent of cookery books. She, on the other hand, used poison as often as not. The contrast made her laugh, this simplicity of what they had so durably created and what she now used to mend.

There was another reason for staying in the studio apart from the footsteps and Enid's pointed ears. Had she lain in her own bed, she might have thought of Francis, the sight of whom, despite her fierce awkwardness and taciturnity and deliberate distance, had always filled her with an almost crazy happiness, and she did not want to think of him. In the studio room was the rosewood pig and its secrets, the jugs of a thousand colours, the paintings, the flags of her existence and anything she had ever acquired with love. Elisabeth wanted to remain with them, covering her bareness with that hidden hoard guarded for more than a decade. Sometimes she was relieved when the room's supply of light was hard on her working eyes. In the morning, the dribble of sunlight showed the paucity of it all, revealed her sentimental addiction to anything flawed, made her possessions look cheap and her taste half formed. Elisabeth shut her eyes, pulled around her the favourite dressing gown, feeling the worn material and the lumpy cushions beneath her chilled back.

The studio reflected the cold of preservation: she had an intense desire for physical comfort, warmth and above all light, in a richer, less shoddy, more secure cocoon than this, even though this was the only room, and these the only things which revealed who she was, intensely, puritanically materialistic and fanatically private. She had never explained this to Francis, nor to any other friend or acquaintance. Elisabeth did not expect to be understood: to date, that negative expectation had not been disappointed. No one had ever asked.

Instead of either memory or introspection, she turned her attention to breakfast, a selection of two-day-old bread, stale milk, fruit which had lingered too long. None of that mattered: she bolted through grocery shops like a convict on the run, lived on the output of corner stores, frozen foods and pasta, a hurried carelessness about feeding which did not result in slenderness. For once she looked at her bare cupboards in dismay, wished her controls of these minor disciplines of life were not as sporadic as they were. When Enid knocked at the door, Elisabeth was victim to a fit of miserable and untimely hunger, a state of physical and emotional grief which had, at long last, brought her to the brink of tears, jerked into life by black coffee. Opening the door was less threat by daylight: there was the half hope that it would be Francis, but, as it was, no stupid woman and certainly not this particular woman, was going to see her crying.

'Yes? What is it? Oh, it's you. Anything wrong?'

The rudeness was transparent. Enid jumped backwards. The cat, ignored as always by its rightful owners, stood at her ankles, cautious, recriminatory, slipping inside in one prudent act of avoiding Enid, who hid her dislike for cats behind a façade of concern and strange, mewing noises. Enid now gaped at Elisabeth, half hidden behind the door, the one forgetting what passed for manners, the other forgetting what it was she needed to say. Enid craned to look round the door, her curiosity to see inside suddenly intensified by Elisabeth's determination that she should not, the sense of rejection and need to know sharpened into a necessity by the disdain of the occupant and the sidling solidarity of the cat. Dumbly,

Enid held out her hand, with a cream envelope. Before she could begin to say, This came for you last evening: I don't know how, but I thought I'd bring it down for you in case it was urgent since you might not bother to come up, and besides, I have bad news for you . . ., Elisabeth's long, pink and pale forearm extended and plucked the letter from Enid's proffering fingers.

'For me? Thanks, see you.'

The door closed so suddenly that Enid's fingers barely escaped injury. She had combed out her curls before she had dressed, but now they shook a little; she had worn a clean skirt and blouse to cope with Sunday and besides she wanted to tell Elisabeth about her battered car. The house was empty: the freer amongst them gone away. On a Sunday like today Enid's husband had left; on a Sunday her son had emigrated; on the Sabbath she had quarrelled with her daughter because there had been nothing else to do. So it followed that on Sundays she deserved at least the courtesy of conversation. She raised her hand to knock again, opened her mouth to speak. The mouth closed and the hand went into the pocket of her skirt. Then she went back to the silence of her flat; the emptiness of a day without shops, friends, neighbours, or anything but envy.

Elisabeth read the invitation inside the envelope, written in a civilized hand on fine cartridge paper. She always admired good paper. The same courteous invitation as those on the answerphone messages: a pleasant, hesitant voice. There was nothing to lose in her acceptance: nothing but fear. The day and the life beyond the day were a vacuum, black and bleak with colours premonitory of winter and her father's footsteps.

Annie Macalpine grumbled about getting out of bed early after a long Saturday. She grumbled and joked more about getting out of bed alone than the indignity of getting out of bed at all, since neither loneliness beneath the duvet nor working on Sundays counted as favourite activities. Annie had never lived alone: in some ways she envied Elisabeth that strange ability which she could not share, especially since her own man of the moment, who had used her bed and eaten the food she presented with such cheerful generosity, seemed to have disappeared on a European trip which probably disguised many purposes other than business, including escape from those sinewy arms which held him. For the moment, Annie did not mind this as much as she imagined she would. Hard as nails, she told herself: that's me; here I am. Any kind of man was better than none at all, but they were all grief and she tried to tell herself she was used to it. Industry was her substitute, along with a thousand and one friends. None of whom, she noticed, was present when needed, but might have been if she had remembered to ask any of those who had shared Saturday night in her kitchen before she had fed and wined them on the profits of a moderate month, and gone to bed less sober than was wise for a person who had to pack up for an art fair in the morning. Annie was not inclined to introspection unless she had a hangover, but on this grey day, within the sound of church bells which somehow suggested the need to think and the need to believe in more than her frenetic and hedonistic existence, she did wonder about her life for all of thirty seconds.

Annie regretted she had not asked Elisabeth to help with this Sunday exhibition in a hotel, because Elisabeth never questioned: you said, Be there, would you mind? and she simply said, When? She would have humped these large framed canvases with her sensitive strength, never dropping or complaining, organizing lights for the stalls and nails for the walls, a workmanlike greaser of the wheels of selling, disappearing before Annie had put on her face, pushed up her hair, donned her pink eye shadow and started to talk the leg off anyone who might want to buy. A temporary, easily rationalized guilt had prevented her from asking Elisabeth Young, a woman who had obliged so many times before. Annie owed Elisabeth Young more than two thousand pounds in unpaid bills. It weighed heavily with them both, heavier with Annie who wished Elisabeth would scream about it instead of being so self-effacing and letting her get away with it, which, in the nature of trade, was what Annie tried to do all the time, without personal discrimination. Even to a friend who deserved better, but after today, she vowed, while she bruised her thumbs and wished she had the use of Lizzie's clapped-out car for the small pictures, after today she would pay Elisabeth and stop spending on those who did not matter. The lights were blinding in the back of the hotel, but half of her own would not work. Liz would have fixed them. Why am I such a bitch, Annie thought, why cut the nose off my face? She arranged the Victorian canvases next to the modern ones on her expensive stand, put

60

on her lipstick, then sat and looked as if she were preoccupied, a person who never dreamed of earning a living which she largely gave away by entertaining all those friends, the Alistairs and the Nicks, in her addiction to popularity. She looked more or less clean, armed with last night's mascara, off-beat arty in her dusty black, pretty and world-weary, sober, sharp and knowledgeable. For the moment, as the first customer swung into view, she felt a passing acquaintance with all of these surface qualities; wished, with that Sunday guilt, she was better at honouring the undemanding friend, especially a friend with a car.

Elisabeth's car stood grinning, the front bumper twisted into a peculiar kind of leer, the front offside door stove in, the back window crazed, with the jack lying on the road behind, the bodywork of the car dusty. A car used for moving things, never for the pleasure of driving, never treasured and never driven fast. After the shock, the hand-in-mouth fear, Elisabeth felt indignation for her elderly, serviceable machine. Phrases came to mind, injunctions from the past: never throw away what has worth, save anything serviceable. I cannot leave it, will not leave it to rot, which is the most economic thing to do. And why did not Enid tell me this? She walks back this way each day from the grocer's and the paper shop. She knows which car is mine; she knows everything, and there was a gleeful message with her this morning. And you have been unkind to both of us, the bumper leered with a permanent smile: you let me in for this kind of rape, don't pity me now. Grim, but nervous, Elisabeth drove the sad red car, the flank

61

scraping on the wheel even after she stopped to drag the metal from the worn rubber with her muddy hands. She did not call the police: it never occurred to her. I am sick, she said, of worn things. When she clanked it shut, the door had shuddered as if live, rattling as she chugged the ten miles eastwards to a garage on the outskirts of London, open Sundays, cheaper than most but never cheerful. There she was forced to leave the grimacing bumper not with the greedy proprietor of the garage, whom she knew well and charmed easily, but with his son.

'Least a week's work,' said the son. 'What a mess. I mean, do what you like, I don't care. Take it or leave it.'

In dad's absence, the son thought his father mad and dangerous: they did not get on well. With some accuracy, he saw his papa as a violent bully and, on this cold day, he did not like Elisabeth or, for that matter, anyone else. She stood in the forecourt at noon, the victim of shrugging rudeness, lack of decision and lack of choice. Leaving the car where it was, she knew faintly, then, what she might have done to Enid by her similar, less aggressive indifference. She thanked the boy pleasantly out of conscience for them both, felt for the letter in her pocket as if it were a talisman. The same letter Enid had brought down with such ceremony, unaware that it carried the promise of a newer car for her indifferent neighbour, to say nothing of what else. Come mend my pictures, the letter said, like the messages on her answerphone, courteously imperative. Stay here; do whatever you please; use the safety of this address, but please work for me. Somewhere, between the lines of this letter and those messages, a voice was shouting, Come on, girl, you can do better than this. You are poor and Sundays stink.

It was, Thomas supposed, a good enough address. In any event, it was his one. Near the river, near an abbey and a cathedral and also close enough to the more temporal lures of shops. London spread beyond him on other days, not today. Sundays were for lies and emptiness and duty. Thomas did not have an answerphone: otherwise he would have checked it every five minutes to ensure there was no message, denied his own confidence that because today was the day he had suggested to Elisabeth, by letter and by phone, for coming to see the pictures, it was the day she would actually do as he dictated. About five in the evening, he had said in his note. The time of day when the cold sharpened and the light had gone, an unenviable time of day for anyone who lived by light. Since there was that large gap of hours between morning and evening, the doing of his irregular Sunday duty bothered him less than usual. He could afford to be generous.

'Are you ready?'

Thomas was opening his own front door to her knock, irritated. Maria would never wait for him to come downstairs, although he told her to do so and he knew she liked to be visited on any other day. On the Sunday mornings when he obliged with his presence as escort, she always came upstairs to him, ludicrously early for mass in the cathedral in case he forgot or left the whole expedition too late. If he was late, she'd probably chew her carpets, such as they are, Thomas thought wryly.

'Ah! Yes, I can see you're ready.'

And so she was. A brown dress merging from beneath a mud-coloured coat, twenty-year-old boots with thick soles elevating her stumpy feet above the pavements she trod with such unease. She wore a hat, of course: a crumpled beret green with age, because she was of the generation which knew you could not go to church without a hat, but even with that decorum she looked appalling. They went to Westminster Cathedral for morning mass, left right, left right, Thomas keeping a strict momentum with his umbrella, she panting to keep up. Halfway there, he stopped suddenly.

'Would you like me to go and fetch the car?'

She shook her head dumbly, pouted.

'Come on, you can speak, you know.' Another shaking of her head: so far she had not said a word. He was not really aiming to encourage her. Out of a kind of devotion, she had aped his own enforced silences when he had been ill and speechless himself and, now that he was not, she seemed disinclined to recover any facility for talking, found she did better without it. Perhaps it was mere laziness, perhaps a form of blackmail supposed to make him feel bad, perhaps her desire not to irritate, but although this dull and persistent silence of hers often provoked the sort of rage which made him want to strike her, poor helpless thing, he did not want her cured of it. Since the last time he had been hysterically, woundingly angry with her, she had spoken scarcely a word. That suited him and suited his current plans even better

'Behave,' he said. 'Or I'll leave you in the square.' The

square outside the cathedral was full of pigeons, fluttering in scorn for the faithful. There were also vagrants, men who begged with little less scruple than the birds. Maria nodded, not deterred. They walked into the main door out of the light and into the hushed, half dark, both of them in silence. She scurried ahead and he restrained her by the arm. 'Shhh,' he said, unnecessarily, meaning, Don't move so fast, stumbling himself in the sudden gloom, the tip of his heavy umbrella striking against the wooden seats as he moved. Finally they sat, the umbrella between them. Thomas refused to move further into the row: already he felt trapped, supposed in a flash of angry and defensive guilt that the pleasure this gave his companion might have reconciled a different, more dutiful man to the pain it gave himself. Maria glared round at him, first angrily and then in a mute appeal when he did not bend his head. 'I will not kneel,' he hissed at her, forgetting his own exhortations to silence. 'Don't stare like that!' She buried her face in the palms of her hands, but not before he had noticed the onset of tears.

'Let us confess to almighty God . . .' intoned the far distant priest, the voice reverberating back through the sonorous loudspeakers. I will not ask for bloody absolution, you old bastard, Thomas told himself as the incense wafted past and his nose wrinkled in disgust at the fumes Maria snuffed with the same enthusiasm she had when she doused herself with holy water at the cathedral doors as another woman might smother herself with cologne in her bathroom. Holy water was Maria's perfume: at the stoup, she reminded him of an ugly duckling in a bird bath.

'I have sinned, Oh Father, I have sinned . . .'

Oh, shut your mouth, thought Thomas. He hated the mosaics of the place, the iconlike walls, with their dramatic but cold depictions of the stations of the cross which, with the cold marble, made the interior both rich and austere. Maria did not like these: she preferred more blood in her illustrations, wanted Veronica who wiped the face of Jesus to come away with a kerchief loaded with gore. I am not sorry for what I do and I shall never confess my sins, Thomas promised between gritted teeth. Next to him, her eyes shining artlessly, her pathetic face illuminated with holy joy and the ardent simplicity of all her muddled beliefs, Maria suddenly burst into song with the fervent sound of an amorous frog.

'Sweet heart of Jesus! We-ee implore,
Make us love thee! More and more . . .'

So she would sing, even if she would not speak. Only no one else was singing: the back of the priest shivered in distaste as he failed to turn from the blessing of his bread and wine. Ho, ho, thought Thomas: this was your bit, wasn't it, not hers. He sat back and folded his arms. Maria went on singing.

'Sweet heart of Jesus, make us know and love thee . . .'

Children from the row in front turned and stared, their adults, more circumspect, facing straight ahead. The round eyes of the children became creased into helpless giggles, stifled into handkerchiefs or sleeves, as one pulled the other, to look again, giggle again, until the snorting was almost as loud as her voice. Thomas sat still, did not join in the chorus of 'shhh, shhh', which came among tut-tutting from the row behind. He did not quite like to feel Maria being so thoroughly despised, which was his own, cruel, prerogative, but part of him wanted to applaud her for being such an embarrassment in any house of God. Look, God, look what you started. Maria persisted through one whole verse and drew breath before starting another. Two ushers were toiling towards her down the aisle, looking like a pair of uncomfortable bouncers.

'*Sweet heart . . .*'

Suddenly she noticed, after the first phrase of the verse she was about to repeat. Registered the heaving shoulders of the sniggering children, in particular the one looking towards her with a chubby hand held over his eyes, the first finger and second parted to reveal one vibrant, transfixed eye. The song died in her throat. Thomas stiffened, unfolded his arms, ready for movement. Too late. She had grabbed the umbrella, seized it halfway down the black material and lunged at the boy. The action was more than a gesture: she thrust the umbrella in the direction of his smile, but the eyes rounded into an *oh*! and he turned into the safety of his stiff-necked, well-upholstered mother, catching the vicious poke in his arm and squealing with pain. Thomas embarked on a fit of coughing, loudly artificial. The mother turned: he glared at her, his hand now

67

holding the umbrella firmly, tussling for possession. They were both strong, he and his sister: she did not relinquish it easily. The ushers hovered. Thomas linked his left arm through Maria's, the umbrella bracing both their elbows like a splint on a fracture, his other arm reaching across her in mock affection. Thank God they had already got past the part when they were all supposed to shake hands, something they both refused to do as a matter of course. The protective glare of the mother intensified: the boy rubbed his arm and began to make small gulping noises of distress. Thomas coughed louder, until at last, in a timely cue, the distant priest signalled the congregation to sing, all of them, with no unseemly solos. There was an audible shuddering of relief as they rose and cleared their lungs.

We will dwell no longer on this amorphous substance of a God today, thought Thomas, catching the confusion and pain on Maria's face as she refused to sing on cue. Damn your God, and all who sail in him. He tightened his hold until his arm and the umbrella were braced like a painful tourniquet. Maria did not seem to mind, bowed to necessity, looked at him with affection and a great big, open smile. Perhaps that was all she wanted, to stand there arm in arm, that little bit of contact, a pauper's mite of affection.

Elisabeth saw people spill out of a Seventh Day Adventists church, full of colour and hats and *bonhomie*, nicely exhausted by singing. The bus home was a meandering hour through Sunday streets and the public life of the East End, littered markets and all their detritus spied from the top deck of the bus. All this rubbish abandoned, all these unprivate lives, herself outside them, not contemptuous, never that, merely aloof. For the third time, she pulled out the cream envelope Enid had delivered. The address was embossed, the paper stiff and smooth. Someone needs me: someone's pictures might want me, and it was pointless to have any other reason for living. Closing her eyes, Elisabeth wondered what it was like to feel secure. Freed from the cocoon of warm transport, walking the last half mile home, she anticipated the footsteps, but as long as her hand curled round the pompous promises of the envelope in her pocket, she heard nothing, saw nothing but a prospect of warmth and calm, light and colour, an image of rooms as yet without shape.

When she got inside, she found herself, like an automaton, putting a change of clothes into a bag, including a working smock without quite knowing why. Afterwards, when she went out again, she slammed the front door. It was unlike her to be noisy, but the reverberations had a satisfyingly and oddly final sound.

The slamming of the door haunted Enid, who heard it in her own silence, resisting the urge to go out and complain. Hours later, she imagined the same sound when she went out into the garden.

'My, aren't we excited? Bedtime, isn't it, sweetie? Into little cat flappie.' Enid spoke in the honeyed, babyish tones she considered appropriate for cats as well as human beings, remembering to modulate her tones even when there were no witnesses, even at the end of her dreaded Sundays, always speaking in expectation of being overheard. Enid never let up: she never even told herself what she thought.

'What's this then, kitten? Is her downstairs being ever so tidy? Shut you out, has she? Rubbish doesn't go out till Tuesday. Why did she put all hers out here in the garden today? Doesn't she know? Pity. She's so popular, but then, she's no one really, no one at all, pussy, no one. Sad, I think, don't you? Putting her rubbish out. I wonder . . . I wonder. Gone away, has she? Her car's gone. I know 'cos I went to see. Some of us don't have the chance to go away. Or a car. Even a wrecked car. I did try to tell her.' Enid giggled. Surreptitiously she moved closer to the cat, disliking but wanting the comfort of response, anything for touch. Free of pretence, the cat moved away from her, leapt nimbly on to a wall, sat there licking and smiling in that half light which was slanted and obscured by the taller houses behind. It was vibrant in its black and white, a great, wide face with luminous eyes, destined for automatic beauty in movement or repose. Caught in the walled garden, owned communally and therefore rarely used at all, the cat on an autumn evening was the only thing of grace among a scrub of newly bared trees and an unmown lawn covered in leaves. For Enid, the cat who loved Elisabeth was a vivid reminder of Elisabeth's self-sufficiency, the colours and the glamour and the invisible sustenance, all her effortless living which took no account of the rest of the world labouring away. Another boyfriend in at her pussy last night, one of a string, but no one knocked for Enid. Nothing but rudeness this morning for Enid, plus a closed door on the avid curiosity which was now running riot.

'Poor pussy,' she said in a half-hearted attempt to persuade the animal down off the wall so that it would look less omnipotent in movement. 'Poor puss. Who's a little skunk, then?' Never mind the whispering of insults: Enid's voice broke along with her control, suddenly bereft of cajoling syllables. The sky had rained, stopped, drizzled again, given Sunday a second chance and then condemned it with rain in earnest as Enid was left shouting for nothing but her furious responsibility for a neighbour's pet, while the cat gazed down, nonchalantly, towards the rubbish mysteriously cleared from Elisabeth's flat. Then further down towards Elisabeth's windows, so often spilling an eerie, neon light into the garden, like some pornographic peep show, but now dark, uncharacteristically and definitely closed.

The lanky youth from the garage patronized by Elisabeth had gone home at five o'clock, every bone in his body stiff with fatigue from going time and time again out to the raw cold from the fuggy warmth of the kiosk on dad's bloody forecourt. His mum and dad were back from their day out and all he understood was that, yet again, numbing boredom and family responsibility had combined to ruin his day. His forehead shone white against the red of his nose and the purplish marks of his acne. The only enjoyable moment of the day had been making that woman leaving the red car look so stupid. A cosy car, he thought: a bit bashed but the heater still worked and no one would be able to see through that crazed, back windscreen. The least he was owed for his pains was the use of dad's motor for the evening, so he could go and see Janet Potter, like him seventeen, who lived five miles away. But dad was only going to listen on a day when pigs had wings. Meanness radiated through his house from the chilly upstairs to the yard full of motor spares. After a row which reached a crescendo of shouting and three blows, Janet Potter's boyfriend ran back to the garage and the car he had not mentioned to his father. He retched his ill-digested food, spitting the aftertaste through the window. Still cold and angry, he drove past his own home and, in passing, waved his fist in the air.

'Aw, come on, Janet. C'mon; feel it again. No harm in it, is there?'

'I don't know about that. That's not what I heard.'

'C'mon. You can feel mine if I can feel –'

'Thank *you* very much. Now why would I want to do that? This isn't half a funny car,' she said by way of post-ponement, sitting in the front passenger seat with her arms across her unbuttoned blouse, the hands which had just pulled down her skirt now tucked under her armpits, which were sweating slightly. 'It smells, this car,' she said, embarrassed by the other smell she would withdraw on her fingers.

'Who says?' he answered, distracted for a moment and suddenly defensive about this vehicle he had claimed as his own, which could go like a bomb. 'Who's saying it smells?'

'It smells,' she said, wrinkling her nose for effect. 'Of

72

medicine and stuff. Ointment. Or that calamine lotion you put on mozzie bites. Germolene, or something. Pooh.'

'Don't be daft. I can't smell nothing.'

'Have you been putting stuff on your spots?' She giggled in the darkness, her hands rebuttoning the blouse with unsteady determination. 'I'd best be going home. And you'd better be taking me. Dad'll kill me if he knew what *you* were wanting.'

He was suddenly furious at her defection, her insistence that this fumbling was something only he wanted; nothing to do with her but only tolerated until she got away from his dirty little desires and the spots she had pretended to ignore, as if she had none herself. He turned on the engine, shoved the car into reverse so suddenly the movement pushed her forward in the seat, her face satisfyingly alarmed. When they reached her house, both of them still speechless, he sat staring ahead, offering nothing as she scrambled out, and he took off again with the same speed and a spurt of mud, denying her the chance to have the last word or even slam the door. He was trying to hold back tears of rage and frustration, the accumulation of a cold day's emotion, swearing at her out loud as he accelerated on to the open road towards home. Faster and faster, this car was old but could go like a bomb, was a bitch, what a bitch, the needle creeping towards seventy and he felt like flying. Then a bend he had forgotten, the red car slewing out of control, bumping off the tarmacadam, everything in focus and the speed slow before the windscreen shattered on a branch. When he came to, he was colder than ice; colder than his hands on the forecourt in December and all the rage had turned to whimpering. He was slumped across the passenger seat, with his head angled down to the floor, blood dripping slowly and copiously from a cut to his nose and one to his scalp. The whole of him was spinning from no point as he sat upright; then he thought he was blind as the blood flowed into one eye. Miraculously the headlights still worked; his first orientation to where he was. They were angled, full beam into the woods less than a mile from home, the car drunkenly resting in the undergrowth fifty yards from the road. Once he knew where he was and knew he was alive, panic made him function, the fear of disgrace far more terrible than blood. Listen: no one knows about this car. I told her a week, but didn't tell dad: if only she never came back for her bloody car. Stumbling home, hugging the side of the road, he was inventing his story of a fight, a mugging, a falling down, a swinging into a lamp post, anything to forestall that evil hour of accounting.

If only she never comes back.

'Why don't you stay? Don't think me presumptuous, please. I'm hardly a danger. Nor our Butler. He is, I think, my greatest concession to luxury.'

The dog put a bony head on his knees. If she ever owned a dog, it would be one like that: big, ugly, flawed, old and affectionate. Elisabeth laughed, cradling the brandy glass in her hand, watching the colours dance in the flames. Gas, he explained: he could not haul coal, but wasn't it convincing? She was warm from a glass half the size of a child's balloon but comfortably weighty, a prism for the light and a catalyst for the taste, held in the hands like a trophy, a generous measure of everything. They were high above the world, in an eyrie, settled for hours in one of the most beautiful rooms she had ever seen, part of the vastness of this strange apartment so large and long it had actually taken time to walk in here from the door. There were other rooms as splendid, bedrooms and bathrooms. Here there were two leather winged chairs, a burning fire, a rug between their feet, a pre-ordained room, uncannily similar to the canvas which by way of dim contrast sat on the easel in her chilly studio. The conviction of knowing exactly where she was had been confusing, as prevalent as the taste of brandy on her tongue, but, along with that similar feeling of knowing him, melded into a sensation of warm familiarity. She loved me for the things which I had done, said Othello of Desdemona. Elisabeth trusted, no less intensely, the man who sat opposite her for the things he owned and for the glorious light, which late in the afternoon still filled his rooms. The rain threw itself against the windows, a harmless onslaught on their comfort.

'I'm so glad you're here,' said the man, Thomas, formally. 'But please do not allow me to force you to stay. But there are bedrooms and bathrooms galore, every etcetera and, as you can see, the nature of my interest is professional. I got your name from Annie Macalpine. Do convince her, Butler.'

The dog ambled across the rug, stood massively by her chair and gazed into her eyes, his rear end wagged by the tail, a persuasion with all the ponderous charm of the master.

75

'We are much above the world here,' he continued. 'Four tall floors. I always loved these vast mansion flats, they were built with a kind of solid elegance. And even in a street lined with a hundred such, it's so quiet, so private. Westminster not far, the heart of London, overpopulated, but not in any way you notice. They might as well not be there, all those millions of others. Safe as houses.'

He laughed at his own poor joke. Discreet, safe, undisturbed: these were descriptions which took on a new meaning, as if they had had only half a meaning before. It made her feel like a celebrity granted the accolade of protection. This Thomas was as safe as his own fabulous abode, as courteous and old-fashioned as his messages.

'You could start in the morning if you liked,' Thomas added diffidently. 'As I told you, all the equipment is here. Less your own foibles, of course, I know you all have them, you restorers, but everything can be arranged, as and when. I love to shop, for anything: I can fetch in anything you want, provided I can carry it. Your predecessor in the task was a wretched, irresponsible man. Left everything undone and buggered off. Debts or love, I gather, both equally pernicious. I've no time for either. I do hope I didn't leave too many messages on your phone machine. One worries so about importuning a woman, in particular, for her valuable time.'

'Oh no, not at all.'

She thought of the rain outside, the leering car abandoned to nothing but more expense, the footsteps which would never sound inside such a carpeted citadel as this, the warmth of her feet, the coldness of Francis, her alienation

76

from the world. Of being guarded and treasured, encouraged to work in private, of being valued beyond rubies. Thought of the pictures to be placed in her hands, the two she had seen, the third, promised. Something brilliant, she had said to Annie: this was better.

'If you're sure you don't mind . . .'

The firelight glinted on his heavily tinted glasses, such a strange affectation for such a small, plain, afflicted man.

'I keep saying it, I'm sure I know you from somewhere.'

'Oh, very likely. Exhibitions, galleries, you know the sort of thing. Might have been with Miss Macalpine. I've been around, you see, for ever. I'm even on the board of a couple of art schools. Maybe from that, you never know. Small place, this city.' Elisabeth thought otherwise: out there it seemed very large.

'We should have discussed payment, you know. I'm told you're far too deferential on that subject. A most unmodern woman, but I shall, of course, be generous.'

She had the face of an unmodern woman, more like the face of a sensuous saint, beatified by events, a madonna praying to heaven, he thought humbly.

'It doesn't matter,' she was saying. 'It really doesn't matter at all. You'll really relinquish that wonderful room for a studio? And you just want these three pictures you've shown me done for a start, particularly the first?'

'There are many, many more. I'll show you another time. If you like. Not yet. Too rich for the eye, is it not? You stop looking, don't you, if you see too many pictures at the same time. Do you like my house, by the way?'

'Like it? Of course I like it.'

77

She had known that as soon as she turned into this street, an avenue of cream and red walls, late Victorian splendour, built for size and privacy. An avenue of trees hiding the lower façades of these huge, austere, mansion blocks, reminiscent of Parisian living, made in the days when whole families lived thus, without ever longing for the freedom or the ground of a house, as she did not. Space in layers, a slice of the sky as the block rose over her head. She knew that inside the rooms would be huge, but until, eschewing the lift, she had climbed those innumerable steps to the fourth and last floor, she had no idea how light, how vast, how impenetrable. The door to this apartment would have admitted a carriage: she had been shown the public part, which meant she had seen the north-facing room, where they sat now, and the room opposite used by her predecessor to restore paintings. She had seen the space and the light, that south-facing light which would continue to pour through the high windows when the other light had ceased to penetrate the sash windows which looked down into the road and across to the livings beyond. She had seen the vast carpeted hallway which hid the sound even of her own steps. She had seen a small, ugly, intensely courteous, unthreatening little man and she smelt safety like a deer at the end of flight. It would do for a while, while she licked her wounds and practised her skills: it made her giddy with relief. Something she recognized as soon as she saw it, like a dress in a window which suddenly incorporated everything she might have wanted to be, an understated sense of all the freedom and privacy money might buy. The only things which Elisabeth did

78

not like were the icons hanging in the hall: they were dark and disturbing, she turned instead to another detail which somehow captivated. The high windows in the south-facing living room were manoeuvred open and shut by means of long, plaited cords made of silk, red interwoven with dull gold, culminating in a tassel like an upside-down thistle with a short fringe, fitting the hand and cool to the touch. The tassels with their ropes were an oriental taste. Summoning the air by these extravagant ropes was like summoning the spirits. Thomas watched her touch these details, his face wearing the mask of tired amusement, delighted in her delight. She likes my house, he thought. She really likes it. The cue, therefore, to introduce Maria, carefully. He chose to present Maria in the wide spaces of the corridor between the north- and south-facing rooms, that endless corridor which had the kitchen on the north side too, a bedroom next to the turret room, another bedroom and two more minor rooms at the far end. There was a bathroom *en suite* with each bedroom.

You could, Elisabeth thought, camp a small army in here. I have never seen such space, or such a natural studio, I love it, I love it. I love it so much I want to shout. As I love – no, that is wrong – as I adore this painting on the easel in this room. The first, the best.

His voice came from a distance.

'Oh, and by the way, this is Maria. Maria loves art. She's very much at home here on that account. Also, she house-keeps, after her fashion. A chaperone! As if it were needed.' His ungainly shout of laughter echoed down the corridor, smothered by the icons and other paintings on the walls and the thick carpet beneath their feet. The mirth produced a shower of spit from his mouth which he smothered with a handkerchief. He was revolting in a quiet kind of way. The relative darkness of the hall seemed a strange place to meet the household, but all that was accidental.

Maria grinned, the smile taking her creases from the chin to the hair, a slightly delinquent grin which poured heart and soul into its shy self, and her great feet seemed to tap welcome in tune with the puzzled forehead and big mouth, shut now but stretched to express itself. She had a twisted upper lip, harelip perhaps, certainly rabbitlike, twitching, a chin covered with a fine fuzz which heightened the impression, so soft it was, skin the texture of orange peel and eyes which disappeared into buttons between heavy lids and equally heavy bags below. She was a benign kind of gnome, a hamster of a woman, quite beyond self-defence or the simple meaning of animosity, grinning and eagerly shaking hands, deliciously excited by this stranger. She stared at Elisabeth's head, mumbled, grinned in an orgy of delight. Elisabeth smiled back, distracted: put Maria into the realm of speechless scenery, with the dog and the chair on which she had sat, not treating her with derision, but with all the indifference of someone with more important things to occupy her mind.

'Maria is not loquacious,' Thomas said kindly, as if the point were not made by all those speechless smiles and her sudden shuffling out of sight. 'She comes in each day. She cannot speak well, untreated cleft palate, something like that . . . Neither she nor I can bear the sound of door bells:

we have a system.' He pointed to a tiny fixture in the wall, next to a light switch. 'Door lights, so that when Maria comes in and out, which she does all the time – she walks Butler, for instance – she presses the buzzer thing, but it doesn't buzz, it lights up here and there instead, a little red light, like a Christmas tree. Oh dear, how ridiculous you must find us . . .'

The same laugh again, the same shower of spittle. What Elisabeth registered was the other woman backing out of sight, not obsequiously but with dignified servitude all the same. It seemed impertinent to question who she was, but since Maria wore an apron round the shapeless form supported in turn by thickly encased legs and shoes which looked distinctly second hand, Elisabeth labelled her as the lady who does. Her eyes went back to the pictures on the corridor wall, where Maria had been lingering. Icons: shady faces of saintly ladies, gilded, ancient, magnificent.

Distracted, she missed the wave Maria gave in her direction, almost in front of her glazed eyes, transfixed as they were by some golden effigy of a virgin. A Greek icon. So said a small notice as if describing the thing for a gallery. 'Central panel of a triptych painted with the mother of God of the Rose', whoever she was. Perhaps Maria's parting wave was some farewell signal to Thomas, a creature clearly regarded not only as employer, but also as some medieval seigneur.

'Excuse me, I'll let her out.' Apologetically, Thomas followed her to the door. There was a combination lock, a battery of buttons which he pressed in quick succession like someone making a hurried telephone call, his back to her. On the last button, a red light came on above the door and the door clicked opened by a fraction. There were murmured words in the hall, goodbye, thank you, see you tomorrow, diffused in Elisabeth's head as she moved away into what might become her studio room. The voices were no more than the sound of buzzing insects on a summer's day, The front door clunked shut.

It took him a while to walk back to the room. She could sense his movements were slow and awkward: he had told her about his stroke, and she supposed him older than he was. She suspected that before he returned, he might well have detoured in the maze of this magnificent place. She did not really notice. Excitement gripped her in a soft vice. Butler the dog had risen and followed master and servant down the hall, came back with master. Elisabeth found the devotion touching.

She turned to the face on the easel in the south-facing room, dark now, clapped her hands in excitement, her face flushed with such exquisite beauty it made Thomas wince. There it was: perfection. Unsullied by life, unimpaired by that strong, Northern voice and colourful clothes chosen less for dignity than for the eye; he would have known her anywhere. Perfection, for once. He had to capture that moment, the first of so many instances he would capture again. For a second, he realized that the beauty was not only in the face and the texture of the face, but in that split-second expression worn with pleasure. You would have to go on, pleasing her with things. In the next moment, with a mixture of sadness, triumph, uncertainty, Thomas knew his trap was sprung.

'Listen,' he said, with a feigned awkwardness which sounded completely explicable. 'Listen, I do feel awful. I mean inviting you to stay. Your bathroom has toothbrushes, all those things, of course, but anything else you need, I do assure you, we can find tomorrow ... I love shopping, did I say that? Do I repeat myself?'

'You can shop all you want for me. I hate it,' she said, turning on him with a smile which shook his solid body to the marrow of an uncooperative frame.

'That's all right, then,' said Thomas. 'I mean that's perfectly fine.'

Serve you right, Beauty, who has chosen the Beast, saint who has chosen Mammon. Serve you right. You have accepted everything. And that means me.

CHAPTER FIVE

She was aware, and was not ashamed, of being faintly in love. With this smudged and shadowed face, the first of the paintings he had shown. Not a sentimental love, but an intense affection quite removed from sex, more like the proud love of a parent for a sweetly enquiring child, an awesome ownership more poignant for the transience of their acquaintance. Elisabeth knew that certain paintings have life, a force which spills from them and envelops the watcher in a strong embrace, the image remaining imprinted on the mind for ever. The face on the canvas had become her ally in a moment of mutual understanding: each recognized the other without criticism. She knew, too, what words she would resort to if asked to describe what she saw. She would do what others did, critics, buyers, collectors: she would describe the qualities of the thing, the tones, the glazes, the subtlety of palette, the brushstrokes, the depth, the perspective, wax lyrical on all

84

of these while carefully missing the point. Which was love, of a sort, a spurt of pure affinity given to the perfect as well as the imperfect, a strange subliminal link with another time and place, but always more particularly, a face, which had, in the mind's eye, been there all the time.

You are mine, with respect and without demand, for the moment. We have a pact of mutual respect.

So did Elisabeth address this face, not in so many words, more with a clucking and a cooing which did not even seem silly. She apologized to it for the washing and undressing which might have to follow, the removal of warts and uncomfortable treatment she might have to afflict. She should not invest these faces with such life: she knew she should not, but she did. Especially this anonymous, beautiful face, with the angle of the head so bizarre, so unportraitlike. Portraits had been her first love, still were, but not an exclusive attachment. Rembrandt wrote his autobiography in self-portraits, and quite a brute he was. Gainsborough described his clients as the continual hurry of one fool upon the back of another, captured their vapidness but delivered them to posterity (she did not applaud Gainsborough for this cynicism), while what she had always liked in principle were those sixteenth-century portrait painters who were paid to enhance the glorious detail of their sitter's clothes, to celebrate riches, status, lace and gold, but never to sign what they made. The artist's identity rarely acknowledged; a feature of those days when he was no more esteemed than any other craftsman, a distressing humility in his anonymity. And anonymity was an attribute of this painting, along with all

Thomas's other paintings, a feature which delighted her beyond words.

'Oh no,' he had explained in the hypnotic light of the fire. 'I did not collect any of the work there. I am the curator. My parents were rich and left me richer.' This was said with a quiet acknowledgement of undeserved good fortune, a humble little pixie, reassuring in self-denigration. 'They were the patrons. Of whom? No one knows. They would not be aligned to anyone or anything, and nor shall I be when I follow suit. They would not flatter any individual or any nationality and, such purists they were, they would not collect for investment. You see, they didn't want either the reputation of connoisseurs or a cache of wealth, there was plenty of that. And they could not bear paying a premium for a name when it was simply a painting they wanted. So they amassed, with two criteria, I think; we never discussed it. One, they should like what they saw, and two, there would be no name. The result was, as you see, varied.'

'How strange. Not the first criterion, the other.'

'Oh, do you think so?' Thomas stood, weight to the left, head on one side like a bespectacled bird, inquisitively harmless. 'Personally, I don't. They were very self-contained people,' he added, as if that explained much. 'They weren't collecting for an audience. Anyway, they died.'

'Here?' she enquired shyly. People's parents, dead or alive, were often the fault line in their lives, the cue for explosions of sentiment, history, fury or weeping. She knew that, remained silent on the subject, allowed no sound of their footsteps, subdued all hauntings from the past.

'No,' he said, spitting again. 'In an aeroplane. They went to Lourdes, with my . . . Whilst I was away from home.'

'What was their living?'

'Oh, my father, he printed missals, holy pictures, religious books. Things like that. Mostly pictures. He acquired, erhmm, an eclectic taste.'

The history was brief, she noticed, not to be expanded for now, and she took it with a hint of disbelief. So Thomas had inherited, humbly, whatever he had inherited: he was whatever charming casualty he was and that was all. Elisabeth had little need to know. There were three hundred paintings in this large apartment. Stored, he said. What she could see was a mere sample. She had agreed to stay because of them, without regard to her clothes or her flat or her commitments, for a day or two. Because of the paintings themselves and because she had become so desperately afraid of the footsteps outside, because it was warm in here and this man respected privacy; he was discretion incarnate. Because some of these three hundred acquisitions might be exquisitely bad, others the vibrant work of unsung masters, the whole collection bearing witness to taste both vulgar and sublime. The only uniformity lay in the fact that none, not one, of the paintings was signed. What she saw was the clue to a humble collection of brilliance, and to treat it was a privilege beyond the purest dreams. The proximity of so many paintings simply made her happy.

It was fitting, oddly appropriate, that she should stand in a room full of light, like a woman blessed, wearing another person's clothes. A stiff cotton overall, not her own folded back at the wrist, made for the longer arms of the previous incumbent who had left for reasons which might have included the lack of kudos in devoting weeks of his life to such glorious anonymity. 'I hoped you would be different,' Thomas said, a hope gravely confirmed. The dog, Butler, stood by, warm and close, affection deepset in his brown-ringed eyes. Among them all she was cocooned. She did not know where she had left her coat, had washed her yesterday's underwear, found within reach all the rudimentary tools of her trade, and was ready to begin. Thomas left her alone in the room with the fine armchairs, the scrubbed wood floor, the perfect light from the low windows and the high. No one listened for her presence: the telephone was silent; there were no footsteps, no step step click, one two click, making their sinister dancing sound, nothing but light, peace, safety, privacy. The face in the painting smiled. Beyond it, in a kind of unfocused sepia haze swam the face of Thomas, closed behind spectacles, still faintly, unconvincingly familiar.

Annie Macalpine was familiar with this sensation, sickeningly familiar. Halfway through Tuesday, with never a client in sight, the Antiques Centre awash with wasted and jaundiced electric light, her hands full of paper and her eyes dizzy with print, sorting and checking the contents of her huge desk. This was the day for doing her accounts, tracing all those slips and notes she vowed she would file but never did until this frightful day of reckoning. Stocktaking, inventory-taking, panicking, the day she dreaded and postponed until it could be delayed no longer, even allowing for the fact that what she told the VAT-man and the Inland Revenue relied heavily on her creative skills, her flair for telling an elegant lie which had been so well rehearsed with the clients. Not that I cheat, mind, Annie promised others as well as her own reflection. She did not cheat, was simply frugal with the truth if the truth was likely to hurt her, and she would abandon truth altogether if the pursuit of it beggared herself and profited government officials. On their behalf, she had no conscience: they were a load of non-laughing hyenas, the lot of them, sent to savage her carcass before it was dead. She had even seduced one once. But for the clients, a different matter. She gave up. Sat on the floor in her corner with the dust and the despair and the shared telephone line. What a shit hole. What a bastard. What a time to tell her he was not coming back. The man who had been sharing her bed for the last nine months, a period other people regarded as the proper incubation period for a baby or a reliable love affair, but which was for Annie the time it usually took to be loved and abandoned. The bastard.

'And you . . . and you . . . and you.' She threaded pieces of paper, invoices and receipts on to a spike, like a short-order cook overwhelmed in a busy kitchen. 'And especially you.' A letter from him, as prosaic as most, ending, 'Look after yourself, Annie. I hope we'll always be friends,' was the one she ripped with her teeth and let flutter to the floor with all the rest of the detritus from her desk.

I hope we'll always be friends . . . Elisabeth had helped her with her accounts before, was a friend in need, an efficient and compulsive keeper of paper who never cheated anyone, not even a government hyena. And whose concern is she? Not mine, not mine, not mine. There was a moment of terrible alarm, a sense of guilt as sharp as indigestion. Annie pretended it was indigestion. Tears had melted her favoured purple and pink eye shadow into the colour of a dead violet on her cheek. What unhinged her now was her own bloody inefficiency. Love had proved bad for the memory.

There was a picture, a sodding picture, just for something completely different, and while she bloody well knew where it was, in Lizzie's house being cleaned or something, she could not, for the life of her, remember who owned it. Annie was not quite a jack of all trades, but she not only sold pictures, she got other pictures restored for customers, she did whatever she was asked to do provided it turned a profit or commission, half of which she declared to the hyenas, while the other half went on friends, wine and men, she recalled, not necessarily in that order. A picture of a room with two leather chairs, a fire and a lot of space, a good but over-detailed picture in her own estimation, but Lizzie had liked it, she who loved the oddest things and was owed two thousand pounds. A picture without a signature which came from some client she could not remember for love or money, damn. Lizzie might know to whom it belonged, that and the other three she could not recall. But Lizzie was owed two thousand pounds which was also owed to the taxman, so Annie did not phone, because she did not want to feel even worse. Coloured tears fell on the floor between her crossed legs. They splashed against the grey-black of her leggings, hugging her rounded calves and thin ankles grown grubby on the bare bone against the floor still littered with the gold flakes from a frame. Shit. She could not bear to forget: could always account for all her stock and all her clients, had the reputation of never letting anyone down and she would have died for that reputation. When Francis Thurloe telephoned, he was surprised by the bruises in the voice, waited for the frenetic conversation he had encountered before, from a woman who was as loquacious as her friend Elisabeth could be taciturn. It was Annie who had sent him to Elisabeth in the first place. She was usually highly efficient.

'Oh. Francis who? Oh, I get you. Hi.'

She did not ask what he wanted, electrified as she was by a brief surge of hope. 'Listen, Francis, I know you've bought from me before, and this might seem an odd question, but did you ever give me a picture for our Lizzie to clean? An interior, with chairs? No? What? Never mind. Just a wild guess, only I can't remember who it bloody belongs to, must be someone highly memorable, can't have been a handsome man like you. You've seen it at her place? Course you have, that's not the question.'

Well, she knew about that: he'd seen everything there was to see in Elisabeth's place, lucky bitch, and hadn't she done them a favour by introducing them to one another, and what thanks did she get? When did anyone ever do that for her, introduce her to someone single, reliable and good-looking? Even Elisabeth had someone now, as well as a painting by some damn owner who would be howling for it soon. Annie did not like the human race at the moment.

'All right are you?' she asked, wiping pink from her sleeve, noticing the dirt on her shoes. 'You want a chat, you said? Something important? Ooh, that I should be so lucky. Yeah, come in any time. A drink? Yeah, when?'

Piss off. Her mind cleared, miraculously. Why worry, why be in such a state when a little mountain exploded into a minefield of molehills? Whoever the lost client was, he would phone, in time. Then she would remember his name, get the painting back, everything fine and the same for the others she could not recall. Francis Thurloe had sounded so concerned. He had, she noticed, a very nice voice and if Elisabeth was as cavalier and unpredictable with him as she had been with other perfectly presentable, unmarried men, she, Annie, might just do something about it. Such as offer a bit of home comfort, draw him out of his upper-crust shell. She wiped her nose on the dirtied sleeve. There was more than one fish in the sea: she didn't have to settle for an eel. Proud of her pun, she rocked with noisy mirth.

Elisabeth squinted in the last of the daylight. Her back hurt, deceived into stooping for longer by that bonus of an hour of extra light which would have been denied in her own studio. That dark room was a foreign place now: she felt as if she had been here for ever.

The face in the painting smiled fainter: Elisabeth knew that same flood of recognition for a friend seen in different clothes. Two days to remove the varnish: how kind of

Thomas to understand the necessary slowness of progress, how rare in a client to see what she had to do. Acetone, dilute with white spirit, to remove the varnish, a different dilution for each small portion of the picture. You can't just wash it all over, she explained: the varnish may not be the same varnish or the same thickness; beneath that, there may be glazes, thin coloured washes with more varnish used as the medium, making pigment more vulnerable in one area than another. I must experiment with this, one centimetre at a time. Look at the drapery behind, and isn't she lovely?

She was indeed lovely, this woman, lovelier still without the varnish which had aged and darkened her. A dark-haired woman surprised, a nineteenth-century portrait, but not with the face staring stolidly at camera or present-ing her best profile. Not the full-frontal or seductive side-view pose, which was all most sitters could maintain. The woman here was leaning over the back of a chair, the chair tilted while she gestured with her outstretched hand, palm upwards as if reaching for another outstretched hand, smiling, beckoning the world into her own. She could have been reaching or inviting: the expression was teasing with-out malice, but there was also a shade of anxiety, the glance of a woman looking back, over her shoulder, turning to something precious from which she had come, giving a warm welcome which would ask questions later. She could have been inviting in a child or a ghost, but the slight matronliness of her clothing suggested a child. Whoever it was, the woman knew the nature of love denied but would not cease to offer it. There was a richness in the dress, the abundant brown hair was coiffed, the brilliant blue taffeta of her gown bunched by the violence of her twisted stance, swirled round her hidden knees in stiff glory, the chair back brittle, creaking with the weight of the gown, not the slender form inside it. Against the stiff silk of the high-necked dress, the skin was olive, slightly wrinkled round the eyes, and creased at the wrist of the hand. She had been messed about, this woman, and her necklace was all wrong.

At the moment, there was a white film covering the varnish-clear surface, the residue of purely superficial cleaning. Beneath that, slightly raised areas on the neck, raised areas in the upper corner of the room into which she compelled the onlooker to enter. Elisabeth concentrated on these patches where the craquelure was less, perhaps betraying later additions and dark suspicions.

It was not only the restorer in Elisabeth who had begun, by Tuesday, to experience the first feelings of unease.

Skin tones: she must look at the skin of this olive neck, where the necklace had yielded a faint trace of pigment on to her cotton wool. There were signs of previous restoration beneath the varnish, so thick and crystalline in parts that she had actually rubbed it off with a forefinger. There had been someone's hands at the neck of this lovely, inviting lady. Perhaps that necklace, the painting comparatively clumsy, was not quite the set of sapphires it seemed. As the tungsten light (new, thoughtfully provided in the comprehensive provision which was contributing to her unease) flooded the painting, Elisabeth heard from the door of the room a gasp of admiration. Maria was watching. Elisabeth turned and smiled.

The small figure at the door was the ghost of the apartment, whom Elisabeth had ignored from the moment of their introduction as an incomprehensible creature who was apparently vital to the ménage, the oil and the cog of domestic arrangements which allowed Thomas to live with almost invisible support. Maria, the servant, the factotum, the walker of the dog, the link with the world who brought none of the world into his home, Elisabeth did not know quite what she was. Maria, encountered on Sunday, out and in during Monday, was suddenly, speechlessly here now. All Elisabeth knew of Maria, or had cared to know, was that she was wiry, middle-aged, stooped, strong, moustachioed, and, if she were to speak at all, would be slow and reluctant to articulate. 'Maria,' Thomas had explained succinctly, 'does for Butler and me. Nicely.' Now, removed from that moment of terse explanation, Elisabeth wondered if Thomas needed around him in his splendid isolation people and living things which were, like Butler and Maria, somehow ugly and incomplete. So far, in her brief glimpses of Maria dragging out the vacuum cleaner like a captive animal, arriving with eggs, milk, frozen foods on which the household dined regularly, departing with tail-wagging Butler, Elisabeth had not detected a hint of beauty, spiritual or otherwise. But then, Elisabeth had not been looking: she was long since blinded by colour into something like indifference for anything which breathed.

'Isn't she lovely?' Elisabeth asked conversationally.

No response. Then a quick nod of the head, an agreement; then a folding of the arms, a self-hugging rather than defiance which revealed another person intensely impressed by what she saw, enough to make Elisabeth like her for ever. On one wrist, there was a large, fresh bandage; the other hand cradled the injury. The bandage callously reminded Elisabeth of the materials she did not have here, such as medical gauze or a certain kind of spatula. Less callously, out of her own profound kindness which bled when others flinched, she asked the only polite question which came to mind.

'Have you burnt yourself, Maria? What happened? Cooking?' She did not know why she asked this: there was no evidence that Maria ever cooked beyond the preparation of frozen suppers which Thomas ordered and she merely collected for this house. Maria opened her mouth to show her appalling teeth, raised the bandaged wrist and made little snapping motions within inches of her fingers, shrugged, cradled her arms again. Elisabeth had no idea what the gesture meant, clucked in sympathy, felt the cut on her thumb and empathized. Maria's eyes were back on the picture, excited.

'Like a mother!' she spat, pointing at the face with her bandaged hand, using the good hand to smooth her own hair which sprang grey and black in all directions. They were all the same colours in this house. 'Like our mother . . . beautiful.' It sounded like a curse, whispered with such effort, such severe approbation, such intensity, but in her ugly face with its deplorable teeth Elisabeth saw the same affection, the same link with that smiling, uncertain, suffering face on canvas that she herself knew. She was right, of course: out of the mouth of babes . . . the painting was like a madonna, a serenely blessing madonna. Claptrap, utter nonsense, life in a painting. Ha! In that one moment of mutual grinning, both with their damaged hands, they were allies of a sort, she and half-dumb, mysterious Maria. Elisabeth had no need of an ally: she had paintings and colour and warmth and light and privacy and tools and everything and Thomas, defective, charming, Thomas. There was a light behind the head of the portrait, cast by a lamp in the painted room, which made that lovely face look as if it wore a halo. From around her wrist, Maria suddenly produced a set of rosary beads, cheap, plastic and garish. She held them against the madonna's face, then against Elisabeth's face, studying the effect.

'OK. Maria, OK, OK, OK . . .'

The little woman spun round, like a weather-house doll propelled by machinery, left the room as quietly as she had arrived, apart from the sound of her beads. Thomas and Butler stood in the doorway she had vacated, framed by electric light from the corridor, all of them drawn and held still by the earth tones on the easel, lit by the tungsten light. Butler shuffled, sat and sighed: it was a kind of mimicry of Maria: Elisabeth wondered if there had been some snapping of Thomas's good fingers to make the dog do that and to make the other woman, who looked oddly like him, move so abruptly, as if she were afraid.

'"Like a mother",' he remarked neutrally. 'I don't know

what Maria might mean by that. Her own, I suppose, poor soul. Do come and have a drink. I know these lights work miracles, but too much of them must be bad for the eyes. Take a rest. You've been working too hard. How beautiful she is.'

Down the long corridor there was a soft thud as a door shut. Elisabeth realized she could not even remember how she had reached the dizzy heights of this floor, was it fourth floor or fifth? By the lift, or by the stairs? Had she walked in humility or allowed herself to be carried aloft, still afraid of those footsteps? A blur, a foggy blur of memory, the few days since stretched into as many years. The colours had taken over. Madame in the picture beckoned. So did Thomas and his silly dog and the prospect of a drink in a fine-cut glass, but for the moment the madonna of the portrait ruled supreme.

'My father's house has many mansions, my mother's house has many rooms.' Thomas's voice teasing and mesmeric and still, dancing before her eyes, that faint glaze of alarm, like a pigment mixed with varnish rather than oil, not quite a solid colour. Soothed, smothered by the brandy and the wine and this lack of responsibility as well as the prospect of work tomorrow. All that.

'Is there anything you need?' asked Thomas, looking like a Christmas elf from behind his darkened glasses.

'Oh no, not yet. But I should go home tomorrow. Things, you know. Other things. I need to collect a few things, tend to a few things.' She found her laugh unnecessarily loud.

'What a pity,' he said. 'Just when we were doing so well. I could go back and fetch anything you wanted, you know. Send dear old Butler in advance. After all, what else do I have to do? A rich man's life can be so dull, you know. Amazingly dull.' The pixie face, puckered beneath the dark glasses, was so rueful, he looked so comic, the disfigured man with his odder dog presenting a paw. She laughed at this solicitude, became suddenly sober, all the same reassured, but resolute.

'All right, not tomorrow. The next day. We could move some of these pictures to my own studio without any harm, you know. Oils on canvas are durable. Do you know the first practical application of oils, or if not the first, nearly, was for banners? They tried using oil to hold pigment and make it spread instead of egg white, which was hard but unbendable, found they could use pigment and oil on the same hemp they used for battle flags, not just on board . . . Tempera was always on board, panels for churches, that sort of thing. Oil paint could bend. Marvellous: you could wrap it up and move it, more marvellous still. The first painters in oil must have been sign writers. Paid the equivalent of what you'd pay a man to decorate your shop today. But you shouldn't bend oil paint on canvas, not really. Thieves think you can, because of films, but you can't, not if you fold it outside in, which is what a thief might do, to protect the surface, and what thieving dealers do all the time. Actually, if you were stealing a canvas, you should roll it outside out. That way, it won't crack, the paint, I mean: it does the other way, especially if you leave it rolled tight.' She was almost weeping

99

at the thought of such destruction, realized she was rambling, the custom of exhaustion, did not mind about anything. Except another glass of wine to replace the first large one thrust into her hand and drunk rapidly. And about anyone going into her house. Her flat was her bastion of stability, her island: she had temporarily forgotten its sublime importance in her life, and she was shocked by her fickleness. She had liked this man up to now: how dare he suggest such an invasion. He did not suggest it again.

'How beautiful she is,' he said, softly. 'The painting. How sweet of Maria to say whatever she said. She probably wanted to bless it. "Like a mother". The best compliment she knew. That's the way to look at it. She is not lucky, Maria.'

'Are you related?' Elisabeth asked, apropos of nothing, on an impulse. His back was turned and his voice a distant negative, 'Oh no, no, not as far as I realize.' A faint giggle. There was that delirious glug, glug, glug, as her glass, a goblet as heavy in the hand as the original brandy glass, was topped up again. My cup runneth over. She forgot unease, forgot any shade of suspicion and her eyes were tired.

'Well, you don't really need anything from home, do you?' said Thomas lazily. 'Nothing tomorrow, anyway. You go home whenever you like.'

'I hear these footsteps,' she announced suddenly, leaving the wine untouched. 'Funny steps. Round my house, strange places. Railway station, places like that. I see someone in the distance with a knife. I always imagine my father and his stick, but I know it can't be that.' She was ashamed of the confession, blamed the wine.

'Why didn't you say? How absolutely, utterly dreadful for you.' His voice was shocked, indignant, full of belief and care, with none of the incredulity she had dreaded. 'You don't hear them here?'

'No.'

He heaved a large sigh: Butler followed suit, the shadow of the man, his alter ego.

'Thank God for that. I feel I should be a terrible host if you did. You must be quite safe here. I couldn't live with myself else. Give yourself a break, please, dear Elisabeth, please. Don't go home yet.'

The frozen supper was turning itself into something eminently edible. There was a waft of it, trouble-free food which did not even have to be carved. She had freedom of his kitchen, had not taken advantage, was hungry and still thirsty.

'You're very kind,' she murmured. 'But no one goes into my home. I forbid it, you see. I'll go back. Not tomorrow. Too much to do tomorrow, but after that I might invite her home, your madonna. If you see what I mean. Lovely here, if you see what I mean, good lights, good everything, but I prefer to work at home. If you see what I mean.'

'A private person,' murmured Thomas in his small and pompous voice, no hint of offence in its timbre. 'Yes, of course, I see what you mean. The last person here went poking in cupboards.'

'I wouldn't dream of doing that.'

They had moved to the room which faced north. He

turned right away from her to take off his glasses and polish them on his handkerchief. Always correctly dressed, this man, a jacket, a shirt, a tie. The fire lit his averted face, small, benign, tranquil, and in that second all the familiarity came together and she knew with a flood of anguish who he was.

Not what he was, who he might have been. The sensation passed, leaving her blushing. She was used to being wrong.

Enid's house was empty, the building free of residents, the cat owners on holiday, the others simply out until late at night, in the bosoms of families such as Enid did not have. All she could hear was the plumbing as the machinery creaked into life. In the long evenings, so much longer since the changing of the clocks, she sat still in her bedroom and listened. There was no ringings of the bell for Elisabeth, none of those irritations, those delicious cues for outrage and intervention, no rug in the hall, nothing to scold, nothing to grumble about when she met the other few and disagreeable retired women in the street. Everyone in this street pretended to spend their lives in a state of constant movement, as if that made them less of a target for conversation.

There was a dripping sound downstairs, into the yard which flanked the garden. She could not even hear those footsteps outside any more. Steps, one two click, one two click, the stuttering footfall of a pirate with a crutch, pausing on the pavement, reminding her of some half-forgotten story. It was as if all life had gone from the vicinity in the absence of Elisabeth, who had departed without so much as a by your leave, a message, a request to water pot plants, leaving that drip, drip, drip. She had gone with the same hurtful indifference to any offer of Enid's ministrations, and the absence hurt as much as the presence.

Enid knew there were strange things in Elisabeth's apartment: she had smelt. She had a vague inkling of flammable poisons, worse, of woodworm, dust, decay, things eating through. That and the curiosity and the silence, compounded by the drip which she really knew was her own problem, drove her downstairs. To listen at the door with a creeping sense of glee and nothing else to do.

Only listening at first. Looking at the door, inviting it to open so she could take this chance and see inside at long last. Then after another day's silence, she went away to fetch a hammer and a screwdriver. Who would know? Who would ever know if she did what she wanted to do? She should have let me in, Enid justified to herself, she should have done that: I only want to help and, besides, she could be dead.

'O sacred heart, sweet fount of love and mercy . . .'

Maria was crooning, less because of her uncritical devotion to religious ritual, than because of the reminders on her walls. The current favourite was an effigy of Jesus, wearing a heart as big as his torso on the chest of a pristine white shift, the brilliant red of it lit from within and surrounded by a graphic crown of thorns. Blood oozed from the thorns; one, long, aesthetic hand of the saviour pointed to his afflictions, the other was raised in benediction.

Flowing brown locks cascaded on to his shoulders, framing a pointed and mournful face and a perfectly barbered beard. There were red holes in his hands, clean little wounds which did not bleed. Now that was art, thought Maria, that really was. Why did Thomas upstairs not collect art like this, the kind which comforted and inspired and told you something? Maria chided herself, because looking at Jesus she remembered the woman in blue, the madonna upstairs. The two madonnas, to be precise; the one in the painting, then the perfect maiden who was Thomas's guest and spent her time washing the other one with such gentleness. Veronica wiped the face of Jesus, Mary Magdalene washed his feet; she had pictures to prove it and, yes, that was perfect art, although of course the lovely girl upstairs who bent with such suppleness about her task could not be confused with a Magdalene. She was too sweet: she would never have been a sinner, and, besides, Thomas said so. The new ménage was all very confusing, but comforting. Good to have this nunlike woman about the place with her quiet humility. Someone who encouraged Thomas in purer tastes.

Maria's own walls held many depictions reminiscent of the beautiful madonnas above stairs. Virgins in robes of a similar blue, differing only, in Maria's eyes, because of the lack of sharp definition in their haloes. A beautiful touch, the haloes: it would be nicer if Thomas had more people with haloes about himself, either in person or on the walls. Nicely *perfect*, like the girl. Maria's mouth fell open with the sudden fear of her own reflections. She could not sing any more.

It was cold down here. Kneeling by the side of her bed on her bare knees, Maria surveyed her own art gallery, offered her suffering up to God. She saw this chilliness as something to be held on deposit against her own sins and those of others.

Lord, she prayed, save my brother. Save him from what he might do. He has always been a sinner, because he cannot believe in what is good. Save him, Lord.

CHAPTER SIX

'A painting is only in perfect condition when it is new and painted by a careful hand. There is a minimum of three levels to the structure; first the support, which may be canvas, wood or paper. This is lined with sizing of various kinds, glue, casein, gesso, to make the surface suitable for oil paint. Then there is the first sketch, in pigment, thinly dilute by oil for the easy creation of outlines. On that is built the picture itself, in layers, the thickest paint ideally coming last. Each layer should dry before the next: the process must not be rushed. The careful artist does not apply a quick-drying paint below one which dries slowly (all mixtures, all pigments vary), unless he wishes to encourage serious cracking of the surface. If the paint is scientifically applied in this manner it will grow its own skin and become perfect because all layers are fused, the one with the other. Later, lack of care in the choice of material will show . . .'

Pompous. Not even quite true, surely? The Pre-Raphaelite technique, to get those jewel colours, was to paint on to a layer of fresh white oil paint while it was still wet. The treatise he read sounded like the history of a man and his emotional and physical development, and there were times, few and far between, when Francis Thurloe found his pictorial possessions irritating, still more thinking about them. He had become excessively tidy out of a desire to control his environment, expected things to stay in place although he no longer anticipated the same from people. Deposits of dust were controllable but the beauty of possessions should be static, and their mysterious movement was beyond him. Perhaps that was why he collected at all, to share that vision of the painter's eye and, then, control it. He did not like 'perhaps'. The word had no place in his language.

What infuriated him now was the shifting of a picture painted on hardboard by some artist who could not afford canvas. Oil on canvas was best, oil on seasoned panel next best (there was some argument about that), and the use of convenient alternatives progressively more hazardous. That much he guessed. The cheaper support of this bargain masterpiece was warped by the heat in the room and the thought made him resentful. Was he supposed to live his whole life in a cool cellar like a case of wine in order to preserve his investments?

Not only warped, but ever moving. It was a figurative picture of a housemaid in a blue dress sitting near a colourful kitchen range reading a book, and it would not hang straight, crept up, crept down or sideways as soon as his back was turned. He swore with loud energy, shaking his fist at the wall. The picture did not respond; remained precisely as crooked and impertinent as before. Museums might employ staff with the express task of straightening frames for all he knew. He, on the other hand, left strict instructions with his cleaning woman not to touch anything hanging on the wall, an order which shamed him as much as forbidding a clumsy grandmother to touch a favourite child. Why not just brace them to the wall, lock them in place? he had asked in bewilderment, innocent in his controlled enthusiasm. He had met the baleful stare of Elisabeth. They are supposed to move, she said: if you keep them still they will buckle and rebel and find some way to shift: the support will shrug off paint to teach you a lesson. They will do what they must, crack if they must; you never really own them, you know.

'Thanks,' Francis said aloud. 'Thanks a million. And for nothing.' Over the past few days he had rationalized the denouement of his unexpected and highly passionate affair with Elisabeth. He liked his ladies slender, he told himself; he liked them fun and he preferred them, like his possessions, to lack complications. There had been a great gulp of conscience last Sunday, all of five days ago, about that conversation with Elisabeth. He had to acknowledge it as cruel because he knew that he would have been ashamed to overhear himself. And he would not have liked to be the target of his words.

'She deserved it,' he had repeated, recognizing in those words an all too familiar, all too shallow, timbre. So said his clients when asked to explain beating their wives. So had said the client today when asked to excuse the wrecking of a stolen picture. Without that case assigned to him by his clerk who knew Francis's art-collecting proclivities, he might have chosen to forget Elisabeth, forget her as another in the chain of girls who had become inconvenient to remember.

'You'll like this case, sir. Just up your street. Culture and all that. Burglary, with criminal damage on the goods. I ask you.'

'I didn't ask you.' Francis was mild in the frostiness which had typified his behaviour all week.

'Well, I'm telling you. Not getting our oats, are we? The client's in for a conference. No one else can do it.'

And the client, oh, the client, little and brittle and sour. Seventeen years old, a seasoned burglar who for reasons best known to himself had taken two paintings from a house, kept them in his bedsit pending disposal, which was difficult because he did not know where to start except in the pub at the end of his road, not an imaginative thief. I could have pointed you in the direction of a dealer or two, Francis thought: some are less fussy than others. Instead, the client had hung his spoils on the walls, admired for a while one picture of children playing, the other of a smiling couple, and, then, cut them to pieces.

The photograph of this carnage reminded Francis of the stark advertisements which revealed, in a depiction of tearing skin, the ravages of multiple sclerosis. To his jaundiced mind, this damage was infinitely worse than burglary, something akin to rape: he had suffered a brief reminder of the outrage caused when he had kicked those damaged oils in Elisabeth's larger, equally spartan room. He had a brief and painful recall of the geography of her apartment, remembered the existence of the other room, her studio, where he had never been allowed and never sought entry. He did not know why he had been so incurious. The client did not know why or how he had done such a thing.

'They deserved it,' he had said. 'They looked at me.'

'Looked at you?'

'Yeah. All the time. Talked to me and all. They made my room crowded, those paintings.'

A very crowded room, the burglar's, cramped as it was with all the impedimenta of living as well as the proceeds of burglaries, a certain siege mentality about these four rented walls.

'They looked at me, them paintings. All the time. Alive they were: they tried to get into bed. Like my mother.'

'Like who?' Francis knew he sounded pompous.

'Nothing. Nothing.'

A painting has life then, as if he did not know. He remembered some traveller's tale, of a place where the inhabitants believed that a photograph took some of your soul, that some little finite bit of you would remain on the print, diminishing the rest. If there was life in this canvas wrecked by a bread knife, but not beyond restoring, like a man injured but well within the competence of an Elisabeth, what price her obsessions? She had found society with her inanimate friends, where the client, this lonely little burglar, this moving unit of harm, found enemies.

'All right,' said Francis wearily to the client, himself out-manoeuvred, his own motives somehow called into question. 'Could you have done this damage accidentally?'

Francis took his route home that day past the street where she lived, saw the blinds drawn down across her windows. I am only a lawyer and an ordinary human being, he told himself, nothing special, although he believed the opposite: I should not be so confused or abused by the silent indifference of any woman. I am like a painting cracked, no longer fused in all my layers and I cannot be bothered to care. My paintings can be fastened to the wall, that burglar's sentence can be minimized, he is only young, but I feel elderly, a little conscience-stricken.

The evening was bitterly cold, a sudden snap to teach the unwary that clock-changing did not merely herald winter but provoked it. Snow soon, they said on the radio. The same who said a stiff breeze tonight, on the eve of a hurricane. Francis Thurloe had his first acquaintance not with loneliness, but with the fear of it. Pictures, he thought: I shall have pictures and undemanding women for company. He was ashamed of his sentiments.

Thomas was faintly gratified, ever so slightly triumphant that Elisabeth should jump when he came into the room. Even more gratified when, once recovered, she could actually behave as if he were not there, carry on with her absorption. Hidden in that was the faintest insult which he could not quite formulate, a lingering resentment of the long-established fact that women ignored his presence. All they have ever done, he thought to himself, is to

111

ignore me and cripple me and control me: I cannot imagine why they should remain so charming. Elisabeth bent with her back to him, squatting on the floor to rummage in the paint box, the broad curve of her rump draped gracefully by the worn blue smock. There were attitudes in women which so emphasized their contours as to make them unreal. Like the *Rokeby Venus* in the National Gallery: the woman lying with her back to the spectator, the valley of her waist accentuating the enormous curve of hip and tapering legs, the dramatic features of nudity, which upright, in clothes, would look merely slender. How small women were dressed, how enormous naked.

'I see you've begun on the next one,' he remarked. 'I don't know why I thought you would do them one at a time.' There was no hint of annoyance in his voice, merely that mild curiosity, tinged with admiration, which she found alternately comforting and uncomfortable.

'Well, no. I want to distance myself from this lady. I've cleaned, removed a bit here and there, but there's all this overpainting round the neck, you know. I'm not sure how much to take off. Don't want to damage what there is underneath. I'll think about it, dabble with it while I start here. I need to stand back from her.'

There was another painting on the easel, the beckoning lady, unvarnished, propped against the wall, the surface blind in the light, forever radiant.

'You did say,' Elisabeth was adding, 'that these three are the crucial ones. The ones you wanted restored more than any of the others. The ones you desperately wanted to see perfect, the best ones. There can't be any paintings better than these. You must find out who did them.'

He shook his head. 'I'm only looking for perfection,' he said. 'Not identities.'

The second painting was no ordinary still life. No fruit, flowers, cheese, game, eating utensils or hung birds, no scrubbed surfaces, pottery, china or brass, but an unstill still life, full of things which seemed warm to the touch. The focus was a bedroom chair, hurriedly festooned with clothes in layers as if they had not been placed there all at once but were the accumulation of a month's untidiness, a lifetime of rushing and flinging. Two odd shoes beneath the chair, a crumpled stocking, a spew of spilt art deco earrings, a few letters sticking out of a jacket collared with fox fur, a glorious muddle of textures. A tidy mind would want to reach into that interior in order to fold and put away, retrieve the spectacles which lay against an abandoned book, straighten the crumpled pages of the letters, sort out which of the clothing needed a wash. All that, visible and shocking, a brilliant and insolent piece of revelation, despite the damage of damp, the patches where the canvas, slowly gorged with moisture, had swelled beyond the endurance of layers of heavy paint and shrugged off the colour. Like the fox collar, where the paint was thickest, and in one corner of the painting, reflected in a mirror, the half-naked figure of a woman, looking at the mess she had made, full of early-morning confusion.

'It reminds me of my own bedroom, sometimes, not all the time,' Elisabeth said. She stood up, curling her spine, her legs straight, bending from the waist, supple. He did not seem to have heard, looked beyond her to the third canvas, propped face inwards against a chair.

'Please don't think you have to rush. There's all the time in the world.'

'I can't rush,' said Elisabeth. 'Look at me. I can't rush, I'm not made for rushing. Even if my bedroom does sometimes look like this.'

'Oh, I don't know about that,' he said, almost flirtatiously. 'About not being able to rush, I mean. And I always imagined – I mean, do imagine you – to be, rather tidy. I mean, you are here. Very tidy.' He was flustering, glad of her back to him. Freudian slip, Thomas boy. Watch the words: you are not supposed to have thought of this woman, much, before you met her. She was nothing but a name in a mouth; you imagined, in the past tense, nothing about her at all.

'Do you need anything?' he blundered on, slowing his voice to a crawl. 'I mean, materials, anything you haven't got here? Even if not immediately, something you may need another day . . . Tell me while you remember. I'm going shopping.'

She paused, reflectively, considered.

'A sable fan brush, sometime,' she murmured. 'I might need it if I have to in-paint much of this fur collar. Can't think of another brush which would do, but no worry. I'll get mine when I go home.' It was two days since she had last mentioned that. Somehow the need for home was being obviated, eroded hour by hour.

'Fine,' he said. 'Fine. See you later.'

114

I shall buy her more paints, he said to himself. Tubes and tubes of paint. And other gifts.

In his departure, she realized again how the footsteps, the one two click, had faded from her mind. There was no scope for footsteps in the vastness of this place, the soft carpet, the warmth, the silent toing and froing. She had not heard a telephone, not even vaguely muffled through doors, the sound of washing machine, flushing cistern, anything. Her right hand throbbed painfully, the cut from the glass stem grasped in the aftermath of the quarrel with Francis exerting a delayed revenge for lack of treatment, protesting at the constant squeezing of finger and thumb round soaked cotton wool, the white spirit a deterrent to healing. In the last few days, she had become habituated to the colours of flesh, round the neck of the olive-skinned woman, so oddly restored before, to give her a new, disparate necklace, or to hide some unsightly scar. Elisabeth had stopped on that painting out of caution. It was unwise to tire the eyes with the same palette, time to refresh them with another.

There was something amiss with the madonna. How much amiss she had yet to find. The unease, soaped away by concentration, filtered back. She gazed at the room in the second painting, willed herself to forget the first, but she was suddenly restless. Thomas in the flat was that rare kind of presence which did not disturb, who gave her the impression she was in all senses entirely alone, the way she liked to feel, although she knew he was there, sitting, reading, telephoning or whatever he did to ensure his invisible means of support, his endless tranquillity. But there was still a different sensation when he went out, an extra depth of emptiness. Guiltily, she remembered she had not even seen the inarticulate Maria today or yesterday; had not asked about that bandaged wrist, forgot her existence. A door, Thomas had said shaking his head sadly. Maria never makes way for doors: she keeps her hand inside until she knows it should be elsewhere. I have never known a woman so clumsy, but then I have not known many women. Poor Maria.

Was she poor Elisabeth? Did he pity her? Was that the reason for all this solicitude, the extension of the kind of pity he gave Maria, whose talents as cleaner and dog walker he otherwise bemoaned? There was a routine in the dog walking, a rigid routine to this life of his which had gradually impressed itself upon her. Butler was guard and loving companion, but theirs was an indoor friendship like something clandestine; they rarely crossed the portals to the outside world together: Thomas stayed in when Butler went out, twice in the day, with Maria, his escort. And then, when Thomas went out, the black and white mongrel stayed indoors, or had for the last days, as far as she noticed. An unprotesting, ever affectionate dog; even his bladder was regimented by love and obedience.

'Butler?'

Elisabeth wandered into the corridor outside what had become her room, her light-filled, colour-filled, excitement-filled domain, the second home, but, suddenly, no replacement for the hard-won first. 'Butler? Walkies?' There was this sudden and overpowering desire to go, simply go. Out, home, collect a sable fan brush, come

116

back, but go out first, walk alone, stretch legs, telephone, go shopping, behave like a person less freakish than what she knew she had become. Post the letters she had written last night, all brief, all cheerful, but vital for herself. Back in time for Thomas and the freshly unfrozen food, the lush warmth, the light, the reflections from her glass. Go home. The dog answered her call, tail wagging, with a slow, ambling gait from a rug in the kitchen, effortful, dutifully resigned. Until she went to the cupboard in which she had seen Thomas hang her coat.

'Walkies, Butler? Would he mind, your lord and master, if you came too? I feel as if I knew him once, Butler, years ago, but I might be wrong, I usually am, better we forget it. I was smaller then and he was much bigger, that man. I doubt he's the same. Are you coming with me?'

Her hand on the nicely underpolished handle of the cupboard door, she bent to stroke: she had been made so familiar here. Thomas said the dog would mourn her departure; he said that the night she arrived. This dog with the ugly face and the limp, the dampish jaw placed on her lap in utter abandonment, was now snapping and snarling, dancing like a tribal man psyching himself for war, a mad dog with drawn back lips and large, yellowed teeth an inch below startling pink gums. The colours of custard and rhubarb, varnish and vermilion. Elisabeth backed away. When she took her hand from the cupboard handle, the snarling lapsed into a low, rumbling growl.

'Silly, what's the matter? Listen, I'm not stealing anything, promise. Silly thing. I'm only going home, for a minute. I need to go home, Butler.'

It was if the dog had anticipated her reluctance to say as much to Thomas. The rumbling increased, the mouth parted, more details of the gums and teeth were displayed. The big, soft, odd-shaped ears were back; the speckled muzzle bore no resemblance to a friendlier self. She had never noticed the potential savagery of that large head, and retreated away from the door. A spare set of keys to her flat was, as always in the pocket of her smock, additional to those in the pocket of her coat: she kept them there always after having once locked herself out, to avoid that unimaginable helplessness which had begun to inflict her now. She could feel them solid in her hand.

The dog growled. Perhaps he wanted to play, but the hand she extended towards him was more in plea than invitation. As she edged to the door, not too cold to run as she was, surely, two or three pound coins rattling in the back pocket, all the human soul required, keys and the fare home. Butler was not convinced. The door to the outside world was more guarded than the door to the coat cupboard. He stood across it with the hair raised into a ridge along his back, showing fangs. It was the first intimation of imprisonment. Looking at the system of buttons to push before the door would open, she realized she was totally ignorant both of how the lock worked and of the combination to work it. The dog was superfluous to such simple detention: he simply reinforced it.

'Maria! '

Was she there? It was difficult to tell. Coffee had been left. The kitchen floor was clean, the carpets pristine, but there was neither sound nor trace of her presence.

'Maria?' Elisabeth's voice rose in a signal for help.

From a scullery room Maria appeared, soft-footed in old carpet slippers, heralded only by the rattling of the rosary hanging round her neck.

'I want to get out, Maria. Butler won't let me out and I can't work the lock. How do I get out?'

Maria shrugged with a rare elegance. You and me both, she seemed to be saying. She walked to the door, pointed at the buttons on the lock, shrugged again. Her wrist was still bandaged and she carried a duster. Elisabeth thought she received the message she was supposed to receive. Only Thomas could open the door, and he would be back whenever he was back: it all depended on him. The grin on Maria's ugly but amiable face seem to indicate that none of this was particularly important. If she accepted this regime of dependence, why should anyone protest?

'Oh, I see. Listen, are you taking Butler out afterwards? Whenever? Looks like he needs it. Yes? Will you post these for me?'

Maria nodded happily. The letters were transferred from Elisabeth's hand into the bosom of Maria's overall, the rosary beads hanging against them. Elisabeth turned away, obscurely embarrassed. Even the paper for the letters and the stamps were Thomas's own. She had taken them from the stock in the north-facing room, next to where the telephone had been. She glanced into that room again now. The phone was no longer there.

Knowing what she did, being what she was, Elisabeth took it with grace, rather than rebellion. Once she was back in her room with the cotton wool and those strewn clothes of the second picture, Butler came in behind her, wagged, dribbled, sat in adoration, rewarding her for good behaviour, the same old docile, ugly dog. Elisabeth remembered the bandage on Maria's arm, and wondered how it was the woman had caught her wrist in a door, rather than her fingers.

Go home tomorrow, do not confront today. Be the coward you have always been in the face of a bully, even a canine bully with a misguided sense of protection, yes of course that was what it was. As if she needed any excuse not to confront, to do what she had always done and hide instead. Darkness had fallen: Thomas seemed to wait until the brink of darkness before his expeditions. The sky was a cloudless Windsor blue, lightened by pink into a subtle glaze, the transition so sudden it was almost tropical. She turned on the daylight light, studied the fur collar, calm now, allowed herself to be compromised, her eyes restored by the colour.

I am immune from loving and needing, Thomas told himself as he walked up the street, but not from wanting. She will have her chance: if she will not take the generosity, if she spurns what I offer her, then she must accept the revenge. Why should she resent imprisonment, she who consigned me to exactly that? She had better not resent it, is all I can say: she'd better not. All my ill fortune stems from her, all my disabilities. She does what she wishes: she believes she has that right. I once believed that, too. From the day I met Elisabeth Young, I have never had that right, nor have I ever handled a brush, although I tried. I broke

120

my heart against that wheel: I made room for the stroke which paralysed what was left and had the women feed me like a baby. I collected all the paintings I could not make: I had people who left me rich, but it was no compensation. She will learn. She must be my share of perfection: she owes me that; we owe each other.

He took some satisfaction in the steadiness of his stride. All those years in the wilderness, learning how to walk again, how to speak: how would she ever know, in her rude health, her unselfconscious beauty, what that was like? Sometimes he wondered if she were actually stupid, with her deliberate ignorance of human motives, her shying from emotion so evident in any conversation. No wonder she had never learned, could not bear to see a human being stripped. Yes, his walking was a work of art. He needed the umbrella or one of his fancier sticks as much for a talisman as a support. He needed it for walking, but not all the time and he needed it now to feel power. One two click, one two click, tapping out the sound of his firm steps which had been so frail, one two click, an efficient, business-like sound. The tip of his Victorian umbrella was polished silver, glinting in the dark, a small ferrule of metal and rubber covering the point which was as sharp as a Toledo dagger, less obvious than the swordsticks of the same age, highly ingenious.

Approaching the correct number in the correct street, he paused and removed the ferrule into a pocket, adjusted the burden he carried under his left arm, increasing the sense of power. The tip of the blade caught the light from a passing car. He took off the smoked-glass spectacles;

121

they impeded his ability to see with the one eye like a cat in the dark. Thomas with one eye, who walked the streets, drove his car rarely and sat at home rationalizing his life in a series of muttered monologues, was highly adept at putting his foot inside the door, and with his little bit of armoury, his umbrella blade, there was nothing he could not do.

Enid responded to the summons by bell, dark though it was. Curiosity always overcame caution: she believed herself immune to threats and every call for attention was confused with the possibility of company. This time, no fringed rug impeded her progress down the hall although she still registered its absence with guilty surprise. Her hair was not tortured into the nightly helmet: too early, by hours. Apart from the stockings she had taken off to mend a minute hole in the toe, she was dressed and prepared to speak, prompted by a dreadful and aggressive conscience. It wasn't my fault, she kept repeating to herself: I had to do it. The cat and her taps, I'll say something to her like that, but I won't be asked, whoever would ask. I had no choice, none at all.

The man at the door did not want her. Rang her bell, but did not want to see her, only wanted something from her.

'I've come to deliver a parcel to the young lady downstairs. Her uncle, madam.'

No, he had told himself: he was not a burglar, nor a particularly good detective, neither now nor when he had stooped to examine the names listed at the side of the door, finding small clues in the dark, smudged letters.

'I've telephoned and rung the bell,' he went on conversationally. 'No joy, though. All right if I just go down and deliver this, leave a message? She's given me a key. In case she was away.' Underneath his left arm, clumsily gripped, he carried the rug from the hall.

He was inside and moving towards the stairs. From the evening conversations with Elisabeth, from his knowledge and intensive observation, Thomas had guessed the geography of Elisabeth's house, the relation of one part of it to another. Enid began to shake her head violently like a demented parrot. No one possessed Elisabeth's key; Elisabeth would have died rather than part with it, but it was not that aspect which alarmed her. She had not intended discovery so soon, or in a manner like this: she had rehearsed often, but the prospect was bleakly terrifying, forcing her too late into shrill haughtiness.

'Certainly not. Absolutely not. Who do you think you are?'

'Her uncle, I said. Don't be ridiculous. I only want to leave a note. And this rug.'

The familiar colours of the hall rug, the fringe dripping out of the crook of his arm, shook her more than anything else. It was a passport of awful credibility.

'Give it to me. I'll give it to her.'

They stood in the glare of the badly shaded light, facing each other like gladiators, she fascinated and repelled by the one, blue eye which stared beyond her and widened. At the very moment Thomas caught sight of the cat on the stairs crouching ready for flight, the light went out. There was a faint thud as the cat hit the hall, raced for the

123

freedom of the door which both of them held half open and half closed in a silent battle. An invisible touch of soft fur brushed Enid's bare, braced legs. She screamed loudly, hoarsely, twisting and hitting out at the wall in an instinctive search for the light, beat the time switch with her fist on the third, frantic attempt. Suddenly they were safe again, all fears suspended in that moment of illumination. Enid moaned and trembled. He controlled his own tremor, patted her arm and felt the additional quiver in response. She was shocked by the strength behind his touch. Something ailed her far more than fear of cat or stranger.

'I'll just go on down, then.'

'No, no,' she shouted. 'No, no, no. She never . . .'

But he was beyond her, taking the stairs with ungainly, shuffling speed down to Elisabeth's apartment. A table by the door, dusty: no shade on the light, no nameplate, an anonymous little lobby. And a red door, scratched around the uncomplicated lock, showing traces of the yellow paint beneath. Provoked by the sight of that minimal, colourful damage, he bent to examine further. Enid reached his side, panting, one arm stretched before as if she had slithered down the last few steps and was still determined to pull him back.

'No, no, no . . . Oh!'

'What happened, lady? My niece been burgled? Or was it the cat did this?'

His voice was sharp as a claw. Enid's face passed from sickly pale to crimson. The outstretched hand fell to clasp the other one in an agony of supplication.

'I didn't mean to . . . I mean the cat was sick . . . No, the tap was dripping, something leaking in her bathroom. I had to, I had no choice. Really, what else could I do?'

He saw in that face all the cupidity, envy, fear, hatred he had ever seen slide across faces far more intelligent than this. Of course there had been a choice or why would she hide, why this compulsive twisting of hands, this look of dementia tinged with guilt.

Thomas struck the door with his umbrella, scoring the paint with the knifelike end, the flash of a blade. Then he hit with the handle, a casual blow with instantaneous effect. Held only by the latch, the door swung open into the dark corridor beyond. A faint scent emerged, the smells and warmth of the departed occupant, perfume, turpentine, calamine, cat and trespass. He turned back to Enid, catching on her face an expression of cowed shame frozen in the instant the light went off again.

'Come inside, missus,' he said. 'You come inside with me. Uncle will look after you.'

CHAPTER SEVEN

Francis Thurloe suffered a number of reactions both during and after, long after, he was spoken to by the police (not an interview, sir, we'd like to make that quite clear), each sensation quite different from the other. First bewilderment, which was humiliating since he was too long in the tooth, he had thought, ever to be bewildered by anything half as prosaic or part of his daily bread as policemen. Strange how one never looked at them when they were simply part of a courtroom scenario, joked about them, never quite took them seriously or saw them as men, always a race apart. In one fell moment, without too much analysis, Francis understood why his clients felt so differently about the police. It was having to look into their eyes and stay still. That made life swim before Francis, as with a drowning man. In the shallows, he thought with a shock of recognition, drowning in the shallows, not the deep water where the divers go for pearls.

'No real cause for concern, sir.' The 'sir' could be an insult or genuine respect. How could even a junior officer such as this tolerate the endless calling of a professional man sir, when he was never called sir in return? Francis supposed it was from training school and hoped they did not mind as he would himself, although he had come through an education where teachers, however inept and second rate, were always designated sir. It was not a comparison he enjoyed.

'There was a note from you, with your address, sir, in the glove compartment of her car. I take it you were . . . friends?'

'Lovers,' Francis stated. He had decided to bite the bullet.

'Quite. She seems to have disappeared. Taken a holiday, perhaps? Only we found her car, Miss Young's car, wrecked and vandalized, not a wheel left, checked out the owner, owner away from home. Lady on the ground floor says she's been gone a week, doesn't go away too often, place locked up, but the lady had a key. Went without a by your leave, but then, why not? She's a free agent. We only wanted to tell her about her car. I expect it was stolen.'

'Perfectly possible. She used it only when absolutely necessary, left it parked in the next street, I seem to remember.' Francis stressed the past tense. 'Could have been stolen any time. She didn't use it every day, only for moving things. We had, by the way, parted company shortly before, in case you need to know. I've no idea where she is.'

'Parents? Dead, I believe? We had to check. Had to go

in her flat, see if we could find something. There was a birth certificate, put it all back, of course. So she hadn't gone to see her people, there aren't no people traceable where she comes from. Far as we know. Young ladies often take off, if they can. Not a criminal inquiry, but if she contacts you, let her know about the car. Any hard feelings, have we?'

'About her? No. It worked for a while, then it didn't.' Francis was shocked, angered by these artless revelations. Who then did Elisabeth visit if she did not visit a family, and were her family another, elegant smokescreen blown for his own benefit? The policeman enjoyed the ability of discomfiting someone he was obliged to call sir. He sighed extravagantly, offensively man to man.

'Just as well you gave her up, judging from this neighbour. If you don't mind my saying, you weren't the only one. Only gentleman friend, I mean. She had a stream of men, I'm told. In and out all the time, if you'll excuse my turn of phrase. Pardon me. As well to know, I always say, sir.'

Later when the first reaction of utter humiliation had died, to make way first for curiosity and, finally, anger, Francis phoned the policeman, to ask the name of the place from which Elisabeth had come. According to her birth certificate. The anger had begun to percolate.

'By the way, sir,' said the policeman in that tone of endless confiding, 'we found a blood transfusion card in her flat. Gave blood twice a year for fifteen years. Good, isn't it? Put it back, of course, for when she comes home.'

'What on earth is the relevance of that?' Francis asked,

frostily, pen poised while his neat hand wrote down CLAY-
FIELDS, the name of the village from which his lover had
originated, a place of which he had never heard since he
dismissed the whole of the north of England as a wilderness. He was surprised by this evidence of public-spirited
philanthropy. Giving blood was not Elisabeth's style.
Giving almost everything else obviously was. He wanted,
very badly, to hit the policeman, stuff the phone down his
throat to end those sedulous and mocking tones.

'Relevance?' The policeman was jocular, as two men
sharing a joke, crudely. 'Well, you might like to know she
didn't have Aids last time she gave blood. And all that
blood in the well of her car can't have been hers, either.'

'You didn't tell me about blood in the car.'

'You didn't want to know, sir. You didn't ask.'

You didn't ask, she had said. Ask, and I may tell you, but
you did not ask. He was fired by paintings, the luxury of
owning things and the luxury of her embraces. A little
weeping in the night he had not questioned. He liked his
ladies fun, but had become less sure about liking them
slender: in the last ten days, walking, driving, his eyes had
been drawn to different shapes, more like Elisabeth's
curves, but why should he care? A daughter of a village
unknown to him. He had spoken of his childhood: she had
listened, avidly asked for more, never volunteered particulars of her own. He had not taken her anywhere near his
numerous relatives: she had not been (how could he put it
now and how did he put it then?) quite suitable. He had
kept her back, although he had somehow assumed she

came from roughly the same stable as himself, comfortable in some uninvestigated equivalent, the kind of family from which people acquired university degrees, the odd bit of furniture, the luxury of cultural interests, financially and spiritually OK.

Francis noticed another crooked picture on his wall, but that was part and parcel of all his annoyance about Elisabeth Young hastening away without as much as a note, and him not being the only one, for the little time he had lasted. And not liking skinny women the way he did; and somehow, being completely fooled by everything about her.

'Let us know if she doesn't come back, won't you? I mean, give her a month.'

'Oh dear, such a worry.'

'Don't fret about it, honest. Happens all the time. Obviously planned. She locked up, put out her rubbish, took some clothes, paid up her rent for a whole quarter. Can't treat that as suspicious. Lovely tea, smashing, thanks. Doesn't sound as if she's much of a loss.'

'You're welcome. Any time,' Enid preened. The iron curls bounced always from her forehead in obedient leaps: she had come up this morning smelling of roses.

'What do I do if anyone wants to get in?'

'Like who?'

'The landlord. Relatives.' She sniggered. 'Boyfriends who might have left something behind. She'd let them in if she was here. She always did.'

'Oh, you let them in, too, I should. If they're genuine, of

course. Not much to steal. Use your discretion.' He winked and smiled. 'Thanks again for the tea. Call us if you need us.'

'Oh, I shall, I shall,' said Enid, sorry to see them go. There was nothing nicer than a man in uniform. A sergeant, too. The lies had tripped off her tongue with pretty ease: there was money in her purse, copied keys in her pocket; she was mistress of all she surveyed, had keys now to everyone's flats, all those lives. Plus a belly full of satisfaction for the privilege of her exclusive knowledge that Elisabeth was not coming back. Uncle said so. He was not quite so sinister in his absence. Remembering Uncle in a pang of horror, Enid went in search of the cat. Only the cat had mourned Elisabeth and even then, briefly.

Annie had found friends among her customers more often than she counted, but Francis Thurloe was not one of them. Two phone calls in a week were not expected: she guessed, pragmatically, that this was not because he liked her for herself, but because of someone else. She agreed to meet him for several, half-formulated reasons. One was because, all of a sudden, there was no one else to meet, and the second was because there was always the chance Francis might want to buy a painting. He had bought before, first in his own right, and then on Lizzie's recommendation, and, having put one in touch with the other, Annie felt faintly proprietorial about them both. Besides, she needed the distraction. The accounts were still a jumble: there were still a few paintings she could not trace through her hectic system, and all of this would be better done with a hangover. She was surprised to be asked out by Francis; he was still merely an acquaintance, rather too up-market and scrupulous for her taste, although he looked divine, and he was, after all, another person's property. Discovering in round one of the conversation that this was no longer the case, that Elisabeth and he were no longer coupled, was faintly cheering. Annie had always been a man's woman as opposed to a woman's woman, not a feature she particularly liked in herself but she did not know how to change. Annie could never rid herself of a predatory instinct and did not wish to try.

'Gone? What? Elisabeth? Gone off with another chap, you mean, straight after finishing with you? Blimey.' She put on the cockney voice which was not her real inheritance. Francis's almost shocking attraction made her do that. Annie's dad had been an accountant – to the market trade, but still a white-collar man, well off, born far from the sound of Bow Bells. She was feeling indignation on Francis's behalf, an indignation he did not seem to share.

'Well, no. Or I don't know. Someone stole her car, smashed it up. Because of that the police went into her flat. There's no evidence she went off with somebody, only that she went. They had to go through her things to find out where she might be, only to tell her about the car, which she definitely wasn't driving, by the way. I suppose she might have been with the person who was.' Francis did not mention the blood, which haunted him. Jealousy flared for the second time, a vicious little flame licking the inside of his throat and making speech difficult. He drank instead, crisp white wine from the Loire, not an autumn drink, but painless.

Annie shrugged. 'She always was secretive. I don't know who else knew her. Lots of people round and about. She did tell me she came from the North, foreign territory to me, funny place, the North, and her parents had died. That was all, really. We talked about paintings, mainly.' This was the point when Annie remembered about the two thousand pounds, payment deferred. A sudden vacation by Elisabeth did not equate with Elisabeth needing that hard-earned cash. Annie's conscience was clearer: she could afford curiosity.

'What about all these men, then? Who told you about that?'

'The police. Gleaned from the neighbours and the inside of her place, I suppose. I never saw the whole of her place, you know: she never let you in where she worked.'

'She was a close one . . .' said Annie suggestively, slightly roguish, as if she were party to more knowledge than she was prepared to reveal.

'Perhaps they found wall-to-wall condoms and evidence of bondage. Whips and rubber. Racks.' Both of them snorted into their wine, giggling with guilty disrespect, swaying with laughter at this weird juxtaposition of ideas. Elisabeth was mysterious, but her large serenity defied any notion of aberrant sex. Then Annie sat bolt upright.

'My paintings!' she yelled. 'She's got some of my fucking paintings . . . Supposing she doesn't come back? My stock, Christ . . . those three naïves she was going to do in a rush. I've got to get them. Mrs Ballantyre'll kill me. And, yes now I know where it is, another one she's had for ages. Listen, can we get in Liz's place? I mean, now? My effing stock, the cow. How could she leave me in the lurch?' Two bottles of wine had been consumed and the night was young. They were looking at each other rather wildly, both bemused into conspiracy, joined by their separate senses of outrage, his the flame of resentful jealousy unquenched by wine, hers a suspicion of theft. Perhaps Elisabeth had got her own back for that missing money after all.

'No,' said Francis. 'No. She would hate anyone to go in her place. Privacy is all with Elisabeth, remember?'

'So you say. You're nicer than I am. What about all those other men? Private, was it, or only one at a time? Anyway, she's probably back already. Come on, let's go.' It was the frenetic energy which made Annie good at business, made her a pack leader, party giver, profit maker, a hyperactivity which disallowed stillness, made resolutions turn to deeds within a split second, to be regretted later but believed entirely for the moment. The second lieutenant in Francis, his capacity to follow a definite lead, made him rise and follow. Annie insisted on paying the bill.

'All right,' he said. 'If she's not there, we'll go and eat. But if she isn't there, how do we get in?' He was being towed in her wake, reluctant, but only a little. He let her enthusiasm break over his back.

'Oh, we'll find a way. I'm good at getting into places.'

Later, he thought how right he had been to believe in this optimism of hers. Not about the task in hand, but about the ease of breaching those castle walls which Elisabeth had made so impregnable to anyone unwanted, she who could remain untouched by guilt or duty to answer either her telephone or the imperious summons of the bell. He had envisaged her there, more than once, a shadow behind the blind, too careless even to hide, letting him walk away if his visit were neither timely nor expected. Before the quarrel, which had been no more than the picking of a scab from a wound, a belated yelp of pain, he had believed in this version of her behaviour, had felt the indifference as he walked away after a chance call. At the time he had respected it: never remained on her doorstep like the schoolboy fan he had felt at first; never imagined she might have been afraid to answer her door. Now the thought that he might have been refused because the territory was already occupied by others felt like a cut from a knife. Walking up that almost gentrified road with Annie swinging her bag as if on holiday, he envied her guiltless sense of purpose. His sense of trespass was drowned in wine from the Loire: all he wanted was more of it. Hoping Elisabeth would be in, yet at the same time wanting to avoid the emotional gulp he knew he would feel on sight of her, he paced behind Annie, like a servant, trying to fuel his resentment and managing to do so, even when their entry was, as Annie promised, unbelievably easy.

'You see?' said Annie. 'I told you so. People always let you in if you either smile or threaten, even if they've got no right to let you. I thought Liz said she had an old bat living upstairs, but that woman was all right, trust Liz to exaggerate. Funny hair, though, and I didn't fancy stopping for tea. Not after wine. Told us to be careful. No need, really, is there?' The look she turned in his direction was almost a leer. It was merely a twisted smile: he knew as much, still felt revolted in a mild way. This was still Elisabeth's flat and they had no business there, all their justifications faded away with the light. Francis and Annie were not a couple: she should not assume they were in agreement about anything. So far he had liked her well enough: now he was less certain.

Going illicitly into another person's flat when the occupant could, in theory, return at any time was unnerving. Francis had dreamt of burglary as a boy: he had never failed to understand the temptation in others. Not a crime, he told himself, this is not a crime. Why not? It has the implied permission of the owner. No, it does not. All right, it is not a crime because we have no intention to rape or steal. How Elisabeth, on her return, would cope with this, was not something he wanted to consider. Elisabeth would never confront: she would roll with the punch, move house and set up somewhere more remote, indelibly hurt by the invasion. Francis wanted to shrug away his reservations, but could not do that, either. It occurred to him that he and this acquaintance were treating Elisabeth as if she were either a criminal or dead.

There had been a faint smell of paint about the door leading into the corridor between her rooms, a plant standing there less dead than he remembered from the last visit before. A week or two seemed a long time.

'Shit a brick. Blimey, what a slut, eh? Sorry, Francis, didn't mean that. Just didn't know she was so messy.'

The kitchen was slightly dirty, the mere dirt of disuse.

Annie never minded anyone describing her as a cheerful slut, as long as they were not referring to her kitchen. She took the word to imply a kind of flattery if said by another woman, implying a good sport with a sense of priorities. Francis, who did not give the same implication to the word, flinched.

'It's not bad,' he ventured, wanting to say nothing at all.

They had passed the bare kitchen and the living room where guests would sit, gone beyond the bedroom where he had also been to his delight, into the open door of the room where he had never ventured. He had not guessed, felt now he should have guessed, that this was the largest, potentially lightest room in the place, and, opposed to the open spaces of the rest, gloriously cluttered.

The studio was hung with tattered pictures like flags. There was a roll-top desk, a table, an easel, four chairs, two built-in sets of shelves as high as his head and another shelf the height of his calf and constructed out of pieces of wood supported on bricks, but fine polished wood, the same as the desk. This shelf was full of jugs, broken bits, colours and more frenetic colours. The head-height shelves contained further pottery plus the implements she required, all in jugs: paintbrushes in jugs, turps bottles in jugs, bottled poisons and powdered pigments in jugs, gauze bandages in jugs, corks, palette knives, rubber thimbles, buttons, string, all jugged. Each jug was of a different shape and shade: they did not stand in sequence and many were chipped. There was no gradation of size or quality or shape: they were simply jugs, so dazzling to the eye, so crazy and cheerful, he laughed out loud.

137

'What's so funny?' Annie did not share his joy. She had tripped on a rosewood pig, standing aimlessly, the snout catching her shin. She kicked it and winced. Francis remembered why they were there, to look for property, a proper barristerial pursuit, stood upright and saluted. There was no mockery in his respect: Annie was so much more logical: and she was angry.

'Where are my pictures, then? Where are those three naïve things, lovely things, though she wasn't so keen, where the fuck are they? And a couple more, now I think of it. And where's that interior? The room, with the chairs and the rug and all . . . I can't even remember who bloody owns it, probably priceless, the one she said she couldn't bring back until the varnish was dry? Oh, Jesus Christ, she's gone off with them all. Probably trading off a barrow in the fucking North, wherever it is she comes from, I don't know. Taking all those goodies back home to daddy.'

Annie plunged her arm into her bag, a large satchel affair, which swung from her shoulder well below her waist, impeding walking and bumping against her knees, her fist grasping for a cigarette, the other hand holding a lighter, the pointed face grim with fury. Her legs were long and thin in their black leggings, a thinnie who, Francis suspected, ate and drank like a Trojan, smoked like an addict and made love with the power of a train. The satchel swung as Annie swung, unhinging a packet of fags with both hands at the same time as three jugs from the low shelf leapt to the floor. One smashed absently, another rolled, the third fell against the skirting board with an audible crack. Annie never took care with things she did not personally find precious.

'Sorry,' she said, grasping the bag into her waist, hitching up her elongated sweater as she did so, apologizing to the breakages as if they were alive, but only briefly, turning her back so the rest were still in danger from the next, dangerous swing.

'Watch it,' said Francis, stepping towards her, arms outstretched, wary of the satchel and the cigarette. She stood with her arms now folded across her chest, the lit cigarette at her lips, the satchel still. Annie was skinny, attractive, bursting with all the positive qualities Elisabeth had ever lacked, realism included. Not a person to say sorry even if she was, because saying sorry after the event was a waste of breath. She puffed, waved her hand, swung round again. Another jug crashed. Francis winced.

'Didn't know she had it in quite so big for all this bashed old china,' said Annie. 'Hope it isn't art deco or anything. Doubt it, she was always a cheapskate. Nothing worthwhile here. Where are my fucking pictures?' Her eyes had scanned the room, alive to the shape of her own, familiar canvases, found neither the colours nor shape of a hiding place.

'Do you know what she is, this girl? My friend and yours?'

Annie's bright red lips, which never seemed to lose their shine, drew on the cigarette, leaving a faint pink trace on the tip. Somewhere *en route* she had managed to renew the lipstick, and if this room inspired in Francis a sense of comical relief, it created high temper in his companion.

Now she was standing by the open desk, the surface of which was covered with tidy piles of documents, letters, invoices, bills, separately bundled in elastic bands, as if there had been a systematic tidying long overdue. On the top of one bundle of letters, she read the words, 'My darling Elisabeth', and read no further. No wonder the police had found their cursory investigation so easy. Then there was a bundle of photographs, their subject matter, perhaps along with the letters, explaining why it was that both the officers of the law and the neighbour upstairs had been so quick to label Elisabeth Young a bit of a goodtime girl.

'Oh,' said Annie, 'never knew she had it in her.'

Black-and-white shots, all showing Elisabeth half draped or naked. A demure Elisabeth, certainly, no lasciviousness in the pose, the eyes avoiding the camera, sculptured portraits somehow designed to show distinctive angles rather than the pouting poses demanded by pornography. There was something both anonymous and vacant about this nakedness, but all Francis registered at the time was the nakedness itself and the spreading of his previous anger, melting into his veins and making him warm in that cold room. Photographs, love letters, pathetic letters. He took another glance. 'Lizzie, won't you please come home . . .' And read no further. He formed the vague but intense impression that she had abandoned everyone who aspired to passionate fondness.

'A thief,' Annie said, 'that's what she bloody is. And a slag.'

Anger cooled into a chill sweat. Francis would not share Annie's condemnation, the same inner prompting which told him to control his temper in a courtroom telling him now he should know better. Elisabeth had never delivered any kind of promise to either of them: what did it matter what she was?

'I can't see her as a thief,' was all he responded, neutrally. 'She might have taken away your paintings to work on them somewhere else. Do you think we have any right to touch any of these things?' With the fading of his own anger, the mind of the lawyer returned, remembering some concepts of a justice in which he believed. Do not accuse with information unfairly obtained.

'Let's go, then,' Annie said abruptly, sensing disapproval. Francis was relieved. Before they left, Annie darted into each of the other rooms, all empty in that quasi-tidiness which should have been familiar to him, but without life was strange. Clean, but not pristine, nothing quite in place, but nothing lost. Back outside in the street, where the cold stung, a different, whipping cold to the chilliness of that studio room, Francis took Annie's arm. They were, in their slightly emotional, slightly ashamed state, back to being allies, unable to abandon each other.

'Listen,' said Francis, grasping her arm. 'We don't mind going into Elisabeth's flat in search of possessions. Ironic, isn't it? We barge in to look after the health of a few pictures . . . Shouldn't we do just as much to try and find out how she is?'

'She's not my concern,' said Annie, breaking step but only for a second.

'Whose concern is she, then?' asked Francis.

They had neglected to return the key: Annie forgot and

141

Francis put it in his pocket. Watching them go down the street, Enid decided she did not mind. She had spare keys now: she was mistress of the whole house.

It vacillated, this anger of his, like a sickness, an ebbing and rising of mental temperature which left Francis exhausted through a dull meal in a weekday dull restaurant, where neither he nor Annie could find appetite. Except for that small, understated appetite for each other, not to be tested on an evening such as this. They retired to their own homes, her cheerful decor and the dozen messages on her answerphone enough to forestall a sensation of loneliness, his, calm, austere by comparison, streamlined apart from the still-crooked picture. A bachelor pad, Francis thought: to be kept thus indefinitely since women were never the gift they seemed. The empty bed was inviting, the automatically controlled heat of his rooms an incentive to sleep. In his own domain he re-exerted the control he relinquished outside in that world of anarchy which was his living, latterly mirroring the world of his emotions. I shall live alone, he thought, for a few years more, to avoid being deceived and to avoid hoping. Also to avoid the humiliation of discovering you have made love to a stranger. Strangers deserved indifference. As he fell asleep, wined and dined, Francis experienced the brief surge of contentment of a man reconciled to his life. He had not, in hindsight, been cruel to Elisabeth; she had been cruel to him. She deserved it, he told himself, this time without a hint of irony. She had a career, a family, a lover: she rode roughshod over them all.

*

At three, he woke with a feeling akin to electric shock, aware in the tingling of one enormous sound. A rending crash and his eyes open, simultaneous, but not synchronized, so that he did not know what the sound was, only that there had been sound, a violent sound to shock him into awareness. There was no cowardice in Francis: it was the impetuosity of him which was controlled: he had always waded into his juvenile fights at once without thinking who might be on the winning side, leapt up now without a second thought, ready to repel the threat, whatever it was. He did not think then of personal attack: Francis had never considered himself important enough for such a foul privilege, nor did he consider he could be held to ransom for his possessions. They did not yet rank high enough to risk his health, his skin or his conventional good looks.

Before he opened the door to his bedroom, he paused for a second, fearless and aggressive, but trying wildly to analyse the sound he knew he had heard, the source of which he could not see nor as yet understand. An automatic prudence had forced his hand to reach for a dressing gown. Francis slept naked: slippers and pyjamas were not his uniform.

So he stepped into the hall of his small and perfect flat, reaching for the light, looking in the direction of his living room and the door, trying first to ascertain if there was a presence which might explain the sound which was still no more than his conviction, the tail end of it reverberating. He was potentially most violent when breathless or roused from sleep, an insult difficult to absorb. When shaken

143

awake, Elisabeth sat bolt upright with staring eyes, clutching herself to herself. He remembered that as his foot passed over the glass and a searing pain roared into his brain. He staggered back into his room, aware that there was no intruder, no breathing presence outside, sat on the edge of his bed while his hand reached for the lamp by the side. He cradled his cut foot and plucked a shard of glass from the now dripping wound which arched in a line defined by droplets of startling red. The plucking out was painless, brought instant relief and the light illuminated the explanation.

The explosion of sound and the implosion of pain were all the result of an old, heavily framed etching in the hall falling from its hook. When he hobbled back to the door, Francis found the carpet sparkling with shards of glitter, the old, brown picture cord frayed into decay, the frame askew against a radiator and his passage in and out treacherous with shattered glass. He had no shoes in his room, nothing but his nakedness. The picture (a print he no longer liked, hence the relegation to the hall) should have been checked to see if the cord was frayed, and then replaced with wire. Everything in glass should be hung with wire, Elisabeth said: everything decays. Don't you know that?

He hovered, finally threw his dressing gown over the glass and skipped beyond, in search of a drink. Then removed his vacuum cleaner from a cupboard and encouraged it to drink up the glass. Remnants still glimmered, stuck among the threads of the carpet. His right foot throbbed; his mind throbbed. You never own them, she had said, they will do what they will. These depictions of things have a life of their own, didn't you know? I don't know about love, she had also said. I might know but I don't really know, I wish I did. Pictures are almost as unreliable as people, but not quite. It takes them years to fall.

This one, thought Francis, has me trapped either in or out of the place where I sleep, because of the glass. Something has Elisabeth trapped where she sleeps. Tramp, harlot, sometime photographic model, born in a place of which he had never heard, recipient of love letters, chameleon, peacock, efficient person, keeper of jugs, colour in her fingertips, no relatives, unable to trust, confide, confront, but equipped with skills which gave paintings life. A borrowed life, thought Francis in his bathroom, not my concern: I am a barrister and nothing is really my concern, but getting this poison out of my foot and getting to court tomorrow.

He relished the peace which followed, the whole relief of not having to fight a living intruder, with nothing to do but dab dilute disinfectant on his wound and go back to bed, leaving the mess until tomorrow. Another battleground survived relatively easily. Life went on tomorrow.

Tomorrow, then, he would check the cords of every picture to avoid a repetition. For now he drifted towards sleep again, making himself think in his precise way of how he would make people laugh when he told of this scare in the small hours, the problem of ridding the carpet of clinging glass. Unbidden, came a scene from Elisabeth's flat: the bedroom with similar, neutral carpet, older than his own

145

but as seen in that last, inquisitive foray, the worn patches covered with a wine-coloured rug. The one from the hall, the tripping-up rug with the treacherous fringe, absent from its place on the Saturday night when he had seen her last. Dry-cleaning, she said: he remembered that, too: the cat had been sick.

The rug. In the wrong place. Some time during this week she had been back. Or some poltergeist. Someone else in there. Bringing back that rug which had always caught his heels. Someone else, but then there had always been someone else. Francis was uneasily awake and then feel asleep again, dreaming of nothing.

There had been no post, either. Something had happened.

It isn't my concern. I don't still love her.

CHAPTER EIGHT

Darkness fell earlier and earlier in the afternoons. Darkness increased the desire not to move. Somehow, she had got used to it all, become absorbed in the ménage until she was part of the walls. She wrote letters, of course, renewing an old habit in herself which had almost died from lack of practice. She wrote to Annie, and nicely to Enid, telling both of them where she was, and once to Francis, a few cheerful pain-free words like a postcard from holiday. The letters, given to Maria for posting, provided a chink in the armour of the environment and gave her at the same time every excuse to do what she wanted to do, which was to stay still. Once embedded in the hostage mentality, once the decision was made to sway with this pleasant regime rather than question, Elisabeth found it was all too easy. Besides, fourteen whole days of trouble-free existence in the sheer exercise of skill, paid at a rate so generous as to be absurd, had the same effect on her as manna from heaven. She had had quite enough experience of the opposite to be easily seduced by this quiet, addictive and intense excitement. I lied, I lied, Elisabeth said to herself, if ever I thought this was not enough to content me. And I did not want to treat the Gainsboroughs, for the rich and famous who would always find their experts; I wanted to rescue the lesser known, as I am doing now. But even so, amongst all this enthusiasm and comfort, she was suspending from her intellect that crowd of suspicions which buzzed around her head like midges in summer. She made them settle, for the moment, around the neck of the blue-robed portrait.

Whatever happened, all thought must be postponed until she decided what to do about the madonna's neck. Elisabeth knew now that some of it had been painted over, not an in-filling of paint to hide damage, but an over-painting skilful and deceptive to the untutored eye until the canvas was held at an angle to show the unevenness of surface. Not only overpainting, perhaps: she had stood back, looked, stood back, looked again, worked on the other painting, and now she knew she was right. One part of the covering paint was newer than the old, more malleable, but still tough, done with an eye to permanence. When Elisabeth painted over damage or filled in a missing piece of lost paint, she did so minimally, using soft restorer's colours for easier removal in a lighter shade than the original to make it less obvious, because to do otherwise was selfish and arrogant. Removing another person's improvements was always a risk. Like any restorer, she was not a soothsayer and never quite knew what might lurk beneath; there were times when the decisions gave her nights of sleeplessness.

But the necklace (at least) on this vulnerable woman was a discordant piece of decoration for such a patrician face, flashy sapphires in a setting of glittery gold, at odds with tiny silver earrings and the colours of the face. Today, Elisabeth had risen early from her comfortable bed, begun to remove these stubborn jewels, piece by piece, watching the pigment on her cotton wool as she worked with a bud, rolling in carefully minute circles, never scraping. A stronger solution of acetone for the new, tough, paint, the smell of it in her eyes and her heart in her mouth.

Beneath all that crusty sparkle, there was skin, and more than that, a slender silver chain, simple in the extreme and used as the vehicle for a single, unset pearl. Perfect for the ultramarine silk which bunched and twisted in the chair below the turned body, a modest choice for a modest woman. The skin on the neck, she could see now, was darkened, but not beyond the powers of her own, cautious retouching. The beauty had been deliberately re-dressed with unnatural finery. Elisabeth simmered with the kind of rage she might have reserved for someone who maliciously persuaded a friend to wear some piece of clothing which would make her look a fool.

'Thomas!' Elisabeth yelled.

There were times, only brief times, when isolation had drawbacks, when shouting was the only thing to do. Times, she realized, when the sharing of something was the only way to define it. In the same spurt of understanding as fizzy as a soda fountain, she thought, I lied too, about not

149

being my mother's daughter. I love cleaning: I have done it all my adult life. Not for the first time she had an enormous longing to show the mother she never mentioned what she had done, to attempt, once more, those failed explanations of achievement, to make good the losses of the years.

'Thomas, come and look!' she yelled again. Shouted words fell like cotton wisps into the carpet of the hall where she stood, and, again, she was perturbed by the inability of sound to carry far in this place.

Nobody heard at first, except Maria, who materialized from the kitchen as she so often did, bearing gifts. Coffee, tea, biscuits, which, Elisabeth realized with a momentary pang of guilt, she often ignored. Maria standing there, looking at the picture with its now damaged throat, her own larynx forcing small sounds of distress from her mouth, pointing in horror. 'Oh! Oh! Oh!' Elisabeth found herself pushed back into the room used as a studio, her arm held, with surprising determination, Maria's imploring face close to her own, the eyes full of tears. In the same moment of surprise she recognized the reason for the distress. Maria's madonnalike picture, the one she often came to admire, now looked far worse, as if vandalized. The plaintive but aristocratic face looked as if someone had scratched the neck below: there was a painful residue of cleanser.

'It's all right,' Elisabeth said. 'Really, all right. Better, see?' She seized the sable brush Thomas had provided, bought from the place she had so exactly instructed, moistened it with saliva, brushed it emptily back and forth

150

across the scraped throat of the picture. The colours emerged in the wet.

'Mend it, see? All better soon.' Maria saw. The distress vanished and the brow cleared. She held one hand in her apron pocket, hidden, pointed with the other to the row of neat paints on a chair. Thomas, bringer of gifts, had brought indoors vast quantities of oil paint. New, tubed paint, a wide range of primary colours, useless. Maria picked up a tube, looked with perplexity, squeezed it, grinned, pointed to the madonna. Then she took off the cap of the tube, still puzzled. No answers, no paint.

'You have to pierce the top,' Elisabeth said, amused.

Maria seized a brush, used the sharp wooden end to pierce the thin aluminium seal of the paint. She did the same with six others, quickly, with the delight of a child playing. Let her play. The paints were of little use for Elisabeth's purposes and they would keep. They were the product of Thomas's compulsive shopping, like other, not always well-chosen gifts. A new blue smock, since he seemed to like her in blue and Maria seemed to approve, soaps, knick-knacks, all impersonal gifts which were met with the same grave politeness with which they were presented. Let Maria play, but Maria had finished. The hand hidden inside the apron drew forth other paintings, a flush of small religious pictures. Elisabeth looked at them with respect. Saw one depiction of a woman with a white chemise and startlingly blue cloak, with beams of light arrowing down from her hands and head and a vivid green serpent toiling in the roses at her feet. The thought crossed Elisabeth's mind, along with her suppressed laughter, that sweet, kindly Maria had similar adornments in mind for their very own madonna, but she did not wish to offend. Maria snatched her treasures away, without offence, but only as if thinking of something else. She proffered instead the rosary from round her neck. Elisabeth accepted it, crossed herself as she had seen others do, and hung the beads on a peg of the easel. Maria nodded with equally grave approval.

Thomas had come from the other end of the corridor, a mile of carpet from that door to this and, with his arrival, the apartment which had seemed as large as it was taste- fully palatial became merely a selection of cells designed to kill noise with the padding of its splendour. The two of them, Thomas and Maria, were both rehearsed in silence, like an order of obedient nuns. Thomas beneath a small chandelier wore the look of a patient gaoler – without the obviousness of clanking keys, but still a gaoler. For both of them. The sensation of that, Elisabeth's smothered panic tinged with disgust for her own foolish imaginings, faded as soon as he smiled. Maria dutifully disappeared with the humble silence of her arrival. We are both afraid of him, Elisabeth thought: both, quietly, unnecessarily afraid.

'You summonsed,' he said, mild and deferential. 'What next?'

'Look,' Elisabeth said. 'Look . . .' She wiped the vulner- able neck in the painting again, so the single pearl showed, damaged but clear, illuminated by wetness. 'Why would anyone alter it?'

Thomas chuckled. 'You tell me,' he suggested.

152

'Vanity,' she said. 'All is vanity. I imagine this picture being hung in the house of a new rich manufacturer, two generations after it was made.' Her voice was gathering nervous speed. 'He might have acquired this picture because of some passing resemblance to a daughter, perhaps, wanted to pretend to others that he had family portraits, a lineage? So he buys his daughter a vulgar necklace and has the same piece painted in round the neck of this portrait. Lo and behold, he has created an ancestor and made the necklace into an heirloom. Families often alter portraits, to suit their own image of themselves.'

She looked at him, watched him watching the slender neck of the madonna as the shine of the cleaning spirit faded and with it the brief depth the fluid had given to the detail. Yes, it was often done, this alteration of portraits to accord with the status of a new generation: there had been no surprise in the discovery, which she had made before, always with the same amazement at the vanity and insecurity that people could invest in the art they placed on their own walls.

He shrugged, the wide smile belying the indifference of the gesture. His glasses, she noticed, were reflective, the kind of spectacles behind which a person hides in order to watch. She had never, in a fortnight of this distant proximity, seen him full face with naked eyes. Vanity, all is vanity. She wanted to ask what she dared not ask, unable in this cocoon to confront what she had come to understand was an indomitable will, even now when he was magnificently cheerful. A gaoler with his dog: she had not questioned, but she knew it so.

'I cannot imagine what foolish owner ordered the adding of the sapphires,' he said. 'But I am convinced that their removal is cause for celebration. Lunch, I think. I mean, out to lunch. Other people do this every day, why not ourselves.'

'But I'd be wasting the light. You're paying me not to waste light.' She did not know why she hesitated when the invitation filled her with such sublime relief she wanted to slump, suddenly dispelling as it did all those multiform suspicions which had been incubating into another state of fear, pushed back, but still fusing into a block, quite different from the fear of intrusion and the fear of footsteps, a fear which grew like a shadow as light faded. He laid a hand on her shoulder.

'I am not paying you to ruin your eyes. And,' he added, removing his hand, still smiling the smile which she had come to see as being faintly relentless, 'I know you've begun to imagine yourself a prisoner here, so I must show you otherwise. Mustn't I? A privilege for me. Lunch, a walk? Maybe you could show me what inspires you? That kind of thing. Come.'

He was turning away as he spoke, that deferential manner of his implying in all its humility his utter conviction of her acceptance. Elisabeth was silent, glad for his movement, his certainty of her compliance and the diplomacy which took away the obligation to reply. He had formulated exactly what she had been thinking ever since Butler had barred her exit, something which Thomas would have dismissed as misguided affection, if he had not, somehow, with the same blocking tactic he used now, prevented mention of it. In all their conversations, he used her own reserve, her shyness, and harnessed it to his advantage, so that even that desire of hers to go home was somehow not mentioned. She knew she was being ridiculous, but there was a kind of security here which she had eagerly embraced on first acquaintance, and, unable to examine the fear that it might have been false, she had held her tongue and her fears, closed her eyes to everything inside her skull, and, when she opened them, all she could see was colour. The olive-skinned woman, the clothes over the chair in the second picture, the third picture which lay in the corner. To leave them would feel like treachery.

Now, he was opening the door, telling her in his guarded and formal way that she was, of course, free to come and go exactly as she wished, if she only chose to ask. All the rest, the illusion of being held so politely as a captive, had been pure imagination.

So they went. 'No fuss,' said Thomas, 'if you please.' There was no chance for fuss. The decision made, movement followed, and she only remembered a vague need to make up her face when they were halfway downstairs. Thomas ignored the lift, she copied him. They were high above the world here: she had forgotten how many stairs or the outside aspect, or anything but what there was within. Inside the turret of her private world the exterior had become a memory. Red brick and brilliant windows so clean they did nothing but reflect; a block maintained to the highest standard. Cream balconies, a plaster shield appliquéd on the wall, nothing of interest to Middle Eastern tenants who occupied most of the other floors. In that moment, the noise of the outside world delighted her. Once they were beyond the vast front door, she looked up to the height from where they had come.

'Is that us?' she said, pointing to the eastern wing of the top floor, where one room stood out above the quiet street.

'That's us,' said Thomas, tersely.

'Don't the windows look small from here?'

'Do they? I never noticed.'

'Where does Maria live?'

'Oh, in the basement. She likes the dark.'

Thomas had a peculiar walk, a movement from the hip on the right side, swinging the leg stiffly but efficiently. The right hand, carried limply, seemed to monitor the movement of the leg, the stillness of the arm a contrast to the rest. It looked a trifle precarious, permanently unstable, but she sensed he was a man who would despise the stigma of any kind of crutch. There were sticks and umbrellas concealed in the cupboard in the hall, she remembered, vaguely: perhaps he had needed them once. Seeing Thomas in the sunlight, she was aware of how little she knew of him, apart from that one article of history they never discussed, she maintaining their veneer of ignorance in case she was wrong. Better not to speak than be wrong. We are both damaged goods, Elisabeth thought, but we have learned to contain the rot. And he is not keeping me prisoner. He is taking me out. Like the dog on the leash, she thought, and crushed the thought in the making.

In the street, she wanted to turn cartwheels, a childish trick she had mastered once, like running and skipping and, sometimes, shouting. In her own flat, she would cart-wheel down the corridor without witnesses, a silly exercise of freedom for the occasional and always solitary state of mild drunkenness. Elisabeth wanted to run now, across the grubby square in front of the cathedral, then across St James's Park where Thomas led with his fast, unbusinesslike swing, but she walked alongside him instead.

'Wouldn't you find it easier if you carried a stick?' she suggested, tentatively, remembering what she had glimpsed inside the cupboard when he had handed out her coat as if the fetching of it were his task and his task alone. Thomas stopped, breathing hard.

'Oh, I don't carry a stick. Not for at least a year. A sign of weakness. I might look it, but I'm not an old man yet.' Then he swung on, so fast she lengthened her own stride to keep up. 'Tell me about it,' she said. 'Tell me what happened to you. Since . . .'

'To me? Since when, birth? Oh, nothing at all.' He stopped and faced her, the loose arm swinging in front of him. 'I suppose you mean this.' He pointed at the right arm with the left. 'Only a stroke, as I told you. I'm informed it happens to the best of men.'

Suddenly he looked grey and exhausted, the dark glasses providing the only focus of colour to the whole of him, Thomas the neutral man, always dressed in dun-coloured clothes as if for camouflage. They were parallel to a bench by the path he had been covering with such clumsy speed. She guided him to it, noticing as she held his left arm that beneath the cloth of his shirtsleeve the muscles were as hard as metal. She did not touch others

157

easily: did not flinch from contact but did not volunteer it, either, for reasons which could include embarrassment or fear of rejection as well as an abhorrence of unnecessary gestures. Touch must have meaning; if not, it became no more than a kind of patting given to a pet, with no other purpose than an awkward comforting. The latter applied in her touching of Thomas: otherwise, the texture of the skin on his wrist, the slight sweat which often shone round his nose and forehead, repelled her. When she had first shaken his hand, she had done so firmly but had relinquished it with relief. Thomas's skin was permanently damp. Looking at him now, sitting with his head forward over his short, plump knees, she did not wish to sit closer although detesting herself for that sharp revulsion which she hoped was not apparent. He folded his arms across his chest, placing one inside the other, a defensive gesture. She wondered, fleetingly, if he had always been such a plain man, the kind of man who was always the wrong side of the line, pallid, short in stature and thin in hair apart from the shadow which always lurked around his chin however recently shaven. She realized with a shock that one of the many reasons she had felt so safe with him from the outset was because he was so quietly, defiantly and definitely unattractive, despite the grooming and the constant smell of aftershave, which signalled him as squeaky clean but faintly silly. As he had stumbled slightly against her in the second before, her hand on his arm had also nudged into that barrel chest which she had, without dwelling on the thought, previously imagined to be flabby, but it too was hard, the consistency of bone rather than flesh. Perhaps Thomas's body had always been misjudged through the assumption that what was essentially ugly must also be sweet and softly safe, immune from the aggression and desires given to more attractive men. For the time, the loneliness of the ugly, his personal isolation as he sat there so controlled but so weak, pierced her with desperate pity.

'Are you all right? Look, just rest a bit and then we'll go home.'

'Go home?' he said. 'Home? Did you say home?'

Thomas sat upright, still with arms folded, looking straight ahead. Then he reached for her hand. For one desperate moment she thought he would raise it in that useless right paw either to kiss or to clutch, but he patted her knuckle instead in a gesture bereft of intimacy.

'Don't pity me,' he said neutrally. 'Whatever you do, don't do that. And of course we don't go home. You've only just got out. Look at those people over there. How very strange.'

He pointed towards six or seven primary-school girls, being bullied into a group to walk through the trees. They were resisting organization, a small school outing on the kind of nature walk Elisabeth remembered in far less structured settings. A parcel of girls, sent out to find specimens of earthly life in the interests of their education, one of them standing on the edge, mutinous and indifferent, clutching a bunch of fallen horse-chestnut leaves, while the other gloved hand held an ice cream, confused as to which burden to preserve first. Elisabeth noticed how the extended finger of Thomas shook as it pointed. When the stray but perfect child turned and watched his gaze, laughing for no reason, the pity which Elisabeth had tried to distance swayed back, sharp and protective, spiked into life by the look of intense hatred on his face. This time she wanted to touch him out of guilt for her own reluctance. He stood before she could make the gesture.

'Come on. Let's go. I do beg your pardon for that little display of weakness. All I need is food.'

If I do not move, Thomas thought to himself, she will see these ludicrous tears trapped behind these ludicrous glasses. She will know how exhausted I get if I attempt to walk faster than her without a stick. She will see too much. For the moment she pities me so much, she will come back with me, all by myself. She will come home, of her own free will, and I shall always be able to say, I did not make her. She called it home and she came home, to me.

As the afternoon progressed, Francis became more aimless. He was doing little more than following his own tracks in circles: he was hungry but not hungry, irritable because of an indifference to a basic need which was never ignored in his carefully controlled days. Francis did not like to lose control. So far he had travelled from Portobello Road to Camden Passage, drifted through arcades of stalls and shops, remarkably unspellbound. From west London to north and back to somewhere in between, without ever being able to make up his mind about buying a single thing. Not even a new pair of socks, never mind a painting. He was ashamed of himself for the waste of time, even more ashamed when without too much genuine desire for the company, he sought out Annie's stall at the back of Church Street. He wanted, but did not want to see Annie. He knew her only slightly and she attracted and repelled in equal measure: there was always a little needle of conflict. Francis told himself he needed to talk about Elisabeth, which was true, but what he needed as much was company.

By four o'clock in the afternoon most of Annie's customers had gone. There was a youth lying on the floor, and a thin woman with peroxide hair sitting on a chair and smoking a blue cigarette, fellow dealers, or Annie's version of friends. He neither knew nor cared which, but somehow their indifference to his presence not only made him feel *de trop*, but also brought upon him the desire to make an impact.

'Look what the cat brought in,' said Annie by way of greeting. 'Thought you might drop by some time today unless you thought we weren't good enough for you. Slumming it, are we?' She was a little resentful of his preoccupation when last seen, turned to her audience. 'One of the posher friends,' she explained. 'Cultured, you know.'

Francis did not like to be ignored, which felt to him like being despised; he invariably set out to charm strangers until he overcame their indifference. The desire to entertain was part of his calling, he supposed, but it might have been the other way round. In any event, the languid youth stirred himself into a man called Ralph who dealt in porcelain; the woman into someone called Jean who dealt in art deco. Business was bad: they had gathered round Annie

161

because Annie liked company. Being bored meant they were highly responsive to Francis, but even if they were an appreciative audience, he could not think why he was fool enough to tell them about the young burglar boy who had stolen paintings, then ripped the canvases to pieces. He turned it into another funny story, appropriate for the company, but as he did so, he knew he should not, because the boy client had been no more than a child and no one had heard that strange *cri de coeur* which had haunted Francis ever since. Then the silly tale of his post-midnight scare with his own broken picture. But they were only interested in the boy.

'Three years! Is that all? Little fucker should have got life.' This from the porcelain man.

'I'd have him flogged. Dipped in acid first, little sod.' This from Jean, suddenly animated, looking like a whip.

'Why?' queried Annie. It had been a long afternoon: she was prepared to act devil's advocate. 'Why? OK, so he pinched the stuff and got fed up with it, but three years? It's not as though the pictures couldn't be repaired sooner than that, was it? Worse things can be done to a painting then taking a knife to it, I can tell you. Did the judge know that, Francis?'

'I doubt it, any more than the boy.'

'Well, you should have told him. Then you should have got the paintings off whoever and taken them round to our Lizzie. She'd have fixed them and then your burglar would have got less.' She was teasing him, patronizing him in her own domain. The languid man stirred, without much conviction.

'Who's this Lizzie? Does she do china? I need a good fixer. Anyone got a drink?'

The conversation moved on: the fortunes of the dying afternoon drained away; Francis forgot what purpose to it there had ever been. The mention of Elisabeth made for no more than an uncomfortable sensation under the skin: the company was better than no company at all in the search for affordable but lovable paintings which had suddenly become such a sterile pursuit. How characterless I am, Francis thought, drinking from a plastic glass, to be so easily diverted. After one bottle of wine, shared but swift to act, he was suddenly charmed in turn by what he had first thought to be unsuitable, shallow, callous company, too feckless to understand law and retribution. By ten o'clock in the evening all of them blossomed into *bonhomie*: Annie's pale skin and pink-shadowed eyes glowed like a siren's. She had taken them home, fed them together with the other four who arrived clanking with cheap bottles of wine far worse than those Francis chose to provide, again to impress, on the way back to Annie's place. Wine was his passport to an otherwise free evening, the same credentials waved by many at Annie's door. And when they staggered home, Francis did not. He seemed to have recovered his taste for thin women and lost his desire for an orderly life.

He could not recall quite when it was the decision was made, the die cast. Maybe it began when she kept pushing past his chair on her way to and from the food she was preparing with efficient ease, ruffling his hair and saying

163

'All right? Comfortable?' with the same possessive condescension she might have used to a child. She had somehow annexed him as her own for the evening, but could not bring herself to show him courtesy in front of her friends, in case the friends did not like him or found him a snob. But they reacted in the opposite way: opened to him, found him delightful (as she knew, with increasing resentment, they would tell her tomorrow). They hung on his words, actually asked his opinions as if he were a kind of domesticated god, which was the way he looked – taller, blonder, cleaner than they, who spent their days wilting behind spotlights and smoking in auctions. It is not fair, Annie was fuming, without analysing what was not fair. He was a hit, but she might have liked him better if he had looked and acted uglier and she could have protected him. In her own small home, he made her selfconscious and himself conspicuous: and every hard-bitten, insecure bone in her resented his effortless ability to attract. She was driven to continue all evening in the way she had begun. Dispensing food and drink with one hand, sneering at him simultaneously. No one else noticed except the victim. Annie often played games.

'Are you sure that's OK for you? Only I know you're used to something better . . .

In truth he ate little and drank too much. The hand which extended his glass for the offered refill of brandy was still steady, Annie's deliberately rocky, so the liquid spilled on the beige gaberdine of his conventionally expensive trousers. 'Oops, sorry,' she murmured, offering as the only antidote a truly filthy dish cloth, which he refused.

'I like my garments battle-scarred,' he said, pretending to laugh. 'You may have to take them off,' someone remarked, and it might have been then the die was cast.

Everyone left. They all expected him to stay. Not that he was in much condition to move. He went instead into Annie's tiny, cluttered bathroom, full of frills and perfumes, feeling in himself a kind of fury. Oh yes, he had noticed the baiting. He relieved himself, looking at an angry face in a smeared mirror, came back belligerent.

'Time you were home, sweetie,' said Annie. 'You'll be needing your beauty sleep.'

She was barefoot. The sweater had been abandoned for a T-shirt which clung over her small bosom, and her angular hips seemed tilted towards him as she sprawled on her sofa among the detritus of her bohemian entertaining. He sat beside her heavily.

'Annie, you've been very kind, very generous, but why the hell have you been such a bitch?'

'Who the fuck do you think you're calling a bitch?'

'The person who called Elisabeth a slut.'

She launched herself at him in an anger which surprised them both, an animal growl in her throat and her fists raised. These he seized and pressed her back against the cushions. She made as if to spit, flailed her legs in the air in an effort to kick, but his fingers were bruising her wrists and his mouth was over hers which somehow opened in a response which was not a scream. When he let go of her hands, she clawed at his back, still subsumed in a violent kissing which was more the grinding of gums and teeth. The shirt ripped, the dampness of his brandy-soaked trousers pressed into her thigh and the smell of them rose into her nostrils. Then his hands were full of her sticky, spiky hair, while hers, satisfied with the tearing sound they had made, with no conscience for the scratches, were in his thick, glossy mane, and the kiss became a kiss. Hands transferred themselves, without words, the whole set of movements becoming less dangerous, more gentle but still aggressive. Finally she turned her head from his far too beautiful, finely chiselled mouth. Each stared into the black pupils of the other, neither in possession of themselves.

'All right,' she said. 'Don't go. But not here. I've got a bloody bed . . .'

Towards which they staggered, still locked in case the other might somehow get away. Fell without any more of the undressing which had taken place like a kind of involuntary shedding in transit. His mouth clamped on one of her nipples while she squirmed out of the leggings, a feat of gymnastics. She felt the smoothness of his buttocks, he the tinyness of hers in a cursory exploration of splayed fingers, making space for himself, without affection. A quick and violent coupling, audible with cries and the slapping of flesh on flesh, diminishing into little moist sounds. He was semi-conscious at her breast, slipping into sleep. She moved him then, dog-tired but wakeful, went into the bathroom he had vacated so recently. Saw in the same smeared mirror her own pinched face, with her dusty black T-shirt still round her neck like a collar.

To sleep, then, there was nothing else. She knew she had not been raped and detested an empty bed: she was pragmatic, not entirely displeased with herself, despite his lying there, angled so he took all the room, like a log. Annie shoved him, positioned him so her back was warmed by his chest and her neck fanned by his breathing.

Two o'clock: two slender bodies in search of something, each bringing to the other nothing more than the availability of flesh. Annie took no thought for their motives, only thought of the warmth.

Until she heard him calling names in his sleep. Elisabeth, Elisabeth, a puzzled, interrogatory murmur in between deep, broken breathing. She squirmed not with resentment, not with guilt, which was an emotion quite foreign to her life, except for this sudden sensation of feeling cold. Cold, like Elisabeth's flat had seemed on her own brief visits, even in summer. The cold of no money and her own dignified choice of needing so few friends. But not real cold, simply skimpy as far as home comforts were concerned, an interesting, colourful place, not built for entertaining and not built to house a man. Post-coital drowsiness brought dreaming into mind a series of discordant images, forgotten obligations, stray thoughts like yowling cats sent to torment. Odd sensations of frost and sudden surges of heat, all conscience, all suppressed thought, all memories, resting their hideous heads on her bosom, as Francis had deposited his. She could have killed him, sleeping thus. Heat took over.

'Elisabeth,' he said quite distinctly, then murmurings which were entirely confused and only served, not to reassure, but to transfix the clarity of her name as he had spoken it. Elisabeth, you bitch. Elisabeth, the stranger in Annie's soft bed, creator of another stream of thought to add to the effluxion of others already out of control. If Annie were like Elisabeth, merely a name spoken in the night but disappeared in the day, a person who had become after so short a time no more than an inconvenient memory, who would look for her? If all those who knocked at Annie's door should find that door closed more than once, how often would they bother to return? Would they turn their world upside down in troubling to find her? Annie, trying desperately to think of something else while the smell of sex and brandy was still in her mouth and her nose, her dead mascara still in her eyes, doubted it. She lay, rigid and chilled in her own home, unable to hug this virtual stranger, remembering how it was they had come to be here. Saturday night and I ain't got nobody: that was why, for both of them. That and a kind of revenge for what they both were and where they belonged. They would not like each other in the morning.

'Don't wash up,' said Elisabeth gently. 'I mean, just don't. For God's sake, I can do it, I'd have done it all along but I thought Maria did it. You still look grey. I thought you were better earlier, but I don't think you are. All that walking. I'm sorry, I've been a bit insensitive, haven't I? It's the brandy you give me in the evening. I simply stagger off and sleep. I never see what you do.'

'Grey? Who said I was grey? Only my hair. And I like to walk. The park was fun, wasn't it? Wasn't it?' He turned his overlarge head in her direction in a kind of fierce interrogation. In that moment, as he straightened himself in his chair, forever wearing those smoked glasses, he looked as he had looked in the restaurant at lunch, in that pink and green restaurant, an occasion managed only by strength of will, while the pity in her had arrived in waves along with the courses, all militating against appetite. He ate like a machine, fussily, in small quantities, a deliberate, choosily greedy feeding and, throughout it all, when he remembered, as he did most of the time, to sit very upright, he looked like a pigeon. He still looked like a pigeon. Or a person pretending not to be weak, a small boy pretending to be strong brushing off help but needing an escort home. Elisabeth had re-entered this zone of light, space, occupation and acceptance out of concern for him: he had not been fit to climb all those stairs alone, adamantly refused the lift: he said it was unreliable and unnecessary but he might have died halfway. She knew this high flat was no longer the place of serenity she had first found, but she had come back with him all the same. Politeness, kindness, weakness, and above all pity, were all stronger forces than that desire for survival which had often eluded her.

'Oh yes,' she said. 'The park was fun. We must do it again. And you really must go to bed. I'm not sure the brandy was a good idea.'

'But it's early, for a girl like you. How old are you, anyway? About thirty?'

You know very well, she thought: you are not so unobservant, but she simply laughed.

'About that. Not too young for early nights. I've got work to do in the morning.' He cleared his throat, rose to his feet.

'Elisabeth?'

169

'Yes?'

He was moving out of the room, leaving her dominion over the fire, talking over his shoulder.

'I do care for you, you know.'

'I know.'

No doors slammed in his progress to rest. Usually, she departed first, to her self-contained suite on the other side of the hall, where the massive doors would close behind her without sound. Being left alone in front of the fire, charged with tidying the room and putting away dishes, jobs he always reserved for himself as a fussy, solicitous host, seemed awkward and intrusive. It should have made her feel more at home, like the relative freedoms of the day, but created the opposite effect, as if he had just given her some kind of authority and responsibility she wanted to resist. Rigid formality had been the hallmark of this liaison so far, a mark of value. In the confines of her own large bedroom, she did not mind: there was everything she wanted, books, warmth and dreams. The night-time silence of the place oppressed her: she was alive to any sound which might disturb it, full of the sleeplessness which was not energy but a quiet distress. Lying down fully clothed, reluctant to wash and render herself naked, she remained immobile on her bed for two long hours, attempting to conjure up those colours which always comforted, the images of what her work would look like at the end, forming a plan for tomorrow's labours, rationalizing nameless fears, listening for him.

She did not know what time it was when she heard him,

only recognized a time of night when she invariably woke, her sleep interrupted, she supposed, by the brandy which had become such a ritual of luxury. Thomas was on the move: she knew it before she heard it from her supine position in the dark. The door to her room, almost opposite the kitchen, was framed in light from the hall. There was a faint clicking sound, Butler's feet on the floor of the kitchen tapping out a subdued enthusiasm for the great outdoors, which was quickly quietened by the master with a shushing sound, no words either spoken or necessary. Then the sound of the hall cupboard opening, then the front door, sounds followed by a return for something forgotten, Butler's lead, she guessed, left in a drawer which was opened now, then closed, slowly. Elisabeth cursed herself for her own immobility, slipped off the bed and moved towards the frame of light. She opened her door while those wordless sounds from the kitchen masked her movements. In time to see his back shuffling towards the front door, ushering the dog before him, pressing the buttons to activate the lock. Thomas's working hand reached out to cancel the light, while under his right arm she saw for one split second a dark object, tipped with silver, flashing on the eye like a blade sticking out behind him before the door was closed and the only remaining light was a dim glow from the kitchen window. There was no sound at all now. Butler was obediently still on the other side of the prison door as she heard it close.

She waited for a full minute, breathing deeply and counting the seconds to keep herself still, one, two, three, four, twenty, thirty, fifty, go, unable to keep the numbers continuous, skipping and going back like someone half numerate. Then she opened her door fully with ostentatious noise, stepped into the hall, turned on the light again, looked first in the cupboard to find her own coat hanging alone above the box full of sticks, dust-free. There was the impulse to go, immediately, to make up for having returned willingly that afternoon, like a credulous fool moved by pity she was no longer sure was appropriate, but she knew, before she hung on to the polished brass handle, that the front door would be locked, mocking her impotence. Loneliness, the splendid isolation she had craved for most of her life, was suddenly no longer an end in itself. I came back with him willingly. She repeated this like a litany. It was shameful. His will overbore my pathetic pretence of having a will at all, and he is keeping me a prisoner. And I did not run, I came back. Maybe with the man who haunted me, that man with a stick. No. Nothing could be as cruel.

Elisabeth turned on the carpet, a graceless pirouette of indecision. Telephone, telephone, she repeated to herself. Find someone and remind them where you are, just in case. In case of what, and who to tell? There was nothing to tell which had not been written in a letter, but it was the voice she needed. Since she had scaled down her acquaintance to skeleton levels, she could only think of Francis. Well, Francis then, Annie perhaps but, Francis first, because she loved Francis. There had been a telephone in the living room: she remembered it from the first night, not seen since, nothing now but the connection point in the wall behind one of the wing chairs. She moved down the hall, timid but bold. Look, she was telling herself, he is only taking the dog for fresh air. Butler may be an incontinent beast; he may do this every night without my knowing, why should I? Locking me in is only the precaution of a man who locks the door each time he goes out himself. Thomas would have to traverse all those stairs back and forth first since he refused the lift: there was time to hunt for the telephone which must exist. His room, she supposed, banging down the long hall, opening the door to what she knew was his lair. A lair within a castle. Or, simply, one more large room.

The window, of the same proportions as a porthole, was wide open, so the sharp breeze struck her first. Then the light showed up cream walls covered in nothing, with the bareness of an institution. There was a set of weights, signs of a regime of rigorous exercise: no wonder his flesh was as hard as bone. One wall was lined with books; there were books by the side of his bed. He had plenty to occupy him here. Looking as she moved, Elisabeth found the telephone by the bed, held her breath as she dialled Francis's number which had been implanted in her memory ever since she had first written it down. She was still counting: twenty, thirty, fifty.

There was no answer. No answer despite her praying into the receiver, then lifting it away from her ear, then replacing it and dialling again. There never had been an answer from anyone whenever she had been in need. The greater the need the more obdurate the silence, she had always found and had thus almost forgotten how to ask. She might have known.

Elisabeth sank on to the edge of Thomas's large bed, rose again sharply, aware of the warmth his figure had imparted to the cheap coverlet thrown over it. A very hard bed, no luxuries in this room, no silk or satin or flounces, no sign of expense, but more like a cell equipped with necessities, nothing more. A bed, a chair, a chest of drawers, stacks of canvases against the wall. Against her will, Elisabeth's mind went back to these, since paintings even now, could not lose that power to distract. Besides, their presence comforted her. A man who kept paintings stored in his room could not be a threat, could only be the harmless, half-disabled patron he seemed to be, a benign, if eccentric collector of beauty. Elisabeth looked closer, saw the first painting in the first stack.

An interior with chairs. Like the room in which she worked here, also like the other, north-facing room in which they sat, ate, drank. Like the picture Annie had given her to restore so many months ago; the one she had been reluctant to return, kept so long that Annie had forgotten it.

Not similar to that painting, the same. Next to it there lay a duster and a piece of stained bandage. Thomas had not quite tidied up. She fled from the room down the corridor, glanced into the open door of the studio. The rosary beads were still on the easel, swinging in some hidden breeze as she passed. Automatically, she crossed herself, ran into her own room, lay down, waited for the light of sanity and dawn.

CHAPTER NINE

Francis could not call this particular waking up a normal ending to sleep. His was the variety of sleep which had been induced by five different varieties of wine and violent exercise. There was an exaggerated slowness to his movements when he woke before dawn and staggered again to the bathroom. The stream of urine alleviated nothing, especially since the mirror was placed in such a way that he was forced to see his face reflected during micturition and did not like what he saw. A pale face, with lines appearing around the eyes and a mouth which was saying to this image, You've got lucky here, old son. He did not like himself, drunk in the house of a mere acquaintance and going to bed with her just because he was being led by his prick and a feeling of disorientation which made this a far safer option than going home.

Part of him supposed, with a grim humour, that he had already paid some of the price. He wondered why he returned to bed since he had already been punished by the heat. Annie believed in comfort, while Francis, indoctrinated in the spartan regime of public school, had a preference for elegant necessities, the minimum of bed clutter and a cool, hard mattress. Not an enveloping cushion which wrapped itself around him as he sank, nor a duvet which could have furnished an Arctic expedition and had left him fighting in the small hours, pushing the cover away while the sweat gathered in the valley of his chest. He adjusted to the edge of the bed with one foot sticking out as a reminder to himself that this was not really a prison but simply a captivity he could escape in the morning. A strange combination of manners and exhaustion had kept him from moving out in the middle of the night although the temptation was there. That, and an overwhelming sense of grief, a sharp pain in his sternum. Elisabeth had been the last lover and he had not lain with her like this, for all his final petulance. Distant though she was, self-contained and cool, he had been comfortable in that bed of hers, serenely intertwined, loving her while she in her own way was loving him. They had functioned thus: they had understood the secret places of the other, loved modestly but well. If she had not opened her heart, she had tried to open part of it and he had not encouraged her: when she had hugged and kissed in the privacy of the dark, she had been with him, in him and around him, both of them giving a quality notable in the absence here. His enactment of the same rituals with Annie was a travesty.

Now he was aware of her adopting a similar position as himself in her over-soft bed, clutching the opposite side to avoid the contact inevitable in the dip which was the centre. The realization provoked the first real feeling of tenderness towards her. It was an improvement, this knowledge of her being vulnerable and also slightly ashamed of such pointless intimacy.

Annie was also far more direct. She could not dwell with unfamiliar guilt, her own or anyone else's. The feeling bored and niggled; she had to spit it out. When Francis fell into a deep sleep just at the time it was almost decent enough to get up and leave, Annie rose, cleaned her kitchen with headachy fury and fortified herself with caffeine. Then brought to the bed a glass of orange juice laced with vitamin C and a cup of dark brown coffee. Francis was blurred on the edge of uncomfortable consciousness when she shook him awake. He groaned, attempted to smile, muttered 'Thank you', and could not meet her eyes. She was not having any of this.

'Well, that was a mistake, wasn't it?'

He gulped on the boiling coffee, burning his mouth, put it down and reached for the orange juice.

'Well, wasn't it?' Her voice was determinedly cheerful, questioning rather than accusing. Last night's bitchiness was gone.

'Yes,' he said. 'Yes, it was, a bit of a mistake. I'm sorry. I behaved badly.'

She shrugged. 'You and me both.' Annie scrunched up her face and tapped her head to indicate incipient madness. He ignored the bright washed sheen of her eyes. 'Booze and bodies,' she added. 'A bad combination.'

'Yes.' He buried his head in the pillow. Not only badly behaved but ignoring any survival code for chance encounters, just a random coupling.

'Too bad. I'm not worried. Too late, anyway. What I want to know is what are we going to do about Elisabeth? Our Lizzie?'

Francis was sitting upright by now, his hand holding the coffee mug jumped six inches, sending half the contents slurping over the rim.

'Pardon?'

'Oh, that's right. Take advantage of my hospitality, then ruin the duvet, go on, why don't you? You heard what I said, as well as knowing what I meant. OK, I repeat: what are we going to do about Elisabeth? Because we have to do something.'

'Why?'

'Because all of a sudden she fucking haunts me, that's why. Lying awake last night – and I know you were, too – I got to thinking how stupid I was. You know, always going around, banging into things, men included, all that kind of stuff. And how friendless I really am. I'm not a good friend to anyone, even though I can make up a party by clicking my fingers, and if I disappeared ... well, I suddenly thought, no one would come looking for me. Single people, you know, living like we live, well, maybe not you, you'd have a mummy and daddy still, wouldn't you?, but if you haven't, no one would bother for ages, would they? None of mine would. They'd be like you, dying not to know. So I thought I'd better begin as I mean to go on. If I take a bit of trouble for Lizzie, who was, actually, always ready to take trouble for me now I come to think of it, maybe, someone, sometime, might look out for me if I happened to get lost. A sort of insurance policy.'

'She doesn't like being called Lizzie.'

'I'll call her what I effing well please, and what a nit-picking lawyer you are. Do you want some more coffee and are you reading me, Spock?'

'Yes. Yes to both.'

'Well, put some clothes on, then. Your skin doesn't go with my duvet.' The brief tenderness which had occurred before dawn in his awareness of their mutual discomfiture flowered now into respect. Within the parameters of his hangover, he began to like her brazen honesty, although none of that quite prevented him from wanting to leave. Or thinking wistfully of a retreat to his own home. In the event he stayed, took the sheet and duvet cover off the bed as Annie was itching to do, put them in her washing machine as if that ended the whole carnal episode, then sat at her kitchen table and pooled information. The stock of their knowledge was pathetically small.

All the dead timber of the week stockpiles on Sundays: Sundays without an art fair or some collectors' venue were as dead to Francis as a corpse. Work was always there to fill the void: perhaps Elisabeth had used it to fill the canyons of her mind. Sitting here with nothing but Sunday and a bad conscience, he saw in a rare moment of insight how becoming a workaholic was a natural progress for a certain kind of life.

'She worked a lot,' he told Annie. 'She worked all the

179

time. She was either working or looking for work. She wouldn't have taken a holiday, not if you had actually given her something to do, she'd honour that first. That's why I think she's simply gone somewhere else. Did we ask that neighbour of hers if she'd left any messages?'

'We did, and she didn't. Come on, Francis, is that all you know? You're pathetic. You're with our Lizzie for how many months, and you've only amassed enough information on her to fill the back of a postage stamp.'

'So? You've known her twenty times longer and don't know that much more. Such as where do you start? Her correspondence? Her contacts, the place where she grew up? I gather, by the way, her parents are dead and she probably hasn't been home for years, although she pretended to me she had.' He was becoming defensive, toned himself down.

'Who told you that?'

'The police, something like that. She never talked about family to me.'

'She's got brothers, I know she has, I once moaned at her, said I was short of men, didn't she have any single relatives.' Annie grinned ruefully. 'She said, yes, she'd got brothers, but she couldn't recommend them and didn't know where they lived.'

'Hmm. Maybe. As for what she likes and doesn't like, apart from privacy, paintings and men, which isn't, come to think of it, quite consistent, I don't know. She didn't steal those paintings of yours, you know. I just can't see her doing that.'

'No,' said Annie, uncomfortably aware that if Elisabeth

had done such a thing it would be no more than a guarantee of debt, common in her line of trade; dealers were always holding one another's stock in lieu of cash.

'The only thing I can say about her with complete confidence is that she never complained,' said Francis, wondering at that even as he spoke. 'Never. Oh, sometimes, in a sentence, about money, never about a person. Never complained, never asked for anything. She wouldn't argue, either; she hid instead, but never ranted, even mildly. Never fought anyone or anything. All she seemed to want was walls of colour and equipment, as if that made up for everything.'

'Maybe it did,' Annie mumbled, unconvinced.

'For what, though? Why is she so subdued, so self-controlled?' He stood up, tall in the confines of the kitchen. 'She loved me, you know. I think. In her way. God alone knows why, I doubt if I deserved it.'

The word love embarrassed Annie. She sneered. 'How do you know she loved you? How does anyone know?'

'You can feel it through the skin.'

Annie looked at him sideways, lit a cigarette quickly and exhaled to fudge the view. He was decent, despite this useless questioning and a level of unworldliness she found shocking. She looked at him again, tried to summon up contempt for his immaturity and the vanity of his motives, could not find it in herself to dislike him. Bodies were treacherous things. If she had reached across her table, she might have touched him. As it was, she remained quite still.

Thomas knew, on Sunday morning, that his guest had

been inside his bedroom to use the telephone. Bodies were treacherous, they left traces. He knew she had been in here and he knew in what mood: he could almost time the moment, after he had gone out in the night, although it was knowledge he refused to digest until morning. If he left the house himself in future, Butler would stay and the door would be locked, as always.

For shame. Sunday, the deadest day of the week, except for the Sunday she had come here. It was only on this Sunday, realizing the implications of her being inside the room which served not only as sleeping space but also as painting store, along with those others locked somewhere, that he knew there might not be an end to this plan. Elisabeth Young wanted to go home. She could feel the bars already and he could feel her feeling them. She was no longer a willing partner: he was not enough, the paintings were not enough. The thought filled him with such sadness that he lay in his bed with his sheet to his chin and wept. His head was huge against the pillow and, from where he lay, his paunchy abdomen looked flat. The mound of his feet, splayed beneath the blanket, gave the lie to his length being anything other than short: one foot, the right, always moved up the bed against his will. His hands, small and neat, gripped the sheet either side of his chin and he had the impression of himself as wearing a bib. I am ridiculous, he thought. I shall always be ridiculous. He removed one of his curled fists and felt his thinning hair, finding no comfort in what was once blond, now grey beneath the black streaks applied every other week. Ridiculous.

Sunday, perversely, was the day he always associated with lies. Sunday in a hospital, gazing towards another face with his one remaining eye, mulishly silent and life hitting the first downhill tangent. Another Sunday, years after, when he had been left rich, but not rich enough to avoid the stroke which shook him from skull to heel as he gestured for help. The wrath of God in the form of the punishment which was not quite death, but felt like death. I never touched her, he was trying to say. I never touched her; however beautiful she may have been, which is not as beautiful as now. I hate her. God, I hate her, but will you believe I never touched her in the way you mean? You have no right to touch me now.

'Touch me!' Thomas whispered. 'Touch me!' The stump of his penis sprang into life beneath the bedclothes, so that the mounds beneath his one sheet and blanket were in line, one left foot, one right foot further up, one indiscriminate hump looking for air. As he watched, it subsided, like a small child sinking behind a desk after some humiliation. Or a dandelion plant the morning after the weedkiller spray, Thomas thought, killed but still rooted, pathetic all the same, that little thing as ugly as the rest of him. He looked at its demise without disappointment.

Thomas swung out of bed and lumbered over to the window. It was a round window, like a porthole; only the top half was ever open, locked like that and he seemed to have lost the keys. They were suicide-proofed, these windows: only a cat could climb through and, out of that fear, Thomas told himself, he had parted with the cat. No, that was not quite true. He did not part with the cat; he killed it.

You had to kill even beautiful things if it was too distressing and dangerous to keep them alive.

Thinking obliquely of that, he remembered his umbrella with annoyance and a hint of alarm. The blast of cold air hit his naked groin as he looked down towards the street. A long way down: a message on paper would float far away, hither and thither, to join London's legendary litter in some distant park. The cold braced him. Thomas made himself stand there until he felt faintly numb and dizzy, his hand holding the window frame. Then he let Butler into the room while he washed and the dog stood guard against the bathroom door.

'They tell lies all over the country today, dog,' Thomas said. 'They stand up in church and sing them without blushing. About God being good and all men being equal, and at no level, no level at all, is this *true*, do you hear me? I haven't told her too many lies, have I, Butler? Not nearly as many as a standard priest. Sunday's a good day for it. Even in that cathedral.'

The dog maintained silence.

'She owes me, anyway,' Thomas continued aloud. 'She started it all.'

The dog growled and his hackles rose, the clue to movement elsewhere in the vastness of the flat. Elisabeth rising, perhaps, going to the kitchen, the Sabbath phoenix rising from the ashes of poor sleep.

'By the way, Butler, don't bite her,' Thomas continued. 'You shouldn't have bitten Maria, whatever she was doing wrong, and you mustn't bite Elisabeth, not ever. You only have to frighten them. I do the biting . . . *Me!*'

Dressed, shirt with large buttonholes made for ease, clip-on tie, trousers pressed, shoes shone, he ambled out of his room towards the kitchen. Oh dear, no avoiding some sort of confrontation today, how she must hate it. Sunday was the day for lies.

She was waiting, of course. Sitting in front of untouched coffee, tired, but as gloriously gentle as ever, politeness first.

'Are you better this morning, Thomas?'

'Greatly, thank you.' He sat heavily, opposite her. She raised troubled and haunted eyes to his, and he thought with a rush of pity, I'm right, I know I am, she cannot cope out there and how beautiful she is. So like the olive-skinned woman in the portrait I bought purely for the resemblance: she, too, would suit an unset pearl at her throat, and how strange, how remarkably unvain, that she has never seen that resemblance. She will make that picture perfect as herself. I need them both.

'Thomas, I must talk to you.'

'Yes, I know.'

She quivered with the effort, the strain transferred to her coffee mug, which she spilt at the moment Francis, a few miles away, spilt his. There was a moment's distraction while she mopped up the mess. During that interval she began to speak. Typically, he thought, beginning with an apology.

'I'm sorry I trespassed into your room last night, but I was looking for the telephone.'

'Oh. Did you get who you wanted?'

'No. He was out.'

'People are always out when you want them,' said Thomas kindly. 'Don't you know that? People are not reliable.'

'Yes, I do know that. Thomas, what are you doing? Why do you double lock the door on me when you go out, like last night? What are you trying to do?'

Sunday was the day for lies. Thomas bowed his head, absurdly penitent 'There's something I must tell you. I didn't want to tell you before, but I have known for a day or two . . . meant, in fact, to tell you yesterday.' He sensed she was holding her breath.

'What then, what?'

The slight shrillness of her tone hardened him: it was all for her own good, after all. 'Listen, dear, purely out of concern for you, I went to see if your flat was safe. It wasn't. Seems your car was stolen and burnt out. Seems your flat was burgled, too. The police went over it with a toothcomb, trying to find where you might be. You understand me? So I went there, too. Took what I could. I only went to rescue your privacy. There was so little left.'

'How?' she asked wildly. 'How did you get in there? How could anyone?' She was feeling in the pocket of her smock for her key, closed her hand over nothing. He watched the fumbling.

'I took your key,' he said simply. 'Oh, and a dry-cleaning ticket. To save you the agony. But the doors had been forced. You must have left some kind of address in the car. I am so sorry, but you don't really have a home any more. I just didn't want you to know, that was all.'

'And now I do.'

'Now you do.'

She leapt up from the table and ran to the front door, tugged at the handle briefly and then let her arms fall to her side. Butler had flung himself after her, pushed his snarling, snapping muscle between herself and the door and stood with his chest heaving. As her movements gradually ceased under the threat of those yellow eyes and teeth, he began to wag his tail, the whole of his rump moving in sympathy. You may bite the hand which feeds, but should stroke the head which bites. Elisabeth did as she automatically did, stroked the big ugly muzzle in conditioned affection, without purpose. You did as you were bid in this house, acted like Pavlov's dog to Pavlov's dog. Especially if you had no home of your own. She did not disbelieve Thomas, although she knew he lied about the timing: she had seen that picture in his room. If what he said was only some approximation of truth, the end result was the same. No privacy, no castle, no life worth the name. She had a memory of sitting on Thomas's bed, listening to the phone ring in Francis's empty flat, and felt a terrible calm anger which could find no words to serve it. The words would have to wait. Elisabeth turned and walked back to the kitchen table. Perhaps she still owed Thomas courtesy, but she did not really think at all. She saw in her mind's eye a hundred smashed jugs of brilliant colours and the inner eye was blinded. The hands were placed flat on the surface of the table, a fine, dark wood table, unsuitable for a kitchen, the surface comfortably cool. Her hands looked sallow and enormous, ringless as

187

became a woman without status, big, spatulate fingers as suited artist or surgeon. Ugly hands for an ugly body, like the rest of her, helpless as a row of dead fishes. Hands which were guilty, neglected, skilful. She saw, out of the corner of her eye, the one good hand of Thomas's, manicured in a way she had always found repellent with a slight sheen to the nails, extended towards her downturned palms. As she watched, the hand withdrew.

'I didn't arrange any of this,' he said. 'Whatever you think of me, you mustn't think that. You're here of your own free will, and is there any point in going anywhere until you've finished the paintings? No, I'll answer for you, no. Just the three. They're all too valuable to me, as you are, for me to let you leave. Can't you see that? I thought you could.'

'Just the three,' she echoed, still looking at her hands. 'Do you think if you let me go today, I would steal them?'

'They found photos of you, in your flat,' Thomas went on conversationally. 'In the nude. Letters to lovers, letters to the parents you seemed to have abandoned. Letters from aunts and uncles, begging for a reply which was not, apparently, forthcoming. Your friends seem to know about these. It's the way with all jigsaw puzzles. People put together the pieces in the wrong order and the result is not slightly different, but totally different. Your neighbours are describing you as a whore, worse than that, a thief who arranged it all. Is there any point going home today, or until they know better? Let them think about you. Just the three pictures, and then I'll help you start again. I want nothing from you. But I do care for you, did I tell you

188

that? Who else cares, who else, I ask you? No, don't answer. Just finish the madonna. Make her perfect.'

'Yes,' she said. 'Yes, yes, yes.' She turned her hands upwards. There were faint traces of stains on the palms, looking like the hairs which superstition said were the first sign of madness, small streaks of purple and fainter yellow, the marks of strong pigments, mixed yesterday. Elisabeth Young got to her feet and pulled the blue smock close to herself by stuffing the hands in her pockets and balling them into protective fists by her sides. She thought of the salvation in those colours, the half-done work, the mixtures which would quickly dry, the careful application of overpaint, the new discoveries, the neck of the olive-skinned lady, the only source of solace left. Thought, too, of the letters she had written on Thomas's fine-head notepaper, and the absence of any reply. It was true, then: they all despised her.

'It's a lovely day,' she said neutrally. 'I'd better do some work. While there's light.'

Maria toiled upstairs. Like her brother she despised the lift, but, unlike him, it was because she was afraid of it. Walking was only another penance which made her in all ways stronger. Her skin chafed beneath the big boots. No socks today, for the added sanctity which was promised by pain. Or so it said in the book on all the saints, a book with pictures she had brought upstairs with her, in the hope she might be able to show it to Elisabeth, by way of explaining the extra accoutrements she felt the madonna needed. Despite the discomfort, Maria was humming in pleasurable

189

anticipation of the real singing in church. Thomas had been neglectful of late, about their Sunday excursion to the cathedral, but today he'd promised.

'Swee-eet heart of Jesus! We-ee implore . . .'

She pressed the bell and waited for a long time. When he finally answered, her face fell. He was not ready, no coat, no umbrella.

'Not today, Maria, I'm sorry.'

She looked down and kicked the door with sudden savagery.

'Shh,' he said. 'Look, I can't. Our Elisabeth isn't well.'

Maria's face lit up. 'I'll look after her,' she volunteered distinctly.

Thomas shuddered. 'No you won't. Anyway, it isn't that kind of sick. She's saying her own prayers in her own room. Be a good girl and take Butler out instead.' He thrust the dog at her and closed the door in her face.

Maria told herself she did not really mind, but she still sat down on the top stair, heavy with disappointment. She had so hoped . . . that they would all go out together, the whole family, Elisabeth, herself and him. There were all these things in church she wanted to show Elisabeth, because Elisabeth was so like all the saints in her pictures and she loved her for being so quiet and nice and good. She could have shown her the portrait of the virgin martyr St Agatha, who was equally good. She had vowed her virginity to Christ and kept her promise even when she was tortured by rack and fire and her breast cut off. Then there was St Agnes, another holy virgin, killed by a sword through the throat. She might even have got Elisabeth to tell her which of her namesakes she preferred, because there were two St Elisabeths, she thought. One from Hungary whom Maria did not like much, because she was married and had children before turning holy, and one from Portugal who was very much better, dark like this Elisabeth, and although she hadn't been a martyr, she had been a queen. With a sinner for a husband, until she made him better.

'Come on, you devil,' she said to the dog.

There was so much else she wanted to say. Instead she plodded downstairs. She could have gone to the cathedral by herself, but it wasn't the same. She could take Butler to the square and watch the people, then go home to the darkness of the basement and pretend it was church. A sense of unfairness went into every step. It wasn't the same.

This basement was a different place, Annie decided, when it was light. On the few occasions she had come here before, including the one time with Francis, she had always entered and left in the dark. This time, in the division of their labour which had become crosser as their enthusiasm faded, each shaming the other while pointing out that they did have livings to earn (and there was, of course, a limit to the time they could spend), she had drawn the short straw of going back to Elisabeth's flat because a woman on her own was less likely to draw fire. Fire from whom was not a question either bothered to answer. Sparks, you mean, Annie told herself, no fire here, only sparks and smoke. In truth, Annie was quite pleased to be going back in there alone. Instinct, the feminine kind, had been inhibited by male company the last time. There were things about a woman's rooms which only another woman could see, and it was, as she noticed, so much better in the light. Darkness, any kind of darkness, hid the stains, the neglect, the cold spots of shame in any house: the shabbiness could shine with pride in the light, never in the dusk.

She had planned to ring the old girl's bell, she whom she had applauded as not so bad, but privately suspected was the sort who would be a concierge in willing KGB employ if she lived in old Moscow, a natural, envious spy. Annie would have preferred not to ring Enid's chimes at any time of day, light or dark, so she waited across the road, hoping against hope that there might be some other way to get beyond the front door. Resentful in her waiting; she was only doing this as a kind of dare, something to shame Francis for calling that name in the middle of the night. Then a young couple approached the same front door. The woman had the keys in her handbag – some large knapsack which took in her arm to the elbow. Annie sped across the road with a big smile. They did not seem to mind her slipping in behind them as long as she continued the smile. They went upstairs before she went down, without the faintest interest in what she might do next. Arm in arm, they trod beyond the common domain towards their own. Annie felt a stab of envy in their unity as she descended and shoved the key in Elisabeth's lock, felt the remains of yesterday's wine, shaken but not particularly stirred by coffee, hitting her with delayed rebellion. Screw Francis. Screw their morning conversation with its mutual lazy challenges and the tasks thereby created.

It did not occur to her, although it remained a possibility

with Francis, that Elisabeth would be back by now. Somehow, Annie knew, through all her speculating in the small hours, that she could not be there, might never be there again, that her absence was quite unnatural; but none of that gave rise to any sensation of fear. What made the hair rise on her neck was the change in the scent of the place. A new warmth, rancid and chemical, not the old scent born on the old breeze. A confusion of scents, a sickly suggestion of aftershave. Then, with a creeping sensation of fear, she heard movement, a scuttling in the direction of the studio room down at the end. Annie's first impulse was to turn and run, but secondary instinct told her that what scuttled here, like a giant rat, scuttled in fear. The corridor was dark: she had the impression of a figure flung from the bathroom as she had opened the front door, the race of someone looking for a hiding place.

'Hallo, hallo! Anyone there?'

Annie stepped forward, leaving the door open behind her. Moved into the studio, where the light showed dust, the same jugs, pictures, equipment. Her eye fell on the rosewood pig with the split back she had noticed before, an intrusive, barbaric but, on second sight, lovable thing. Then her eye fell on the figure in the corner, a creature making her small self smaller, huddled behind a chair partly hidden by a cupboard with the easel pulled in front in a pathetic, hurried attempt at concealment. As her own alarm subsided in the face of the other's fear, Annie was slightly amused. She recognized Enid, the concierge woman, with a head full of iron grips to keep the hair straight. For what, Annie thought, for what? Why does anyone do that? She had little sensitivity for the vanities of anyone much beyond her own age.

'Hallo,' she said again, keeping her voice deliberately neutral. 'What are you doing there?'

'Oh,' Enid whimpered breathlessly. 'Oh, you did frighten me. I thought it was him . . .' Then she began to recover, became brisker. 'What do you mean, what am I doing? I could ask you the same thing.'

'I came to look for Elisabeth. Who did you think I was?'

Enid stood up, brushing something from her skirt, which was crumpled, Annie noticed, in contrast to her appearance the time before. Oddly, Enid's left forearm was heavily bandaged. The fist at the end of it clutched a plastic bottle. Annie's eyes fixed on that.

'Have you hurt yourself?' She tried to sound sympathetic, but the woman defied pity.

'Yes, yes, as a matter of fact,' Enid babbled. 'That's right, I did. Cut my arm, clearing up. I only came down here to see if she had some ointment. She does, you know – Elisabeth, I mean – keep that sort of thing, for when she gets dermatitis. Problems, she has, with her skin, sometimes, because of all this lot, I suppose.' Enid waved a hand towards the bottles and jars. 'I only came to borrow,' she added. The lined face, naked of the heavy makeup which Annie knew would be habitual in a woman who tortured her hair, looked pinched, sick, crafty but vulnerable.

'Who did you think I was?' Annie repeated with understated curiosity.

'Uncle,' said Enid rapidly. 'No, the landlord. Him. I thought he'd come back for his umbrella. I only came down for some calamine. What do you want? You shouldn't be here. It's all right for him, not you.' She shuddered on the verge of manic giggles.

'I'll be gone in a minute, promise. How did you hurt your arm?' Annie smiled, the full saleswoman smile, rarely known to fail. Enid stood, still trembling, malice and uncertainty combined in her face.

'Never you mind. I'll go now. Please give me back the key. I'm supposed to look after this place and take care of it. I've got a right.'

'Yes,' said Annie. 'Of course you have.' She was too tired to ask questions and still too resentful, turned her back on the neighbour, hearing rather than seeing Enid's crablike departure. The desk had been disturbed, but she could not recall if it was herself and Francis who had done the disturbing. The piles of correspondence were in a different order, the photographs of Elisabeth still prominent. Annie looked at these again, thought she understood them in daylight. Art school fodder, a small, dated portfolio which had been sent around to show the sender's availability for work as a life-class model, lots of poor students did it, nothing prurient there at all. So why had they been left out like this, as if to give such a deliberately wrong impression? Annie sat down, mortified, tried to think clearly. Were I a detective, what would I do? Look for bloody clues, is what, but there was nothing worthy of the name. All personal letters seemed to be missing; there was no sign of an address book. Absently, Annie stuffed into her bag a pile of receipts, confirmations of goods bought in a variety of shops, all saved, she supposed, for the tax man. Don't lose these, Annie told herself, remembering her own nightmarish battles with business accounts: it wouldn't be fair. She remembered how Elisabeth had spoken about getting phone messages from a dealer, and, feeling clever, opened the answerphone on the desk, to find there was no tape. Her sense of alarm grew. Crossing back to the door, she collided with the rosewood pig, stopped and looked again. Deep into the fissure along the back, there was paper, easy to miss since it looked like old-newspaper stuffing, but as her fingers explored with a careful probing, they encountered letters. Trust Liz never to discard a letter, even if half written. Perhaps poverty made her such a hoarder; something did. Annie pulled out the first, discarded an envelope postmarked CLAYFIELDS, wherever that was, read quickly a juvenile script on good paper. 'Dear Mr Artist,' she read, 'I am so very sorry . . .' and that was all. Hearing steps in the corridor, Annie scooped out the rest, the good paper with the cheaper, pink paper, hidden envelopes and all, crushed them down in her bag along with the other papers from the desk. Enid was back in the room, panting from a scramble up and down stairs.

'Are you from him? You must be from him. She didn't have any girl friends. Only men.'

Annie stayed calm in the face of this nervous malice.

'From who? Oh, yes, all right.' It seemed better to deny nothing.

'Only he left his umbrella. This thing.' Enid extended a rolled umbrella, of exceptional quality to Annie's cursory glance. 'Take it away. I don't want it here.'

'Fine, yes fine, no problem, I'm going now. You go first,

I'll lock the door.' Enid had the instinct to obey any orders if firmly given, left for the second time, forgetting to repeat the request for the key, while Annie paused, simply to examine the umbrella. The handle was carved and topped with ornate silver: the fabric curled neatly into the dimensions of a thick cigar and the tip was six inches of silver hidden beneath a ferrule. Removing this out of sheer curiosity for anything so immaculately designed, Annie revealed in the afternoon light a spectacular little dagger, double-edged and glinting, brilliant but stained. Such an ordinary brolly, such a neat little weapon, so effective, she felt a distinct aversion to carrying it. But it was beautiful and valuable and had been thrust into her hands, and none of those factors were of the kind which Annie could resist. She had never turned away a gift in her life, especially a gift which could be sold. Out in the street, some distance from the house, memory tugged at her like wind in the hair. She recognized what she possessed, but not in any kind of focus, experimented with it by holding it as she would a walking stick. It was the right size for a woman, though heavy; the sound of it was pleasantly officious, one two click on the pavement, one two click, as if she meant business. While she struggled to remember where it was she had seen something similar before, imagining it was on some stall in the Antiques Centre, she thought with conscious amusement of how it looked so innocuous and contained this stained and lethal knife.

It was the sort of decorative thing which gave its owner a sense of power.

CHAPTER TEN

'Bring me my bow of burning gold,
Bring me my arrows of desire;
Bring me my spear, O clouds unfold!
Bring me my chariot of fire.
I shall not cease from mental fight,
Nor shall my sword sleep in my hand,
Till we have built Jerusalem,
In England's green and pleasant land.'

Francis had been born in the soft belly of the South-east.
There had been no great rallying cries in the Church of
England agnosticism of his childhood, only exhortations to
learn, do well and become what was expected, all of which
he had followed without any need for rebellions. The tune
of a hymn sung at school in Surrey, running through his
head with irritating insistence now, was somehow more
apposite to the industrial lands beyond Nottingham which

he had largely ignored except to comment on the mystery of the accents. From his own affluent ghetto, Francis had only visited the North because England was too small a space to ignore that half of it and there had always been some friend or relative marooned up there. Looking now, with adult eyes, he saw how beautiful was the colour green, how scarred in parts as the train slid north of Loughborough. Inside the safety of his carriage, slipping up the first vertebrae of the spinal column of England, he felt strangely peaceful, but then excited and ashamed to be what he was, an Englishman born and bred, a dealer in the flotsam and jetsam of his own society, an educated man but, to put it in the words of the couple on the next seat who were arguing in fierce undertones, as ignorant as a pig in shit.

'You don't know nothing,' the woman was saying to her companion. 'You don't know bugger all. I don't know where you was born, but it weren't the same planet as me.'

Their argument was unclear, only the fuel which oiled it in the form of four tins of something from the buffet. Listening to the public rows of others made him want to close one ear and open the other wider, but the jeering accusations seemed directed towards himself although he had never stared at the shapeless protagonists in any obvious way, no more than two sneaking glances. Conscience, perhaps, troubling him. The train hummed and rocked: he had brought some work to pass the two and a half hours it took to reach the town nearest the village from which Elisabeth came, but the motion of the train was enough to prevent concentration on anything other than the argument, the tune of the hymn and the knowledge, increasing by the minute, of how little, how desperately little, he had ever discovered about other people's lives. Passing farmland, drawing into ugly towns along with that sickening burning smell of train brakes, he knew he did not want to disembark. The hymn continued, the tape rewinding itself in his skull with all the known words of it he remembered, always going back to the beginning.

And did those feet in ancient time,
Walk upon England's mountains green . . .

There were no mountains, green or otherwise, and there was no bus to a place called Clayfields for over an hour.

Francis got a taxi. He flashed by shops and through new roads, past neon-lit supermarket complexes of aggressive proportions, a high-spending, low-culture, nuclear-free zone.

'Don't get much call for going to Clayfields,' said the driver, who seemed given to laughing at his own words. 'What do you want there? Got family?'

'No. I'm going to look for one.'

'Tha'll be lucky out theer.'

'Is it far?'

'In a manner of speaking.' He laughed louder. Francis could not see the joke. By now he was unable to control a sickening sensation of acute embarrassment, a rising flush which made his face red. What did he think he was doing on this foreign territory (he would throttle Annie for this bright idea), what was his alibi and what was he going to say? There was no glamour about amateur detecting: God knows there was little enough about the professional sort, which he had never given sufficient respect. Before this expedition he had somehow imagined the desert of the North outside its major cities to be an interlinked series of cosy little complexes, ugly but convivial, informed by familial *bonhomie*. Not vast tracts of isolating roads, towns mushrooming from the embers of others and taxi drivers as truculent as taxi drivers anywhere, but in the North speaking slower, with their stranger voices, the accent belying the speaker's intelligence to the Southern ear . . .

'I were born in Clayfields,' said the man. 'Oh my dear, yes.'

Another laugh. Francis felt his heartbeat slow, race, stabilize. 'And you live there now?'

There was a strange sound from the man in front, an explosive chuckle. 'Not likely. That'll be eight pound.'

They had stopped on a steep slope at the bottom of a street of terraced houses. Four miles from the station, when Francis was feeling the heat on his face, they had turned off a busy dual carriageway, which hummed below as the only sound in the still air. They were parked by a bus shelter with broken windows: Francis could see through the gaps to the next, identical street. Turning round to look back at the road on which they had arrived, he could see it leading downhill to a valley in the lee of the traffic, a gulley at the bottom piled with rubbish as if the whole detritus of the streets had slithered there, cars, beds, broken objects of vibrant plastic and swirling bits of paper. Looking up and beyond, there were the strange and featureless hills which were made by man, slag heaps covered and smoothed, but unable to sustain trees or crops, a barren undulation which went on and on. Francis felt exposed, threatened and bereft: he could not quite move and knew the driver watched him in the rear-view mirror as he might have watched someone poised for theft.

'Eight pound,' he repeated, grinning.

Francis mumbled an apology, reached for his wallet, still looking out. Grey red houses, black grey road, an iron sky and the hills nothing but washed-out green growing on black, looking like weird stubble on a dirty chin. There was no real colour, the whole thing viewed through a bleaching lens, no depth, no vibrance and a terrible silence as if the rinsing-out of pigment were an ongoing process which depended upon no birds, no trees, no sign of human life. Francis met the stony, black-rimmed eyes which examined him through the mirror. He had no code of manners guaranteed to work here, no power to entertain, no officialdom to quote, and was unable to tell a lie. The taxi man was ageless, a small whippet of Northerner in a large car, his eyes rimmed with coal, a cynical face and a muscled body, response unpredictable, apart from incessant amusement. Francis constructed a brisk version of his fabled charm, thought of Philip Marlowe and his fictional ilk, smiled at this crazy comparison.

'I heard you,' he said. 'Eight pounds. Ten or fifteen if you'll show me where I might get a drink. And have one with me. I'm looking for a family called Young.'

'You never!' The way the driver threw back his head

and roared with laughter was quite unnerving. He seemed to find most things funny.

Maria had once liked to laugh, but that was a long time ago. Now she lived in a little and limited world which had suddenly expanded to include another person if only that other person would notice. Such a good and lovely girl. You knew how good and lovely, because she had no possessions, no clothes but a smock or two, no vanities: she lived small.

Much of the time, but not all of the time, Maria loved Thomas with an unquestioning love, compounded by fear, which was one of the reasons why the other person should notice her, because she, too, was becoming part of the family, or so Thomas said. But it was not a holy family with a saint amongst it (as Thomas had obliquely suggested), nor one where you declared who you were. What puzzled her, although she should not resent it in the least since his word was simply law, was his insistence that no one should know that she was his blood sister, and yes, she did mind that. Martha might not have minded, Agatha, Agnes and Veronica might not have minded, but she did. A bit.

Only a sister would have looked after him sixteen years ago as she had done – more so, latterly, in the worse times of his disablement. Only a blood brother would house her as he did. There was no need to state she was his creature, not for someone who had been so loyal that she had even copied his stuttering speech, kept silent in sympathy when his own speech had been denied him, a habit she had seen no point in reversing, which made it so much easier to obey his strictures on not speaking now. But she knew what he could do. He destroyed things which were good: there were these things he could not stand, and he had got the dog to help him.

Butler, that beast. She had been prepared to love Butler with the same lack of reserve, but the love had not lasted. He was not a good dog, but had a mind of his own. What Thomas was was a madman with a soul in danger and a mad dog: that was what she had to get across. She wanted to talk to the girl, because Thomas had given up talking to his sister, did not even take her to church any more, and that boded ill. But if she did get this across to the beautiful girl who stayed there, without a dress or a piece of jewellery to her name, who worked with the humble dedication of a nun and was so serenely beautiful – if she got anything across to Elisabeth, she would be taking a risk herself, because there was nothing outside Thomas. Nothing but this park in which she sat with its disturbing amount of space, the square with all its vagrants outside the cathedral, which she crossed by herself with less terror each time and an even greater sense of belonging.

Thomas might just kill the girl, Maria decided. Once she had done those three paintings he had bought just before she got there, he would kill her, because she was so good and so beautiful and so like the madonnas, he would not be able to stand the presence of all that virtue and simplicity. He would do away with her, in the same way he had made away with all those paintings which used to festoon the walls when this had been their parents' house. All those saints there had been then: perfect paintings, the sort which Thomas could not abide and Maria adored. All he had left was three of the icons and she was supposed to be satisfied with that. Thomas, she decided, simply killed or destroyed anything which was perfect. He killed what he liked best. He destroyed, too, or jeered at, whatever Maria liked, so it followed, Maria told herself, that she should not reveal how much she was coming to love that girl. And for both their sakes, she had better try to get the girl on her side. Even if, God forgive her, she had to tell lies. No, she never told lies, especially on Sundays.

Butler bristled. Maria was learning the symptoms now, wiped her eyes with caution while making soothing sounds. The dog was programmed to react as he did to any kind of emotional display; reaction must be avoided. He had bitten a naughty child here in the park once, although Maria had to admit, she had encouraged him. No, she did not love Butler. She had offered Butler to God long before for being not only bad, but stupid. If you gave him anything that smelt at all of food, he took it and ate it: you could have given him cyanide.

Absently, Maria took from the bosom of her coat three or four of the letters she had been given to post over the last fortnight. The rest were in her room. Butler liked the smell of beef casserole. Without such scents he would not have been so easy to convince: she had dipped all letters in the gravy of one of those half-eaten, mushy, frozen meals on which Thomas seemed to thrive. He could eat only mush, because he could not handle knife and fork, while this crazy dog would eat dusters. No wonder they were both so cross; they needed so much. She handed one of the stained envelopes to Butler as if it were some kind of tasty morsel, teasing him with it. What did a plain and simple girl want with letters, anyway? St Bernadette, St Agnes, St Theresa never bothered with letters: they were too busy. Be good, sweet child, and let who will be clever. Butler took the stiff parchment envelope, chewed, swallowed some, spat out the rest. It would probably make him sick. He might then bite her. Good.

'Why, Thomas, why? Why did you lie to me?'

There were two prerequisites for making Thomas talk, apart from her own courage. One was that the talking, however banal the content had become, should be initiated by him in the room where she worked. The second was that all voices should remain muted. Although she had lost the habit of shouting, it was harder, now, to keep the voice from ascending.

'All the paintings, Thomas, they were not collected by your mother and father. They were collected more recently than that. I know by the auction stamps on the back. You know auction houses do that, don't you? They stamp the date of the sale on the back of the canvas or the frame, and I am perfectly capable of turning round some of the pictures on your walls . . . Nor was the equipment in this studio left behind by someone who came and went: it is mostly new, and no restorer has all new equipment unless he is a dilettante in the game, someone you would not have used Otherwise we all have our little eccentric bits which are peculiarly ours, to service our individual methods. And then you gave me the illusion of freedom, which I followed because I wanted to believe, but I know, I do know, that you are taking steps to stop me from leaving. I think I have played into your hands, but what game you play, I do not know. Tell me, Thomas, do you hate me so much? Did you think I lied about you to make them do as they did? If you are who I think you are?'

It had hung in the air since yesterday, the hatred, crackling since breakfast, ever since he had seen her look of despair when the door was barred against her. Elisabeth cursed the blindness which had prevented her from seeing in Maria's ugly face that daily aspect of fear, that bold reluctance to come back again into the lion's den, although she had no illusions now about the limitation on Maria's choices. The regime was now perfectly clear.

'Why, Thomas, why? Is it because you know how valuable these paintings may be? Do you think I'd leave and bring back burglars? Do you think I'd bring back thugs from dealers to take advantage? You're not so helpless. Can't walk far without some sort of stick, but you've the strength of an ox. More brain, though. You might spit as you speak, but you know what you want. Which I do not.'

She had removed the rugs from the floor, in case they should be damaged and also to give herself the advantage of knowing when he passed across the threshold from carpet to wood. His steps across the wood, still honey blond like in the picture which had been part of her seduction here, were small and precise: step step click, step step click, carrying a different stick. Waiting for Maria to come back with the dog before going out himself, he had given up pretending. The sound of the stick rang like a death knell: her bravery faded between heart and mouth.

'I collected the paintings for myself, originally,' Thomas began. 'First I had tried to sell my own work, but once I was left with only one eye, I could see, perversely, that I was never going to be any good and no one wanted paintings by me, least of all myself. But you do not need to be an artist to love a painting. I started to collect the anonymous. I was always going to be anonymous, so it seemed appropriate. I thought of you even then, imagined that would be a touch you would like. You're a very honest girl, wouldn't ever go for the greedy investor. Then I saw you and it changed everything. I had the stroke and dwelt with dreams of you, and, once I could, I bought from the dealers you dealt with, I sent you pictures to restore, I watched, I listened to what people said.'

'Thomas, what do you want from me?'

'I want to look after you in the way that no one ever looked after me. Abdication, that's what it was. Apart from a constant diet of religion and a house full of hideous religious art, there was a sort of neglectful spoiling for me. Let the boy do what he likes. If he thinks he's a latter-day Van Gogh, let him think it, be it, live what craziness he pleases. At least when you were a child, you had your guardian angels, did you not? Oh, I got my education, but I was left to drift. Without talent.'

Thomas stood before one of the low windows. He did not move a muscle, or change the direction of his eyes when she threw back her head with a snort of laughter.

The hysteria made the sound drunken: she started and could not stop. Only then did Thomas cross the room. Adept with the tip of the ferrule, he scooped up a tiny amount of the paint on her palette on to the tip of the stick.

'If this is flake white, be careful. Highly poisonous. You cannot kiss a painting full of lead. The stuff of cosmetics for dead ladies. I told you, just the three paintings. Won't take long, will it? After that, go if you must, with my blessing. Just these three. You make me repeat myself like the teacher I was. You may as well stay for now, where else would you go?'

She had checked her laughter, nodded. His face broke into an unearthly smile. He took off the smoked glasses and rubbed them on a silk handkerchief. 'Good. I'm glad you agree. You owe me that.' She opened her mouth to speak again. Thomas waved his wicked-looking stick, casually, teasingly. 'No,' he said quickly. 'We won't talk about it now.'

Francis had lost the embarrassment, that rising hysteria which afflicted him in the taxi. Instead he felt drunk, but doubted if that sensation was anything he could call an improvement. The beer was execrable; so was the pub. It was small, dark, plastic and hung with Christmas decorations which he imagined for one dizzy moment as a fine piece of forward thinking for early November until he realized they must have been in place for at least eleven months. The dust betrayed the tinsel into something lazy and still, an addition which aimed to be festive all the year

209

round. This place could make a fortune once there was a vogue for ugly, 1990s, festive memorabilia. As it was, the only souvenir of another age was the man beside him laughing all the time, none of that braying sound a comfort.

'You want the Young family? Well, you can have 'em. Now then, lad, listen, it was ever such a big laff, the best we'd had in a month let alone the year. Down the road, three from the end there, that were the Young family. Young! That Mrs Young was never young since the day she were born, poor cow. She was right for him since he must've been old when he was five. This was a pit village then.' He waved expansively, as if there had been a time when this pub had been lively and these streets a metropolis.

'A mining village, to you,' said the man, more kindly. 'And of course everyone worked down pit. Not he. He had something wrong with one of his legs, limped a lot, got a job on the surface, white collar, foreman, like, carried a stick. We most of us never liked the surface men, especially not him throwing his weight around and quick with the orders, so no one sympathized that much when he got himself landed with three kids and his mother and father and all under one little roof. They're small, these houses, small and very dark inside, they face the wrong way for daylight: you can see from what's left, and none of them Youngs, apart from the mister, was what you'd call tiny. He ruled it like an army camp, he'd been in the army, see? The place was clean as a whistle, no waste, no mess, never a dog or cat, especially a cat, Mrs Young said she couldn't abide the smell. I think the kids queued up for jobs and food, they were organized every minute of the day, even bathtime, I heard; can't have been any secrets in that house. He was a bitter man, was Ernest Young, nothing ever good enough, wore his white collar like a saint. People like that expect the earth; they never, ever get enough. I tell you, he frightened me.'

The taxi man took a long pull of his beer. Francis tried to follow suit but found the beer disgusting.

'I don't know why Ernest pinned all his faith in that daughter, but he did, from the start. More than he ever did for his sons, which was odd, but then they turned out thick as planks while she had brains. You'd have thought she'd be spoiled like the youngest often are, but oh no. Drilled, dawn to dusk, like one long parade ground, all to make sure she were going to go as far as she could, no letting up. She was the one, that girl, always the one.' Another pull of the pint. He looked down at it in surprise. Francis went to get another, feeling the scrutiny of the woman behind the bar. The place was empty: he felt uncomfortable.

'Anyway, the laugh was this when I get around to it. Young was as pure and proper as a gravestone and just about as sober, so was the missus, and both of them as good as a tribe of vicars. What they had was what they had, right? No HP, no credit; he said that was like stealing and, by Christ, they were brought up honest, even if the boys did turn out nasty. Old man Young could no more borrow than he could climb Everest, never in debt to any bugger and they were all going to get on. He always said his sons weren't going to go down pit, but that was all they wanted, so he concentrated on the girl instead. She wasn't going to be no factory girl either, not like most of the girls round here, she was going to be different. A scientist, he said, he was always going on about science. Something, at any rate, our princess, who was so good at homework while the rest were out chasing boys, showing off tits before they were ten. She were a bonny lass, for all she was kept so close, never allowed to play with rough kids, always indoors with a book. She was cleverer even than he thought, did well at school, but of course that didn't make her liked any better or them either. Stuck up was what they were, better than the rest of us, coming out of that house with that kid all cleaned and pressed in her school uniform, who did they think they were?'

For once the man did not end his sentence with a laugh.

'There was no warning when the pit closed. Well, there might have been if we'd listened, but . . . I'd worked there, my father and his, we didn't even know how to fight the ending, went round like zombies. Of course, Ernest Young got another job straight away, which didn't make anyone love him better, since most of us didn't. I suppose being white collar one place is much like another, but there was a bit less choice for any of us who knew nothing else but shifting coal. Black coal, black rings round your eyes and, as far as we could see, no job for ever, except for him, the bastard. Made him more determined than ever that none of this was ever going to happen to his darling girl, kept her even closer. This pub was fuller for a year or more; sweet all else to do. But about then I heard she was saying how she was interested in art, couldn't stick all that science stuff he rammed down her throat. She tried painting and all sorts, went out with a book and paper all over the place. He stopped her, of course, said she wasn't going in for any of this arty-farty stuff. Short path to the dole queue and he wasn't having any of that. He took to saying on the bus that she'd be going to university. University? First from this street, I can tell you, bloody university and none of us sods with the hope of a job, and even while you had the same bad dreams over and over again, the whole place was changing.'

The taxi driver was a good raconteur. He knew when to wet his lips, saw Francis's neutral expression, grinned.

'You mean, what were wrong with it changing, couldn't it do with some improvement? It wasn't so bad, you know, but suddenly, it wasn't a pit village any more. A slag heap slipped and took out three empty houses at the end of one row. They made it safe with all this landscaping and four of the other houses came empty because families with sense moved off to look for work, and then, all of a sudden, strangers moved in, people from town where Young's daughter used to go to school. So did the other girls, but all that nonsense stopped as soon as they were fifteen, they had to go to work, specially then. One of these new people was an art teacher, from town again, there never was a school here since Queen fucking Victoria. He was a right one, this little bloke, said he wanted to live alongside us to soak up the "industrial landscape". Started off coming into the pub every night until he got frozen out, even told us how he liked the slag heaps from the open cast, wonderful colours, he said. Daft bastard! The "landscape", as

213

he called it, the stuff I could see from my window, was a lot of people hanging about with nothing better to do than get drunk and fight while the life bled out of them, but then this artist was well off, wasn't he? Artist, art teacher, who's one of them without having money of his own? Paid to live in one of our houses, talking rubbish and painting slag as well as all sorts of weird things, like stuff he did in his back yard with pints of paint, along with his cat and his plants. We never had plants, but he kept a cat which he kissed and fed fish: he wasn't what I would call a man at all. Couldn't stand the bastard, but live and let live, I said. Ernest Young's two lads, just old enough for the pub, well, they didn't agree.'

There was a pause, a distasteful licking of lips. Francis rose without signal and fetched another pint. In the absence of any other customers, it was quickly done.

'First, they got his cat. Put paraffin on its tail and set it alight, better than a firework on legs running down the road and fizzing in a drain, poor thing. No one spoke up and no one told him, but he might have found out. That was when he seemed to realize what we thought of him, stopped going to the pub after he knew he'd been seen crawling along the backs of the houses with a dish of sardines shouting, "Pussy, pussy, pussy . . . come home!", silly as arseholes. He didn't talk so big after that. Stayed indoors, making funny things with paint, never did a real painting or a single useful thing in all the year he was there. Somebody loved him, though. Young's daughter, about fourteen then, used to go visit him, this so-called artist. Seemed fascinated by him and what he did, couldn't keep

214

away. Some said later that she was really trying to make up to him for what her brothers had done to his cat, but I think she just fancied what she found. She might have meant it, about liking art and liking people who did art stuff, but she'd have to like it a lot to fancy him and all those great big pictures he'd started to make, all mess on canvas as if someone had rolled round in it. I saw some of the stuff he did in his back yard once, and if I'd done it myself, the wife would have got me committed. Anyway, after a while of her being in and out of his house, her dad got wind of it, got mad about it, not that she'd take any notice, told him to sod off, until one day in summer, when she was late home, he sent his lads round. Seventeen and nineteen, they were, built like brick shithouses, one of them already with a baby. All they ever did was draw dole and spend it in the pub, spoiling for a job or a fight.'

Francis, sensed the crux of the long story, gestured to the glasses. The man nodded, smiled.

'Young's daughter may only have been fourteen but, I'm telling you, she was well stacked. Had a chest on her fit to cause a riot, not that I was supposed to notice, but of course everyone did. The lads, her brothers, went to the artist's house like their dad said, only without knocking, and there she was. They knew trouble when they saw it: they'd been brought up proper and they never could take their drink. "Did he touch you?" they said. "No, no, he never," she said. "He just put this paint on me. I've got to stand still. If I don't mind, why should you?" She'd got a mouth on her in those days, could still answer back, she'd stand up for herself, not like later. And do you know, he

215

had? This artist put paint all over her or let her put it on herself, same difference. She was wearing nothing but her knickers, her skin covered all over in pink and gold, bright reds and purples and this bright shining green, her lying on the floor while he was supposed to be painting another picture of what she looked like, whistling and singing when they came in, like he often did when he was busy. "He never touched me," she kept saying. "He never touched me." The dirty blighter.'

He took a massive swig from his glass, laughter gurgling inside his chest.

'So they pasted him. You know that sound? Same as a wet sponge in a polythene bag beat against a wall, that's the sound you get when you keep hitting. I suppose, I don't know, mind, it was a bad business. No one ever said, but I know they took one of his eyes out. And the rest. They said one of his eyes was right outside his face, somewhere near his chin. Like his itty-bitty, arty-farty house that should have been lived in by a pit family, he was a right mess after with a great hole where that eye should have been, but he didn't call for the police or anything like that. Young's cousin was a copper, did I tell you that? And, anyway, even if that teacher were stupid, he knew enough to know there was no point in calling the law. No one liked him, see? And he'd no business living there, really: only himself to blame. Mind you, she might have been right about him not touching her, what with him not being like other men and having no paint on himself, they couldn't have been kissing, it would have shown. She was screaming, fighting, trying to stop them: there was blood all over the floor, all

216

mixed up with the paint. The lads were well drunk, but she still kept saying, "He never touched me, let him be, let him be." They didn't let him be, not until they'd finished with him which took a little while, but, to be fair, they did call the ambulance after.'

'I thought,' said Francis, with the gorge rising in his throat, 'that this was a funny story. A laugh.' Another pint arrived, this time after a signal, followed by money left on the table, silently. No change was given.

'What? Oh yes. Because after that, you know what they did? They walked her home, just as she was. No clothes at all but little knickers: my, she was a fair sight. Blue paint on her titties (you could tell that even if her arms were crossed), red on her face, pink on her bum and that lime-green over her eyes. They made her walk the whole length of the village and back. Someone gave her one of those plastic bin liners, but her dad, walking along and waving his stick, he took it away. There's only three streets – only two now – up the hill in rows, the pub and the shop, that's all there ever was, but I suppose it was big enough. Past the pub twice at seven on a summer's evening, she did make heads turn, every single head of the fifty families following her round. Laugh! I thought we'd die. After that, when everyone had a good giggle, I heard they took her home and made her sit in the kitchen on newspaper until she learned better and got her turn in the bath. I laughed till I cried. Even her mother smiled and so she should because she looked so funny and, anyway, she laughed too. Tits like a ship in full sail, painted pink and green. Thought of it makes me sweat.'

217

His present laughter rang round the pub as the door opened and cold air came in with two men. The taxi man lowered his voice. The woman behind the bar grinned at the newcomers and moved to the pumps without waiting for instructions.

'What happened next?' Francis asked, composing his face into a rigid smile which was obviously a less excited response than the raconteur demanded.

'The teacher bloke left, of course. Went home on the train from town. Came back for his things with a stick – no, not a stick, a fucking umbrella, I ask you. Funny glasses for his eyes, too, made him look like a robber. I saw him then, waiting for the train. He didn't speak, but then there weren't much to say –'

'Never mind him,' said Francis with the first touch of impatience. 'I meant, what happened next to the girl, Elisabeth Young? What did she do?'

The taxi man seemed to have forgotten the girl. He was well into the depths of the story, in which the girl had somehow become irrelevant.

'Her? Oh, I reckon she'd learned her lesson. So her dad said. He'd not brought up a brainy daughter of his to take off her clothes for no bugger, even an artist. Any road, she seemed to settle down, did more homework, lost her mouth. Used to see her at the bus stop, going into the town to school when all the other girls had stopped, never wearing anything but school uniform up to her chin, always standing with her arms crossed across her chest. Got all those exams, she did, stuck up little madam, didn't pass the time of day much. You might have known she was Young's daughter and couldn't take a joke, but you couldn't look at her without seeing that paint and those titties. Oh, what a laugh . . .' This was illustrated by a choking sound into his glass of beer. Francis wondered about the wisdom of leaving Clayfields in this driver's car, thought there might be a choice, and if there was, he would find the bus.

'Lime Lizzie! That's what she was called, after the paint. Mind we still heard a lot from Mister and Missus about how she was going to get this wonderful job, and she did go to college. But you know the last laugh? She never did so well after all, probably went to the bad, never got anywhere, never got married and never came back. Oh yes, for her mother's funeral, dressed like a scarecrow. Never did nothing, her dad said in drink, never made money, never got them out of this hole, just pissed about, never did nothing with all that learning and all. Lives in a cellar, the poor tart.'

The driver drained his glass. The hand was steady, the eye clear, the laughter still brimming. If I had been born here, thought Francis, in a place which had decayed around me, I would not laugh: I might cry and be more bitter than this windy beer. He thought it timely to take the heat out of his interest in the Youngs.

'But you,' he asked, turning his charm upon the storyteller. 'You got out of Clayfields? Got another job? You must have been a young man, then.'

'We most of us got out,' said the taxi man, rising and grinning. 'Those with sense. Even old man Young. Went to live with one of his sons in town after he retired. He was older, you see, more difficult to move, even with his stick.

Do you want a lift back? That'll be fifteen pound, you said.'

'Thank you, no,' said Francis, handing over the twenty he guessed was expected. His clipped Southern accents, sharpened by his own disgust, rang round the plastic pub. The two other drinkers looked up briefly, without amusement, went back to their combined, well-rehearsed silence. The woman at the pumps was filing her nails. Francis tried to imagine what the bar would look like full of people as he took his feet to the door, his crisp, patrician 'thank you very much' met with a leaden nod of mere acknowledgement. The thought was threatening rather than appealing. The company of the man who talked too much was not what Philip Marlowe would have had. By now, the detective and he would have been friends, not like this, separated by centuries and a conditioning which made a chasm a mile wide. He walked back with the taxi driver to the car because it seemed a sociable thing to do.

'Tell me summat,' said the man with his strange, nervous, ever-present laugh, still grinning. 'Whatya want with the Youngs, anyway?'

Francis cleared his throat. 'Their daughter's gone missing. Lime Lizzie. I came to see if she'd come home.' The driver shook his head.

'She'd not do that. Not her.'

'How do you know? She might. Families are where you go when you're in trouble, aren't they?'

This time the shout of laughter was so loud it was obscene, cutting into the chill grey air like a whip. The reconstructed, featureless hills of slag were colourless in their artificial curves, patently the clumsy amends of men for other men's carnage.

'Not her!' he repeated, hauling himself in behind the wheel. 'And how do I know? That'd be telling, but I know. Is the daft cow in trouble, then, and you're the boyfriend, is that it? She won't have gone far. I heard she lived in a cellar and fiddles with pictures, like she always did. Down South. You going to marry her? Is it yours?'

'I might marry her,' said Francis evenly. 'How do you know the family so well?'

'Like I said, that'd be telling. Anyway. you've got competition. Some other bugger's been looking – not recent, mind.'

Francis gripped his coat around himself, wished he had scarf and gloves, wished the North was not that much colder, wished too he were a hundred miles away from this brutal, smiling face with its addiction to laughter. In a mimic of the other's nonchalant attitude, he shrugged his shoulders as if there were no urgency in this one, last enquiry.

'Someone else? Who could that be? No accounting for taste.' The taxi engine roared, over-revved. Maybe the driver was not as sober as he looked. Francis felt strangely drunk on two pints to the other's murky four. The reply was cast away out of the open window as the car stuttered down the ever empty street.

'Who else? That fucking little artist, that's who. She always said she'd go and look after him. That's who-o-o.'

The voice drifted away with the engine and a final bark of laughter. After the sound died, the silence was deafening.

Into it crept the sounds of dereliction, nothing but the hum of traffic, a place isolated by the cars in the dual carriageway below, no birdsong, no wind in trees, simply these streets and this valley full of rubbish. They were not bad houses, Francis thought as he walked up the first row and down its parallel terrace: all equipped with the yard behind, a little younger than the D. H. Lawrence version, ugly as sin, but built to last and constructed for living. Some were lit: it was that kind of wintry day in which hibernation seemed routine for reluctant humankind facing nothing but winter; some were dark. He tried to picture their windows full of Christmas lights and a thriving family life inside, replete with the wherewithal for the season. Then he attempted to reconstruct the scene on a summer evening with the houses equally full, the valley with a rusty stream from the pit and a girl child paraded, clutching her large, bare breasts covered with paint, the skin more highly coloured than the blank eyes of her reflecting nothing. Oh my lovely Elisabeth, was that enough to make you what you are? No memory left but the colours of that evening, the lack of colour in the rest of life? I never knew, I never knew. You never asked, she had said. You never asked and no one ever listens. I manage by myself: I always did.

Francis Thurloe, a barrister in a camel-hair coat, stood at the bus stop, finally, where a scratched sign warned him that the wait might last another hour. As he waited in the mid-afternoon, three children toiled up the hill from the Opposite bus stop, home from school elsewhere. There was the barest semblance of uniform, but nothing pressed, starched or regulation, no caps, a disparity of training shoes. They were chattering like sparrows, but fell into silence as they walked by. One of them looked as if he had been in a fight, possibly with the other two. Once further uphill, they were in a huddle, looking back. Francis ignored them, aware with a sudden surge of embarrassment that he might have looked like some kind of official: he should not have worn a suit under this coat. Another quarter-hour. Nothing to look at, nothing. Just as he began to regret that he had relinquished the ride back to town with the taxi driver for another kind of purgatory longer but less acute, he felt their presence behind him. A small stone grazed his neck, sent to tease rather than hurt. Precious little to bait in this part of the world. He turned towards a shuffling and the banging of a door, looked stolidly towards the makeshift hills. Another stone, larger than the last, badly aimed, rolling by with a large noise. No more shuffling, a greater sense of threat. He dragged together his worldly wisdom and stepped purposefully downhill, on to the anonymous road, began to walk in the direction of the town.

CHAPTER ELEVEN

Letters had seemed to spill into her hand out of the back of the pig. Annie forgot she had ferreted deep into that fissured back, like a nurse delving in a septic wound. Some of this was poisoned paper, dyed in the venom of familial hatred, while other sheets, covered with Elisabeth's own writing, were coloured with the fainter shades of pathos. Gradually, Annie could discern the difference between the various hands, although she could not guess at first who the other writers were. Elisabeth's writing was familiar, a neat script with subdued flamboyance, the individual still clear in these juvenile letters. Annie would have thrown away such missives had they been hers, consigned into litter anything which reminded her of tears, shame or subservience, let them drift, like other detritus, but Elisabeth had kept all souvenirs of conscience, recrimination sealed down in the intestine of a wooden pig, so heavy a load, she might as well have carried it like a coffin. Perhaps she had hoped the paper inside might finally revert back to being wood.

'You're a little tart. Lizzie Young, that's what you are. Someone sent us photos of you, you ungrateful little tart. Too good for us, are you? After all we did. Found any good artists lately?'

And more, on pink paper.

'Your father doesn't know I'm writing, Lizzie. Thanks for the money. Don't reply, please.' More pink paper, yellow at the edges, cheap and nasty, like all these sentiments. Better paper for the letters Elisabeth herself had written but only to have them marked on the ivory parchment envelopes 'returned to sender'. Annie remembered Elisabeth still used the same type of paper now, despising what was cheaper, maintaining a preference for quality which seemed to have been formed during that dim, adolescent age when the handwriting was frozen in the premature wisdom of her years.

'Dear Mr Artist, they will not tell me where you are, I have tried, sent a letter to your old school, oh please say you got it and you are well. I do so need to know you are well. They tell me so, but I don't know, I can't see anything when I shut my eyes but colours, I dream of them. Please, please promise me if you cannot or will not write to me, that you will tell me if you need me and I shall come and look after you for ever. Please, please. Let me do that. I am so sorry, so sorry, so sorry. I told them you did not touch me, it was not like that. Please tell me if you need me, please.'

Someone else wrote too, if not grammatically, graphically, on that anonymous, unsigned pink paper.

'Lime Lizzie's a tart, that she is. Lives on muck, is muck, goes with men. Your mother's dead, you know. Those photos killed her . . .'

They were art-school photos, Annie yelled, those photos on her desk, even I know that now, and she was a girl, a girl, not a woman of sound mind, you bastards. You stinking crapulous, evil-minded bastards, leave her alone, do you hear? Leave her alone.

Annie did not know and could not guess at the history of the carefully preserved letters and did not care. They were written by brothers, aunts, all pens dipped in some universal ink of condemnation. They were like the anonymous letters of mad people to a murderer. Elisabeth's replies, cringing apologies, had faded into silence.

If Annie had not read these first thing in the morning before she had embarked on the rest of her day of discovery, she might not have begun as she had, which was with curiosity and a mind open to impression. Or seen so clearly in the course of a few hours how everybody else loved this erstwhile friend of hers, everybody. All those little people, difficult to explain, as if Lizzie had been a different person to each. (Annie was slowly learning to refer to her as Elisabeth, simply because the letters used Liz or Lizzie as a term of insult.) Elisabeth's present acquaintance loved Elisabeth. No, not loved: love was not so easily born or sustained, or so Annie was beginning to learn, but this brusque and serious restorer of paintings seemed to

226

inspire enormous affection (to say nothing of the lust) wherever she went. Annie had begun by sitting on the floor of her living room, glad for once to be alone, and checked off the list of the places she intended to visit that day. Namely, all the small and obscure shops which Elisabeth had ever patronized in the last few months according to the carefully preserved invoices she had stored with such businesslike efficiency and Annie had collected the day before, along with the contents of the rosewood pig and an application form explaining the photographs. A backstreet girl, Elisabeth Young: addicted to the smaller scale of things, as if she could never walk up a main road and confront a big front door, even of a shop.

Annie, having slammed out of her flat as far as the road, groaned. Rain pissing down as if the Atlantic had come to roost in the nearest clouds. Back to her own door, cursing, fretting for keys, not knowing what to put down first. Remembering the umbrella thrust into her hands by Enid, the one as beautifully antique as the other was not, she grabbed it, started out again. The rain stopped immediately. Turning right at the end of the road, she ignored her normal route, following the correspondence in Elisabeth's extraordinarily tidy personal business file. She was led both by the need for action over inaction, to compete with Francis's larger contribution of actually taking a train and going North, and by a growing curiosity for the way this woman lived. Elisabeth had kept receipts and invoices for every single purchase, a record of everything acquired, decorative or prosaic; she kept notes with the dedication of a clerk. In the neat bound pile of these, Annie had found invoices for pottery and paintbrushes, medium and varnish, bandages, acetone, carbon tetrachloride, swatches of material, tiny quantities of gold leaf, wax – all acquired in different places as if the shopping were an art in itself. And in all these places, Elisabeth's human contacts were light and undemanding but precious to all concerned.

The first was a hardware shop, the sort of place Annie imagined hung on to existence by a line thinner than the picture wire it sold by the yard. There were nails and screws by the gross, copper piping, lead piping, soldering irons, pure white spirit, pints of linseed oil, cables, electrical fittings, security grilles, shelves, wholesale paint and preparations, stuff for restoring houses rather than portraits. A crude, chemical, dusty, metallic set of smells to it all. Annie never minded barging in and stating her business without preamble: she was usually immune to embarrassment.

'Excuse me, I'm looking for a friend of mine, buys stuff from you, Elisabeth Young, seen her by any chance, recently?'

It was the shop where, according to the invoices, Elisabeth bought glues and poisons, a shop where, in common with the staff in other shops even more obscure, they stopped and smiled at the mention of the name. An old man in brown overalls which made him look as if he were dressed in wrapping paper beamed. Elisabeth, oh yes, our friend Elisabeth. A willingness to talk all day about our friend Elisabeth. Will you call if you see her? Annie leaving a card and backing away from the kind of affection she knew she could never inspire. The same in the shop where Elisabeth bought gauze, and in the next where she bought pigment, better known and loved in shops than anywhere else. Known by name, face, shape and charm, for the magic of her smile. It began to rain again. Annie opened the umbrella with distaste.

The madonna of the portrait was not complete: she was slow to give up her secrets. Each of her secrets gave way to another and Elisabeth shied from the decisions. She had half formed her suspicions, waited for them to be fully formed. Acting on instinct, she turned the madonna to the wall, hiding what she had recently, and ever more boldly, done. She started work on the third painting, which she knew, really, mattered to neither Thomas nor anyone else. A Victorian landscape of heathery hills with a brown road leading away, heavy-handed asphaltum, suitable only for thin glaze spreading, painted thick like this it cracked to the core with crazing so wide and deep she could insert the tip of a brush handle. Asphaltum, beloved of the age for paint and tarmacadam roads, which reminded her obscurely of all her little shops and things she did not have.

In the kitchen there was a list for Thomas. One heat probe, Thomas, please, so I can attempt to reconstitute this asphaltum rather than pick it out and start again, get it from Macey's, address supplied. Two kinds of restorer's colours, only those two, Linney's have these, address supplied. Some gauze for the holes in the still life, medical suppliers, Devonshire Street, address supplied, all convenient. He liked shopping: it gave him satisfaction. The realization that he might well have followed her around all those shops was a knowledge she was trying, if not to dismiss, at least to digest with cautious slowness. She could remember that clicking metal, like her father's stick: so like her father's stick she had assumed it to be the same, following her round on all those errands.

Maria was back. It was raining outside, the dog's claws pattering in the kitchen, Thomas's voice murmuring to Maria, sounding peculiarly like an endearment. The front door opened and closed, the sense of his having left only apparent from the sudden lightness of her own breathing.

In the kitchen Maria uttered the kind of comforting noises which made Butler change back into a shambling old dog as she fetched him water. Over the sound of his long pink tongue slurping and splashing liquid on to the clean floor, Maria found herself thinking. Oh, if only he would not come back. The dog drank as if he had just run a marathon in a desert. Maria watched for a moment, crooning to herself, then, swifter of thought and movement than usual, sidled quickly out of the kitchen door and slammed it shut behind her. Immediately Butler began to howl, one long note of fury. The door shook as he flung himself against it. 'Bastard!' Maria yelled, kicking the door in sudden delight. The sound brought Elisabeth running. There was a silence and Maria began to laugh.

The two women stood in the hall, silent as the dog fell silent, Maria's mirth a soundless heaving punctuated by wheezing noises which brought tears to her eyes. Elisabeth put a hand round her shoulders: Maria clutched her and the two of them stood in a fierce embrace, patting each other like strangers at a funeral, unknown to each other, but suddenly locked in a mutual affection.

It would be all right, Maria thought wistfully, if my brother did not come back: I could love this one instead and she would be kind to me. I know now what I must say. I know what I can show her.

By some process as mysterious as the making of paint, they had become friends of a sort, Maria and she, through the passage of little gestures and smiles. Elisabeth had used up her small supply of gauze to bind that injured hand, whilst daily, Maria watched over the other, apparently helpless. Maria's mind was racing into dreaming. Oh, if this girl trusted her and did not trust Thomas, they could just set up home here, full of the right kind of pictures: they could do without him. They blinked at each other, laughed again.

'Shopping?' Maria stuttered. 'He? Shopping?' She gestured towards the door, stabbing with her finger.

'Shopping. Maybe an hour, maybe not so much.' Elisabeth replied with gestures of her own hands, exaggerated, as if she were talking to someone deaf. The information was understood. Maria sighed. Beyond the kitchen door the dog barked again, then changed the tune to a slow, ominous growling.

'No tea,' said Maria, face clouded before they both smiled again. Maria felt redeemed in the presence of a kindred spirit who understood vital things, such as love of the madonna in the picture, a love of other saintly virtues and a hatred for that dog. She pulled at Elisabeth's arm, furiously smitten by the shortcomings of her inarticulacy, wanting to communicate so much that she shook with the effort. Why have I ignored you, Elisabeth thought, why pushed you to one side when you were so kind and could have told me so much? I ignored you because I was preoccupied and the fact you cleaned for a living, but then, so do I.

'Come with me, come now . . .'

'Where, Maria, where?'

'Now, now.' The insistence was distressing. Finally, Elisabeth took Maria's hand, allowed herself to be led down the long corridor towards Thomas's room. At the door both shrank back, but the mood of hilarity prevailed until Maria opened the door and pulled her inside. By day, the room was bleaker still, as quiet as a deserted cell, colder than a grave as the half-open window admitted a knife edge of breeze. Light made the ceiling higher. There was no sign of the telephone, hidden, along with Thomas's strange psyche and all his scars, somewhere in this room.

Set in the wall opposite the monastic bed with the smooth white coverlet where Elisabeth had sat in the middle of the night, there was a large cupboard, in front of which she had seen those familiar canvases. Now they were gone: perhaps Maria had moved them in response to orders, orders which were issued and obeyed every day while she worked undisturbed in her studio room, like a queen spinning straw into gold inside a fairy-tale tower. Maria leapt toward the vast cupboard doors and flung them open.

'Here, here, look!' Elisabeth looked.

It was more a dressing room designed for the Edwardian gentlemen who might have occupied these spacious apartments with the necessary servants. A valet could have walked in here in the morning and sorted out the wardrobe for the day, pressed and suggested the appropriate apparel for the evening, almost dwelt in here. It was the size of an old-fashioned linen cupboard, too small for human habitation and airless, but still three or four steps from front to back when empty. Large enough, even full as it now was, for someone to enter, then stop and stare.

Here were the three hundred, the rest of his cache of paintings, oils on canvas and wood, panel, paper, ranged by the dozen, neatly if sometimes dangerously stacked in their profusion. The light which followed them in from the window seemed slow to penetrate the cupboard room which had no light of its own. The chill, far removed from the luxurious warmth of the rest of the flat, inhibited Elisabeth's eyes: she was like a wine connoisseur suddenly invited to inspect the labels in a dark cellar, excited but half blind. Light sprang from some of the nearest canvases: light was hidden in them with vivid colours. She turned away from these, reluctantly, responding to Maria's heavy hand on her arm, not there, here, pulling away her eyes and the fascination of all her senses, damping down her euphoria, that of someone who has stumbled into a treasure trove and wants no more than to look and dream of riches.

'Here, here . . . Look. Oh, please look . . ..'

To the left there was the neatest and the largest stack,

from which rose a pungent smell. Elisabeth, eyes now attuned to the angle of the light, squatted on her haunches in front of these. The nearest were old, dirty, damaged. Some were icons on board, scratched and neglected, bashed and ignored: they were among the odoriferous ones, reeking of kitchens, onions, oil and coal fires, must and mice. But the ones behind were aggressively clean, sharp with the scent of new varnish and nutty oil. The first of these was exquisite: a woman lying on a couch, reading a book and patently at ease. Behind that another portrait, then another and another. There were faces male and female, handsome, flawed, smiling or grim, posing or preening, relaxed or cautious. All were rich in colourful garments – official or unofficial robes, boots and spurs, a nightdress. They were *déshabillé* or fully clothed, but, however dressed, they were all bursting with the richness of flesh, had in common the prime of life, their portraits celebrations of the impudence of beauty or success, mostly beauty. None of the pictures was framed; all eighteenth or nineteenth century, none showed signs of bloom, damp, heat or neglect, but all had been rescued and restored, not left in attics or held in safes, that trick of millionaires who do not know that a picture must breathe or else rot.

Elisabeth could feel her heart stand still and the skin prickle at the base of her neck where the breeze from the window chilled the sweat seeping down from beneath her hair. In two or three of the portraits, she recognized her own hair, like the hair of the olive-skinned madonna which she had worked on and had invested with love, mahogany-coloured hair pinned back to hide an embarrassing, uncontrolled richness. The olive-skinned lady with the wounded neck and vulgar jewellery had something else which she shared with Elisabeth, but not with these staring foreheads and mouths. None of them had eyes.

Someone had gouged out that evidence of life with knife thrusts so small and precise that he might have been trying to prise out the brain beyond, like a man teasing lobster flesh from the claw, ferreting greedily with a pick. They were sad, staring and angry, these distinguished, beautiful faces: their lives full of vigour had been punctured into death. Where there had been sparkle, amusement, discretion, taste, vanity, fear, there were now only these neat stiletto holes.

A human finger cannot resist a hole. Of the holes which had been eyes in the first three of the murdered portraits, most were big enough to admit Elisabeth's smallest finger; she could not resist a gentle if compulsive touching of these neat wounds. Only eyes were lost. These had been delicate attacks.

'Murder.' Maria echoed her thoughts. 'Gone to hell. Poor things.' She sounded remote with her strange voice, sympathetic, but also obscurely satisfied. From the back of the cleaned paintings, those without eyes and leaning against the ones which smelt, Elisabeth dragged a single canvas, held it aloft, falling back on the addictive, professional alter ego which was her constant defence, the guardian against horror. Before her was another olive-skinned woman, painted with a palette so similar to the one she knew that she would recognize the colour of those absent eyes, would know how to reconstruct the carnage of that face with her gauze and her pigments. Thinking this deferred a sensation of madness.

'I could mend this,' she murmured.

Maria shook her head violently and stamped her foot in an agony of fearful impatience. Didn't she know, didn't she know? More gently, but insistently, she took the painting from Elisabeth, holding it by one corner and quickly stuffed it back into its place beyond the stack of reeking canvases. She held it with finger and thumb, so light was a stretched canvas without a frame, the solidity of the paint surface so cunningly deceptive, but Elisabeth winced. A painting should be held by the sides, always. Was she so obsessive she could think of that, even now? The premonition of danger, suspended by the familiar colours, returned. Maria was hurrying, rearranging the dressing room to hide every trace of their presence, shutting the door firmly and brushing her hands down her overall. The smell lingered over them both. When Maria turned back to Elisabeth, her eyes were full of tears.

'Poor, poor, poor,' she said. The words of sympathy were crooned, urgently. It was imperative but impossible to explain, but she knew she must try, throwing her whole ugly body into the attempt, spittle flying with the gestures. Survival depended on it.

'He cleans,' she spat, rubbing the air with an imaginary cloth. 'Make clean, perfect . . . And after, when it is *Perfect* . . .' She stopped, and began to drag an uncomprehending Elisabeth back down the corridor to the cloak cupboard by the front door. Inside, Maria rummaged and spat, attacking the box of sticks. Cupboard upon cupboard, this place so full of tidied-away secrets, doors upon doors. Maria abruptly produced one black umbrella, then a second, then a third, finally a stick tipped with silver, which she flourished before she looked at it again and shrugged.

'Not this one,' she spat. 'But like this, he does this . . . She held the cane like a fencer, thrust with it in the direction of the kitchen, making small, lunging movements accompanied by aggressive grunts, 'Huh! Huh! Huh!' There was a rumble and a crash as Butler's growls increased and he hurled himself against the door. 'Bastard!' Maria yelled lunging harder and breaking into a peal of laughter. She dropped the stick and crept closer to the door. 'Big bastard, and your master, your mother was a cat!' The effect was more comic than tragic: Elisabeth laughed, too, until they whooped with crazy giggles even as Elisabeth was thinking of stranger sounds, her eyes mesmerized by the silver top of the stick as it lay on the ground. Now that she understood more than the half, she found the rest intolerable knowledge and her fingers became nerveless with fear. Step step click, one two click, the footsteps in the mind, like the dance before the sacrifice. She did not know how long they had been in the dressing room by Thomas's bed, how long standing here while Maria let rip her hidden talents and played the fool, but her mind was filled with the sound of footsteps, the flash of silver which had threatened so in the deserted railway station where she had first seen it, the steps in the street, one two click, one two click, haunting for weeks, encouraging, even manufacturing her escape into this confinement. He had lured her here through her fear of the outside. Slowly and by common accord, the two of them stopped laughing. Elisabeth, copying Maria's action with the painting, took the fallen stick and replaced it exactly where it had been found and closed the door. Then, as they stood looking at each other, wondering how they might broach the monster in the kitchen and the monster beyond, they heard a sound at the front door. Butler became silent. Elisabeth and Maria, the latter with a finger over her lips and a head frantically shaking, fled to the studio room. Elisabeth picked up a rag and a bottle of white spirit: Maria stood behind in a pose of uneasy nonchalance.

'Thomas?' Elisabeth gaily called as the front door opened and Butler began to bark again. 'Thomas, is that you?'

He did not answer. Elisabeth began to rub at the third picture, already clean, the actions of her fingers automatic, keeping her back to the door. The light had already faded: she had not turned on the tungsten light for the earth colours of which this picture was composed, panicked. Too dark to work: he would know she could not work at this hour without light, but she stood still, hoping against desperate hope that the half light and her shaking would not betray her. His footsteps were very slow, guessed at rather than heard over that sound-muffling carpet, teased by Maria's vacuum cleaning into thicker pile and greater silence. It was his breath she heeded before the sound of his steps on the wooden floor of the studio, his presence, directly behind her, looking at Maria's immobile face, then at Elisabeth's back in its pretended concentration.

'Maria, what are you doing here? You mustn't disturb Elisabeth, I told you. Elisabeth, your shopping. And I bought you something – well, a present . . .'

She turned with what she hoped was a grateful smile. Beneath the glasses his nostrils were dilated: he carried neither stick nor umbrella, and she thought for one wild moment she might be wrong, she and Maria, about every thing. The nostrils continued to twitch. His sense of smell, Elisabeth had noticed, was peculiarly refined: she had watched him sniff food as if its odour were the most essential element. In guilty response, she raised her own hands to her nose as if to brush away dirt. Her fingers reeked of onions, fires, kitchen smells, including must and mice, the scents which had impregnated the old and battered canvases in front of those which were newly restored but disfigured. Oil takes up smells, she remembered: an oil painting will smell for ever of where it has been, the fumes of the air, heat, cooking, coal, all drunk into the medium. You could tell how an ancient kitchen smelt, she remembered, by the painting from above the fire; paintings lived to tell tales, and so did the present state of her hands, her smock, Maria's overall, all stinking with the odour of other generations.

'Go to the kitchen, Maria. *Now.*'

Maria tried to appear surprised. 'Go,' he said. She remembered Butler in the kitchen, cringed, put her hand over her mouth.

'Tea,' said Elisabeth brightly. 'Tea. I'll go.' Thomas smiled and shook his head in a wide, lazy sideways movement, like a horse disturbing flies in summer. With one hand on her shoulder, he propelled Maria out of the room. Elisabeth stood still, unsure of what to do. The front door was unlocked now: she had imagined Thomas escorting Maria towards it, as he did most evenings, telling her what time to come back tomorrow, guarding his secret of the lock's combination. All she had to do was run behind them both and, when the door was open, run some more, past the two and down the stairs. The paralysis melted: she felt in the pocket for her house keys, remembering even then, she had no house, merely a roof, but something, anything where she was not captive, a park bench, was better than this. She recalled the sensation of Thomas's hand on her arm, shuddered, prepared to move. The timing was crucial: with the good arm Thomas could stop a train.

Then she heard the kitchen door open and slam shut and realized what he had done. The air, still air in this flat on top of the world, was rent with screams of terror. Thomas stood outside the door of the kitchen, looking at it in puzzlement, smiling his silly smile, as if it were not he who had slammed it shut on Maria and that dog.

The last stop of the day was the garage and the rain had begun again. A fool's errand, Annie thought halfway. Elisabeth's car was dead, so why would Elisabeth have come here at all, although her invoices showed she had been here twice in the last year? She could not have been contemplating buying another car before her own was stolen, or could she? Annie was damp, sick of the sight of buses and trains and the weight of the umbrella. It was not meant to be held aloft, too much metal even if the metal were silver. Annie found the garage desolate. A fat, middle-aged man sat in the kiosk on the forecourt, his shelter so small there was no room inside for anyone else, so Annie stood outside. The man was distracted, staring into the distance away from her, so she tapped on the window, awkwardly, with the umbrella. Rain shone on the silver tip. The man turned, saw Annie and shrank back into the swivel chair he occupied. The cheap upholstery of the chair was torn, and foam stuffing poked obscenely through.

'Elisabeth Young?' Annie began, brightly enough, but her smile was wearing thin. He shouted at her to go away, but she stayed while he put his head in his hands, muttered, wept. She persisted.

There was this car, her car, he said. Which she had brought in and which his son had taken and never said anything about it. Never, until this man came in, with that umbrella, and took him to one side. 'Why couldn't the boy have told me first?' the father said. 'I could have covered up for him. But that other bloke, he was frightening and in the end the boy told us both. Frightening, asking about the car, said he was Miss Young's uncle, but he was not, she could never have an uncle like that, I said. She was too nice, I said, but the boy, well he was terrified, he told him things he'd never tell me. But when I found out from listening what he'd done, my boy, with that girl's car, I beat him good and proper. "It was broken, dad," he said, "it was already good for nothing, that car; stoppit, stoppit." But I didn't stop, I was angry, wasn't I?'

It didn't make sense to Annie, any of it. Only about the uncle having the umbrella she now carried, which he had stuck in the kiosk seat to make his point. An uncle tying up the loose ends of Lizzie's life, seeking to pay her bills. Someone who had been through Elisabeth's correspondence and all her records as carefully as she. Annie understood only about the boy running off, taking another car, driving the way he tended to drive when he, too, was hurt and angry. And not coming home again, making his father cry with guilt. Absent, like all those similarly haunted by a man with a blade concealed in his innocence.

CHAPTER TWELVE

Francis had heard worse stories, even in his relatively few years of practice. Many worse, of burnt babies and abused children, brutalized beyond hope of a moral code, no possible salvation in a society which was meaningless to their lives. All of these histories he had absorbed with professional disinterest, reproduced where necessary in mitigation or quoted to friends, sometimes with less respect than others, but more often with incredulity. Compassion was dulled by ignorance and distance: he could not afford to let pity swell his senses and make him forgot his lines.

It was different, though, when that life about whom a tale was told had touched his own. 'Is it yours, then?' the taxi man had jeered. Is she pregnant, will you marry her, is she in trouble? As if that were the only kind of trouble.

Francis had not once thought of marrying Elisabeth. The love which preceded marriage was surely quite different from the emotion he had so signally failed to nurture towards her. A marriageable love would be a question of compatibility, similarity, not at all like the initial crush of amazing intensity which had blazed his trail to Elisabeth with her softly accented voice and all those artisan but artistic qualities. No she was not suitable, with varnish in her fingernails, her abrupt common sense, her frequent lack of the charm he possessed himself in such abundance; was instead a person stuck in limbo, the professional from working-class stock, neither fish nor fowl, seeming so ready to face the world, so immune to public opinion, seeming indeed, like someone who could protect herself with all that sublime independence which had been half of the attraction but fifty per cent of the irritation. No promises of any kind had ever entered his transactions with Elisabeth, but somehow the thought of her being pregnant was not unpleasant and he almost wished it were true.

The country seemed to flower into colour as his train drew out of the dismal, unmanned station which was a shaming contrast to the new concrete richness of Clayfields' nearest town. Culture here was carried in polythene bags, Francis thought, and chided himself for his snobbery. Night fell as the train roared south. He dozed with nightmarish visions before his eyes, visions which defied logic but included an image of the Velasquez Venus. Elisabeth had led him to it in the National Gallery, pointing out the very faintest of lines which showed where it had been restored, then shown him later a picture in a book of the same Venus, hacked by the knife of a maddened suffragette. The Venus had a dazzling body, lay on her side with the long curve of her perfect back facing out, head resting on a hand as she gazed at her own reflection in the mirror held by Cupid. Such flesh that Francis and a million others wanted to touch the hollow of her waist and run hands down her thighs. The suffragette had sliced into that tactile flesh with a blade, ripping through the buttocks and the spine with systematic strokes, but Venus had not wept or died: she had lived to enchant, hung there now, with those infinitesimal marks on her back, restored because she was priceless and beautiful and the blade had been so sharp, her shadowed face still smirking into her mirror.

To the rhythm of the train, the erotic body of the painting became Elisabeth's with none of her anonymity: the bile of the image choked the back of his throat as if he had swallowed lava. Elisabeth, lying thus, cut across her curves with knives, red blood welling on olive-skinned flesh from wounds a foot long. Elisabeth, led silent round her dying village with paint obscenely smeared on her breasts, covering her scars for ever. Francis had heard worse stories, could not recall a worse dream.

Annie had been crying, sitting in her flat snuffling. For the people who loved Elisabeth, for the boy in the garage and his howling father, crying out of a nameless fear and an equally indefinable guilt which belonged with the letters inside the pig. It seemed to her that Elisabeth was dangerous to all she knew, but Annie was growing to love her with the love she preserved first for the victims of bullies, and second for all those men who might never love her back. Annie listened to Francis, who told the saga of his day, omitting the manic laughter and the last remarks of the taxi man. Annie told the details of her day, omitting anything which did not give her credit, such as the silly crying and the resentment with which she had begun in the morning. Then she showed him the letters.

'Great family,' she said, spreading out the letters on the floor, her collection from the intestine of the rosewood pig. 'Really lovely. Just like yours and mine, I guess. Sweethearts, every one. Load of bastards.'

The letters, various colours and ages, were now scattered. Annie liked the thought of watching Francis pick them up, but was denied the privilege. Her phone rang in the other room and she went to answer.

Francis bent down from the chair and scooped a few sheets into a fist with less elegance than he might have used if Annie had been watching. For all their common purpose, they were still making each other reluctant to take it seriously: here in the warmth, it became more of a game they could play and they were as aware of one another as mating cats. The frozen North, which had slid away from him in the train, the shower and the taxi came back with the bitterness of the wine and the crinkle of cheap paper. Pink.

Annie's face, when he raised his head to her footstep, was equally pale, two nodules of crimson blusher standing out on her cheeks.

'That was a shopkeeper,' she said shortly. 'One of those where I went today, following my little trail of devotion. Do you know we could get half of London looking for Lime Lizzie if we wanted? Anyway, someone came in on an errand.'

Francis jumped. A vivid but guilty hope enlivened his face.

'No, no, not her. Just someone who came in for a special kind of gauze, the kind Elisabeth uses. They don't get much call for it and there aren't many art restorers that go into medical-supply shops, are there? That's what Yvonne said, a friend of Lizzie's. They all call themselves friends of hers.'

'Don't call her Lizzie,' Francis said automatically.

'Suit yourself. They didn't have what he wanted, so she offered to send it to him if he paid in advance. He said he'd collect. But he was a funny little man, Yvonne said. A bit sinister, she said, told her he was a restorer, but he can't have been, she said, because he looked blind, had a funny stick and dark glasses.'

'And? So? Maybe every art restorer uses the same things, I don't know . . .'

She sat down abruptly. 'Oh my God. Oh my Christ.'

'What?' said Francis.

'I forgot the glasses. I always forget glasses. I know who he is. There's this man, bought a picture from me, just the once, ages ago, asked me about restorers, I told him about Lizzie. Only I've lost the paperwork, the way I do. He gave me a picture for restoration . . . I passed it on for Lizzie to do . . . it's the one that disappeared from her place and I couldn't remember whose it was. Drove me mad. You know the one I mean. Don't you remember I asked you

247

about it? She had it for ages. Two chairs, a wooden floor . . .'

'Yes, I know the one, I know. I wanted it, picture of a room. But why, what?'

Annie flourished from behind her back the silver-tipped, beautiful, lethal umbrella.

'He had a stick with silver on, a bit like this. A funny, fussy, not very memorable man to look at, that's why I didn't remember him, far too unmemorable. Apart from the stick. And the glasses.'

'Where did you find that?' asked Francis, gesturing to the umbrella.

'In her bloody flat,' said Annie. 'And it wasn't there last time, was it?'

He took the umbrella, examined it like a judge with an exhibit. He pulled off the ferrule, carelessly. The blade beneath scored the palm of his hand and together they watched the forming of a thin line of blood.

Thomas had left the flat with Maria, taken her away. He said he would be back soon. The door clunked shut behind him. Elisabeth squirmed with shame. Tossed her head and arched her body with the agony of it; shame, guilt incarnate in her own sweating flesh. Neither the lights over the picture nor the heat of a tropical sun could have made her perspire so much with this guilt, this shame, shame, shame. To have listened to those screams and remained still, struck with the paralysis of violence, doing as she was told there-after, the cowardly mopper of blood. She thought, I cannoned into Thomas as he stood outside the kitchen door. I may have shouted at him, but not for that long; I did nothing to persuade him to move until he was ready to move and open the door, and there she was crouched with her ugly mouth, whimpering now, not screaming, for which I dared be grateful. The dog, licking its foul lips, as if he had not liked the texture of her hairy skin, experimenting with the aftertaste. Maria's stumpy legs were bleeding, a little mashed around the ankle, small puncture wounds which did not penetrate to muscle, nips rather than bites, but still wounds which would turn black, blue, throb for days. There was also an ugly scrape on one shin which might have hurt worst of all, but looked less significant, the skin red raw from the tom edge of the plastic rubbish bin behind which she had hidden to shield herself from the worst. With passable success, but not enough to dismiss the terror from her face, make her voice more audible than a kitten's mewing, or the mouth more human than a slack and dribbling line. Thomas had laughed. Behind that soft exterior of consistent civility, the madness and sadness showed like the wounds on his servant. He laughed as if it were a joke, the comforting but forced laughter of an adult in front of a child in order to pretend that falling down was not really serious, that the child was not really hurt and should not make a fuss. Laughter to surprise someone into smiling and forgetting, carrying the promise of a treat if they complied. He had put his arms round Maria's shoulders. And then, most obscene of all, worse than her screams and her bleeding legs, was her response. She placed her arms around his neck, her face against the barrel of his chest, and let him hold her, sobbing.

'There, there,' he said. 'Not to worry. All better soon, all better soon. Say a prayer.'

Maria let him touch her. She seemed to be comforted, seemed to like it. You would do anything out of fear: you would embrace the devil himself. Most moving, living things, Elisabeth thought, can become trained in savagery. Dogs, cats, rats, anything with a sharper instinct for survival than a sheep. They can be forced out of character by events or a ringmaster: their savagery is infectious, father to son, man to dog, woman to man. Thomas had been gentle once, but that was a long time ago; part of the man had died. Elisabeth could feel the infection of cruelty.

In his absence, she had raced round each room of the flat, including the bare, spare rooms she had examined before, followed by Butler who was snapping but not biting. So many windows, so many locks without keys. Suicide-proof, he said, and the only windows wide enough for exit were those in her studio, too high to reach up sheer, smooth walls. Then she flung open kitchen and cupboard drawers, looking for knives, screwdrivers, hammers, anything heavy and sharp enough to attack the solid door to decimate that lock, at least make sounds Nothing but plastic, innocuous implements. Dear God, no one ever even used knives in this house: they never even ate what could not be eaten with fork or fingers. She went inside the hall cupboard to look for his umbrella with the blade, his swordstick, anything he might have, but found only sticks, one tipped with all too malleable silver. Beat on the door with one of these, a thumping hollow, futile sound while the dog behind her ripped her blue smock with his teeth. While she screamed, beat back at the yellow jaws, more out of resentment for the interruption than out of fear, the door opened. The light flashed in the hall, like the cue for a patient to see the doctor or an applicant an official, and there was Thomas back, still smiling. He pushed her back before him into the kitchen with ridiculous ease, still smiling.

'You can't let her go like that.' Elisabeth shouted. 'What will she do?'

'Oh, she's not so bad,' said Thomas. 'I've seen worse. She shouldn't have shut him in, she ought to know better. And this is Maria's home. She'll come back in the morning like she always does, though I may give her a day off tomorrow. It's your home, too, you know.'

'No it isn't. Let me go with her. She should go to a doctor.'

'She wouldn't go to a doctor, I promise you. She'd refuse. There's nothing for you to do but finish the painting. You have to do that. You can't go, either.'

'Why? Why? Why?'

'I must have something perfect in this place!' The voice had risen to a shout. 'Perfect!'

'Why?' she shouted back, tired of that interrogative sounding in her sore throat. 'Why? You aren't perfect. Nothing is . . .'

She looked at him, bemused. Thomas sat down heavily. Elisabeth could only stare at him, solid herself with guilt and fury.

'Nothing is perfect, I am so far from perfect and that is why. I am surrounded by imperfection. That is why I seek the opposite. I am . . . . I am an ugly, ineffectual man, as I have been since I was young. Since you made me so.'

'I did not, I did not –'

'Oh, I don't blame you, but you must surely have told them something, something to suggest I'd seduced you, or something filthy of the kind, to make them be so savage, you must have done that. You must have done, it was only natural, you wanted the attention.'

'I didn't,' she whispered. 'I didn't, I didn't, I can't have done. It wasn't true. I was a little girl who bothered you. That was all. You know that was all. You know I was incapable of telling lies.'

'Oh never mind. I said I don't blame you. But I'm entitled to something aren't I? Something perfect, like – oh I don't know what like – you, for instance. I have no entitlements. I'm surprised that being so ugly doesn't disenfranchise me from the vote. No entitlements at all.'

She found the desire in herself to jeer at him, wanted to hurt, as she was hurt, a sudden rallying force.

'No entitlements? To what? Only to riches, pictures, rest, recreation, a place like this. And light, never-ending light. No entitlements?'

'No. You don't understand. Between those who can attract, those who are physically acceptable, and those who are not, there is a chasm a mile wide. No entitlements. Not to respect, not to anything. I have to acquire perfection. I have not got it in me. First an eye then an arm . . . So I want a piece of beauty. You, perhaps. One perfect picture perhaps, without all the singing and dancing.'

She was calmer now, found words.

'Thomas, you want perfection, you want beauty, but what do you do with it? You can't stand it, can you? All

252

those paintings, restored, made as good as they could be and then you carve them up, don't you?' She tried to subdue her voice, but it emerged as sharp as an untuned violin. She sounded like her father and winced at the memory.

'Only it isn't that easy, you know,' she went on tunelessly, recklessly. 'I mean, it's no good sticking these perfectly restored portraits of yours with a dagger to destroy their eyes. Takes more than that to kill a painting, you know. You'd have to burn them. Smother them with acid. Something more final than a knife. You can't kill a painting as easily as you can a human being.' Even now she could not resist communicating this little fact. He must have known where she had been in his absence, she and Maria, poking about in the murk of his privacy, but he was looking at her as if he had no idea of the implications of what she knew.

'What paintings?' He stood up again. Such a small man, lower to the ground than she, but twice as powerful. She wondered how money could be converted into muscle.

'Your paintings, of course. The ones in the dressing room. The ones without eyes. Those.'

Thomas was walking across the kitchen to look through a window which was identical to his bedroom porthole, small, partly open to allow a breeze, but unmovable.

'Those paintings? I suppose you think . . . I suppose, they were, well, fairly perfect.' He began to laugh, an ugly, raucous, unstoppable laugh, different from the crooning laugh he had used to comfort Maria, louder and louder there were forced tears at the corners of his eyes, little drops of mirth.

253

'Look at me. Don't laugh at me.'

She walked towards him, the savagery rising, ready to attack. Thought of the paint beneath her nails which would leave traces in a scratch on his plump cheek, but the shame curdled the rage, the impotence of the way she had stood there minutes before, preventing nothing, merely looking at the blood. A little on the floor, a little ignored round the muzzle of the recumbent dog, as if poor Maria's blood were scanty, thin and smeared, like her smile. Maria had been escorted to the front door, her sobbing muffled, her head against his, her back to Elisabeth. There had been a mute accusation in that, a contempt for her failure to rescue a friend, which mirrored Elisabeth's own sentiments about herself. She was never swift enough to intervene: she was cowardice incarnate.

'I'll go to Maria now,' she said, moving to the door. 'Let me out, tell me where she is. I shan't ask twice.' There was a hesitation in the air, more palpable than the breeze from the window.

'You promised you'd stay with me, if ever I asked.'

'No I never promised that. A different person . . .'

She was moving, aimed in absolute resolution. All she had to do in those seconds was to reverse the nightmare by an act of will, but she hesitated, let her arms fall and her fear show. Felt in the crook of her elbow the coldness of metal, shook her arm free and then felt her elbow pinioned. Easy. A second's indecision and the arm was hooked by the cold metal handle of his stick. His face at her shoulder and a shower of spittle on her neck, leaving her rigid with revulsion.

'Don't be silly, Lizzie, don't. Paintings matter more than anything. You know that. You have to stay, you have to finish. Where's your pride? No one else answers when you need them, only me.' He laughed again. She would have done anything to stop that laugh. 'Give me a chance,' he said. 'Give me a chance. Listen, I bought you something nice . . . Look at it, please. You never gave me a chance.'

She moved her hand slowly to wipe her neck. Her hand was heavy. Pity, guilt, shame. All of them the same weight, the creators of inertia.

So the door was locked and Thomas was back in his room while the light had gone from hers. The light had gone from everything: the madonna did not smile even when Elisabeth looked at her, put her back on the easel, knowing now what she had to do, what there was to do. Before that, she prowled round the windows in the room, those she could reach. She had so delighted in the obedience of the high windows to their silk ropes, for the blessed light they let into the room so late in the day. Now she loathed their inaccessibility. They reminded her of the high windows in the rooms of her old school, and the classroom duties to open or shut them with a pole, although never with tassels like these, shiny, red, soft, golden, a texture so fine and cool she held it against her hot face. The lower sash windows on the right of the room were locked to open no more than a foot, wide enough for her head and all her hair as she gazed down. Opposite were the blank windows of an identical block of flats, windows she had never seen lit or opened shielding the empty rooms beyond. Down below she could hear the hum of

255

city dwellers cutting through this otherwise silent street at the end of the working day, accustomed by now to the early dark, rejoicing in it. She could see the textures of their dull coats, which contrasted with the cars that juggled for position, flat rectangles of colour pausing and revving with controlled power, waiting for one another to make space. She wanted to be part of the crowds she had always despised as she had barged rudely through, repeating the mantra words of a child. Don't look at me, just don't look at me. I am a strange animal who knows no herd but has to hug the flank of one, needing but despising. Look at me now. She could dream from this height that one of them, only one, might look up and see her at the window and know she was trapped. Come upstairs, demand entrance, and prevent all those tentacles of fear from taking hold. Come home with me, they would say, come out of here.

Francis, coming up those stairs, saying, I wondered where you had got to, darling. Come home. Francis, who could not answer a letter, even one on headed paper which he might have understood. Careless Annie: no word, either.

If she smashed the window, she could scramble out and fall. There was always that option for oblivion, but she suddenly treasured her life and all the little it was. And there was Maria to consider, Maria and the madonna. Elisabeth looked at her room. Look in, not out: there is no point in looking out. She had placed half her materials on the floor: tidily now she added to the stock the extras of Thomas's shopping. The heat probe for the asphaltum, but he had forgotten the gauze. Forgotten the gauze, as if he intended that neither his prisoners nor his paintings should have bandages for the wounds they might acquire, but he had bought a gift. In a minute, that other bag. She could fire this place, stain this wood, ruin these floors and desecrate these handsome chairs: she could examine the garment in the bag, Thomas's gift, which she had briefly touched, withdrawing her fingers as if they had been stung. She looked at the madonna again, shuddered and knew what she would do. She would find calamine lotion to soothe her hands: she would finish the painting. Then he would scar it.

Drawn to the window again, she made herself look down, suffer the vertigo of longing.

No one was looking for her. They were all busy. She turned away. Francis, look at me.

'All right, all right. Supposing this man . . .'

'Is the artist who caused so much trouble.'

'And got half blinded, came off worse . . .'

'Well that's an arguable point, isn't it? About which of them came off worse. He only lost an eye . . .'

'Well why the stick, then? Was it worse, what they did to him, or did something else happen to him after? Could he blame Elisabeth for that?'

'We seem to be assuming he blames Elisabeth for something. No evidence, no evidence at all. If it is the same man, that is. Might not be at all.'

Annie pushed her hand through her hair, feeling the dry texture. Too many changes of colour, and she had singed the fringe with the extravagant arcs described by her cigarette. There was the slightest scent of burning.

'Why shouldn't it be the same man? Listen, the descriptions seem to tally and how many one-eyed men do you count amongst your acquaintances? Oh no, sorry, I forgot, your acquaintances are all middle-class, middle-weight, middle-brain sportsmen . . .'

'Don't get at me, Annie. All right, so what if he is? Why wait all this time and then go round terrorizing her life? Orchestrates, or at least knows about, the destruction of her car . . .

'And scares the living daylights out of her neighbour . . .'

'You didn't tell me about that.'

'Yes I did, Francis, baby: you weren't listening. You were so damn full of your own martyrdom.' He ignored that.

'Yes I was listening. I was. I'm a paid listener.'

Annie got up, cramped. 'Not to me you're not. And you'd better go home. Late, work tomorrow, all that.'

'We haven't decided what to do,' he ventured, delaying.

'We don't really know what the fuck to do. Sleep on it. She can't be in danger. She'd have written. She's a great letter writer.'

And you don't really want to go home. Annie did not say so, simply thought so, the conclusion forming itself in her mind with a quiet amusement and some satisfaction. No, he did not want to go: she was not making him particularly comfortable, there had been nothing flirtatious in her attitude, but he had just discovered loneliness and he did not want to leave for the limited company of the pictures in his flat. He was harassed, worried, guilt-ridden, all of these sensations new to him. Not a graduate in the school of hard knocks, this one, Annie thought, oh no. For a moment she despised him sitting on her floor, drinking her wine, his back against her furniture, but then the moment passed as she ruffled his thick, fair hair. It was a gentle reminder for him to move. She was suddenly resentful of the dominion of good looks. Those of Elisabeth which she had never envied at all, and had learned to appreciate now, but those of Francis in particular.

'You could get away with murder with a head of hair like that,' she said, the remarks in the making as thoughtful as venomous. 'Your alibi would be the way you look, that rueful, vulnerable smile which isn't even calculated, which you've probably worn to good effect since you were three months old, you legitimate bastard.'

'Don't be silly,' said Francis, surprised and not flattered.

'A good-looking man has the world to eat before he even begins on his oysters,' Annie went on, suddenly remembering the little man with the limp and the stick, seeing in one terrible gulp of realization the comparative impotence of such a man. Men who looked like Francis had the power: men who looked like the creep had to create their own. Somewhere in there some clue was lurking, the germ of an explanation for all the fictions and wild analyses which had employed their evening.

'I shall go back through all my damn books and look for his address. If I can't find it, some other dealer must have it. If he's bought from me, he buys from others. I'll get it. I know what kind of pictures he likes, I can tell from the one he brought in to me. You can always tell. You're so

259

predictable, you collectors.' Her eyes widened with her yawn, another realization smothered in the gasp.

'I bet he likes what Elisabeth likes . . .'

Francis closed his eyes. The reluctance to go was not feigned, but he did go. Work and all that. He went armed with the sorrows he had unearthed and the reflection, not quite enough to dispel the thought of Elisabeth from his mind, that Annie was the kind of girl who knew how to look after a man, who answered back and that might be what he needed Also the shameful thought that he was a man who had no idea of how to look after anyone, a boy who had nurtured nothing but good luck. Not even, he thought, a dog.

When St Sebastian died (he was, of course, martyred, like all her real favourites, they made the best pictures), the death had not been quick. Maria looked at his depiction, thirteenth from the left, three down from the top on the wall against her bed. Sebastian was tied to a tree and shot with arrows, none of them fatal. He did not die from one wound, because he saved himself to be beaten to death afterwards. All in all, it cannot have been a pleasant way to go. In the pictures of him with his arrows, his face was contorted with agony, his eyes turned to heaven in a silent supplication, and he could not slump because of his bonds. But he must have moved each time another shaft pierced muscle, thudded into his side to create those rivulets of blood as red as the feathers on the arrows themselves, and he had been brave because he was a saint and saints were, perforce, brave people. Did he remember his God? Did he really suffer in silence, as she should have done? Maria thought of other saints, remembering the lesson that there was no salvation without suffering, no heaven for those who were beautiful, no reward in the other life for vanity. So Sebastian may not have minded much this mutilation of his beautiful body, because it was only an initiation for the bliss of the afterlife, a necessary atonement. She would not mind, either: suffering and mutilation were only preliminaries to heaven.

Maria prayed to another picture (three along), which showed a swooning saint praying to God in thanks for the stigmata on her hands, the tidy wounds blessing her bare feet. Maria envied the stigmata. She had stigmata in the wrong places: puncture wounds on her ankles and the healing holes on her wrists. The dog should have gone for her hands if she were ever going to acquire sainthood. The other way she had denied sainthood today was to scream, to whimper and to lie. She had in all ways lost anything which could ever be termed a holy dignity. The thought was distressing, so she moved on to Bernadette of Lourdes, who saw the Virgin with roses round her feet, the same feet which stamped or danced on rock to open the miracle spring at Lourdes, a nicely humble saint, but the ankle hurt, hurt, hurt, and not from stigmata. Life had to be hard to earn the right passage, but need it be this hard?

She prayed to the Jesus of the Sacred Heart. Maria asked him to help and he smiled back at her his faded, benign smile. He looked lovely, Jesus. He was telling her, as he often did, to do what she could about the world, the flesh and the devil. But mostly, of course, the flesh. Her own was as mottled as ever. You could not get to heaven with any other kind. If you had something better, you should hide it.

Well, Maria thought, if I am a little bad sometimes, you must all help me, but will you please help my brother, because he is worse? She worried for her brother, began to think of what he had said when he brought her downstairs. Her cruel, misguided brother: she agonized for his soul and he told lies on Sundays. The thought struck her afresh. He had told her, on the Sunday before Elisabeth arrived, that Elisabeth was a sort of saint in disguise. Saints were often humble people, like Joseph the carpenter, artisans, cleaners, like Martha. Now he was suggesting that Maria should not speak with this good person, because she was not . . . good.

But then, he told lies on other days of the week as well. He told them all the time.

Thomas was frightened. He could feel his fear penetrate the hackles of the dog, which growled without moving.

'Shut up, you brute,' he muttered. 'Don't you dare growl at me.'

Perhaps he had gone too far in training the dog as he had in everything else. Let us review this little life, Thomas. It is not Sunday any more, old man. There is no need to tell so many lies, the way you always have, to get whatever you wanted. What have you done? Think about it. When did the madness start? It was time to think, because he had never predicted this new conspiracy between Maria and Elisabeth: that had not been on the

262

cards at all. Even so, it might not have been wise to speak to Maria the way he had earlier on. His troubled mind dismissed that problem, went back and forth in a kind of sweeping motion over his conscience, like the windscreen wipers on a car. Oh, he had hated Elisabeth. Hated but loved this girl child who hung around him so piteously in that misguided dump in the North, at the time when he considered himself a rebellious socialist, an artist with the God-given talent as well as the right to paint the secular world as he saw it. He already hated the spiritual. Despised Elisabeth then for inciting those two brothers of hers, even though he knew, once the wounds were healed, that she would have done no such thing. There had been no one to look after him when he came home to this empty flat. Except his neglected sister, Maria, the saviour then, who had never quite left home with all its corridors of holy illustrations. Maria, to whom he was bound for life, for all her goodness to him.

When had it begun, his old, new fixation? When he was trustee of the art school, and saw, by chance, those photographs of *la belle* Elisabeth? Known from those austerely erotic prints, duplicated by himself and sent to her parents while the rage was still hot, that she had grown well. When had it got so much more complicated, with himself collecting portraits which contained some element of her, either the skin, the hair, something reminiscent? He had to get Butler to guard them all. Against all manner of things. And there was still Maria, whom he could not cast out, because, yet again, she had been the only one on call – nurse, cook, haphazard but effective, the only one who would do this with an element of love. He could not bear her in the house. That, too, was accommodated. Everything was accommodated.

'I only want to look at her.' He detached his finger from the hole which was the eye, replaced the painting exactly where he had found it, wrinkling his nose at the smell, went back into his chilly bedroom.

'I only wanted to look at her,' he repeated, standing tall. Yes, her, and a hundred canvases or more, all with their little bit of resemblance of perfection. He only wanted to look until he had begun to follow her, watching the details of that limited life, hating it on her behalf. It had swung from a longing to a sense of responsibility, to a sense of ownership, of entitlement. And in the middle of these wild arcs, still swinging now, there was the hatred which had begun it all, the sense of loss, the wanting to look at that perfect face all the time, and the other moments of not being able to bear it.

'I only want to look at her!'

Yelled, this time, with a shower of spit, as if he were an orator and there were a thousand to convince. No, it was not entirely true. Yes, he wanted more, could contemplate anything except letting her go, but he wished, sometimes, that she was dead.

She would look lovely in the blue dress. Better than the madonna.

She would look perfect.

CHAPTER THIRTEEN

They had delayed. There were the obligations of work which they could not ignore on this or any weekday, but still the delay was wilful and they both knew it. It became a self-perpetuating delay, to hide the fact that they did not, quite yet, want a conclusion. In the end, it was Francis who found the address. Annie was infuriated by the ease of his method. She preferred doing everything under her own steam; it made the effort more honest somehow, more worthy of a reward. Nor could she have done what Francis did, because she was incapable of finding the right words to persuade a single policeman to help her across the road. Officials, any officials, somehow sensed her hostility, and became anathema, an alien breed. Francis, on the other hand, was born to delegate. He did not expect people to take his burdens from him: they simply volunteered. The detective whom he had saved from embarrassment was happy to assist over a pint after court. Go and see this garage owner (address on this old receipt). Establish if the girl did bring in her car and whether, more than three weeks later, a man came asking what had happened to it. There was no scope for a proper inquiry yet, the detective warned.

'I mean she went away, meant to go away, no one's reported her missing. It would be different if she'd hired the boy to ruin her car, for insurance money or something, but no, I see, it wasn't that kind of car.' No commercial value at all, thought Francis sadly, rather like most of Elisabeth's possessions. 'You would just like to know, would you, sir, if the man who called to enquire about the car, left a name and an address? Your friend had asked about this before, but the garage owner was too distraught to say? He was an uncle, you say, this man?'

'Yes,' said Francis, 'an uncle. Definitely an uncle with an interest in her car. Probably sent by her. I just want to know where she might be.'

'Easy, sir. The garage is on my patch.'

On my patch. Francis realized he had no sense of territory, no sense of being born anywhere, belonging anywhere which commanded profound knowledge or a fierce loyalty. He did not envy Elisabeth the territory of her birth, but he did envy those who stayed still in one place and knew it intimately. He knew perfectly well that if it had been he who had vanished without trace for weeks, a plethora of acquaintances and family would have noticed: there would have been more than an inquiry by now; there would have been a nationwide hunt because

266

people like him did not disappear without a flurry of indignation. Yet with Elisabeth Young, there were shrugged shoulders and the vague feeling she would turn up, as if people without family connections were faintly disgraceful and owed it to others not to be so inconvenient. The thought of her afflicted him, together with wondering what it was like to be her, waking to the horror that there was no one, not a soul, rooting or searching. But with the uncomfortable conscience of such thoughts, came the sentiments of a hundred criminal clients: she deserved it; she wanted the isolation; she could always use a telephone or write a letter.

Not if she was not in the habit of asking, she couldn't. Not if she had always prayed to a mountain of silence. And why should she phone you, you supercilious bastard? You cut those lines of need as soon as you saw them. With a knife, boy, with a knife.

The pictures on the walls of his flat seemed to unite in rebellion, especially the ones she had restored, hung as crooked as a row of thieves' heads on spikes, mute accusations in their unexpected delinquency, as if they missed the loving touch of her hands and reminded him that love was not too fine or foolish a word for it. Love in various forms was something he considered his own. He had taken hers in the same spirit, left nothing behind but the vacuum of expectation.

Annie would be angry with him, he knew. He did not like that, either.

The detective called Francis at his chambers the same

afternoon. 'No address, sir, none. But his name is Thomas Milton. Lives near Westminster Cathedral.'

Doubting Thomas. Francis took to the telephone directory. Nothing. Took to verbal enquiries which were both feasible and possible because of his patrician voice and the way he asked. After that, there was one address, only one.

The sky, late on a Tuesday afternoon, was bluer than summer. Where he lived, in Kensington, trees played against the windows. He ignored the beer cans in the gutters, the figure recumbent across a doorway as he skirted his way home, sights which would normally occasion a fierce irritation but now caused a mild embarrassment. First, he telephoned the number he had researched, somehow knowing, even as he dialled, that there would be no reply, not even bothering to consider what he might say if anyone answered. Despite the predictability, he felt absurdly disappointed, almost hurt, imagined a telephone disconnected and placed in a drawer by someone who wanted to be left alone. It felt like a rejection by Elisabeth herself, slowed down that sense of urgency into a kind of paralysis.

Elisabeth was trying to recall that state of mind which had ever found the noise of a telephone irritating. She longed for its disturbance. The anger with which she had greeted interruptions seemed alien now. It seemed such a bizarre thing to do, hide a telephone, but Thomas had removed the one from this room on the second day she was there and she had not even considered it odd at the time. So many normal reactions had been eradicated from the

268

moment she entered this flat. Such as now, when her reaction to receiving a gift became the opposite of what it might have been. Elisabeth's youth had not accustomed her to receiving luxuries, but when they were given she would experience a moment of euphoria. Francis had not been a giver of gifts, did not seem to know how soon they could create a frisson on the way to loving. But this did not apply to large, blackmailing gifts, given by a man who held the keys and hid the telephone. There was no frisson but hatred for Thomas's gifts and Elisabeth could not bear to touch what he touched.

She had been deliberate in ignoring the second parcel Thomas had brought home with him the day before. The sleek black and gold bag had stood on the floor of the studio like a cunning accusation. There was no sign of Maria. Elisabeth felt a sick wave of longing and anxiety when she thought of poor Maria. Thomas pottered out and pottered in: twice he took Butler, but mostly he hovered in a mutually maintained silence. They teetered on the brink of speech, like a pair of ballerinas waiting for a cue, warming up, but every ounce of energy had gone from them both. Elisabeth thought of it when she bent in the morning, touching her toes, clasping her ankles and aligning her torso with her knees, an automatic routine of stretching to prove she was still alive. Yesterday was yesterday. She had slept somehow, briefly, but the sleep was poisonous, full of the sound of Maria's screaming, visions of the colours of hellfire and bruises. All the pictures merged in her mind: the madonna wore fur which was stained with blood while the strewn clothes of the second picture squirmed at her feet, and the madonna carried her heart in her hand like a hideous torch, gazing with a face which had no eyes. There were holes instead which ran like corridors into rooms with strange windows at the back of her skull. In the end, Elisabeth had lain with her own eyes open, forcing herself to think of nothing but the completion of that one single painting. It was her secret, but by the end of the previous day, the madonna had become a fleshy creature, a beckoner-on, on, a powerful, non-virginal thing. Not the benign and sensitive matriarch she had first seemed. Something else. It was as well Thomas stayed well away, took out the dog, came back, ignored her. Except once, outside the kitchen, armed with a stick.

'Maria's not coming today. I told her to rest.'

'I'll go shopping, then, shall I?'

'That won't be necessary. Be reasonable.'

'Reasonable!' Her voice faded and she shied away from him.

'Shh,' he commanded, turning away, ending the encounter, going to his own room. Then his voice floated back, drifting over the carpet.

'Oh, don't forget I brought you a gift . . .'

'I don't want it, I don't want it . . .' She was chanting like a child, clenching her fists, remembering the power hidden inside that physique of his, resenting her own lack of weapons. There was nothing sharp or heavy in the kitchen: she had looked and looked.

'Try it, please. Please. Try.' The demand softened to a request. And that was all. A day without Maria seemed particularly empty. The third presence had been more of a distraction than she knew, more a reminder of the outside world and a conduit to freedom than she had ever understood. Without Maria, there was less hope and more fear. Elisabeth worked savagely. There was nothing else to do until the light faded. Then, in the late afternoon, when she had done all her eyes would allow her to do and regarded what she had done with strange fascination, she stumbled across the bag and remembered the gift again. Curious, dithering, idle, lonely and frightened: whatever her reservations, she could not quite ignore the bag where the tissue paper stung her hands. Men gave gifts to mistresses, did they not, although none had done so for her: she had never been owned, never would be and, in the context of this confinement, any gift was revolting, but then, as the light had faded from the afternoon, so too had her power to sustain her calm by normal functioning and feverish but deliberate work. Avoiding the last light of the studio room, accessible to Thomas in theory although he had not come near all day to her acute relief, but in the privacy of her bedroom, she let the gift slither from its wrapping like a live thing.

The robe (somehow, the words 'frock', 'dress', 'outfit' were all inadequate as descriptions) could not have been purchased in one expedition. It belonged in a play, designed for effect. There were elements in it of the kind of ball gown in which you sat for your portrait, if you were the kind who ever sat thus. You sat in your best, from generation to generation, and often showed plenty of your flesh. Definitions for the garment defied her. A robe for the house or the opera. Her relief to find that it was not what she dreaded most by way of gift, some vulgar piece of negligée or film-star nightie designed for tearing off, gave her a temporary sensation of release, licence to look and admire before thinking. No woman could have failed to do that, even a woman with Elisabeth's lack of vanity, and certainly not one with an eccentric but profound addiction to almost anything of beauty. She was a prisoner seeking oblivion, stealing into the kitchen looking for something to drink, a *soup*çon of alcoholic courage. White wine in the fridge. Furtively, she seized a bottle, glass, plastic corkscrew, went back to her room and looked again, but only after the first glass had hit the back of her throat in an icy stream. After that, it was not enough to look. Even in self-disgust she could not stop there.

There was a huge wardrobe in her bedroom, made of walnut, with one mirrored door. As she stood, dressed in the robe, without quite knowing how she came to be so dressed, she looked as if she were inside a picture, framed by the moulded wood surrounding the glass, the bevelling of the edges catching the bedside light and throwing her shadow behind her. The robe was made of silk lined with silk, thick but fine and immediately warm to the skin. The collar stood up in a fan of pleats behind her head, down across her collarbones and across her bosom to the top button of the fastening. Tiny buttons of bluish pearl surrounded by the same silk, two dozen of them, descended past the moulded waist to the floor. There were no tucks, no darts, no obtrusive seams, simply panels of cloth which created the fluid shape of the thing, fluting out to a rich volume round her ankles and brushing the floor on which the toes of her bare feet curled in involuntary delight. The sleeves were pleated at the shoulder, full in the upper arm, buttoned at the wrist: the whole garment was shimmering, Elizabethan, medieval, modern, Eastern and Western, barbaric, severe but sensuous; the material moved as she moved, twisted, turned to see the panels which contracted into the small of her back, accentuating her waist, and, when she stood still, the cloth fell back softly into draping folds with less noise than a lace curtain in a breeze. It was both a European court and the kasbah, herself the queen or the odalisque. In the course of fastening the buttons which slipped easily into tiny, hand-wrought button holes, Elisabeth consumed another glass of wine and, as she stood transfixed by her own reflection, another and then another. The gown fitted but skimmed: she could move without breathing in, piled her hair on top of her head with the two combs which usually served to scrape it away from her face and keep it from trailing into paint or chemicals. The scent of this garment made her giddy: clean and fresh with a hint of roses, so divine she loved it while hating all it could signify. There was something insidious about the domination of this dress which even in the wonder of it made her angry. The blues shimmered and danced in the shadows of folds – ultramarine, the most expensive blue of the painter's palette. Elisabeth wanted to sob as she regarded herself. Ludicrous, the whole scenario obscene. The captive dressing up like a child before a party. Entertaining herself before the scaffold.

The opening of the bag, the trying on, the examination of how the dress, gown, robe, was made, took her from the last of the half light to darkness: from the time when the windows in her bedroom changed from solid planes of blue to black, and the dress, dark against her olive skin, shone in the unassisted glare of electric light. With her hair still pinned in untidy magnificence and her feet still bare, Elisabeth stepped unsteadily over the wide corridor outside, ready to share the madness of Thomas. The dress moved with her in a thousand shades of lapis lazuli.

Thomas sat in the room which was for night. He had lit the fire and sat in one of the wing chairs, not waiting, simply acting the role of a man in a reverie, turned away from the door.

'Did you get my note?' he said sharply. 'I left it in the kitchen. Communication by note seems better than none at all. Maria is back tomorrow. I thought you'd be pleased to know. Listen, we must talk.' He did not look round, but was addressing the steps he had heard. The arrogance made her furious, his strange, not quite discourteous failing to turn, confident enough in his captive to assume she would not be sneaking up behind him with a kitchen knife. It might have come to that, she thought, if I could have found such a knife, but I could not. It might still come to that, violence less alien than it had ever been. Butler, the guardian savage, made more response than the master, ambled across the carpet with his tail raised in greeting, a study in slow hypocrisy.

'Oh . . .!'

The sound emerged from Thomas almost like a cry of pain as she crossed before him to the sideboard where a row of decanters gleamed. 'Oh . . . darling . . .' the last syllables a sentiment rather than a word, breathed on an outward breath, choked back into a cough as if to deny it was said at all as he stood up awkwardly, supporting himself on the arm of his chair, sat back again abruptly, his body pushed in the chest by an invisible hand. Elisabeth found the sherry decanter and poured a generous measure into a wine glass. Way too much after half a litre of wine, but the alcohol had congealed rather than inebriated. All the same, her hands were clumsy. She crashed the sherry decanter against the brandy as she replaced it. The sound was sharp: Butler stirred. There was a louder rustling of silk as she moved.

'Well?' she said aggressively. 'Well? Is this what you wanted?'

He stared.

'Is this what you wanted?' she repeated. 'A piece of perfect horseflesh, dressed in your colours? Something to look at until you can't stand it? Something to feel? Here I am.' She sat. The robe rustled. She stood again, the sound of the fabric a deafening whisper as she swigged a throatful so recklessly that tears came to her eyes. The fire caught the reflection of their moisture: the tiny pearl buttons gleamed.

'This thing must have cost a thousand,' she added conversationally. 'And I don't know for what.'

'For you,' he said into a long silence. 'Only for you. You and you only.' The humbleness of the singsong tone grated on her nerves: temper, subdued for years, flared into desperate life.

'For me!' she shouted. 'For me? What crap. It's for you. It has nothing to do with me. It's all for you, and all your mad obsessions about beauty, to hide you from all those realities outside. Something to save you from being a poor little rich man, from being a pathetic creature as mad as his bloody dog. Oh for God's sake at least try to be honest. Don't try and tell me it has anything to do with caring for me or any rubbish like that. You can't care for me and trap me like a butterfly. You can't care for Maria if you make Butler bite her. You can't be a loving gaoler, there's no such thing, you bastard. Come on, then. Come and get me.'

He hesitated, struggling for words, moistening his lips as if to retrieve the spittle in advance.

'What do I want? I want you to be as beautiful, perfect, safe and happy as you can be. That is my pleasure. I also want you to be loved.' His face by the fire was a mirror of sly, earnest devotion, lit by the constant smile. The room was as hot as a furnace.

Elisabeth's voice rose to a wail. 'Loved? Is that it? Loved by you? Oh how simple. Just a quick fuck, or something more complex? If only I knew. I'd rather be hated: it's easier to deal with.' She threw the rest of the sherry down her throat. Butler growled. She looked at him in contempt.

'And this damned dog is the guardian of your morals too, is he? Let's see what you want and get rid of all this splendour at the same time, shall we? Since you don't know the truth, finding out is trial and error. Only I can't stand dishonesty and I can't stand the suspense.'

The alcohol suddenly burned as her fingers gathered speed

undoing the buttons. She began by bending, unbuttoning from the ankle, her forehead almost touching the floor while the combs escaped from her hair, the hands moving faster and faster. The robe was designed to be worn next to the skin: it was moulded thus and thus she had worn it. She stood with the garment undone and her hair over her face as she freed the last fastenings at the cuffs, and then, with a dexterity owing more to the rage pounding at her temples than to elegance, she was suddenly naked. Not shyly naked, either, but taunting, standing tall and straight with her arms by her side, not coyly covering herself. She bent again with her full suppleness, retrieved the combs from where they had fallen among the glorious folds of ultra-marine at her feet, raised her arms above her head to secure the hair back as it had been. Her breasts were raised with the action of her arms, hung heavy, soft and golden. She was perfectly calm.

'Was this what you wanted, Thomas? Come on, let's get it over. The attempt, at least.'

His dead eye burned. Elisabeth stepped out of the dress neatly. Thomas did not move. She crossed over to the sideboard again, refilled another glass, this time with brandy. Dutch courage, alcoholic nonchalance: she felt she could drink a lake, thought of acrobats on the flying trapeze psyching themselves into bravery. She waited for him, determined now to say nothing, let him do whatever he would do. It did not matter much any more. A body was only a body. Freedom was another matter altogether.

Movement, as slight as a sigh. Heavy movement,

Thomas hauling the barrel of his body out of his chair, Elisabeth bracing herself, looking at the yellow colour of the sherry under glass in the decanter, like a specimen of vintage urine. Thomas moving, slowly, like an old man. A click of his fingers, a signal to the dog, who shifted too and then slumped again. She heard Thomas pause in his dragging footsteps. The door shut and only then did she dare look away from the wall she faced and move to the fire.

The dog lay across the dress, making himself comfortable, sticking his wet nose among the folds, lifting a hind leg to lick in a vulgar instinct of cleanliness. Elisabeth stood alone by the fire, resting her head on her arm as the warmth hit her body and the light of the flames played over her naked skin.

Butler did not like the smell of the dress. Elisabeth went back to her own bathroom, where she was violently sick.

The flat faded back into silence.

No fire for Maria: she did not deserve a fire. She had nursed the legs for a day, not because she wished to do so, but because she was obeying his orders. His instructions, her own lord and master. There had been more than one saint named Thomas, she was thinking inconsequentially before he arrived this morning. First, there was doubting Thomas, who had insisted on touching the wounds of the risen Christ, touched with his hand the wound in the side, to prove that it was indeed he who had died and risen again. Then there was Thomas Becket, who should have been an example to her own Thomas. A dubious saint, she thought, one who had first served his king until he changed his allegiance back to his God and was murdered for that devotion. Oh, there was time for her own Thomas yet. He would free himself of all temptations yet. Maria liked saints who learned.

She had shown her Thomas a picture of his patron when he had ventured below stairs today, but he was not interested, brushed it away. He had only come down to tell her to stay where she was and not bother him. Elisabeth is being difficult, he had said: she is not such a good girl, all spoken vaguely, with an air of distraction as he sniffed his distaste for the meanness of her surroundings. Oh, she adored him; hated him, too. Since the morning she had been sitting still for most of the day, thinking.

On the single rickety table lay a selection of metal things she had rescued from the pockets of her coat, where she kept everything secret. There was a kitchen knife and a penknife, both preserved from confiscation, used to trim the edges of her paper pictures. She always preferred knives to scissors. There were also the keys to the window locks in the flat upstairs.

Maria addressed her picture of St Sebastian. 'He'd be very cross if he knew,' she chuckled. 'Very. He thinks he knows everything. He's keeping me hidden. Why? What's he doing?' Thomas had been so impatient to be gone when he visited today. 'She is not the good woman we thought,' he had said to her so earnestly the afternoon before. 'She is not what she seems, Maria. You must *not* make a friend of her. Don't talk to her, Maria. Don't talk to her, don't tell her things, the way you did. That's all. What were you trying to do? Make her hate me? I don't want her to hate me, sister. I don't really want her to hate you, either. But she will if you talk to her. So don't.'

Maria had nodded, just to make him hug her again, but he didn't. Now, she was bored, and her legs ached less, so that she had to scratch to make sure there had been a real reason for all that pain and still some pain behind it. She looked with satisfaction. Just like St Sebastian: it would go on for a long time. But into that strange contentment came a worry which hurt more, a chronic mistrust which was becoming second nature. Maria tapped her nose, not a natural gesture but one she had seen used. 'I know,' said the gesture, and at the same time she said, 'I know, I know, I know. A thing or two. Just a thing or two. Maybe three.'

Not what she seemed. A woman, not a saint, Elisabeth. Someone who might drag him away back into the worldly muck from which Maria had rescued him. Drag him with the ease of all those pictures. He was so vulnerable to his own eye.

The realization hurt more fiercely than the wounds: she could feel the flush of blood rise in her chest and a stickiness of sweat form in her groin and beneath her arms. What were they doing up there, brother Thomas whom she tried to save and the girl who he said was no good? Oh God, was he killing her soul? Doing what else with their loneliness? Being what? Maria stumbled towards her tiny bathroom. No, no, no. She used the soft toilet paper which Thomas encouraged her to buy along with his own shopping, scrubbed at her face, crotch, under her arms, and sat thinking with the paper scrunched in her hand. She did not put any depictions of Jesus or saints in the lavatory: that would be sacrilegious, so the walls were bare and there was nothing to look at, less to distract. Her ablutions in here were always done with a modest speed, often, like now, without light. Struggling up and out in the dark, she struck one shin on the door and howled in pain. She had tried to save his soul. She had tried to save him from all the temptations of the eyes. From flesh. She had loved that girl and she was betrayed.

Enid did not cry. It was more a snorting sound, which Annie found contrived. Francis and Annie sat before her like the inquisitors they were, both of them rigid with lack of sympathy.

'The car,' Francis was saying harshly. 'Can you remember when she last used the car?'

Enid coughed, recovered herself. 'The car,' Francis repeated.

'No, I don't remember. Only that she took it when she went. And . . .' The voice, made deliberately girlish and plaintive, trailed away while she wafted a hand in front of her face as though trying to flick away a fly. In a shocking gesture of familiarity, Annie leaned forward, snatched the drifting hand and deposited it back in Enid's lap. The effect was as salutary as a public slap from teacher.

'No. It was all smashed up, I tried to tell her but she wouldn't listen. You know, someone hit it when they came round the corner, they're always doing that, everyone goes so fast. But that man, well, he knew about it being smashed up. I wondered how he did know. I think he said it. I tried to tell her . . .'

'Does he come here in a car himself? The uncle?'

'No, yes. No, not as far as I know, not usually. I asked him, because I thought I'd seen a car before, I mean, when he used to wait outside . . .'

'He used to what?' Annie's voice again, sharp and snappy.

'Wait outside. Walk up and down, with a stick. I didn't know it was the same person then, of course. It was only later when he came, and I thought about the stick. I used to hear it. Anyway, when I asked him about the car he said to mind my own business, but then he said, yes he did have a car, only ever used it at night, when he could park, and on Sundays. He came here once on a Sunday. With his dog. I kept asking him where she was, I was beginning to worry, but when I cried, he made his dog bite me . . .'

'Some uncle,' Francis murmured.

'Ah well,' said Enid, more comfortably. 'I don't know about that, do I? She knew a lot of men. She might have had a lot of . . . uncles.'

'You're a wicked old woman,' said Annie quietly. 'A horrible old bitch. Why didn't you warn her about someone walking up and down outside? You nasty old cow.'

Even Francis was slightly discomfited by the venom in Annie's hissed words and threatening stance, as she leaned forward like a snake about to strike. Enid's composure had mended itself only to dissolve completely and the snorting sound gained a genuine grief. Enid was afraid and did not want anyone to hit her.

'How could I tell her?' she blubbed. 'When I didn't know there was anything wrong? I didn't know that the

282

someone outside, hanging around, was this uncle, how could I? Besides, she wouldn't have listened to me. She never would.'

'Why not tell someone else, then? Like us when we came here, instead of all those lies? The police even?'

'Because she wouldn't ever listen to me. She wouldn't ever listen to me or let me in. She wouldn't let anyone need her and I needed her. I couldn't tell anyone else because it was me broke into her place, just to see. Uncle knew that, but he said it was our secret, so he gave me some money to paint over the paint where I'd made a mess, told me it was my place now, took some of her clothes, pictures and things, squared the landlord, took her post away, told me what to say. I had to, I had to. I couldn't tell that nice policeman it was me after all . . . I couldn't. Could I?'

'No,' said Francis, without meaning to reassure, sorry for her at last, thinking of all his clients and their various justifications for the sudden suspensions of free will. 'No. I suppose you couldn't.' He rose and towered above her, pleasant but menacing.

'Give us the telephone number, then.' Enid shrank back.

'Come on, the number he gave you. Or did he give you a card? He must have done, Enid. He'd have wanted you to get in touch if anything happened, wouldn't he? Like a fire. Like when the police searched, or someone like us coming round and asking a whole lot more questions than we did. Come on, come on, give.' He clicked his fingers while she watched him, mesmerized. Then slowly she got to her feet, went over to her mantelpiece, as heaped with ghastly glass ornaments as the chintzy tables in the room, brought back a card which was laid face down. The only calling card she has, Annie thought maliciously, hardly surprising. By now, Enid had crumpled completely. She looked very old.

'Only I wasn't to phone him,' she said. 'Never. I was to write him a postcard. Or I was to phone his sister, in the evenings. He'd call back next day. There.' She pointed to a second number under the embossed digits of the first. Both Annie and Francis looked at the card as if it might contain the answer to everything.

'The dealer,' Annie murmured. 'The fucking dealer who left messages. The chap who probably bought paintings. The one who took his messages out of her fucking answer-phone. Oh fuck.'

Francis was registering the telephone number with a shock of satisfaction. It was the same as the one he had, the confirmation he needed, together with the address. The very same.

'But I've never phoned,' said Enid sadly, revealing the desert of an entirely uneventful life. 'There's been no need.'

No, thought Francis. No need in nearly a month's absence, no hue and cry, how appallingly, horribly dreadful. They had got what they wanted here. Bullying, pushing, persuading, insulting. Enid remained more than faintly repellent. Annie was set up and ready to go. Her bag swung dangerously and indifferently near the glass ornaments. He watched it with anxiety. She needed taking away. They moved.

'He wanted something else,' Enid volunteered.

'What else?'

'The cat. He wanted me to let him know if no one looked after the cat. He was worried about the cat. I s'pose that's one reason why I never did phone, not even after you came.'

Francis remembered the cat, insolently possessive, but someone else's cat.

'Why should the cat make any difference?'

'It's gone. Went off. Lost. I didn't dare tell him.'

'Thanks for the tea,' said Annie, with a sweetness which reminded Francis of the cloying and sickening taste of saccharine.

In unspoken accord they walked swiftly down the street which had lost all of the summer and most of the autumn clothes which gave it any pretension to dignity. Now the trees were bare, and the houses revealed in faded splendour, big, old, shabby and spacious, made for their occupants' gossip before the success of moving on. With the same unity, they found themselves hailing a taxi at the same moment. Part of the original plan, argued over before they had set out, was to go once again (for the last time, Annie said) down to Elisabeth's flat, but they had not had the heart. The original plan had gone for nothing when Enid had appeared, poking a lizardlike head out of her door, and Annie, with the instinct of a terrier, had pounced on her and shaken her about until all that snorting and confessing began. It was not a pleasant way to spend an evening: both of them were in a state of subdued shock. Francis directed the cab back to his flat. At least there he could vouch for the quality of the wine and the remnants of order. The sense of urgency was again a paralysis. They felt like two people pursued by their own shadows: they needed each other and the rights or wrongs of the needing were irrelevant.

'What have you got to do tomorrow?' she asked wearily, leaning against him as the taxi swayed. It seemed as good a topic as any until a drink could give her a sense of direction. Francis was beginning to notice this aspect of Annie, found it endearing. Anger crackled from her like static electricity: she became vibrant with it, almost incandescent, just as she did with company around her, but afterwards slumped into a kind of formless passivity only one stage short of sleep. He leaned back. It was late. Both seemed to have taken it as read that they could do nothing else significant that evening.

'Tomorrow I've got to be in court, like today but more so. I'm not pretending, not prevaricating, I just have to be there. It's a kid, only a kid, pleading guilty, but it's important. I've been neglecting what I do best. I can't cancel.'

'Maybe we should go there now. We've got the address. Or should we phone this sister first?'

'It's late. Tomorrow. Makes no difference.'

Francis could feel the dust of his own establishment. It hit him like the smell of smoke when he opened the door. Annie did not notice: her priorities were different. She aimed for the fridge and its promise of dry white wine as if she had been in the place every day of her life and knew where everything would be. Elisabeth never liked it here, Francis was thinking. She stayed once or twice and I

286

always had the impression she wanted to be gone, back to her own cave. Or maybe I never made the point of allowing anyone to feel at home, in case they closed in on me. To think I felt I could criticize her for the same.

'Cheers,' said Annie. 'Here's to Enid. May she rot in hell. Along with Uncle. Oh Jesus Christ, I'm tired.'

He did not resent her making so free, nor her failure to comment on his domain, his taste, the choices which illuminated his personality in the form of all those pictures, half of them crooked. He sipped cold white wine, thought of Annie's diminished fire and was glad to see her as she was. What strange, intense fondness had grown out of sparring. Then he picked up the telephone and dialled the first number on the card announcing the elusive existence of Thomas Milton. No reply. Annie watched, drank as if the wine were water. He dialled the number of the quoted sister, whose existence, if believed at all, was equally elusive. She had no face, no stick, no sinister mannerisms: she might be all right. She wasn't.

'You want Thomas?' said a voice. 'You want Thomas? You can have Thomas. Not here. Telephone tomorrow, see? Tomorrow. It's late now, very late.'

So it was. Annie was relieved it was easily late enough to give an excuse for doing nothing more.

'Is there someone with Mr Milton? I was looking for Elisabeth . . .' Francis ventured with a high politeness in his voice which reminded Annie of an intoning priest. It struck her as ridiculous, this particular voice of strained deference. In the background she laughed loudly. 'Aw, come on, Francis,' she muttered and laughed again.

'What do you want with Thomas? He is sleeping. Telephone tomorrow. You've woken me. Go *away* until the morning.'

Maria listened to make sure the voice obeyed. Then she put the phone down, thinking hard. She is not alone like me, this girl. Not what I thought: someone is asking for her and no one would ask for me. He is doing something very wrong, my Thomas. If other people knew, it must be so. If a message came from the outside world in the middle of the night, there must be something wrong and the wrath of God was calling down the line. Tomorrow, tomorrow, tomorrow. Someone with him? they asked. In what sense? Laughing, they were laughing at something they knew. Maria was hesitant, concerned; hot and sweating all over again, she went to the bathroom. Elisabeth: that name, synonymous with betrayal.

Elisabeth vomited three times, and slept because her body would allow nothing else after the last reflection of her face in the mirror had shown a thinner self: cadaverous some-how, the form of her shrunk to fit the dimensions of the dress which would not have fitted ten days before. The last thought before the hazy, sickening sleep with that fruity, putrid taste of brandy in her mouth, was the dog lying on silk like some fat, decadent prince.

Some time before dawn, Thomas went to find the dress. He called it a robe for the house, nothing fancier than that, a housecoat. The robe, so similar in colour to the one worn by the madonna of the painting, was sticky with Butler's saliva. A few other mild excretions: he was jealous of his master and he had not liked the smell. His claws needed clipping: they had shredded the material of the bodice, involuntarily, not out of malice, as he tried to make a nest in there, a resting place for his imperfect form.

Thomas dragged the robe away. He smoothed the crumpled silk with his hand, hung it over his arm and carried it back to his room. Once there, he folded it carefully, with difficulty laid it on the end of his spartan bed, and watched as if it might move, until his eyes, too, closed.

CHAPTER FOURTEEN

'Are we being silly? I don't know about you. I don't know much, as it happens. I don't have a conscience about this, either. Not now. Is it like two people being able to talk openly about a friend, as critically as they want, provided they both know they love the friend? Why don't I feel bad about this? I don't know what you think. Listen, we have to go there today, whatever happens, we have to go there and not be put off. We're the only ones looking, you know, absolutely the only ones and we shouldn't have wasted time. After I've been to court, can you . . . can we . . . go and find her? Annie, are you awake? Annie, you're a lovely lover, but you know why we're here, don't you? We've still got to find her. You are awake, aren't you?'

From the depths of his hard bed came an unselfconscious groan, choked on the beginnings of a yawn. Stretching like a cat, Annie emerged from beneath his duvet, all head and collarbones, thin shoulders held together with wire, awake, unrepentant.

'"Lovely lover". Thanks for that. But oh God, not conscience again. I can't stand it. Listen, don't you dare apologize to me, it's so condescending. I wanted to be here: it's the story of my fucking life. Wanted and not wanted. Bit like our Elisabeth, isn't it, but different. Pity I like you. Pity I've come to be so fond of her. Is it morning?'

'Yes, it's morning. I've got to go soon.'

'I suppose you do. So do I. Got a clean shirt, have you?'

'Yes.'

'You would, I suppose. Christ, this bed's hard. Why do you have a bed this hard?'

'I don't know. Why's yours so soft?'

'Soft, like me. It's in the hormones, can't help myself. Soft. I need my soft head examined.' She grinned, ever more catlike, amazingly talkative. 'For Christ's sake, this isn't a confessional. Look, we were both frightened: we *are* frightened. So we go to bed together, so what? I wanted to get laid and you wanted to make up for last time, which you did, thank you. And we both love Elisabeth and nothing's altered. Right?'

He put his arms around her thinness. Her face, puffed and sleepy, was the same challenging face, which Francis had never liked or trusted as much as he did now. He hugged her with brief sincerity, feeling the strength of her bones. Annie pulled the duvet round herself like a nest. He was momentarily amazed to have made love so thoroughly with so little confusion, and no, there was no conscience, simply a sense of extra strength.

'She never came here, you know,' he said softly. It was almost true but still a lie, one he considered necessary. Annie nodded. She had needed him to tell her that and did not much care if it was accurate.

'Can I let myself out? What time is it? Where do we meet then? Listen, what are you saying? Of course none of this makes any difference, it never did, but I liked it and we both needed it, so there. Course we've got to go and find Uncle today and see what gives. Give us a time and place. This afternoon, did you say?' She yawned again. He paused, looking and smiling, feeling anxious but contented.

'Go on,' she said. 'I know you only live here, but fuck off. You talk too much.'

They agreed that they would meet at Westminster Cathedral at three o'clock. Not the abbey with all the buried poets, but the cathedral with its priests and smaller crowds of fervent tourists. By the McDonald's, Francis said. A strange adjunct to a pigeon-covered square through which the faithful trod to a modern basilica. Yes, she knew where he meant, exactly. There were all those streets full of mansion flats just behind. She might go inside and pray first, she joked, as if praying for her own soul was not as alien to her as priests were, and anyone else who purported to direct the lives of others. Yes, yes, she knew where he meant, now go, now, please.

After he had left, Annie abandoned her nest. In the bathroom she scrubbed at her body and examined a face not improved by the ministrations of soap and water in the absence of her usual battery of cleansers, toners, moisturizers. None of these things in an austere bathroom like this. None, either, in Elisabeth's place, she recalled, but then Elisabeth would emerge with the face of a wise angel, not the sharp chin and spiky hair which announced the devil in herself. Just wanted to be fucked? Some people believe anything. No she hadn't: she'd wanted much more than that, but she was only a pragmatist and took what she could.

Annie whistled. 'I'm on your territory, aren't I, angel?' she said. 'Never mind, I'm going soon, leaving no souvenirs. He just wanted somebody, and so did I. Call it dutch courage, we aren't giving up on you. You just united us, body, but not soul. You can have him back when we find you. And I'm sorry for the delay, but I needed to find out. What he would really be like. He's OK. Bit young for me, but OK.'

In the kitchen there were only dry biscuits, coffee and a carton of dead milk. Better go home for breakfast. Before that, she wandered through the space of Francis's flat, straightening all the pictures on the walls, lovingly. She was not sorry, she was not even disturbed: she felt buoyant. A little loving, that was what it had been: a little genuine loving. Now she knew what it was, this thing which so moved the souls of others, she would know how to recognize it again. Not in the man, whoever he was; in herself.

Breakfast. The thought repelled as much as the day. Elisabeth had not noticed, but registered now, how eating of all kinds seemed to have fallen out of fashion in this strange establishment which was her prison. How she and Thomas had come in the last three days to forage separately in the kitchen while the other's back was turned. Bread and cheese for her, eaten on the run back to her studio; latterly, only the cheese. Which went part of the way to explain this hollow sickness, a condition with more to it than an indiscriminate consumption of alcohol vomited away in disgust.

Something must be resolved. There was light sneaking from behind her curtains like a temptress, but she was weak. When she rolled from her bed, her legs felt woolly, and the lukewarm water of the shower hit like needles as she drenched her hair in an effort to wash away that pervasive scent of shame, disgust, humiliation. The hostage temperament of guilty imprisonment. It was early, the day still half formed, her mind feeling the infancy of the light and her thoughts. without direction. There was something she must do, something to bring matters to a head, the combined sickness of the house. Thomas had not wanted a lover; she might have known. He had never wanted a lover: he had wanted a spectacle. He might not know what he wanted. Except that it was some vision of beauty which he would be forced to ruin. Then so he must. And if it was her, then at least she would have done what she was compelled to do and honoured something. She would honour the madonna if she honoured nothing and no one else.

In the studio room, she played with the tasselled ropes of the high windows, tugging without thinking to allow air into the room. She had worked in here long and hard yesterday. The continuing urgency overcame the sickness. The madonna was on the easel, safe. She had wondered about that, wondered if she would still be safe, this siren on canvas, now that she was revealed. It was not what he wanted: the original madonna was what he had wanted and that madonna had changed. The changes were not extensive, but they were radical. The first thing which Elisabeth saw this morning was the ultramarine of the gown, that silken taffeta bunched gown, twisted as the woman turned her stupendous face. The skirts were as full as ever, liquid as the sea, but the bodice had shrunk in the preceding days, offered little protection now.

But Victorians did have dresses like these. There was nothing strange, only you did not quite expect to be able to change the garments in a painting as you might alter a model's. Victorian fashions were made to last: if you had a ball gown with a daring dé*colletage* for your first dance, it could and would be altered to include a fichu of lace up to the chin or a new piece of material serving the same purpose. Sleeves could be made to hook into shoulders which had been blissfully bare, while skirts could be taken up and down, flounced to reveal a different colour of petticoat. They did not expect their finery to expire with the demands of climate and fashion; they expected it to last in dozens of variations, until, as it rarely did, the stuff decayed. They were not feckless: could mourn, walk, talk, receive, in one dress; laugh, wed, dance, dine, preside after dark in another. How easy. No need for a lecture to explain this painting, Elisabeth thought. I know all that. I knew all that when I wore the gown last night, stuffed as I was with all the envy in the world, for the chance to wear something half as beautiful, but not with the expectation that I should wear it again and again and again . . . I only mention it, because you have to see, Thomas, anyone, whoever you are, that there are possible explanations concerning the madonna you might not otherwise be able to follow.

You see, she was not dressed thus when she was first painted. I uncovered for you the redone neck of her dress and took away those vulgar sapphires which clutched so oddly to her throat, lying where a necklace could not quite lie. I know about these things, I have looked, I have seen, although I have never worn myself the necklaces other people try around the antique stalls. At first, the neck of the dress revealed only that slender stem encircled by those bright sapphires, but they were the wrong blue: bangkok sapphires, not pale blue, but dyed to make them artificially, durably darker. Now, you do not have coloured gems of a different blue to go with your best, ultramarine, silk-lined-with-silk dress, the one which might have to last you for years . . . This was not a lady unused to thrift: we understood each other. At second glance she wore that demure pendant to go with the little earrings, but by then, only because I had looked at those colours for so long, I knew that the whole of the top of the bodice was wrong. So skilfully wrong it was difficult to detect. Beautifully done, and not long after the thing was first painted, probably by the same artist with almost the same palette, within a year or so, but not with quite the same pigment. A different lapis lazuli, lumpier, paler, a slightly cheaper alternative. Maybe he, too, resented these changes and left his clues. I confess that I have not undressed this lady lightly. It was because I felt she was dressed as she wished to be for her portrait, and if she later changed her mind, or her keeper changed it for her because he wanted her effigy hung in the dining room rather than the bedroom, that was up to her. She might even have been a kept woman who became a kept wife, but she was the woman first. But I did want to get back to the way she was when the artist first put brush to his pristine canvas, and saw her as she was. Before he was ever called back to save her from disrepute, he or the brother artist who could paint in exactly the same way . . .

There was so much *less* dress to the original. I did not detect that from the craquelure, those crazy cracks which come with age, when the paint breathes and dries like a human skin. I guessed more from the colour and a little from the lumps and bumps which betrayed a thicker surface where there was varnish not of the same source, things you guess through your fingertips. Then there was the impasto round her head, where he had introduced an extra layer of light to soften her and hide the fact that her coiffed hair had been untidier at first. The artist spruced her up, and with all this removed, all these optional extras, what is now on the canvas is not a madonna, not an elegant matron leaning forward with some entreaty to a child, but a woman with her handsome bosom curving forth over the undone bodice of her dress, her hair slightly wild, beckoning some man back into the circle of her arms, back into her bed. Not a chaste wife, but a mistress.

Perhaps, Elisabeth thought, I should have let well alone.

Little wonder this artist was also paid to hide his name in the draperies behind the chair. There was nothing anonymous about her: it was obvious what generous manner of woman she was and who had painted her, but it was too late now, far too late to do anything but admire. Elisabeth had kept this canvas turned to the wall, pretended to work on the others, and now all there was left to do was revarnish completely, to protect and make the colours of this earthly creature glow and shine, reveal the density of her glory, make her perfect for Thomas's admiration and destruction. There was nothing else Elisabeth needed to do and nothing else she could do, so while the light outside was still milky, and the busy world still half dead, she began to varnish. Precisely, deftly but swiftly to provoke the crisis.

When Thomas woke, for the tenth time but after the longest and darkest sleep, he could remember few of the nightmares, only the sensations and panics of his dreams. They were the repeated sensations of the worst, most terrifying episodes of his life, the sharp end of the terror, not the dead end of all the realizations which followed, when he looked in a mirror once to see how he appeared as a man without an eye, or when he woke, the other time after the stroke, to discover he was still alive, not in pain, but speechless, to all intents a worthless lump of man. The ultramarine dress lay across his chest: twice in the night, after he had wept his way to bed with that diminished garment, he had woken to find it wrapped round his throat, as if the garment crept with a life all of its own and forced itself into the intimacy he had refused from Elisabeth herself. On the first occasion he awoke to a sensation of total blindness that reminded him of when the boys had taken out his eye; he pulled off the silk cloth and screamed. When the dress was in his mouth the second time, he recalled the dumbness, and when he woke in the morning, with the dress draped over the bottom of his bed, that was still what he recalled.

Thomas thought, in a rare moment of clear thinking, that he might have become as anonymous as he was because he was so used to no one listening. Ugly persons listened, yes; people from whom he was buying things, yes: they looked into his eyes and tabulated the amount of attention they would have to give, but nothing even roughly similar to that slavish affection he had received from a beautiful child in a dying village. Someone who did not find ridiculous the aspirations of a plain little man to create, or acquire, things of beauty. The aspirations of the same but half-crippled man to have about himself a woman of beauty would be viewed as obscene. Oh yes, that was another feature of his appearance and diminished ability to make demands on his world. He was not allowed to despise those who were also ugly, or even dislike them: he was supposed to join with them, to play their kind of games and he could not. He was supposed to empathize with Maria and he could not: he was simply bound to her in a barbaric way. He was supposed to adopt, along with the preternaturally ugly, the solace of religion and he despised it in every shape or form. Tore down his parents' icons instead, slandered Maria's saints. Bitterness reared with the same old fury.

Oh, Elisabeth, why can't I talk to you? Listen, all will be

well if you will only listen. Slowly, surely, the optimism always latent in him renewed itself. Listen, look at me if you can. All right, I am holding you captive, but there is more to all this. Please let me explain how I do my best and get it wrong. I did want, I do want and can only have . . . You cannot go yet, not under these misapprehensions, you cannot: you think worse now of me than I could ever have imagined. You cannot go until you begin to understand how I have to live. Suddenly it was easy. Of course she would understand.

Thomas made his toilet. He was in a hurry. The sleep after dawn, when the body finally gives up the tussle with wakefulness, was the harshest, deepest sleep of all: he was late and clumsy. Blood flowed from his chin. Maria would be coming upstairs in a minute. Could he send her away for today? No, he could not. He would promise her church next Sunday, tell her to be quiet and frighten her, which had always worked. Tell her to finish the cleaning, get her to go out for a long, long walk with the dog to underline the point. Then she would be fine while he went out to shop for Elisabeth, set the scene for his confessions. When he shopped, he would leave behind Butler, this foul, snotty, terrible dog he was supposed to love, like he was supposed to love her, this sister, with her blackmailing devotion to their dual, immortal souls.

He mopped the blood from the one-handed shaving, put on a clean shirt, clean trousers, did not have the time it took to manage a tie – dear God, it was nearly eleven o'clock, only minutes to spare. He blundered down the corridor with a swatch of soft toilet paper to his chin, saw the light signalling Maria's presence outside. Opening the door, he could feel his voice descending to a hiss.

'Get in there!' Pointing to the kitchen. 'Clean up. No, clean up later . . . Are you all right? Good. Take the dog out sooner rather than later, keep him out for at least an hour, he needs it. He's bursting and I'm busy, do you hear? I want to shop this afternoon. You can finish the other rooms then. Please do as you're told.'

She nodded, the radiant, crooked smile fading. Stepped into the kitchen, watched him walk towards the studio room. I do not like this, Maria thought. I know a thing or two, maybe three. Thomas knocked on the door. It had been closed of late, and since dumbness was not new to either of them, he had not intruded. At the moment, cheered that the blood had ceased to flow on his chin, he had a plan, and the one talent he thought he could count on was planning. Planning, the thought of any kind of action, made him high. He had forgotten that the plans took on a life of their own and, like some hermaphrodite, needed no input in order to reproduce other plans, fledgling plots, of which this was one. A special dinner, an occasion for speech (he forgot Elisabeth's relative lack of interest in food). Thomas did not wait for an invitation before he marched in. On the easel was the madonna, part of her shining with new varnish, part of her dry. The light fell on her, leaving her half obscured. Those major parts, unvarnished, which still did not reflect, were invisible until anyone came close: the light disguised her cunningly.

'Listen, Elisabeth. Listen, I do not care about finishing

the paintings, *I do not care*, do you hear me? But you can't go yet.'

He is lying, she thought, it makes his voice loud: he cannot come close and hides the lie by making such a show of not looking, but the light in here hurts his tired eye. Thomas never once turned to the depiction on the easel; he looked only into Elisabeth's similar face. He had something to say: his face was contorted with the effort.

'I don't even care about me, but the least I can do, before you go . . .' – he paused for effect – 'before you go, when you go, soon, I think, is to ask you, oh, I don't quite know what . . . ask you, ask . . . to listen. Someone must. So you must stay, for today. If you please. I'm going to shop for supper. Something delicious. You don't eat enough. Don't talk to Maria when she gets back with Butler. She does talk a lot of nonsense, you know, really.'

Despite the pomposity of the 'if you please' and the smile which split his pudgy face, his intensity, together with his lack of tie, the blotted remnants of blood on his chin like battered mosquitoes, the aspect of this little man who looked both harried and somehow hideously pleased with himself, was more frightening than all his disarming manners. Once buoyed with the excitement of self-deluding optimism, Thomas could excite neither pity nor guilt. He looked immune; he looked demonic. The demon pixie, planning his errands to buy poison.

Elisabeth stood dumbly. She had stood for more than three hours now: the light and the sheen and the smell of the varnish were spinning themselves into sugar before her eyes.

302

'Go?' she said. 'Can I go?'

'Not yet,' he said firmly, the smile stretched over his teeth in a rictus. 'Not yet. Listen, I have things to do today.' His mind was busy, his eye registering neither what was on the easel nor the expression on her face. He spied instead the shining cleanliness of her hair, caught up in combs at each side into damp but glorious colour as she retreated before his advance. I was wrong about buying her a dress, he was thinking, completely wrong. Why does she need such things? They give her all the wrong ideas. I shall buy her something else to redeem that mistake and then I shall be able to explain. Something for her hair, less suggestive, shoes, perhaps, or some tool of the trade, a set of brushes, something she will take and use, make her see I would never . . . His nose wrinkled: there was a strong smell in the room, despite the open windows above their heads, and the strength of the smell distracted him momentarily.

'Were they any good, those paints I bought you the other day?' They had come in with the other gifts, or was it before? She could not remember. Maria had played with them. When was that? A long time ago.

'No,' she said quietly. 'No, but never mind. When can I go?'

He was disappointed. Somehow he had made himself believe that she would be infected with his cheerfulness, but there she was backing away, and she did not even like his paints. No more paints, then: that would not be today's gift. Something else.

'Not yet, please listen, you cannot go quite yet, but

soon. I'll leave you in peace now.' He was planning furiously, talking half to himself. 'Ye-e-s, let's see . . . Maria takes out dog, then I'll go out, about noon . . .'

'No! You cannot let Maria take him out, you can't do that, Thomas, after what happened. Not after her being bitten, Thomas. Please. I'll take the dog, if you like.'

She said it without thinking, but Thomas stopped, sorrowed, although not downcast, by the blatant cunning of this ploy. It dampened his enthusiasm, but only for a second. He felt he could afford to overlook it.

'Maria will be fine,' he promised stiffly. 'Please be patient. We'll eat about six this evening. I'll call for you.' He made it sound as if he would be coming from the other end of town. Elisabeth could only nod, feeling the sheer exhaustion of his presence, weak with hunger, the varnish smell and these sudden changes in his demeanour. Thomas closed the door behind him.

Doors. The only sound which penetrated anywhere, except occasional murmurings of conversation. Doors clicking shut were the only herald of human activity. Elisabeth sat in one of the armchairs and closed her eyes. The light was stronger: opening her eyes, she could see the window ropes swinging in the breeze she had let into the room, the tassels blurred. Maria, she was thinking. I must do something about Maria, cannot let her stay as a tortured servant here, whatever happens to me. I don't believe a word he says, about me being free to go, free to do anything. She closed her eyes again in a wave of dizzy nausea. With that acuteness of hearing which only came when she was not looking she registered the fact that doors were slamming, an epilogue to raised voices. First the kitchen door, then the outer door, then the softer sound of Thomas's bedroom door, then silence. Peering into the corridor, she saw that Thomas had retreated. Maria, Butler and his leash were gone. A tiptoe dash into the kitchen, then she was foraging for coffee and a lump of dry, stale bread to still the specks dancing in front of her eyes, hoping that Maria would come back soon, unscathed. How selfish I am: I must not think only of myself, I hope she is safe. And then because it was imperative to finish, she went back to the varnish. The madonna called for her final touch. Whatever else happened today, something had to be achieved.

It might have been two or three o'clock, with pauses and dreamings and long interludes when the applying of the varnish consumed her whole concentration. Careful now, careful: go with the direction of the paint, follow the brush-strokes made by the artist or you do not cover every millimetre of surface. Not working from top to bottom, but from the centre to the outside as the artist had done with his final layers, until all was covered and all was revealed. The last portion was so absorbing, Elisabeth did not hear the further, softer, opening and closing of doors until, with the canvas complete, she stood back from it, adjusting the easel to the light to examine the surface better.

This time there was merely a hint of noise: they had not spoken as one came out and the other in. It was not an empty silence, but a shuffling silence, no human voice, but

Butler sniffing at the door and the consciousness of some-one else sniffing with an almost pleasurable disgust.

They had returned to their mutual instinct for the other's comings and goings, Maria and Thomas, so that this time, when she had demanded entry, coming back with the dog, he had been waiting for her, so impatient was he to be gone himself. In the meantime, he had left his room and quietly done his ineffectual best to tidy the living room where he had sat last evening, fiddling with duster and damp cloth the easier to pass time. He read the paper which came in with Maria in the morning, planning, planning, writing list after list of what to do, what to say and how to say it. When the door light showed (and he was checking every minute), he let her in quickly. 'Late, Maria, late, where have you been, two-thirty, too bad.' But the voice was very soft as if he were speaking secrets, so she scored no victory in her tardiness. He had one of his sticks and a shopping bag in hand, looked cheerful, held the door open for her, did not say anything else, but slipped outside in the same breath.

Maria was startlingly, alarmingly angry. Her ankles hurt after the walk with the docile dog, a dull ache like a for-gotten bruise knocked into life. She had guessed what went on, became more sure, but still looked for confirmation. There was his behaviour when she had arrived this morn-ing, ordering her into the kitchen while he talked in secret to Elisabeth; the same dismissive cheerfulness of him now, the antics of a boy who had just been given a prize, the benign and smug face he wore when he was naughty. She

306

paddled down the corridor, dropping Butler's lead, poked her head, lizardlike, into the living room and stopped. So, cleared up in here, had he? Taken away glasses, messes, sticky things which suggested drink and no food, straightened rumpled rugs, taken trouble to hide some orgy? The level in the decanters was low, there was stickiness on the floor like a snail trail. Maria moved out of there quickly, hurried to Thomas's room. The same tidiness, the bed carefully made, the breeze running strong from the window, disturbing the fanlike collar of a brilliant silk robe which lay on the end of the bed. Maria moved slowly towards the garment.

Brilliant, virginal blue, like the robe on the madonna, the pristine and pure blues which always decked her little pictures of the mother of God, Mary with the roses round her feet, with her blues cascading from her shoulders as her arms were held forth in blessing, revealing the innocence of the white robe underneath. Maria touched the material, instantly warm as if it had just come from contact with skin. Then she held it aloft. There were moisture stains on the front: the unbuttoned bodice was torn, partially ripped in several places as if by fingernails. Maria remembered the care Thomas took with his hands, could almost hear the small sounds of fine fabric tearing. She did not drop the garment as the truth burst, but flung it from her as a thing diseased, watched it land with arms outspread on the pillow of the bed. The bodice was covered, as if ashamed. She stood and looked, expecting the thing to move. From a great distance, she heard her name called.

'Maria! Are you there? Maria, where are you? Are you

all right?' Maria darted from bed to door. Elisabeth was running towards her with arms outstretched, ready for an embrace, the voice light with welcome and a wrapping of relief. For a moment Maria wanted to smile, feel arms around her in that rare luxury of being touched, but she remembered where those arms had been, what sins of the flesh they contained along with their blood and bones. She could not ever receive that offered warmth, flying towards where she stood with her fists clenched.

'No!' she shrieked. 'Get away from me! Get away!' Elisabeth's hands were on Maria's shoulders. Maria pulled them away, stepped back.

'Maria? Are you all right? Are you hurt? What's the matter? Maria, look at me, look at me . . .'

But Maria was twisting her head away to avoid the contamination of a glance. A stain of bright red colour rose through her face. Her hands were clenched white.

'What is it? Maria, look at me, please,' Elisabeth repeated. 'Please.'

'No.' Then, with a cunning which surprised herself, Maria forced a kind of gentler resignation into her voice. It was a slurred voice, difficult to follow.

'No Not today. Thomas says you must work today, and so must I. Be good, Miss Elisabeth. We must be good for today.' Elaborately, Maria put her fingers to her lips. It took a little time to say all this. Maria was proud of herself, but Elisabeth turned paler, her olive skin a shiny sallow. She dropped her arms and let Maria stalk past her without ever once catching her eye. Butler followed after her. Elisabeth hesitated, fought the desire to go after her, to say, Look, we are both in the same boat, you must trust me. She thought of what harm she might do if she won her plea for a return to their friendlier conspiracy, the partnership which had seemed to exist. She sensed that Maria had been threatened: if she were to make her go against some explicit order of Thomas, delivered in a raised voice that morning, might she not detach the woman from her small supply of survival instinct? Might she not cause, as she had before, more bites, more dangers? Elisabeth felt she owed Maria more than that, and, besides, the defection of her one and only ally, the one source of hope and simple affection, hurt with a winding pain. It doubled her like a punch: the coffee and dry bread rose like a sluggish, dirty tide. Hand over mouth, she rushed through Thomas's room into the *en suite* bathroom, leaned over his basin, heaving.

Weak, very, weak, the sweet taste of sherry suddenly foremost. She sat in there for what seemed a long time, holding down the rising threat of panic. Minutes ticked by with the specking in front of her eyes, while she wished Maria would come back, if only to tell her to keep to her own quarters, anything for the comfort of conversation. Speak to me, whatever the words. Look at me, look at me as if I were not alien, please, I care for you. Then thinking with the crystal clarity which came with the cold in here, she lifted her head and went back to his bedroom.

Dully, she looked at the ultramarine robe flung to the top of the bed, saw it without shock, but the same onset of panic which had paralysed her before. She sat on the bed and touched the robe, turning it over and seeing the marks of claws. Oh, Thomas, destructive Thomas, he could not even leave a dress alone. Was the perfection of the inanimate always too much for him? How long would the madonna have, or herself, unless she were somehow scarred? Then clarity returned in its strange snatches and, staggering like a drunk, she moved over to the dressing room. There was a series of fast-moving thoughts: he might have hidden the telephone, the bathroom, look there; it must be somewhere, it was here once, by his bed, I must phone; he cannot have thrown it away. Then she felt the mesmerizing draw of those paintings without eyes, as if only the sight of paintings could give her courage. She knew by instinct she was right about the bathroom, but she still delayed and stayed by the cupboard.

They were there, the eyeless ones, this time in front of the others. Perhaps Thomas liked to remind himself of what he had done: perhaps it was the thrill of his tiny existence, the thrill denied by sexual contact or love or any equivalent, even friendship. She gazed at the first, the alternative madonna by the same hand, another portrait, modest but not saintly, the eyes stabbed out of existence with repeated, savagely precise thrusts. And still on the floor, as she had seen the first time and forgotten to notice on the second, a duster, a shred of bandage.

She placed a little finger inside an eye. The holes. Not made with a swordstick, surely, lethal though they were? How then? With Thomas's less than steady balance sometimes, he would have to stand so far away from the dreadful task that he would take the risk of inaccuracy.

Were these not the inflictions of a smaller blade, the vicious stabbing of close quarters, much too precise for Thomas's one good hand? Squatting on her haunches in front of this disfigured beauty, Elisabeth lost her bearings for a minute. Wondering how it was that someone, even with the strength of Thomas, could have held down the painting while he struck at it with such precision and force. How very nearly impossible he should do that all on his own. Or with his disablement, the useless arm and the less than focused eyes, at all. The clarity in her mind was that of a person suddenly seeing life under water: the clarity of someone not quite drunk, on the first tier of drugs, the perception which leads to confusion, so blinding in its conclusions. She thought of the vulnerable, taunting, beseeching, sinful madonna on her easel in the studio, freshly shone with varnish, and she ran.

CHAPTER FIFTEEN

Annie waited outside Westminster Cathedral. She was as clean and neat as she could make herself in black leggings, stiff tan cotton shirt and heavy woollen jacket, also black. She looked efficient in a masculine way, betrayed only by the high-heeled boots hiding her thin calves as she strode up and down, competent for nothing but fooling the world that she was far fiercer than she felt. It was the uniform of movement, striding about, an ample disguise for the shivering soul within, where anger flickered and faded into a profound irritation, first because she was early, and secondly because Francis was late. The day was sharp November, full of brilliantly brief appearances from a sun abruptly masked by black cloud, Annie noticed, although rarely an observer of anything as irrelevant as weather. In the meantime, the aggression which made her laugh, sing, dance and shout stored up a residue until he arrived, melted slightly when he appeared, as she was afraid it always would, but the trick was not to let it show. That way lay madness, so she flexed the cold muscles and scowled.

'You said three o'clock.'

'I know I said three. I'm late. I'm sorry. Is that enough? I had to stay, I thought it would be sooner, but he went to prison, my client. I had to talk to him, I'm sorry.'

'You missed a slice of life here, I'm telling you.' Annie led the way, talking to hide the fact that she had not liked the waiting, had actually been afraid, not a physical fear but an alienation. In the course of twenty minutes, she had seen a weekday wedding, hats and all, spilling out of the cathedral in the wake of a smattering of tourists armed with bags, others gawping as they sat in the cold and ate their hamburgers. The newly-weds were importuned by the itinerant population of the square, whose sleeping bags and cardboard arrangements littered the alcoves of the nearby shops. These were frisky to the point of desperation in the afternoon, too long after the hostels closed for business in the morning and too many hours before they opened. Winter was cruel, Annie thought, not uninterested as three of the itinerants began to fight, swaying with drunken malice, slugging with ugly, dizzied blows and roaring threats until a policeman came and parted them. Each melted, muttering, into the corners of a dirty square suddenly vast and sinister in their absence. The edge is near, all life lived on a precipice. Annie could not admit her fear. Where will Elisabeth go if we find her? What is the release if she is captive? Back to her flat and her interrupted life? Stay with her captor? She had better do that than ever join these, and yet Annie could see her here,

313

picking up her bedding and moving on at the first sign of conflict, a city refugee with no lineage and no defences. She shuddered, wanted to put her arm through that of Francis, who looked, in his suit and winter coat, a fortress.

'Prison, you said?' she questioned over her shoulder, still leading the way and wishing he would go first. 'Poor sod. What for?'

'Grievous bodily harm,' said Francis.

'How grievous?'

Francis stopped, a spasm of vicarious pain on his face, not echoed by the cynical, professional shrug of his shoulders. 'Oh, he threw ammonia at someone, nearly blinded him.'

'Nice friends you have.'

He stopped. 'No, I have no friends.' The remark felt like a blow: it made her angrier than all the waiting. He grinned to defuse the effect he did not guess. 'Present company excepted, of course.' The words were sincere, as far as he could be in his state of nervousness, but they sounded like an afterthought. Annie mimicked his shrug and walked on.

They were halfway down an avenue of colossal mansion flats. 'Next turn right,' said Annie tensely, who had looked up the route they should take in her *A to Z*. It had been something to do.

'I know,' said Francis. 'I looked, too.'

There were such dense, such silent streets. Aberdale Mansions, Churchill Mansions, the environs of Westminster and the Houses of Parliament, blocks of flats which had

314

fallen out of fashion and crept back in, built to a scale which was expensive to maintain, inhabited by foreign residents, *pied-à-terre* owners, the right honourable member for such and such, or his mistress, people who only lived anywhere half the time. The mansions all had the same red brick, the same stucco round their huge doors, the same eccentric numbering: a row of them resembled a layer cake sandwiched with the uniform cream of their windows and useless balconies. It was cooler in the valleys made by these dwellings: cold and calm. Grafted on the massive doors of two such blocks Francis saw the twinkling symbols of security: a video entryphone, a combination lock. The building they sought would be the same, locked and barred: he could feel it in his bones, hear the echo of distant closing doors.

'I don't know what we're worried about,' he said flatly. 'All wound up like this. We won't be able to get in.'

Annie stopped, swung her great satchel bag in front of her, rummaged in it for cigarette and lighter before moving on.

'So what? We'll wait. Oh Christ, look.'

She swung round to face him, jerking her thumb over her shoulder, pulling on the cigarette as if it were a source of life. 'Look,' she hissed. 'Him coming up the road. Behind me, twenty yards down.' Francis looked. There was a sole figure walking from the opposite direction, carrying a carrier bag, along with a cane. Walking up the street in his dark glasses, melting into one of the massive front doors. Francis wanted to run towards the man. Annie sensed it, put a warning hand on his arm.

315

'Don't,' she hissed, the more cautious for once. 'Just don't. It might not be him. You ring the bell, just like anyone else.' When they found the right door, the door they guessed he had entered, they found it was double-fronted with glass panels in the upper half. Through this door, painted black, they could gaze into a hallway with stairs curling out of sight. The numbers of the apartments were painted in gold on a black background alongside the battery of bells for fifteen separate residences. Francis looked up, thinking to himself that magnificence was not homely. Annie, bolder, bent forward on the top step after pressing a number on the elaborate entryphone system drew no response, peered rudely into the hall.

'We'll wait,' she said. 'Won't we?' Francis was silent. He wished he had run when he had wanted to run. His own anxiety, fuelled by Annie's twitchiness and then subdued by her, curdled into the mixture which makes men want to fight.

The sight of the madonna on the easel seemed to disturb Butler. Scurrying back to the kitchen in a state of hopeless, quavering hatred, Maria did what she always did when she felt like this and busied herself with the necessary, put out Butler's food hours early, slopped water into his bowl. The door of the room where she had so often spied Elisabeth working like an angel with an aura round her hair, quiet, industrious, the very soul of virtue, the door which had led on to the most wonderful presence of that virgin mother on her easel, had been closed latterly, barring Maria's silent presence, and it was only with thinking about it that she had begun to mind. Rushing past now, Maria did not notice how Elisabeth, in her own headlong rush to meet and greet, had burst out and left the door open; but if Maria did not stop, Butler did. He went in, saw with his fuddled, elderly eyes some great focus of light, a shining, threatening plane angled to face the door. Some canine instinct suppressed the barking: the threat was not moving. He stood with the hackles forming ridges along his spine and his throat full of a slow, heavy rumbling. Yards away, in the kitchen, Maria was wrinkling her nose in distaste as she spooned his tinned food into his tin bowl, noticing, only with the last spoonful, his absence. She was, in her perverse way, using the same spoon she used to scrape up the leftovers of all those frozen meals to eat herself; she stood with the implement in her hand, wondering why the dog was not there and salivating. With the refinement of instinct they sometimes had for each other, she caught the vibrations of his mood and his sound, the same way she tried, had tried for years, to do with her brother.

Leaving the spoon, Maria stamped back out into the corridor, sensing another terrible rejection. Perhaps the hated dog was siding with the new enemy, but there was silence in the corridor, where the carpet was flawed with footprints. She saw Butler backing out of the studio room as if afraid, the light streaming from it as the clouds outside suddenly parted to reveal a ray of shifty sunlight which glowed and faded. Enough for Maria to see from the door the smile on the face of the painting, catch from the brilliant, temporary glow, the skin of the bosom and the naked neck, the eclipsing of the halo round the head and the aura of flesh and dreadful wickedness. The madonna was defaced, stripped of all purity, her eyes bright with temptation: eyes which were already damned but still luring some other down all those well-worn routes to hell, the wide roads, not the narrow paths strewn with thorns. The eyes of the madonna, no longer glazed with Maria's interpretation of holiness, but like all the other eyes; they challenged and pleaded, lustrous with their own perfection and all the threat such perfection implied. The madonna was all the temptations of the flesh, thrusting her own into the nearest hand, asking it to curl inside that bodice and knead the swollen nipples. Beside the canvas on a chair, well below the point of that half-bare breast and unbuttoned bodice, lay Elisabeth's tools, palette, palette knife, all those paints in tubes which Thomas had bought to tempt, perhaps even to seduce. And this, it seemed, along with other gifts, was what they had done, seduced. Both of them, the madonna and the girl, blasphemers of the saints. Of all that she had seen, this was the most hateful and hideous sight, a defacement of what she had loved as well as revered, and the rage exploded.

Maria was looking for a knife. Any knife. In that mushrooming of existing fury, she could not uproot herself from the site of this outrage to go away and seek a better tool for the task, a pointed stick, or even search for the knife she had put in her pocket this morning in some half-formed precaution of self-defence. Then the palette knife was in her hand punching towards the smiling face, the wooden handle held firmly in her fist. But the knife stuck

318

to the canvas, skidded first on wet varnish, proved futile: there was no edge to this blade. Other blades might achieve as little. Maria could not think clearly: there was none of her former precision, no ritual in this destruction. Her glance lit on the tubes of paint; her shaking hands were still able to unscrew the cap of something brilliant red, not for the colour but because it was nearest. It was a large tube; she had handled it before, awkwardly. The paint inside was viscous and smooth as it blurted into the palm of her hand and was smeared, from there, over the mouth of the non-virginal face. The other handful was next, over the nostrils to stop them breathing, but the paint lay on the surface like an insult, a thin disguise, more of it on Maria's own skin, in her fingers, the smell in her nostrils. She applied the nozzle of the red tube straight against the face. All gone. Seizing another tube, yellow, she added that, spread it all round with the palette knife. Bitch, bitch, bitch. Mother of God, do not have mercy on this sinner. The red danced before her eyes, mixed with the yellow. The eyes of the painting were camouflaged with the new, vulgar colours: she felt as if she had just lanced some enormous cyst or caused, beneath that luxuriant hair, some massive, satisfying haemorrhage of foul, infected blood. She seized another tube, another red, spat that towards the hair.

Viewed from behind, Maria looked calm and industrious in the eye of this violent storm. A calm, squat creature, busy about her easel, like an amateur painter in evening class. From the relative darkness of the corridor, it took Elisabeth a while to see the vivid, puslike decorations to the canvas, hear the guttural breathing and angry snorting which accompanied the artistry, deafen herself with her own scream of terrible rage, feel under the dry palms of her own hands the massive power of Maria's damp shoulders as she leapt on her with all her own weight to pull her away. Maria was rock-solid, reminiscent of Thomas in her physicality, a powerhouse of ugliness, stronger than Elisabeth and fuelled by a fury which was not mortal but divine retribution, receiving directions from some single-minded God. Who directed her then to propel her elbows into the softness of Elisabeth's bosom, to turn and punch and then to claw, with her paint-filled hand first towards the other's eyes, then to her clothes. There was deadly method in her fighting; in Elisabeth's, none. The easel overturned on them both. The canvas hit Butler as he slunk away from furies far worse than his own. His paws on the wooden floor took up enough paint to make him skid. He stood beyond the door, whining for escape while the wrath of God triumphed. Knocking over chair, table, pushing the ever resisting Elisabeth before her, delivering with soundless speed blow after blow to the abdomen of her quarry, Maria finally rammed her against the wall below the high windows. Looking up, fighting back, Elisabeth registered the dying of the sun-filled light pouring through. Her eyes were filmed with oil: the light was a vision of hell. Maria punched once more, this time with full force. Elisabeth's unshod feet slipped from under; she clutched at the window cord to break the fall, hitting her head on the way down. She crumpled like rag and for one full minute slipped into

320

another, blacker world, where colour was, for a matter of seconds, extinct.

She was conscious now, kneeling against the wall as if at prayer, her vision blurred by the paint in her eyes, hurting, drunk with shock and pain. Maria was holding her hair and seemed to be smearing more paint on Elisabeth's forehead. Elisabeth suppressed her scream, instinctively remembering to avoid the poison of paint in her open mouth, spat instead, tried to claw back, but her hands were pinioned above her head, towards where the high window swung and tugged at the cord which bound her wrists. Clever Maria. Mixed with the smell of oily paint, the overturned acetone bottle and its scent of almonds, was the pungent smell of Maria, a stench of uncleanliness and urine. Mad, bad, about her business of disfigurement, grunting like a pig. Somewhere in that blurred vision, there was the glittering of a real blade, not the dull palette blade, but a blade waved in front of Elisabeth's face as if held by the hand of a malevolent hypnotist, the movement accompanied by a kind of singing. A stubby set of fingers felt their way round the sockets of Elisabeth's eyes, forcing one eye open, then the other, feeling for purchase. Elisabeth did not know what Maria had done. She knew her cheeks were covered with thick fluid, dripping from her eyes, and she was whimpering. All her sight registered was the reflection of a blade cutting through a pool of glutinous red. The pain was intense. Maria's fingers slipped, probed again. Then she was speaking, her guttural voice whispering, Look at me, look at me, look towards me . . .' The singing resumed. 'Sweet heart of Jesus, make us know and love thee . . .'

Elisabeth tried to close her stinging eyes tight shut. She imagined the name of manufacture printed on the blade. Kitchen Devil. The pain was greater and now she had no sight at all. Then all motion stopped. In a wave of terrifying silence, the singing stopped, then changed to a sobbing.

'Maria! Come away. Enough!'

He had seen, from the door, a face covered with trickling gore. A forehead streaked with wounds. Deep red sockets where there had been eyes, the bloody wreck of a face destroyed, so hideous, the vision made him preternaturally calm.

There was a glacial quality in Thomas's voice. A rustling signified the abrupt abandonment of whatever he carried, while a whimpering howl might have been from the larynx of the dog, or from Maria herself, a furious, frustrated, half-repentant keening from a figure paralysed by discovery.

'Put it down. Now.'

A clunking sound as the glittering thing fell from her hand to the floor. His voice, developing a tremor, rising higher, but still calm.

'What have you done? You will go to hell, Maria. Another knife? I told you, no knives. Where did you steal it? What did I tell you? Get out of here, go to hell. Get out, and never come back. Do you hear me? Out!'

The last words were orders over the shoulder as he stumbled across the barricade of fallen furniture to where

Elisabeth attempted to struggle to her feet, disorientated, half blind. Maria's keening growls rose to a wail of despair: there was nothing from him, no pity; he did not even look towards her handiwork on the fallen easel, or to her. He went instead straight to Elisabeth, murmuring like a lover, 'Oh, darling darling child, I'm sorry, so sorry, I didn't know, I should have known, I couldn't guess, speak to me, speak to me . . .' He was trying with his one hand to raise her from her stance of awful subjugation, her pathetic, shameful kneeling attitude of sacrifice. Maria watched, all fury gone, nothing left but pain and loss. 'Get out!' he screamed at her. 'Get out! Go to hell!'

'She is bad, Thomas, bad . . .'

'Get out! You evil cow, get out!'

He left Elisabeth, moved towards Maria, making in the depths of his chest growling, threatening sounds, more animal than human. The sounds became confused with angry sobs. His glasses fell away: he was angrier, more lethal than she had ever seen him. 'Get away, you monster. You ugly devil. I'll kill you . . .'

Maria screamed once, a rising cry of grief, which prefaced the following of his order and the sound of her crashing out of the room, out of the flat and down the stairs, into the distance, falling against the walls at each bend of stairs. The dog streaked before her with a greater grace, terrified of them all.

It had taken mere minutes of waiting for them both to be bored, restless and ready for recriminations. To deflect the accusations she knew would come in her direction, Annie tried to pass the time by constantly looking through the windows of the big door. Finally, she was rewarded.

'Look,' said Annie. 'There's a dog in there. Coming down with someone. Quick. When they come out, we go in.'

Francis nodded grimly. It had been silly to imagine they could wait indefinitely. Both of them, he in particular, wore with their sombre clothes an aura of tension, a mixture of anxiety, embarrassment, and dread. As they stood with an assumed innocence of purpose, the door was wrenched open and an ugly dog shot forth. Followed by an uglier woman, gasping for breath, staggering, yelling at the dog to wait, but the dog did not wait. Francis gripped the edge of the door in the nick of time before the woman could let it slam behind her. She looked at him and he recoiled in revulsion. Not only ugly but warped with malice, streaked with wild colours, the eyes narrowed. Maria did not know why she spoke or who they were. She only saw a man looking fair and handsome but repelled, as all human beings were repelled. She wrenched out in her breathlessness the final words of mischief.

'Upstairs. He's killing her.' Words flung back as she stumbled down the last steps into the street, leaving him holding the door. Francis was fit, Annie not. He bounded beyond her up one flight of stairs, the next and the next, horror mounting with each flight. There were smears of blood, it seemed, in the corners where the stairs turned, filthy-looking smears of red along the cream-coloured walls evoking a bleeding body dragged, telling of cruelty, flogging, humiliating violence. And at the very top, an open door on to a sea of cream carpet, also smeared. From inside, the underwater murmuring of voices. His head was pounding: the dream of the Venus was back. On the long way upstairs, led by the trail, he had been propelled by the vision of a body sliced to the bone, blood welling through canvas skin.

Following the sound, Francis came to that room where the light was fading with a sudden darkening of a freak shaft of sunlight. At first he saw only one thing: Elisabeth, standing and pinioned, leaning silently against the man who seemed to hold her while reaching clumsily with one hand towards her bound wrists, speaking low with words which might have been reassurance, but could also have been obscenities. The man was fumbling: Thomas with one hand could not undo the window cord; he was realizing he could not. As Francis watched, Thomas let go of Elisabeth, reached for a knife which lay on the floor, looked up without retrieving it. His formal jacket looked incongruous; both he and the knife were smeared with colour. Elisabeth's hair was matted with touches of red. The face, also turned towards Francis, looked streaked with blood, the eyes half closed as in the image of some heavily beaten prisoner not yet cleaned up for presentation on television. Bowed and bloody, she was trying to speak. Francis launched himself at Thomas as he rose upright with the knife in his hand. He had lost his dark glasses: the undisguised face glowed with a sinister innocence and Francis saw without room for surprise that the chubby cheeks were streaked with tears. Regardless of that, he struck the face and body repeatedly, pummelled blows with his strong fists into that chest, seeing red as he struck, seeing stars, wanting more than anything to inflict the maximum, disabling pain, unable to stop. He scarcely noticed the feebleness of resistance: he was black with vengeful fury, hysterical with righteous rage, and his blows were somehow more justifiable for the woodenly muscled flesh with which they seemed to connect: the token resistance enraged him more, so he wanted to do more, hit again and again. Then he remembered the blade, seized it in his left hand, made a clumsy, threatening aim towards the hateful baby face before him, dimly, but only dimly, aware of Elisabeth screaming, 'Leave him alone, leave him alone . . . He didn't touch me . . . Leave him alone.' A plea which rang in his ears later, penetrated only when he saw Thomas crouching at his feet, a thin line of blood emerging on his forehead and across the hand which had endeavoured to protect his face. Thomas, kneeling and silent with blood pouring over his red hand, down on to his filthied shirt in a redder stream. Then Annie was behind Francis, pulling him away, latching her elbow round his neck, he remembered later, while Thomas crawled like a dog and then knelt again, with one hand over his face, the other held loosely over his mouth, like an animal's paw.

'He didn't touch me . . .' Elisabeth's voice, breaking, pleading. The room was full of breath, silent for seconds which resembled hours as the whole tableau slipped into the place of nightmare memory, all of them panting, from the running, the fighting and the fear. Annie, heart bursting from the stairs, undid the knots behind Elisabeth's back, holding out arms to support her in case she fell. Elisabeth said something which sounded like thank you. She stood stiffly, a drunken person wondering how to take the first step. And then came the most obscene episode of all, to Francis, far the most shocking, so hard on his soul it took away the last of his breath as he watched what Elisabeth did. She did not stagger across into his arms, nor did she take the support proffered by Annie, but moved trancelike towards Thomas. She crouched with one arm round his shoulder, the other lifting the hem of her skirt, searching for a piece of unsullied material to hold against the blood which flowed between his fingers, mingled wetly with hopeless tears. She shielded him with her own body, rocked him, held him, pressed him against her. 'Thomas, Thomas, Thomas . . . there there, it's all right. Not your eye, please, not your eye. Look at me.'

Then she turned to the others, her terrible face streaked like Thomas's with greasy rivulets of tears, and spoke with maddening, insulting control, a voice full of weary but accusing despair.

'You stupid bastards,' she said. 'Can't you see? He never touched me, he never. Do you hear me? He never actually touched me . . . never, never, never, you stupid fools.' She turned back to him then, ignored them, murmuring to this disgusting apparition who crouched there, sobbing. She pulled him to his feet, led him two steps to a chair, placed him in it. A handsome wing chair, Annie noticed, the only thing unturned; it was on the tip of her tongue to make the prosaic observation that you'll get that chair dirty if you aren't careful, but she did not speak. There was nothing to say. Whatever this mess, whatever she had suffered, it was Elisabeth who was in control. Speaking to Thomas, soothing, questioning, deciphering his mumbled replies, then issuing orders.

'Would one of you please go into the bathroom attached to the bedroom at the far end of the flat? There is a telephone in the cupboard under the basin. You plug it in wherever you can find a point, and phone for an ambulance . . . .' Thomas stirred, clutched her with the pathetic paw, mumbled. 'No, you don't. You phone for his own doctor. Can you, Francis, go into my bathroom, bring me a towel? I just need to stop some of this paint getting near an open cut. If you see what I mean.'

Paint. Annie stared at the floor. Merely paint. Near her feet was an overturned bottle of acetone, releasing the smell of almonds, the spilt liquid whitening the polished stain of the wooden floor. She knew nothing but humble confusion and a sense of horror, looked towards Elisabeth in a kind of plea for enlightenment before she obeyed. She was rewarded with the ghost of a smile.

'It's all right,' said Elisabeth. 'It's good to see you both. I just wish the circumstances were different.'

Outside, the sky had darkened. When Annie turned on the light on her way from the room, nudging Francis into life as she went, she could see it all for what it was. Paint.

'He never touched me,' Elisabeth said. 'Never, never, never, did I tell you that? He never touched me.'

She was crying with the helpless sound which took the mind of Francis and reduced it to liquid. Like spittle.

CHAPTER SIXTEEN

They were listening to him, so it had to be a dream Two women, listening, hanging on to his every word. The blurred image of Elisabeth was listening to him: he could smell her scent from fifty paces, perfume, calamine, turpentine, could guess the colours of her skin, wanted to touch but did not dare. When the light had gone, perhaps she would not notice.

The other face was puzzling, womanlike, sharp as a ferret, but far from ugly. I am enrapturing two beautiful women, Thomas thought. I do this simply with my own face, the way I look has them bound to me. I am not dead, so it may not be a dream; although I wish I might be allowed to die for the mortal sin of failing to acquit myself well with any human being, but how fine to be so handsome that I draw such an audience. His face twisted into a grin; his body heaved slightly, with laughter. His hand was compelled to travel round his face, feeling for the sockets of his eyes to recognize the same deadness of the one containing its orb of glass, wincing when his fingertips encountered the other and felt the tracery of stitches, whose insertion he could not remember at all. They felt like stiff spiders marching up towards his hair in a line. He wanted to brush them away: tiny predators on a fresh corpse.

Although he could see, he did not really want to open wide. One of the spiders twitched in the corner of his eyebrow, a distracting tick which made him want to scream. The gust of a noisy panic rose in his chest. Then another hand took his own away from his face, placed it by his side; held it there in a clasp which was loose, warm and dry. He could not feel love, but he could feel rapt attention.

'Thomas, we're going soon, for a while. Talk to me, Thomas, tell me why.'

'I didn't touch you, did I?' Thomas said loudly. 'I never touched you.'

There was a moment's hesitation, a clearing of throat, another pause.

'It depends what you mean.'

The sharp face had disappeared with a snort. How can she? Annie thought. How can she touch him after all that? I do not, cannot, fathom the nature of such forgiveness.

Walking back across the square flanking the cathedral, a route he had crossed innumerable times in the week since he had trodden that way first, Francis thought how much he hated it. Shops, church, fine dwellings, God and Mammon juxtaposed. He could no more go inside that place and pray, knowing what he half knew, than he could have worshipped the moon, even though he would have loved to have prayed for forgiveness for the savagery within him. Francis was acting as errand boy: he had been taking things from one place to another today, a plethora of things: he was the key man. In his pocket were the instructions for the combination lock on the front door of the flat where he was bound: he had dismantled it once and now he would mantle it. Francis was hoping that Elisabeth would love him for his practical skills, his dependability at least, or his humility. As long as she could love him for something, because he had little enough reason to be proud of himself. As he covered the square with his long stride, he looked neither left nor right. There were pigeons and human beings strutting beneath an iron-grey sky. Winter was upon them.

He had missed the moment earlier when a woman had been arrested in the corner of the square. She had not been drunk, only seemed so. Disorderly without the intoxication, she kept trying to get inside the locked door of the cathedral at night, singing hymns loudly. A new one here, not a regular. The others would have pounced on her forced her to move on outside their territory, but her dog frightened them, protected her although she abused it all the time. The dog was chased off, finally, and Maria taken away after she began to beat her head against a wall, banging her forehead, scratching her groin, still singing. She said she was called Bernadette, looking for holy water. Then she said she was Sebastian with an arrow in her

crotch and that made her laugh. Then she said she was
called Francis but the pigeons would not come to her.
There was no way she would give her name, did not seem
to know it. In lieu of identity she carried holy pictures in
her pockets. She had been seen at church: it was assumed
she was foreign. Maria liked the custody of her cell and
since she did not appear to be waiting for anyone to come
and claim her, it was assumed, again, that none would.
There were other fights in the environs, battles in night-
time doorways voided by day. They would keep her away
from there, they said, as long as they could. The dog ran
free: he was caught again in the park, snarling at children.

It was far colder. Thomas could feel it through the open
window. Another week gone and all those shufflings of
departure. There were no spiders near his eyes. Now he sat
in one of the winged chairs. In the north-facing room: he
could not bear the brighter light of the other.

'Must you go? But of course you must. A nurse you
said? You will leave me with a nurse? Where's Maria?'

'I don't know. I have neither asked nor reported. You
must do that. Go on with the story. We only began last
week.'

'I don't want to do anything.'

'Tell me about her.'

'Look at me, then.' Elisabeth saw a face without spiders. An old man baby face, a head too large for its body,
another livid scar, still pink. Not ugly, but not appealing.
She saw a belly in a chair, dressed in brown and a hand
with a wound of alizarin crimson. She did not see a friend,

but she did not see an enemy, either. Rather a mass of colours, to whom she owed nothing. She heard an appeal which was for so little and still too much, but she complied.

'They did not love us much, our mother and our father. They had instead that perverted love of religion which has nothing to do with the real kind or the quality of goodness. They prayed; they shored up the walls of churches; they were part of the foundations. The making of their children was in furtherance of some order to increase and multiply, not, I think, the conclusion of desire. They did not approve of the physical; sex could not be mentioned in this house. The walls were adorned with icons and pictures of saints: they collected these as others might pornography, symbols of the opposite, of purity, promises of heaven and terrible threats of hell. That was our inheritance, but I was a boy, therefore educated; Maria the girl they wanted to give to God. She is older than I: enough difference in the years for her not to be a companion. At some point she went missing, pregnant, miscarried, hauled home bleeding, in disgrace from wherever she had run, kept here in safety while I spread my wings. Oh God, she was made to repent: she was encouraged in a sort of flagellation which was an extension of theirs . . . They died, these parents whom I resented, *en route* back from Lourdes with her. They believed that the intervention of saints could cure that lip and what they considered the cancer of her soul, but she survived, madder, sadder. They left everything to me, nothing to her, God knows why, but their God did. She lived here alone: I was never going to come home. But I did, of course, after Clayfields, I had no choice, and there she was, the only person in the world who loved me, would be with me, let me act as her second reason for living. Telling me meantime all about how I would be punished by God for what I had dared to do, because I had taken away almost all the icons and certainly all the saints which lined these walls. I did that straight away, could not bear them, vulgar, crude, threatening. Maria said I had killed God in this house . . . I laughed at her, collected more paintings like a madman, anything to dispel the gloom. Oh and I spent money like water to make up for all the comforts which had never been here: they were spartan, rich saints themselves, our mother and father. They taught one to turn the other cheek against any blow, despise the riches they had; they believed only in suffering and sacrifice, compulsive martyrs. I put silk where there had been cotton, pictorial scenes where there had been icons, all but a few, left to placate her. She hated that, Maria; loathed everything I did, but the paintings worst of all. Perhaps some small part of her was right: I keep my bedroom spartan, bathroom more so; I have never been quite easy in the luxury I can afford.'

'Not even the brandy?'

A ghost of a smile hovered, but it might have been automatic.

'Ah yes, food, brandy, but never much and never with cigars. Paintings were the luxury: I chose paintings of those with luxurious lives, so I could capture their mood. Like primitive man, do you think, painting the animals so he could tame a little of their spirit? A brandy would be nice,' he added.

She fetched it, spilt a little on the carpet. He was aware of another, alien presence, blenched.

'Maria?'

'No. My friend, Francis.'

He did not move, detached his hand, sighed and gripped the glass.

'He's just going, aren't you, Francis?' The voice held an order. A door closed and a shadow walked across Thomas's grave, lightly. He sipped the brandy. She would leave soon and go to her younger hunter, and he himself had turned the other cheek. A life for a life, he supposed. 'Go on,' she said. 'I'm listening.'

'. . . Maria.' A little of the brandy landed on the arm of the chair and Thomas resolved to be more careful.

'I ignored her, but you cannot quite ignore the one soul who loves you. Nor can you say you hate them. I put her downstairs, could not bear her so close; there was always plenty of money to do things like that, set her up in some sort of style, but she made her own place into a kind of monastic cell, liked it like that, whatever I urged her to do. I had my little life, my endless rounds of rescuing fine and anonymous art, doing this and that before I saw your photographs and then saw you and then had this stroke. After that, there she was again, in power. And I in her debt. Without speech, only dreams.'

'Did I have a predecessor?' Elisabeth asked gently. 'Was there really another restorer here or did you make that up?'

'Not quite. There was, but they were not his things you found. I bought them all, after he had gone, for you. He came in and out, but he left when . . .'

His face became still and he closed his eyes. Growing away at the undyed roots, his hair was white. 'Go on,' she said.

'Of course he left, that man. Maria had her revenge, you see. She hated my paintings, the ones more human than divine, resented the lifeblood of them. Found them, stabbed them. Of course the restorer went. Why would anyone work for someone else to destroy what he did? But long before that I had seen you, knew what you did . . . watched. I had got the dog, got him to guard my room from further carnage. Not only to guard against Maria indoors, but to protect her and keep her safe when she was out . . . She could shop, but that was all. I got the locks to stop her coming and going as she pleased. I threw out every single knife or potential weapon, except my umbrella which gave me such power and she never touched, and besides it was too large for her to take away and hide: she respected it as my weapon and mine only. But I needed her as she needed me. You cannot send away your only sister whom you have disinherited. Where would she go? She was good for a long time, growing sane while I was grow-ing mad. After I saw you. Do you believe me?'

'Yes. Why didn't you tell me she was your sister?'

He hesitated. 'Shame, I think. I had little enough to endear you as it was. Is it Sunday? I only tell lies on Sundays.'

'No, it isn't Sunday.'

'Is it light or dark?'

'Dark now. I'll be back soon.'

'There's no need. Really.'

336

'It's my choice.'

'Not approved by your friends, I take it?'

'No.' She was retreating, her hand withdrawn from his. He wished he could not feel her relief in that polite, but quivering anxiousness to be gone. He spoke with a sudden urgency.

'And you've taken the pictures?'

'Yes.'

'Go with God,' he murmured. 'Go with your own God.'

She was next to him again. 'Thomas? I'm sorry for what happened, both times. We could never be side by side, you know. We seem to trigger destruction, you for me, and more particularly, I for you. Have you noticed?'

'Yes,' he said. 'I know that. Take one of the sticks when you go home. It's dark and dangerous out there.'

'I detest your damned sticks, Thomas.'

He chuckled. 'They make a weak person powerful. Never despise a weapon. You are too gentle for your own good, and so was I. I can't ask you to come back, even once in a while, can I?'

'No you can't ask, but I shall.'

'What can I do about my sister?'

'Report to the police, then nothing. A convent, per-haps?'

'Yes. Elisabeth, how do I make up to you?'

'For what? Pictures, Thomas: find me pictures to mend.'

Annie Macalpine was spring-cleaning in a fever when Francis called. Not just the kitchen but the whole of her

337

apartment. There seemed to be fewer frills than before. As soon as she had opened the door, she uncorked a bottle of wine and the telephone rang. *Plus ça change.*

'Who? Michael! Yes, fine, fine . . . Sorry, not this evening, sweetheart. I'm washing my hair. Ciao.'

'Denying yourself company, are you?' Francis asked her, teasing. 'That isn't like you.'

'How do you know? You don't know what I'm like.'

He flinched. It seemed these days that he went from friend to friend seeking his self-respect but revealing his ignorance. Annie softened and patted his head like a distant grandmother.

'No, you're right. It isn't like me. Saturday night is party night. It isn't the company I mind at the moment, but the quality of it. Beggars can be choosers, I find. Any news of that madwoman?'

'No.'

'Going round to Elisabeth, are you?'

'Yes, later. After she's come back from Thomas. You're welcome too, you know, if you want.' She ignored the invitation.

'I don't know how she can go and see him,' she murmured. 'But then again, maybe I do.'

They were easy together: he could feel the same old reluctance to leave, but she wanted him to feel welcome in her home and, then, go. She wanted to hear all about Francis and Elisabeth while not wanting to know at all. She was the only person he felt did not judge, who had understood the full and dreadful force of closet violence in every man, but she wanted him to go now, so she could

338

miss him in private. Hanging in the corner of her living room he noticed a brilliant-blue gown encased in dry-cleaner's polythene with the shining silk of the long skirt trailing on the floor. 'Ah-ha,' he said, 'you are going out, after all. What is it? A ball?'

She jumped, looked as guilty as she was ever capable of looking, then relaxed. Elisabeth had been about to throw away that dress during the days when they had been organizing Thomas and his abode, but Annie said no, give it to me: it's too valuable to throw away; if you hate it, I don't. She was remembering now that Francis did not know either the history or existence of this dress; only she herself knew, with Elisabeth and Thomas, and Annie was not about to extend the range. She was good at keeping secrets and she was not going to let any kind of sentiment stand in the way of an acquisition.

'That? Oh, I'm keeping it for someone. I might have it mended and altered for me.' And wear it, she thought, only for someone special who really did want me, so there, and why don't you go, Francis, please? The longer you linger, the worse it is for me. She sprang up. 'Here, take a bottle of wine for Lizzie, and oh, I almost forgot, this cheque I've owed her for ages. Tell her I'll see her next week some time.'

'Lizzie?'

'OK, Elisabeth. I can call her what I like. Now piss off, I'm busy.'

After he was gone, she felt the impact of his hug from her knees to her head, attacked her cleaning again with renewed vigour. Handled that one well, didn't you? she told herself. Didn't you just? You're a brave girl, Annie, you're all right. The phone rang. She hesitated, then ignored it. If they wanted her, they would come back.

Francis, too, felt the print of hands on his back as he walked up the road towards where Elisabeth Young lived. He was quite hopeless with his longing for her, back to where he had been with her in the very beginning, gripped by the crush he now had to call love. Humbled by his own misjudgements, his capacity for violence and the terrible harm he had almost done. Bemused by the complete irrelevance of law, order and judgement in all their messy private lives. Not one of them, himself included, had once considered calling for official help, still less official retribution or family assistance. No one had called anyone to task for their lawlessness. He was unsure of what code he could live by next, what he would find himself holding in lieu of a belief. People or love, crooked paintings and damaged lives. Something like that. He walked slowly, full of the anxious anticipation of seeing her.

Enid opened the door for him. He did not know why she did that, but she did, scuttling back inside her own premises with a nervous smile as he made his way downstairs, shaking his head. 'Why should I be cruel to her?' Elisabeth had said. 'Look, she is old and sad, I was unkind to her, I who should have recognized the casualty she is. She had her revenge and now we're quits. Why shouldn't she come in for tea? What have I got to hide?'

'And your father?' Francis asked. 'What about him?

Does he come under the mantle of universal tolerance and forgiveness, like me, now you can think of him clearly?'

She stopped for that one. 'No,' she said slowly. 'Not yet. There's a bit more work to do on that one.'

The door was open wide. Francis could smell polish and sweet smells. 'Hallo! Hallo!' The blond man bearing gifts, his own wine, Annie's wine, food and flowers and a vulnerable heart fit to burst.

'Hallo,' she shouted back from the studio room, where the door was also open wide. Working after dark: it was long after dark. The half light which still lived when he had knocked on Annie's door was long since gone: now it was night. He recognized the glow of her tungsten light. On the beechwood easel was the madonna. Stacked in one corner were all the eyeless portraits, the sight of which made Francis quiver. Thomas had paid in kind.

The madonna glowed in haunting beauty. She had lost the pus of paint, stood there, varnished again, beckoning with her provoking smile, a man's ideal mistress. Elisabeth turned from the easel, smiling her own completely different smile. There was no resemblance at all.

'It's all right, I'm just finishing.'

'No, no, you carry on if you want.'

She had been applying the last touch. He put his arms round her and his face against her hair, smelling the shampoo, perfume, linseed and all the scents which were hers and rose from her warmth. When he looked up, he met the glance of the painting and automatically shook his head.

341

'I love you, Elisabeth. I love you to pieces. But I can't have you, can I?'

'No. Not all of me. No one has all of anyone. You only get a fraction, and that's usually more than enough.'

'A fraction of you, then.'

'Perhaps.'

He kissed the nape of her neck, satisfied for now. She put down her tools and turned to him shyly. She brushed hair out of his eyes.

'You could do with a haircut,' she said. You are, Francis thought, the most voluptuous, desirable, compassionate person in my world. I might have to spend a long, long time acquainting you with just how beautiful you are. The inhabitants of your world to date have shown strange ways of convincing you. I have to do better.

'How was Thomas, then?'

'As you saw. I'll tell you what he told me today. Might help me to understand it.'

'Do you actually like him? Or love him, in a way? You don't have to answer.'

'In a way, both. He's a part of me, is all. I admire his inner eye. I'm glad he's alive. I want him to have a better life, and I want him to be safe.'

She turned off the tungsten light. The existence of light was less important if it was all your own share of light. You could only do so much in a day. Keeping your eyes to another day was more important. Property was important only if you loved it. The fog which had dogged Francis's footsteps up the road now sealed itself against the windows.

'I just wish he wasn't so lonely. It makes people mad,' Elisabeth said.

'Hmm,' said Francis.

'I do want him to feel safe. I feel safe. I want everyone to feel safe. At least sometimes.'

A small, squat figure sat huddled in a doorway, listening to midnight and watching the fog. It was all the thicker, closer to the river. She had felt it sidle up from the ponds in the park as she had wandered through, hiding behind trees and calling for the dog. Once off the grass and on to the pavements, she remembered to be quieter with the stick. Someone had given her the stick, or maybe she had found it. You could always find a good stick if you came up behind someone old who was resting on a bench. Near the cathedral, Maria detoured, bolder now. The stick made a sound, one two click, one two click. She liked it: it gave her a sense of power to go with this equally dizzy sense of power which was her freedom. When she found the dog, she would beat it. Maria had grown in confidence, and with her stick she had walked for miles. She knew the centres of London in a way she never had, and all those years of frugal life and deliberate courtship of penances such as cold and pain stood her in good stead for survival now.

She thought she knew where the madonna was. Dead, she hoped. She also thought she might know where the girl was. And if she was wrong about that, she did not doubt that they would both come back. Everyone always came home, she supposed: they had no choice. For tonight, she was not in the doorway of her brother, but she was close.

From the opposite side of the road, even in the fog, looking up, she could see the lights from everyone else's windows.

Look at me.

Let's Dance

To Angela Nightingale,
for being alive

CHAPTER ONE

There was no other way to describe it. A perfectly beautiful house which also managed to be ugly. There was a glory in its pretence to be a truly grand house whilst being, in reality, a mansionette masquerading as a mansion. There was no spitting of gravel as a car turned into the drive, since the gravel was half submerged into the weedy earth, leaving a smooth tread and puddles. The tennis court was similar, erupting with moss, the pond to the side choked with weed and a haven for frogs, while the lawn resembled a green lunar landscape, spongy to the feet, riddled with mole-holes. Round the back, where the red brick of decaying outhouses met the pitted surface of the stable yard, a berry tree was shedding an early autumn crop so plentiful it was ignored even by the birds. The grounds were sweet smelling, as edible as the house. Like good rich food, a blessing and a curse.

The front was a two-storey elevation, mostly glass window set in sandstone below a shallow pitched roof of dull but definite grey. The front door had altered with the generations, undecided about fate, looked temporary, far too small and cheap between a pair of fat columns. These had once been surmounted by stone lions, added and then taken away at the same time as the stone globes on the gateposts. Humility followed pretension.

The out-of-scale Corinthian columns alone appeared to announce not only a huge reception hall, but also twenty bedrooms of liberty hall, instead of the mere five. As it was, a small vestibule was flanked by two fine front rooms with enormous windows, one living room, one dining room, each with fifteen huge panes of old glass in elegant, thin frames, currently dirty but none the less magnificent. It was the kind of hospitable, slightly blowzy house which invited the colourful domination of virginia creeper and weeds, never the sinister overtones of ivy. But the creeper had been killed: there were trails of it growing up against the mellow gold stone, like a trail of debris on a handkerchief, holes in the upper slabs where foliage had been held if not controlled. Each brick of this perfect example of English eccentricity, *folie de grandeur* and sheer, if muddled, taste, came from the valley landscape where the house stood as if growing out of it, unable to live elsewhere, insulted by the suggestion. Invisible from the road, the house withstood all weathers, and was perfectly isolated.

There were one and a half bathrooms for all those rooms, one lavatory in the servants' quarters. Three servants at one time, plus gardener and stable lad, plus any assistance needed from the village, now hamlet, lying one mile away and the town, five miles beyond and visible from the hill. Some gentlewoman had once considered it a struggle to manage with a staff of five. Those were the days.

Serena Burley lived in it alone. A man called George, who was not paid for his labours, drove each day from the town to look after her and her dog. No one knew where he came from or why he had done this for the three years of Serena's erratically developing dementia. Janice, who was paid, although not handsomely, also attended. Robert and Isabel, Serena's far-distant children, visited for frantically busy weekends in which they mended things and went away, saddened, appalled and relieved. George was such a Godsend, they never questioned either his identity or his motives.

They worried about their mother while half tolerating, half detesting one another. Most of the time, the detestation won. Robert was a bully and Isabel was weak. He regarded her with all the contempt held by the strong for the meek who had also managed, by no effort of their own, to inherit the earth. Robert would inherit little from his mother: the house was held on some obscure leasehold arrangement. Isabel's inheritance came from someone else. Neither of them could quite believe Serena's diagnosis, since the rude health of both of them made them deny the existence of anything incurable. And because Serena Burley had been such a password for magnificence, it was impossible to imagine that she would not, somehow, re-emerge from this senile chrysalis and laugh at them.

'It can't go on,' Robert kept repeating. 'It simply can't. She'll have to go into a home. You'll have to make her. Or go and look after her for a while until we decide what to do.'

'Go and look after her? Why can't you go and look after her? What's the difference between your responsibility as a son and mine as a daughter, and besides, you're the one she adores . . .' Isabel would feel the lump of tears whenever the conversation got to this point, which it did on every telephone call. However would she acquire a family of her own if she went home to her mother? Almost on cue, as if someone was squeezing them for effect, there would be the sound of screaming children in the background of Robert's home.

'That's why,' he would hiss triumphantly, a stage-whisper of a hiss, intended to be heard by his sensible wife who loathed her sister-in-law as much as she envied her. '*We* have no power to shove her into a home, because she's still just about sane, and I couldn't possibly go and look after her because I have family responsibilities . . .'

'That was your choice!' Isabel would yell at this point, also intending to be heard, but the guilt crept up into her throat at the same time and made her voice tremble on the edge of petulant hysteria.

'. . . I have kids and no money and a tough job, none of which applies to you . . .'

The words 'you lazy slut' were never quite announced: they hovered there, over the wires, to be repeated at supper by Mrs Robert Burley, but they still entered the iron of Isabel's soul. A son is a son till he takes him a wife: my daughter's my daughter for all of her life.

'She's fine as she is. She's got help . . .'

This was Isabel, avoiding confrontation as she usually did, denying her mother's example, that of her aunt as well. She was unequal to it at the best of times, which was never like this, hampered by guilt and the luck of life which evaded her brother, hampered even more at the moment by the denouement of yet another love affair. All Robert could do was moan about the responsibility of having kids: all she could dream about was the utter privilege of what he

4

claimed as an affliction. Whether it was love or babies that formed the subject matter of dreams, she could no longer distinguish and was not about to try. Her own mother had told her not to come home and, apart from brief visitations, she had done her best to comply.

'How can you say everything's fine? The house is falling down.'

'All you care about is the things inside the house!' Isabel screamed this time, despite herself, the high notes of her shrill voice warbling like a raucous jungle bird.

'Better than caring about nothing but yourself. Like you.'

Staring into space after such family chats, Isabel imagined her beloved mother, her eyes which grew paler and paler with age and the arms outstretched in the great big greeting which would be Serena's welcome. No one else had ever inspired such huge and unrequited love. Or such pride.

There was a series of photographs in tarnished silver frames on top of Serena's desk. Some of them talked, some did not. The one of Mab, Serena's sister, for instance, showed the solid, uncommunicative face of a woman to whom life had been scrupulously unfair, right from the day when her mother had decided to call her Mabel, because of that Mabel Lucy Atwell look: deliciously fat cheeks, snub nose, eyelashes to kill for. Later Mab was still best seen in profile, because even as an adult that plumpness resembled the moon, with features set uncertainly in a squashed circle, a currant bun of a face with a frizz of hair.

Next to Aunt Mab were Isabel and Robert, clinging to her fat thighs. Serena had taken that photo herself: no one showed to advantage. She featured alongside, inside a better frame, wearing a black ballgown, with husband on arm, receiving adoration. That was preferable. Serena had been venerated wherever she went, the subject of a thousand schoolgirl crushes and a hundred leering men, while her sister Mab blossomed into the kind of child people called bonny, or so she had explained to Isabel, leaving her niece to wonder what it might have been like to be sibling to a younger sister so beautiful she made men and women alike catch their breath. She was not aptly named. Her name suggested tranquillity, whereas all her life Serena had howled at the moon. There were more than vestiges of a former, sensual beauty about her eyes, her hair, her carriage.

The photograph of fat, capable Mab began to talk. Well, Mab said, cheerfully, I had to develop in other ways. And I was, I am, happier than my sister, in the long run. My sister is not going to like being old, you know, but for me it makes no difference. No one will notice. Serena turned the photo down so she could not see Mab, smiling.

'Bedlam!' Serena shrieked. 'What rhymes with bedlam, George?'

'I dunno. Can't you think of something easier than that?'

'Tart.'

'Part?'

'Fart!'

'Oh, very funny. Better write it down quickly. Where's your pen?'

Sitting at her desk, Serena was suddenly protective. She leant forward over a pile of paper, shielding it from view. 'You'd better not look at what I'm writing, George. Secrets.'

'I know, I know, but I can scarce read, remember?'

'Don't believe you. You're a clever fucker. A right smart *bugger*!'

He chuckled, good-natured in the face of an outburst. 'Language, Mrs Burley, my lovely sweetheart, you gotta watch that language.'

She relaxed, put her head in her hands. 'Language is the root of all good and evil, George. Which is a shame, because I can't remember the verbs.' She looked round, wildly. 'What do I mean, George. Verbs? Words?'

'I think you mean words,' he said gently. 'And never you mind. You got plenty of words left.'

'What's happening to me, George?'

'You need feeding, that's all.'

He plodded out of the room, making an effort to behave as if he had no right in there and she had not called him in in the first place. As far as anyone else was concerned, he never went further than the kitchen. He had a place by the fire, along with the dog. He was not paid to do what he did. He was not supposed to do anything for Serena: he did what he did for the dog. Or that was the way it had started out.

The house had a strange and lopsided magnificence, certainly in comparison with any he had ever known, although he had never been familiar with a wide variety of houses. At home he could not have kept a hamster: the rules, imposed by the authorities, the lack of air and the neighbours, did not allow. Here the place smelled blissfully of animal and warmth. There were falling-down outhouses outside, a coalhouse where a boy could keep a rabbit, a backyard and a whole acre of land. He saw it as a kind of flawed heaven and inside it he had this strange sensation of vitality. Mrs Burley was a good woman and she needed him when no one else did. She was mad only in other people's estimation. There was no one else he would rather obey.

'Things she does!' he informed the dog, as well as anyone else who would listen. 'Course she isn't mad. She's sane as you and I. You know what? I got there this afternoon and how do you think she was doing? On her hands and knees, she was, planting plastic flowers outside. I said to her, I said, you shouldn't be doing that, you'll get your knees muddy. Fuck off, she says to me, why not? There's fuck-all else growing here. If I put these lovely things here, then the others will know they should grow. Makes sense, don't it?'

And that was the fact of it. So much of what Serena did made sense. To Serena and also to George. They shared a common and secret logic which did not require even the effort of mutual tolerance. George, Serena and, to some extent, Janice, conspired to maintain a façade and to keep Mrs Burley where she belonged, and, although Janice did not know it, to preserve George in relative safety.

He was back in the kitchen. There was a fuel-burning stove of indeterminate age at one end, with a sweet nursing chair in front of it, the sink at the other end and a badly done, uphill sloping quarry-tiled floor uniting the two. There was also a refrigerator, an electric cooker and a series of old kitchen units littered against the walls, a couple of deep, walk-in cupboards built into the fabric of huge sandstone walls and a series of doors which had once puzzled him until he knew better. One led to a pantry, a miserable little room, full of fuse boxes, a washing machine, what still passed for a freezer and shelves full of stores, all dusty and deficient, the place a masterpiece of bad design. Something called Fablon, a kind of stick-on polythene, coated the pantry shelves, curled at the edges, making fingers stick and grime collect. Looking out from the pantry window there was a spinney, beginning with a small bank on which he had

8

seen the ferret play last summer, both of them enchanted with the sunlight.

The wood had been cut back and now took revenge by crawling forwards in a thicket of sycamore. Nearest the window were the purple autumn crocuses which he could call his own, the bulbs he had planted signalling a new ownership of this wild territory. George watched the ginger cat crawl among them, pause where he had planted out the Christmas tree the winter before, willing permanence on both its withered branches and his tenure in this blessed house. The cat strove to survive, just as he did. Serena said it would grow up to be handsome, which was more than anyone would ever say about him. George had done his growing in another world, and in this one acquired a new skin and an identity which, for the first time ever, pleased him.

The other door, aside from the one that led into the corridor, an avenue that bore signs of Serena's eclectic taste, led down to the cellar. In saner moments Mrs Burley had told him about people keeping food down there before the advent of the refrigerator, why didn't he go and look? He had looked, closely, once or twice and never again. Janice said there was a cheese press made out of half a ton of stone, because it had once been a dairy. Stone shelves, a back cellar full of junk, a little window covered with dank weed, a place where things were put and left for ever. Until Serena had a party, magicked glasses, knives, forks, out of there. Oh, really? There had been no parties here in three years: George would have hated a crowd. It was the look of the steps down which so appalled him. They were stone, but so worn that each of them lisped into the centre, lethally slippery, the outward edge forming a wavy line, glistening with damp. It was the thought of how many people, how many hundreds of thousands of footsteps, had created that effect by constant traffic that had unnerved him. George did not like darkness, or servitude.

The dog got up out of her basket, cautiously enthusiastic. She seemed, like her mistress, to lose the capacity for barking in the afternoon, made a noise only for those she liked.

'Fine bloody watchdog you are,' he grumbled. 'C'mon, ol' girl. You and me against the world. C'mon.'

She moved her fat rump, thudded her tail, looked up beseechingly. Cold, outside.

'Walkies,' he said. 'You'll feel better for it after.'

They went out the back. Past the pump that no longer worked, over the fence into the park, her paws clipping on the remnant of concrete by the stable yard. There was a fine powdering of frost on the grass: the cattle had been taken indoors, so the land was theirs. In the distance was the treadmill of the town. He raised a fist to it.

In all of the vexed, fifty-odd years of his life, George had never been this happy. He needed this status quo, and without giving it much thought was determined it should remain exactly as it was.

Janice did an evening shift after George had gone, four hours a day. She was a comfortable woman and a natural diplomat, a necessary talent for one who pursued a patient career in looking after the elderly, albeit one that was founded on her nervousness about doing anything else, except clean things, which was what she had once done here. Patience was certainly a virtue. What did these poor old dears have to do with jargon about being mentally challenged? She looked at Serena Burley over the rim of her spectacles and then averted her eyes. Serena would have responded better to a man: Serena lit up in the presence of the male sex, but for a woman Janice did better than most when it came to persuading her to eat. People who had not entirely lost their table manners, but were still aware enough to know they were doing something not quite right, were embarrassed to be watched, although Mrs Burley used mealtimes as a great attention-seeking exercise. It was as if she wished to prove her frugality by never admitting to hunger. She lived on chocolate, and the only thing she could cook, albeit with maximum labour, was fish and chips. As one who had cooked for two fussy children and one bottomless pit of a husband for what seemed like endless years, Janice did not think this diet a sign of madness in itself, in fact it seemed a sign of sanity. All the same, these antics over a meal could be irritating to anyone else, who had failed to eradicate impatience as Janice had, leaving a vacuum filled with nothing but endless affection, loyalty governed by prudence and a fear for what she held dear.

'Too hot,' Serena complained. 'Ooh, far too hot. I can't eat this. Why is it so hot?'

It was not hot: Janice had ensured it was merely warm, so that Mrs Burley would do what she usually did, which was tear off chunks of fish and feed them under the table to the ever-waiting dog. It was *de rigueur* that half the meal would be given away: proof to herself, in some benighted way, that Mrs Burley was a civilized, delicate and far from greedy woman. Janice kept quiet, apart from saying, mmm, this is nice, by way of encouragement. A bit like running water making people want to pee. She did not like the thought of Mrs Burley's fingers, covered in dog saliva, putting chips

11

into her own mouth, but there was nothing she could do about that and it was better than the old girl eating nothing at all. Janice supposed that owner and dog must be immune to each other's germs after all this time. It was the dog looked poorly. That was the daftest thing the daughter had done, buy that dog which had grown into a fat and indiscriminately friendly bitch, as pleased with male strangers as Serena was herself. Janice cleared the plates.

'Would you like some ice-cream?'

'Too cold,' said Serena. 'Isn't it?'

The sky outside was black, that time of year when darkness began to rule and daylight in the evening faded into a memory. The days had been grey and cold, limiting the mean allowance of light to a few hours of indifferent illumination per diem. Would Mrs Burley still be here in the spring? Janice dreaded winter. The house had begun to unnerve her after dark: she had dreams about it. She looked with longing at the outline of her red car, blurred by the wavy lines of the glass on the kitchen door. Should have put it away in the dilapidated garage round the back, where the sight of it would not fill Serena with envy. She patted her pocket for the keys, which the old dear kept trying to pinch; still wanted to drive, poor old duck. Janice did four until eight, Mondays, Wednesdays and Fridays, and it was almost time to go, but Mrs Burley always began to talk when they were both on the downward run, and then she did not quite have the heart. Tonight she was going to be bold, strike for freedom ten minutes early. There was something oppressive, intense and mischievous about her charge this evening, and her own movements around the sink became brisk.

'I've got one son and one daughter,' Serena began, 'and they don't love me any more because of the words.'

'Never, Mrs B.,' said Janice, making her chatter into a parody of cleaning-lady talk because Mrs Burley liked it that way. 'They love you a lot, but they got to work, you know. And they live a long way away.'

Janice did not believe that sons and daughters owed it to their elders to interrupt their lives and turn themselves to the ignominy of the kind of service that was her livelihood. Only those who did not know what it was like would ever expect that, and she would have killed herself rather than have her children do for her what she did. They could do it for some-one else, but they were never going to do it for her. They were never going to see her eat with open jaws and suck her fingers as she gave chips to the dog. You had to have your compassion paid for to do this job.

'Don't go,' said Serena. 'Please don't go. I'm frightened.'

There's a ritual, see? Janice would tell her husband. A blackmail ritual, when she tries to stop me going, only it doesn't correspond with my hours.

'Course you aren't frightened. You don't know the mean-ing of the word.'

'What verb?' Serena was suddenly angry; terribly angry. Janice paused with her hand on the door latch, looking out to the comfort of her red car. In that, home soon. Sooner the better.

'A bit cross, maybe. Never frightened, not you. Don't worry about it, love. See you soon.'

That was a ritual too, the use of simple words and simpler promises. She remembered closing the door on that sullen and disappointed face with its sharp features, big soft eyes hinting at the splendour of all that former beauty, blowing kisses as she got in the driving seat and went hell for leather out of the rutted drive and on to the road across the fields.

13

By the time she was halfway to the church, the music blared, making a cocoon of the car, making her relax too much. She missed one of the biggest potholes, bounced into another, felt a thump on the bottom of the still new car.

The wages of guilt. She was not only ten minutes under time, but fifteen and that included getting out of the house. She stopped by the church, got out to examine the car in the thin light of the winter sky, bending and squinting beneath it as if what she might see could make any difference. Really, daughter or son had no cause to come back and take on this old lady, but, supposing there was any money in the till, they should fill in the potholes in the road so that other people, on their wages, did not have to ruin their cars when they happened to be in a temper themselves. Then she relaxed, let her breath out: there was nothing she could do. Why rush home anyway? Home was where the heart was, but it meant more demands. Home was halfway sustained by Mrs Burley's cash: she could not afford to feel churlish, or wish for the end of this era.

So she stood by the graveyard in the dark, smoking the cigarette that was mandatory in the Burley household, forbidden in her own, watching the sky. Outside the sky was a different creature from the sky observed longingly from the inside of window panes. It was lighter and brighter, full of comforting mystery, not really dark at all. Hope in October; must have been the crocuses out of the pantry window, made her think that way.

At the end of that lumpy drive over the fields, where the track met the car park next to the church, she faced a cottage. Nice couple with absent children moving about in there, and nothing else but her smoke and the dim knowledge that she

14

should not, in this sudden delirium of free time, lean against the other car parked alongside. There was movement behind the cottage windows. Horrible curtains, she thought. Cheap.

She remembered, with a slight and guilty amusement, the relations between these worthy neighbours and Mrs Burley after the latter had written off their motor car in a head-on collision. Mrs Burley did not like giving way. End of Serena's driving licence; end of neighbourly goodwill, since she had not seen fit to apologize. Difficult to forgive someone who wrote off your car: she could see it now, all over their front lawn. She sniggered silently at the thought. Then there was a soft crunching of footsteps, which made her freeze without real fear. Bloody George. Appearing behind her as if she needed supporting.

'You shouldn't smoke,' he said. 'Bad for your health.'

'So is sneaking up on people in the dark, you silly bugger. What you doing here?'

Only George, the harmless one who had given her the creeps at first, until she found they got on fine, running the place comfortably between them, provided George was given the illusion of being in charge and also given his manly credit for being the only one who could possibly make Serena obey an order she did not already see the advantage of obeying.

'Dunno. Coming back to the car. Don't it feel like midnight, and we haven't even reached the news on the radio?' There was a mute accusation in that, a reminder of the time, five minutes over eight, but twenty since she had left the house.

'Serena told me her husband's buried in this graveyard. She told me a while back, so I planted this crocus. Thought I'd tend to it, so I went to see Sal at the end of the road, to get some water in case they needed it.'

Janice wondered how it was that George always got to know everyone's name. She must have been coming here a good many years, but George, in his three, knew the names for all the faces she had ever seen. It was not a mere semblance of control, she realized; it was complete.

'Then I thought, you can't have weeds on a grave. I'll have to go on tending Edward's grave, I thought. Not that anything's growing, apart from the crocus. Funny, innit? You and me here. No one else.'

Glory be, thought Janice, listening with admiration and a faint sense of outrage: he's on first-name terms with the dead as well.

'I bumped my car, George. Be an angel and have a look at it for me, will you? I don't understand these things.'

He had turned away from her, not that he ever came close, hands in his pockets; harmless, a bolshie little man, short of leg, squat, powerful and utterly benign, keeping a good distance. 'Look at them stars,' he said. 'Better than my crocuses, and longer lasting.'

He had a torch, ever well-equipped, lay on the ground and pulled himself under the car without a word of protest. She could hear his breathing, a grunting that turned to humming as the light played. The humming stilled her conscience that he should be so willing, but she was still pleased when he emerged, stood and dusted himself off. George never seemed to feel the cold and nothing was ever too much trouble.

'Nothing,' he said. She doubted if he knew anything more about cars than she did, but allowed herself to be reassured.

She moved within three feet of him, never going closer. The sky was clear as water, dark while luminous. They pivoted together, noticed of one accord. A flickering light from the house half a mile away, nothing more than an unnatural glow.

16

'George,' said Janice, querulously, 'what's that?'

'She's on fire,' said George, almost admiringly. 'That silly old love is on fire.'

The fire had taken hold of the outhouse nearest the kitchen door. It had a back wall made of brick, wooden beams which burst and splintered. Serena, who had put the ash from the fire into the bin designated for that purpose, did not think of her own actions as being the cause. She had found the first burst of flame, from the lawn-mower petrol, also stored in there along with a mercifully short supply of coal, slightly alarming, but now the sheer sound was exhilarating. She had trailed across the yard from the back door to within three yards of the heat, repeatedly carrying a mug of water which she flung half-heartedly towards the inferno. Wind blew the smoke away from herself and the house: she knew no sensation of fear, but the work tired her, so she stood and watched. Then went indoors to her desk, looked for paper to burn, all those letters, all those useless words, but when she reached the door of the dining room she forgot what her errand had been, went back and got that thing that played tapes from the kitchen. The flames died so quickly: it seemed such a shame that this vision of heat and light should be so short-lived.

When the fire brigade arrived, Serena was dancing. The tape machine was bellowing forth a military march, to which she waltzed and smiled, and invited them to join in. Serena had fond memories of bonfires. And dances.

'Isn't it lovely?' she asked them. 'Will you dance?'

They stared at her, bewildered, themselves distracted from this fire, full of mild anti-climax. The coals glowed in the dark: it was more like a cheery blaze, a frivolous waste of

17

household fuel and the beams that had once supported a roof. Then, while others unloaded the hose and went to work, George took Serena in his arms, and waltzed her slowly across the overgrown lawn.

Janice watched them laughing and felt sick, with a feeling of terror she could not define. It was not so much that she knew she could not bring herself to work for a pyromaniac because she was afraid of fire, but it was a tide of frightful premonition. It sounded so well, Serena and George: it was a combination of will-power and victim and she could not work out for the life of her which way round it was.

Then she went indoors and screamed down the phone to Mrs Burley's daughter a litany of recriminations she did not feel, accusations that were unjust, warnings that were a reaction to shock and a situation she could suddenly see was untenable. She did not look for a result. She was not searching for fairness, justice, resolution. She was screaming against the fire which could have engulfed her and might not have happened if she had left on time. Your mother will die here, she shouted.

And that was how Isabel Burley came home to look after her mother. Because the appeal to do so came not from a bullying brother, but from someone else, who could no longer pick up the pieces. And, of course, because of her own agenda.

The flames had been fun, but it was no good trying to be clever. Difficult enough to concentrate on being good.

It was never as bad in the very middle of the night like this, when there was nothing to see but darkness and she could imagine that tomorrow everything would be back to normal. She was energized by the dark, like the evil spirits fostered by Bibles and fairy stories, but Serena Burley did not hold with God, never had. No merciful God would ever do this to her. Only a sadistic creator, motivated by malice, could first tease his servant with the irritations of age and then exercise this power for terror. It was the work of malevolence, and although she would address respectful pleadings towards any handsome deity of the male sex who would give her back her mind, she would not curtsy towards a psychopathic dictator.

'Damn, bloody, bloody hell.'

In the early hours of the morning, her mind was as clear as a bell. She could think in whole sentences and could even tell herself what a shame it was to have no belief, because it would be exquisite to pray in words and have the illusion of someone reading the despair. The fact that her mind was clear for as long as this in the hours before dawn could be construed as a gesture towards mercy from her cretinous creator, she supposed. During this time, designated as the darkest for the soul, but in reality the only time when there was no distraction at all, the words did as she asked and turned into phrases. Perhaps this God kept different hours. On second thoughts, she considered it was a refinement of heavenly cruelty to give her spells of clarity like this, at these invariable times of day, when she could remember who she was and what she had done. Serena adored these interludes and dreaded them.

She called for pen and paper, snapping her fingers towards the imaginary servant in the corner; the pen appeared in her hand and the paper on her lap. She wrote, furiously.

Who was she, then? Serena Burley, aged seventy-five, one-time intellect and beauty of this and other parishes, citizen of the wider world where she had travelled with her husband as the culture and the foil to his grand but limited mind. He dug oil wells and gave lectures on petroleum science: she filled houses with books, flowers, letters and charm, because that was her vocation. She provided en route the statutory two babies, who were not a vocation at all.

'I quite forget how we did it,' Serena remarked out loud, shaking her head, laughing. Her hand paused; she rubbed her wrist. The paper was curiously blank for all those words. She continued the record. Speaking out loud assisted the business of writing.

A goodish life, she wrote, in which she had been well served by long-suffering people. Her sister in particular, plus others. They had chosen to love Serena and all who belonged to her with a level of self-sacrifice that had been vital to her growing children, and a source of excruciating irritation to herself.

That was what charm had achieved for her. Enormous charm. She thought with a brief smile of self-admiration how it was she could define guilt, but had no experience of it.

What a joy it had been to use her witty talent with words to threaten, cajole, flatter, achieve. So few had the skill to communicate: she was one of them. Words made demand meet supply. She wrote laboriously: 'I . . . absolutely . . . adore men and I love the poetry of words.'

Shitting, miserable, fucking arseholes . . . Spit. Cunt. Rats.

The writing seemed to have slipped on to her wrist. She shook the Biro and spoke to it sternly.

If she had a tape recorder, like the one she'd used for Edward's *lectures, she would be able to say exactly what this condition was like. It was the nightmare of an operation where the patient is merely drugged, not anaesthetized, rendered immobile and helpless in the face of hideous pain and the knowledge that the surgeon is removing the wrong leg. Or trying to push the baby back in. The image made her cry and giggle at the same time and reminded her that there was no time for crying. Crying only served to eclipse this hour into more of the bumbling confusion that filled the day, apart from those crucial minutes, sometimes a whole thirty at a time, when she could control the clouds and make them move away from the sun.*

'TTT. Tutt tutt!'

The moments of reprieve were never long enough for her to do the things that were imperative. Such as phone Isabel and tell her never to come home again; make her promise faithfully she would do no such thing, the less she saw, the better. Tell her that she had not been a good mother to her daughter in that awful, pious sense people meant and she had no expectation of the silly child being a good daughter either, so there. She had never been a good wife either. She had never learned to cook, but could drive with all the aplomb of a chauffeur. How good she was at organizing parties. She hummed to the tune of a dance. Mantra words, lovely words. Rabbits, cats, dogs lavatory poo and big fat pricks . . .

'Crabb'd age and youth, Cannot live together.' Who said that? Crabbed age cannot live with anything. Serena felt as if her breath would kill a plant: only the plastic variety would survive. It was no good luxuriating in all these words; there was the real business to be done. Crabbed age should die.

Oh, for one of those recorder things, simply to prove to some-one in the morning that she could still articulate. She could go downstairs now, telling them all about it at the same time. Such

*grand facts to record for posterity. Such as, this floor is very cold,
these stairs grow steeper and longer, this carpet is rough and
someone has stolen my shoes. She paused for the black moment
by the living-room door when she did not know where she was
and the terror hit in waves, and then, in a flood of perspiration,
it passed when she saw familiar objects, waltzed round them,
touching and nodding, saying hallo. The hallway leading from
the stairs at the front of the house to the back was colder still and
the floor in the kitchen was a chill that burned. Someone had
stolen her shoes.*

Bitch, cunt on wheels.

*So cold, she would tell them: the light of the moon, coming into
my kitchen like a damn thief and if George had hidden the
knives again, she would fillet the man with a fork. Empty threats.
This was the place where she started to fail. Serena had always
been less at home in kitchens than living rooms or any place
where she had been hostess, dispensing of herself. Talking, flirting,
listening, touching. It seemed that darling George had begun to
trust her again since she had become more careful. There were
knives in a wooden block, standing upright like exclamation
marks. What she should really be doing now was what those
Japanese men of honour were supposed to do and that silly bitch
Madame Butterfly did. Kneel, thrust the thing into the breast-
bone, yell something final. The thought of the pain was
frightening, and anyway, the dog would laugh. Not a bad thing,
perhaps; she would have given her back teeth to make someone
laugh out loud instead of that sometimes respectful, sometimes
insolent stare, tinged with puzzled sadness, which she got if she
was lucky.*

God was an arsehole.

*Hari-kari, whoever he was, had no fucking business in a
kitchen; she would be deafened by the whimpering for a start,*

herself, the dog or the cat, made no difference. Back upstairs then, colder and colder, the cat in her arms. Although she protested, cat had cold steel against her throat. Nothing could be colder than her feet. Serena spoke softly to Ginger, explaining that this was not selfish; it was just too bad she was needed for practice. Serena had always loved cats, admiring the way they refused to heed a single social obligation, but, all the same, something had to die first to make sure she got it right.

She nodded, regally, at the grandfather clock on the way upstairs.

Back on her couch, concentration failed while she wondered what to relinquish in order to get the full use of her hands. Fur or knife, knife or fur, find the slippers, get feet warm, don't let go of anything, although the wretch wailed, knowing she wanted her throat. Cats were always feminine, to Serena's mind, regardless of sex. Females should be stoical about life as well as death.

And then she coughed, big, explosive spasms, out of control, too many cigarettes, too much age, and the knife lunged into the pillow and Ginger was off like greased lightning. She howled, shook her fist, but the cat stayed on top of the wardrobe, licking to get rid of the taste of Serena, just like everyone else did. Look, she said, we were in this together. The cat had no imagination.

'No bollocks!' she yelled.

Bums, cunts and bums. Fucking bums.

Back to the writing-paper then, restless.

There was another thing to do with the knife. She would stick it right up her private bits, turn it round and round and round, dig it in. Killing herself this way might be no worse than a big bleed and certainly better than having a baby. That was tomorrow's plan, then: she would get ice from downstairs; something to put on top and dull the pain while she bled away slowly from

23

below. Three hours at least before anyone would find her, six if she said she was tired, and by then half her vital fluids would be in the mattress.

Tomorrow, promise?

First she wanted to tell them, so that when they found her she could point to the paper. The sounds she made these days were so ugly. Dawn edged prettily round the window with the promise of a fine October day. She wrote busily.

Fucking bloody arseholes, fucking cunts. Bums, bums, bums. It's all on that paper, there; her whole life history on the paper which she put under the pillow for transferring to the desk.

She even told them how dawn had looked before another day of horror.

Grey, colour, shot with light, streaked with excrement.

Curious.

CHAPTER TWO

Isabel Burley began most conversations by saying she was sorry. It was not always clear why, but she was usually in a state of apology about something. She was thirty-three years old and honed into fitness and a slenderness she wore well without anyone remarking how extreme it was. The joints were too big for the body: experts would notice a closet anorexia; the rest were either bewitched or bewildered by the long legs, ballerina features and gauche lack of grace, as if life had frozen her adolescent years into the stance of either a frightened gazelle or a clumsy foal. She had a nervous laugh and was widely perceived as reliable, if stupid. If she turned up for an appointment damp, breathless and late, she still turned up without fail. Poor little semi-rich girl, sometime aerobics teacher, sometime cosmetics saleswoman, sometime student, victim to her own good looks, her own incessant concern about them and a constant anxiety to please. There was more than an element of the dizzy blonde, except she was dark. Whenever she passed a mirror, she checked her long hair.

The riches, such as they were, consisted of Aunt Mab's inheritance, received with bewildered gratitude over a decade before, to the fury of Mab's nephew Robert, who received nothing. Aunt Mab had been a schoolteacher who knew very well how to invest her stipend, so the fruits of her prudence and her pretty cottage had been enough for Isabel to buy a London flat and thus avoid the need to earn more than a modest living. Isabel always served her notice, but she preferred jobs she could leave. What others spent on mortgages, she spent on clothes. Her brother Robert said it was amazing she had never tried drugs, since she was extravagant and they were not fattening. The riches were not of the endless sort, but they were sufficient to set her apart from striving contemporaries. What was left of her inheritance, Robert said, was all for pissing downwind, like the fool she was. This was not entirely true: Isabel had invested carefully, and although she knew where the bottom of the barrel was, she was never going to scrape it.

Men loved Isabel, who had been brought up never to be a nuisance and rarely was. Despite the feeling of inadequacy that made her twist her mouth in front of a mirror in the morning, telling herself over and over, 'I am not silly, I am not silly,' a practice learned from a self-help manual and rendering at least one lover paralysed with laughter, she could never quite encompass the truth of her own denials. Isabel Burley was not, after all, a fool, but she had two inhibiting agents to that hidden, mental chemistry which was not brilliance, but certainly intelligence. Firstly, education had centred around dancing class, whatever Aunt Mab had done to redeem the lack in school holidays; and secondly, she loved her mother in an unconsolable way. She had always hoped to emulate Serena when she finally grew up; she had never lived up to the image.

The ability to drink men under the table was only one of the characteristics they admired; another was her constant availability. She was good at delivering men back to their own doorsteps, or taking them to hers, where they lay, impotent and groaning, for twenty-four hours and she, sweet thing, did not mind. Later they would translate this experience into the memory of a good time, remember her with affection, while not quite recalling anything she said. 'I love Isabel Burley,' was not a sentiment shouted from rooftops. She dispensed enough kindness to deserve greater loyalty, but she did it without either thought or finesse.

As for the friendship of women, that was difficult. There were waifs and broken-hearted strays, but otherwise women could not see Isabel as either safe or unenviable.

'I love you Issy . . . You know how much I love you.'

'No, I don't know. If you loved me, you'd be married to me and not to someone else.'

It was Joe who caused the problems by being really mad about her. Married, of course, engaged initially on the first sight of Bella in leotard. He had a couple of nights out on the town with Issy, simply to relieve tension, which it did, before she sent him home to his nuptials. Despite his marital bed, Joe could not get her out of his mind and after six months came back howling at the windows of her posh flat for all the heart he had found there once. She had let him in, and two years of passionate vacillation followed.

'How could I leave her? She would never manage without me . . .'

On the evening of the night when Isabel received the phone call about her mother and the fire, Isabel had bitten Joe, on the thigh. The bite was ugly, and a perfect reverse pattern of Isabel's teeth. It drew minimal blood, although the scratches to his chest and the head wound from the edge of a jug, thrown across the room with considerable force, bled furiously. This occurred in the interval between after-work hours and going home, the traditional time for a married man to call upon his mistress. By ten that night, Isabel was contemplating the wreckage of her blood-stained bedclothes and her whole, loveless existence. It was not the first time her occasional propensity to violence had horrified her as much as what she had become and what little she had ever achieved. Bimbo. Airhead. Cheap. Everything her mother had never been, let alone what Aunt Mab would have wanted for her. She was in a state of self-hating chaos. Her love for her mother, Robert's endless chastisement, and the reservoir of guilt which always lapped against her backbone, made her a soft enough touch already.

Life had never thrown Isabel in close conjunction with any form of mental ailment except that encountered in the street. In the midst of her desultory packing, she remembered briefly what she had once known with uncomfortable clarity, namely that Serena had never approved of her, was one of the majority who considered her a fool. She put the realization back inside a box and into the attic store room of her thoughts.

The thought of Mother's flesh, roasted rare, black on the outside, pink in the middle, tipped an unwary balance poised on the cliff of a wasted life. By midnight, going home to look after Serena seemed the only thing left to do. And the only thing that might redeem her pride. It was her mother who was the one who might give love and want it back and it was for both the privileges, the getting and the giving, that she went home.

'Love you, Mum. Now, what are we going to do about your hair?' Isabel had entered a world far distant from the anonymity of London and it was difficult to call it familiar. Yet ten days later the place she thought of as home had reclaimed her, made her forget how anxious she had been to leave it in the first place: how nothing between the ages of eighteen and twenty-one had ever worked; how miserable she had been. All she could recall now was her arrival. No sign of Serena. No greeting. Instead a clash of sound from the tape deck in the long living room, reverberating and echoing over the whole house, shivering the timbers in a series of violent discords. Mother shouting above it, 'I don't need you, I need words!' thumping the wall to make the kind of row that drowned thought. Isabel had paused, then rushed towards the noise, which stopped before she reached it. Serena's eyes, defiant, met hers.

'The words are over there,' she had begun, looking towards the desk, before a big beatific smile dawned in that stretched, ugly-attractive face and she had sprung towards her daughter with an energy that defied her years. Her hair was dull and her make-up odd: thick, pale foundation, brilliant blue paste over the eyelids. There were subtle changes in the month since Isabel's last, fleeting, visit. Now she was here to stay. Make things better; do something properly.

'Darling! You're so thin! My lovely child!'

There was the strange sensation of being greeted by a duchess. A hostess who hid the fact she was expecting this guest and had been anticipating the arrival for some time.

Isabel had melted into her embrace, drowned herself in it. 'Shh,' she had said, 'shh, Mummy. It's all right now.' Saying the words and making the gestures she wanted for herself.

'I do love you,' Serena had said. 'I do, I do.'

Had she ever said that before? Isabel could not remember, only knew how sweet it was to hear.

'I know you do. What a big hug! You never used to like hugging.'

They had swayed together, Serena's soft bosom surrendering the smell of lavender, her arms surprisingly strong.

'You never used to like music so much, either, sweetheart. What's got into you?'

Serena had withdrawn slightly, to arms' length. Enough distance to look into Isabel's face, caress her cheek, pinch it playfully, but in a way which hurt a little. Isabel had a dim memory of scratches over her buttocks from a lover. Affection carried scars. She had not flinched. The analogy of a lover continued, with her mother's delicate hands on her own slim hips, the swelling stomach of the older woman pushing forward with great insistency, spreading against her own waist, the voice urgent with whispered confidence.

'Darling, you've come home at last. Let me tell you things . . .'

Today, the wind blew.

'Let me tell you something,' George said to the dog as they plodded back across the fields. 'Number one is that there's far worse things than being on your own. Serena and I know that, don't we? Believe me. And there's worse things a dog can do than run sheep, or a man chase women, but I'm glad you've lost the habit.'

The dog squatted, strained with total concentration.

George looked at her with concern: trouble with bowels was a sign of age in a retriever, so he'd heard. Serena should stop feeding her pap. He thought how he would break up into little pieces if anything happened to this old bitch, and not only because she was the formal *raison d'être* for his being in Mrs Burley's house. There would be far less reason for him to be there on a daily basis if there was no dog to walk: he could hardly take out that vicious little ginger cat which needed no guardian and already ate, slept and ran where it pleased.

'The worst thing you can ever be,' George told the dog as they resumed progress uphill, 'is too crowded. Penned up with a hundred other people, never left by yourself for a minute. Not when you squat, not when you sleep, not when you eat. I didn't know what hell was, but I'm telling you now, that's exactly what it is. And if that's hell, this is heaven.'

The wind gusted strongly in their faces. George challenged himself not to walk slower in the face of such force and an uphill gradient: it was a discipline to walk at the same pace at all times. Get the heartbeat going, set a steady pace and keep it up for at least an hour, make a bit of a sweat, but not too much, and just keep going, enjoying the sensation of muscles at work. Once he had established a pace, then he could look around. See nothing but the fields, feel the mud beneath his boots, catch from the corner of his eye the fungus on that tree, the squirrel leaping from one bare branch to another, the fat blackbirds near the house. When the dog lumbered away in comic and futile pursuit of a rabbit, George almost doubled up with pleasure. 'You can't explain it to no one else,' he told her. 'Not to no one who doesn't know what you mean already, why you should chase that thing, and I should be so happy. I doubt if Mrs Burley knows it either, but at least she never asks questions. You can't explain being happy, that's for sure.'

He had the dreamer's knack of forgetting. Out here, or in the garden with the dog who was the receptacle for all his secrets, George could think of his own home with less revulsion. Not a home, more of a billet, a bed-sit in a hostel for so-called hopeful cases, people from abnormal lives on their way to what passed for normality. He had lived there for four years, a halfway house in a new town which had become home. Get a job, they said, ha, ha, ha. Should be easy for a well-built man like you, factories around here not fussy about a record as long as you work: amazing, but it's still difficult to find someone willing to put in the hours and besides, you won't have much opportunity for your little game among all the heavy machinery. He had stuck it for a month, then gone berserk, run out of there scream-ing, sacked next day. We don't mind the record, the boss told his social worker, but he can't stand being crowded and we can't be doing with the disabled. Which George somehow dimly knew himself to be. Despite his physical strength.

'And how did you get to be here?' That was Janice asking. He could laugh at the memory of her curiosity, the affront to her of something happening without her knowing.

'Oh, I was just walking by. Saw Mrs Burley trying to trim that bush outside the gate. She couldn't do it, so I said, give us those shears, Missus, I'll do it for you.'

Something like that, a lifetime ago. He did not mention the lassitude of those long walks before Serena had found him. Long walks in the countryside reached in his battered car, the only solace he knew for despair. Those empty days before Serena had asked him in for tea and behaved as if she had known him for ever, no questions, no judgement, simply acceptance.

Greyer clouds rolled forward over an already grey sky, the beginning of the afternoon darkness, and George marvelled at how much of these mean days he was able to spend with the light on his back. His red hair was thin on top, his ears stuck out, but he refused the benefit of hat and gloves which Serena pressed on him. Makes me too hot, Missus. He swung his legs over the gate and marched round the back of the house. There was the familiar smell of homecoming, and also, in the sight of Isabel's jaunty little car, the sulphurous smell of a crowd, and the whiff of danger. He frowned. He was trying to extend towards Isabel Burley some of the vast affection he felt for her mother, but he could not. All right: he hated her and she disliked him. She was not a patch on her mother: she had no class, and she made him tremble with the old, familiar shame.

He could hear the murmur of voices from the living room. On the kitchen sideboard there were letters waiting for the postman, at least two letters a day. He always took them, posted them in town. He had collected the post, too, from Sal at the end of the road, but now, he supposed, Isabel would object, once she noticed. Fear clutched at his lungs. Already he was relegated to the kitchen as if he had never gone beyond; Isabel's rule prevailed. He saw the erosion of his tasks and also saw, with contempt, that there was one envelope addressed in a clear hand, larger but similar to Serena's microscopic script. Her own were important letters, Serena said. He looked at them as he scooped them up in one large paw, ready to leave without a word, sick with a kind of envy. George wanted his house back. He was also waiting for an accusation from Isabel. She gave me those things, he would say. Gave them me. I never took them.

'Serena Burley has Alzheimer's disease,' John Cornell told his son, with a slight satisfaction he found difficult to hide. 'She's on her own,' he added unnecessarily, 'and going barmy. Now that isn't a good thing.'

'She might not have Alzheimer's,' said his son, looking up from the catalogue. 'Rumour has it she's been getting very strange and eccentric, that's all.'

'I know what I'm talking about. I had several drinks with Doc Reilly. It's not eccentric to set your own coalhouse on fire: it's mad. The doc says it can only get worse.'

'Well, I think that's very sad, because she's always been a charming woman, and anyway, I don't always believe in Dr Reilly's diagnoses.'

What an unholy alliance they were, his father and Doc Reilly.

Cornell senior snorted into his coffee mug and kicked the rostrum where Andrew sat.

'Just as you don't really approve of the good doctor. Or filthy commerce, or earning a living. What *do* you approve of, Andy?'

Better to shrug, pretend he was not paying attention, distract Father with something else, to stop an early-evening conversation, at that time of day when Dad needed a drink, from escalating into the kind of destructive exchange of words that was more a swapping of insults than a row which achieved something. Not even a clearing of the air, since the air between them was always thick with misunderstanding, beyond the curing of either of them. Andrew did indeed struggle with the unpicturesque partnership of Doc Reilly

34

and his own dear old Dad. It had begun over the years while Father graduated from wheelchair to sticks: from fallen glory to wily strength. He and the Doc were a pair of small-town, clever rogues in a constant process of graduation to something worse. If they had lived in a Wild West town, Dad would have been an undertaker and they would have carved up business between them. Doc Reilly, for instance, did not abide by any code of confidentiality when one of his patients was dying, especially a patient who might possibly have a house to sell and furniture for the picking. The auction room in which they sat contained three sets of deceaseds' effects, all of them erstwhile visitors to Doc's surgery, asking for him in particular, and while most of the stuff was reasonable rubbish, some of it was always far better. Andrew could see his father now, hovering over Serena Burley's ugly house and exquisite furniture like a fat vulture unable to wait for the victim to be entirely without movement, too impatient for the last sign of breath. Nearly dead was as good as dead.

'Too early for fog,' John grumbled.

He did not even look like a Steptoe; that was the problem. He looked like an old gent.

It was a rich little conurbation in which they lived, prosperous market town on the one hand, ugly on the other, full of Midlands contempt for anything fancy. The ugly end had made John Cornell his money after he had built the two cheap estates in the sixties, houses that still changed hands with monotonous regularity. Were people so easily fooled, both then and now, when houses were so lacking in quality but full of gimmicks, Andrew wondered? He was equally amazed at his father's level of business cunning, which diversified his empire entirely as fashion dictated, but always slightly ahead of it. Cornell had once pandered to the over-whelming desire for something new, while never forgetting the dual gods of nostalgia and greed. First, the new houses with an old look, then old furniture made palatable.

'We've got a good lot of stuff coming in this week. There'll be more after Christmas.'

Because the elderly died in winter. Andrew had spent almost eight years of his life nursing his father after a car smash which had never curtailed the drinking or dulled the old man's wits. Doc Reilly said that this was how the boy had learned his love of a good antique. Both of them had resented it. John was not made kinder by disablement and the youthful Andrew had been poised for flight, which now felt too late for the prematurely middle-aged man he had become. He had never possessed an ounce of his father's wildness, weighted as he was with the absence of his father's conscience.

'What kind of a reserve price do we put on Mrs Jones's sideboard?'

'I don't know. A lot, I would. It's handsome, like she was, once. It won't go first time round unless a dealer buys it.'

Strange the way his father leered over furniture the way he lusted after women and yet, in a public way, was so capa-ble of appearing to treat both with respect. A façade, while his son felt a frisson of pure affection when his blunt fingers ran over polished wood, sorrow when he examined some-thing damaged. Andrew would feel the fracture in a fine chair leg with all the sensitivity of a vet with a favourite lame horse, the Doc said, while with women he was useless: tongue-tied and shy. A clod of a boy, his father confided; a man to waste all his hormones stroking inanimate objects.

John Cornell lumbered to his feet, leant heavily on his stick and made for the door of the disused church that served as an auction room. He had never had time for the clergy, but he had to admit the buggers could build. The door alone would stop a tank, and if his son's docility was going to deny him the satisfaction of shouting, then he might as well leave.

Andrew was fingering a blue vase. Put it back in the cabinet where small items, some they had bought, some for sale on commission, remained.

'Dad?'

'What?'

'Don't you think you should have asked a few more questions about this?'

'That was three weeks ago, son. And he seemed a harmless enough fellow: friend of Derek's. Been in before with the odd bit and piece. Puts his cash in his sock.'

'Yes, I know, you said. A few small items over a few weeks. Nothing he would ever own himself. How do we know where he got them?'

'Nothing very valuable. Why worry about fifty quid's worth? Friend of Derek's. Bound to be OK.'

'For Christ sake, since when was being a friend of Derek a recommendation from the Queen?'

'You know what, son? You've got homophobia, that's your problem.'

He was halfway to the door, nonchalant about getting the boy to react after all. Good to see him there, stiff with righteous rage.

'Dad . . . Another thing . . .'

'What now?' He loved this door, so difficult to shift, a challenge.

37

'You won't get your hands on Serena's stuff for a while, you know. Her daughter's come home to look after her. Your lovely old Mrs Burley could go on for ever.'

Triumph indeed. John Cornell's shoulders shook with the kind of mirth that could only be created by knowing more than someone else. It was a source of solace he had perfected in illness. He changed tack, looked at his son sorrowfully.

'I know, son, I know. Don't ever think you're first with the news. And her brother's asked us to do a valuation. When you've time, that is.'

'He what?'

'You heard. It's only me with licence to go deaf, you know. Not you, at your age.'

He went, the door left open behind him, the suggestion of scorn and restrained laughter heavy in the air. Inside this church there was no odour of sanctity, and much of desecration. Andrew Cornell sat at the rostrum, once a pulpit, staring at a room full of old furniture. He did not bother his head with thoughts of where his life had gone wrong, how on earth it had diverted itself up this avenue of exploitation and discontent. He thought about Isabel Burley, imagined her beauty against his plainness, then thought with less intensity about her mother, and what an inestimable pleasure it must be to lose one's memory, provided it included the forgetting of all those times one had been either coward or fool.

Do you love me, dear parent?

Home is where the heart is. The homes of Isabel's childhood had been in other houses, before Father's affluence and Mother's wish had landed them in this place. Father had lived for present splendour and ignored his pension plan. He

38

had died on his one last trip abroad after Isabel had left this house. Her memory of him was blurred.

Do you like me?

It seemed an urgent question to ask as they sat by the fire, but she could not bring herself to put it into words. 'Do you love me, Mother? Do you? Did you ever?' She did not ask it: it was impertinent, she knew, but in the face of Serena's studied indifference it seemed a worthwhile query. Isabel wanted a reward for what she was doing; wanted her mother, forgetful as she was, to remember that her daughter's presence in this remote house might have involved some kind of sacrifice, might even have been seen as noble enough to be worth someone saying, Thank you, well done, that child. But no one had, Mother least of all.

Over the first week Isabel had met the butcher, baker, vicar, George and Janice. The latter two seemed to resent her presence, Janice to the tune of downing tools altogether, while others took it for granted with amazing speed, as if they were suddenly relieved of a burden themselves. Isabel had come to realize that there had been an informal but efficient network that looked after her mother's interests and that, frankly, the whole gang was sick and tired of the task, except daft George. Serena's wider circle of party-going friends seemed to have disappeared. Perhaps it was the fear inspired by people who were ill to the point of madness, as if they were contagious, and this made Isabel indignant, deflected her thoughts. She could not yet begin to understand that aversion. Her mother was simply a case of warped magnificence, not in the same category as anyone else.

'Who are you writing to, Mum?' Isabel was careful; tried to be sensitive. Mother's desk was private and she was never going to try to look inside it. Privacy was sacred: she must not invade it. A pause, a guttural reply. 'People. Lots of people.'

'Do you remember writing to me?'

'Oh no, darling, I never wrote to you. Did I?'

The image slipped out of focus.

Isabel felt an overwhelming sadness. Where was the creature of power and beauty, bending to kiss her in a waft of perfume before leaving to go somewhere else? The writer of the great wad of exciting letters, sent from all over the world, displayed with pride to friends as the product of the fairest hand on earth?

'Mum, I think we should have a party. What do you think?'

There was no reply. The darkness outside was complete. Serena sat in her armchair by the fire, a writing pad on the table in front of her, one hand shielding what she wrote, her eyes squinting through her glasses at the page in the light of the standard lamp behind her. Her fountain pen scratched across the paper with a sound which had begun to irritate, like the distant sound of a dripping tap. Isabel noticed how her mother's glasses were scratched and dirty: the sight made her feel deficient. Ten days here, busy with re-organization and novelty, bathed in the glow of her own virtue and she had not noticed that her mother's spectacles were less than useless. Or that what her mother wrote in these evenings and afternoons was likely to be scribble.

'A party, Mum! What do you think?'

Serena sighed and put down the pen.

'A what?'

'A party!' Isabel found herself yelling. Ashamed of it, she lowered her voice. 'A party, Mum, for your friends. You know.'

Realization dawned on Serena's face. 'A party? You mean a party?'

Isabel found herself shouting again. She was looking at the paper Mother covered with writing, remembering the wonderful letters received at school, her own window on foreign worlds, the borrowed sophistication she had felt on receiving them, thinking at the same time of the letter she had written to Joe this week, the craven apology and all the anger dead. Do you love me? Does anyone to whom I have surrendered myself love me?

'I said, a party! I meant a party!!'

Mother smiled, then shook her head.

'Lovely. But we couldn't have a party without George. And George wouldn't like it.'

'What does George matter?'

'George wouldn't like it.'

'I'd like it.'

The eyes behind the scratched glass looked preternaturally calm and magnified into an owlish wisdom. The face was transfixed into a wide smile of artificial politeness as she picked up her pen again and spoke with dismissive precision out of the corner of her mouth.

'You'd like it? But you don't matter at all.'

Isabel counted to ten, slowly. It was not the first of the insults, only the neatest and, even in the euphoria inherent in the knowledge of doing good, being for once in her life Virtuous with a capital V, she had noticed them all. She dismissed them as she guessed she was meant to dismiss them, as part of Mother's little insecurities. Less than that, in fact, simply a form of teasing, meaning nothing, surely, characteristic of the way her mother had always teased. The wounds and the hugs were synchronized.

41

'Love you,' Serena said, without looking up from her writing, murmuring with the sighing distinction that only occurred in the evenings. 'Love you lots. Do you love me?'

Isabel did not reply. Then, 'We need some more coal for the fire,' she said.

'George got the coal in earlier. He brought it from the new place where the coal lives now. Bucket by the back door.'

George did everything. He was polite, coyly deferential to Isabel, and did not flaunt his indispensability. He scuttled away when he saw her, but he still did everything. It was he who understood this domain, he upon whom Serena relied.

No. She needs me.

The kitchen smelled, of stove and dishcloth and chips and warm dog. Beyond that door, the evening was bleak. Winter glowered. She did not like leaves drifting against the back door, the constant domination of the vast garden, the mud which clung to shoes and the silence of the stars at night. Hush, child: things done in the name of love are well worth doing. Loving and being loved; that was life. By the time she came back from the kitchen with the bucket of coal, the living room was full of sound. Mother's tape deck was turned up high and Mother's plump body blocked the fire, swaying to the sound. She clutched her skirts to reveal her stockings and wiggled her hips.

'Did you say party?' she asked. Beamed.

'Pretend you're a man,' she said. 'Let's dance.'

CHAPTER THREE

Home, sweet home. People are looking at me.

George felt the cold sweat of panic. Not the rage of his claustrophobia, the panic of guilty conscience.

I wanted a friend, he told himself; someone to talk to, but people like Derek can only be enemies. Who loves ya, George?

George knew he should not have left those letters in his room, not for a minute. Nothing could be left in the hostel rooms, unless it was old clothing no one else would want. Dirty socks, even underwear, walked away from the washing machine in the basement. The laces from George's training shoes had gone. And so had the letters, probably for the sake of the first-class stamps. Inside prison walls there had been some code of manners. Here there was none. He could see Derek, laughing.

But then anything, even a piece of paper, was currency to small, skinny Derek. George found the envelopes, less the stamps and the contents, in the waste bin under the kitchen sink, along with the remnants of Chinese takeaways and polystyrene containers for hamburgers. Derek might return the letters, but he would want to barter, and any material that he could glean from the letters, such as the address from where they were written, would already have been absorbed. George hoped against hope that Derek's erratic concentration did not make any connection between the address in the letters and his own daily destination. He also hoped the information had not been shared. Derek had the morals and the curiosity of a cat. George had befriended him before realizing the pathetic mewing was the preliminary to a scratch.

The prevailing smell in the kitchen was soap and nicotine. George did not drink or smoke, the others' single largest expenditures, and he cooked proper food. They called him Miss Tiggy Winkle. He was the only one who brought inside what he called proper food, namely the raw materials, meat and vegetables, bread that failed to stick to the roof of the mouth, ingredients that required preparation. The length of time he took making his evening meal made him the object of some derision, deflected in part by the element of admiration maintained for anyone who persisted in eccentricities, and the fact that he left what he did not eat, including apple pies and cakes, which were more popular than stew made from scrag-end of lamb or vegetable soup. George earned himself peace and an element of anonymity with the deliberate leftovers of his solid, nutritious food. He flexed his muscles round the kitchen sink, just to let them see he was guarding his back.

The kitchen was as far removed from Serena's as any kitchen could be. Galvanized steel cupboards, an industrial cooker with eight stern gas rings, an oven big enough to roast an ox. Two sets of utilitarian formica-topped tables flanked by stacking chairs, set on a grey-and-white lino floor, always indifferently clean. Bright neon lights to illuminate the spartan comfort and show up all the faces as they set about the business of eating. Attempts had been made towards homeliness, such as posters on the walls and two plastic plants, but the room remained, at best, like a school canteen, at worst, when the day was grey and the smell was bad, a miserable basement room, always warm.

Warmth drew Derek here, away from the loneliness of his own room, which always smelled vaguely of bodily fluid – sperm, sweat, blood and urine – masked with disinfectant and deodorant, as did all upper three corridors of the hostel for otherwise homeless men, some *en route* between prison and the real world. The smell of sperm came first, like the wafted emissions from a factory making glue. The scent of fifteen loveless men was undisguisable, even when they showered, dressed and stole each other's toiletries. It was an unreal rite of passage to the real world.

'Hey up, George. How've you been?'

'All right, thanks. And you?'

'Oh, fine. I won the lottery again, did I tell you?'

George was a freak: he shone with cleanliness in poor clothes, he kept his room anonymous and he did not cry in the night. Derek, a resident for six months now, had adored him. George did unheard-of things; he ran a self-serviced car, often up on bricks (someone must have given him that car: Serena had given him that car); he had somewhere to go every day, from where he returned, refreshed and fulfilled; he fried mushrooms which he collected himself because he knew how; and last week he made a pie, for nothing, out of blackberries. That made him rich and, in the hinterland of

45

people with nothing to lose and no idea of what they stood to gain, enormously enviable. George had a secret. George was happy. That was something that had to be fixed. People liked George: that would have to be fixed, too. Derek, small and sweet, skinny little runt with a handsome face, everybody's gofer, with just enough sense not to turn tricks in public loos in a small town like this, admired the stockiness of George and the muscles on his arms, fancied himself in love. All George wanted was to keep his bum clean, but he had been flattered and loved the easy flow of words and jokes. Derek had made him laugh.

'There was a bit of a fight in here, dinner time,' said the man who had greeted him and watched, hungrily, as he peeled potatoes.

'Oh dear,' said George, not inviting further particulars. There were often squabbles. It was dangerous to be a one-eyed man in the country of the blind, perilous to be in possession of his own particular source of peace. He knew he had to watch it.

He should never have talked to Derek. Have let Derek take him to the old furniture place to sell stuff, as if he was a fellow thief. Have let Derek find out, from his own, unguarded, tongue, what there was to envy.

'We've lost the letters,' Serena said next morning.

'George took them,' said Isabel for the tenth time.

'I want them back.'

'You can't have them back. Never mind, you've written some more.'

Which she had. Two, three letters a day. Or pieces of paper stuck into envelopes that bore addresses Isabel could not read and doubted if any postman could, either. Isabel was not going to point this out. Letters were therapy and Serena was entitled to whatever secret life she wished to lead behind those scratched glasses.

'I want to go to town *now*.'

'Come on, then.'

'I'm driving, aren't I?'

'No, Mummy, you know you can't. Be a good girl.'

It horrified Isabel the way she had so quickly got into the habit of talking to her mother as if her mother were a child. It seemed to rob them both of dignity. Mother was a petulant child this morning. Isabel had been craving a child of her own for the last few years, her body had been crying out for such a burden, but not a child like this.

Isabel's car, which Serena loved and envied, to the extent that Isabel locked it out of sight in the ramshackle garage, was the vital link between town and home. There had been three or four fairly successful forays to the shops: today they would try the market. Isabel had grown accustomed to the rutted track, knew how to avoid the worst of the holes without dipping over into the fields, even enjoyed the challenge. There was nothing between this small, powerful bullet of movement and the sky, nothing at the end of the track but the church and the graveyard, the farm and the cottage and then five miles more to civilization. A party, Isabel thought again, suddenly longing for company. She shivered slightly. However many times she had visited her mother here, she had never done more than nod at the neighbours. Makers of hay and tillers of the earth, nothing in common with either of her parents. She shivered again. How exclusive they had been.

'Are you warm enough, Mum?'

'What?'

Of course she was warm enough. Serena wore an ancient fur coat, a hat suitable for a wedding, with a scarf tied beneath it, huge earrings, shiny black boots. She needed no help with washing and dressing, although the end result was alarming. Her eyebrows were painted black; the remainder of her face pale with thick powder. She was docile in the car as long as music was played.

They both watched with pleasure and curiosity as countryside gave way to the outskirts of town, the sight of people inspiring Serena to point and squawk as if she had never seen people before, while the presence of populace made Isabel homesick. The pointing and gesturing was fine inside the privacy of the car, less so when she guided Serena into the marketplace. Years before there had been some pleasure in shopping with her mother. Isabel looked forward to it, failed to comprehend how different it could be now.

'I want lots of things!' Serena yelled.

'Shh, not so loud. What sorts of things? We need soap and tights and fruit . . .'

'Things!' Serena yelled again, waving her arms about, hitting a man in the chest. He staggered to one side and swore. She darted to a stall, where autumn apples lay in polished splendour next to glowing oranges and bright bananas. The day was grey: the colour of the fruit, artfully assembled in serried rows, beckoned invitingly. Mother wanted the grapefruit at the back, scrabbled at the display, clawed and pawed until the careful symmetry was destroyed and oranges bounced on the cobbled floor of the market square, apples fell in dull successive thumps, plums softer in their quiet bruising. The woman behind the stall was shouting before Isabel pulled Serena away, amazed at the strength she needed to shift her from this orgy of desecration. The shouting made Serena pause; the restraint made her wild until she stopped as suddenly as she had begun. She stood back, looked at the plump owner of the spilled fruit, pointed at the double chins and cawed with laughter. It was a loud, abrasive sound, cutting into the silence.

'Fat!' Serena screamed between her laughter. 'Fat, fat! Oh yes, very fat!'

There was no right reaction. A child can be slapped for bad behaviour. Slapped and made to cry in public, but not a seventy-five-year-old woman. Isabel placed herself between her gesturing mother and the stall, blushing with shame, murmuring apologies, picking up the fruit. A plum squashed beneath her heel: money changed hands as the woman, too, realized that she could not shriek at senior citizens, or at least not for long.

Behind her daughter Serena clicked her tongue and stamped her feet impatiently, as if she were cold and there was nothing more important. 'Hurry up, hurry up,' she was chanting. 'Hurry up. Got to get things.'

The stallholder watched, fury transformed into contemptuous pity. The outburst had a calming effect on Serena. Fear, Isabel told herself, seeking an explanation to suppress her own anger. Surely that was all it was when Mother was faced with crowds of people, colour and choice becoming mingled into one mad abstract canvas, violent in impact. The aggression of frustration.

'What was all that about, Mum?' Her voice cooed. She hated her voice for having to make that cooing sound: she loathed the stallholder for the final benediction of her pity. Mother was marching on, carving a path for herself. She was gazing into the faces of shoppers, smiling widely at each with startled recognition, as if they were long-lost acquaintances, greeted with delight. People avoided her gaze as Mrs Burley sailed down the central aisle of stalls, giving away smiles like presents, Isabel following like a bag carrier, suffused with misery, catching up without wanting to catch up.

'Why did you do that to that stall, Mum?' It was a pointless question for a piece of petulance already forgotten.

Serena stopped. She took her hands out of the pockets of her coat, looked at them slowly. Made fists of them, then let the fingers uncurl, one by one, counting under her breath.

'One, two three . . . I wanted five thingies, Issy. Only I don't know what they are.'

'You wrote them down, darling.'

Serena looked puzzled, then definite, shook her head. 'No, I didn't.'

'Yes, you did. In your pocket?'

'No, I didn't. I don't do that.'

Was that what all that fury was about? A forgotten list in her cramped script? Was that all?

Isabel cooed like a pigeon. 'Don't worry, I can remember what it was you wanted.'

Serena looked at her with the same pity she had herself received from the stallholder, the glance given to a lunatic.

'Of course you don't know what I want. You can't possibly have any idea. I want to go home, is what I want. I want George. Now.'

The voice had risen a pitch. Serena rubbed her eyes, smeared the blackened eyebrows, making her look like a clown.

So they set off towards the multi-storey car park, Serena giggling and pointing again, forgetting the imperative of haste. A ludicrous progress, akin to a pair of drunks, Serena clutching then pulling away, as the mood struck, Isabel embarrassed to restrain her. At one point Serena darted away to stroke the blond hair of a teenage boy: he reacted as if she had slapped him. Isabel hated him, too. Then Serena homed in on a posse of women, engaged them in earnest conversation until they fled in various directions. Then she sabotaged a group of children: she stood by the exit of Tesco, pulling faces, crossing her eyes, putting her fingers in her ears. The youngest child did not object, the eldest giggled with shifty embarrassment. By the time they were back at the car, Isabel had learned to keep a firm hold on her mother's arm and maintain an adamant, insincere flow of loud chat. Serena refused to get into the car, claiming it was not hers, hers was bigger. Persuaded, finally, she slumped into a sulk in the passenger seat until Isabel remembered the music. Pausing to pay at the booth, Isabel aware, for the fiftieth time, of the now familiar glance of pity from the attendant.

'When are we going to have this party?' Serena asked, suddenly sane again.

'Never. Not ever.'

There was a pain throbbing at Isabel's temples: she wanted either to weep or to sleep. It was wrong to feel thus, the opposite of virtuous or forgiving. Wrong to feel this dreadful shame.

They were turning into the homeward stretch at the beginning of the fields by the church, Mother twitching and humming and finally unearthing from her pocket the shopping list which she greeted with a crow of pleasure. She wanted to go back, she announced.

'Back where?'

'Shops.'

'No.'

'Shops. Yes! I know what I want. I want to go back.'

'No. Absolutely not.' No cooing in the voice, merely desperation.

'I want to drive the car!'

Serena had refused the seat-belt and Isabel had failed to insist. She had no preparation for the lunge towards the steering wheel, Serena's ringed hand catching her face, the temporary blindness of her hat in front of her eyes, the screams emerging from her own mouth as the car rocked, bucked, slewed from side to side on the track, romped off the road and into the field. They stalled to a juddering halt. Serena's head hit the windscreen with a gentle crack. In the breathy, sobbing silence that followed, Isabel could feel the soft flesh of her chest pinioning her mother's hard knuckle to the wheel. Beneath her left breast, the fingers began to move like tentacles.

Serena began to whimper.

They were out. They were out and Andrew was pleased; there was an enormous release from his own sense of not quite looking forward to this. There was an old car outside by the stable yard, back door unlocked, but no one in. Good. Andrew was tentative, but unashamed, of trespassing. The house remained as he remembered it, the outside obdurate, but a house which drew in strangers like a sponge drew water. He went into the kitchen. Same old stove, same old quarry tiles on the floor which sloped into the corridor that led through the centre of the house towards the relative grandeur of the black-and-white tiles spread back from the front door. He moved to his left, into the living room, remembered with startling clarity the fact that this was the first place he had kissed

Isabel Burley, when she was twenty. How they had managed to make contact in the vastness of this room puzzled him for a whole minute. Maybe such things were best forgotten, as was the infrequency with which he had kissed women since. He shook himself, remembered he was here to look at furniture, not reminisce.

He sat on the vast sofa with the broken springs. It was so deep, the springs could be avoided: it was for sprawling and snoozing, arguing and making up, this beast. He was a sentimental man: he saw the surface of the cover was not entirely clean, a feature he was almost ashamed to notice in this pale, distinguished place as he rested in it. Lay back against the pommel of the arm, cradling the left side of his face against the right palm of his hand. He moved his fingers over his face, testing the position of his eyes and bones as if he were his own lover exploring his features. She had felt him thus, examining the parameters of his face with the palms of her hands warming his cheekbones. Andrew drew his knees to his chest and opened his eyes. The skin of his palms and his face was suddenly soft. This was indeed a beautiful room, full of beautiful things.

Windows on two sides washed the whole place with light. Three hundred square feet, he reckoned, mostly covered with Indian carpet, whitish, greenish, with some faint design, fringed, frayed, faded, valuable and friendly. Sunlight bleached fabric, warm with age, the Knole sofa, covered with damask, similarly worn and soft. To the left, Serena's rolltop desk, a perfect, well-used piece, like this sofa, glorious wood nevertheless. On the other side, a fantastic rosewood credenza, a bureau, a chest, an assemblage of gossiping chairs by the west-facing window, each different, as if designed for an individual occupant. The chatelaine loved chairs, he remembered. One squat chair with a scrolled back, one gorgeous piece of curved tapestry which belonged in a lady's bedroom, one low-slung bergère armchair. They were married into a group by their sense of expectancy and the plump cushions that invited guests. Old tapestry covers, like the kind found in church, he noticed, not uniform but united by colour. Where had Serena found them? There were curtains which were never drawn, but which drew the eye, a fireplace and, even with the chill on the room, with such comfort implicit in it, he wanted to remain. Carpet worth one thousand, chairs two, bureau three, and so on. He wished it was not so automatic to place a monetary value on things at the same time as admiring them.

Splendid rooms, surely. These were the rooms that gave the house a reputation for beauty, he thought, crossly. While all the time it remained essentially an ugly house designed on a grand scale without much sense of proportion.

He swung himself to his feet and moved across the hall to the dining room. Sat on a carver chair that had seen better days, as had the scratched and glowing walnut of the oval table. This room had the feeling of disuse; it needed flames in the hearth to encourage the latent warmth, a fire and a crowd, candles down the length of the table adorned at the moment with nothing more than two superb silver candlesticks and a vast grape ivy plant with dusty leaves. Andrew looked at his watch. Table worth at least a thousand, matching set of eight dining chairs considerably more. There were fingerprints and smear marks on the table, as if someone had stroked it.

He could venture this far, he decided, but he felt he could not go upstairs without someone to take him. Bedrooms were private places: people kept their secrets there rather than in desks. He could invade only the public domain, and even that was beginning to feel intrusive.

'Excuse me, but what the hell do you think you're doing?'

He turned to find himself looking at a small, faintly familiar and very belligerent red-headed man carrying a stick in one hand, resting the knob in the other palm, flanked by a dog. The voice of inquiry was challenging but polite, although the position of the stick and the square-legged stance of the man left Andrew fairly sure that the benefit of doubt he was being granted was only tempo-rary. The stick was not for decoration. Beside the man, the dog looked redundant. Petal did not bark in the afternoon.

'I'm sorry,' Andrew said pleasantly. 'I came to see Mrs Burley or her daughter. Perhaps I should have waited out-side, but the door was unlocked.'

George clicked his tongue. 'They've gone to the shops. What was it you wanted?' He still held the stick, reluctant to relinquish authority.

Andrew shrugged. 'Nothing that can't wait. Only Mrs Burley's son asked us to look at the furniture, check the insurance. After that fire, you know.' He produced a card.

'Oh.' George was disarmed, also curious. 'She's got some nice things, Mrs Burley.'

'Yes. Yes, she has. Valuable things.'

'They're all old things,' said George, dismissively. 'Worth a bob or two, I expect, but not much. And she won't be having any more fires. Not with me around.'

George decided he did not dislike this harmless-looking man with thin legs under the suit: there was none of the air of understated threat with which George was so familiar, but still he wanted him out of the room.

'I can fix you a cup of tea if you come into the kitchen. No one eats in here any more.'

'And who are you?' Andrew asked meekly, following him.

'I'm George. I walk the dog and look after Serena. Mrs Burley.' George said this with a note of defensive pride.

'Who does the cleaning?'

'Nobody much at the moment. Oh, Miss Burley moves things around, but Mrs Burley did most of it herself. She's not mad, you know.'

The back door stood open, so they heard the car above the sound of the boiling kettle. Music blared as the doors opened, then ceased abruptly. There was the sound of one weary voice, one angry one. Serena was framed in the doorway, crushing her hat. There was a lump on her forehead; her mascara extended past it into her hairline; she staggered slightly. George leapt to her side, clucking anxiety. She gave him the full force of her smile.

'Hello, my lovely. I hit my head, didn't I?'

Andrew did not know the format of this household, nor its hierarchy. He could only interpret the look George gave Serena as one of tender affection and the glance thrown in Isabel's direction as one of murder, which Isabel, three steps behind and clearly struggling for self-control, failed to notice. Her face was blotched: she looked like someone suddenly familiar with defeat. And she was still beautiful. Andrew forgot to notice the complexities and palpable tension of this trio as he stared at Isabel, last seen, how long ago would it be, a dozen years or more, the memory largely ignored in the interim, as if it could ever go away. The long brown hair with the oriental sheen, tied at the nape of her elegant neck, the perfect, slender figure over which she had agonized even then, and the huge, deep-set eyes which defined her face. A house is only as good as what you put in it: Andrew's father said that to customers. Isabel would give credit and dimension to the most unpromising of rooms. She could be hired to lean against furniture, like a model posed against an impossibly expensive car. Good bones: she would always look like an uncertain girl. The nose was a shade too long, he told himself; the mouth too wide. It would devalue her price at auction, but why was it that bidders did not stare after her in the street, and why had she ever let herself be touched by lesser persons than princes? Andrew could not fathom. She was edibly gorgeous, yet removed. Never looking at herself without anxiety. Never looking round and saying, What power I have.

At the same time, he could not believe how he could have been so hurt by something as insubstantial as a letter. He was one person for whom the demise of the letter-writing habit in modern life was not a source of grief.

The resurgence of fascination intrigued him. Isabel Burley had been nothing more than a promiscuous bitch who had wounded him and others. Gone through half the promising men in town and chucked them away. He had thought he would no longer mind in the least about that, and had arrived prepared to treat her with the distant courtesy of the professional he had become. He would have suffered no pain at all if he had not dwelt in those empty rooms first and she did not look first so impressive and then so . . . diminished. While Serena, bruised but plump and glowing, looked as if she was already guzzling on her daughter's vitality.

'What did you do to her?' George was asking, his voice dangerous.

Isabel did not look at him. 'I didn't do anything, George. She did. She tried to grab the wheel and took the car off the road. I managed to get it back. No harm done.'

Then she noticed Andrew. I am always the last to be noticed, Andrew thought.

'This chap says he's come to look at the furniture,' George muttered, dismissing him as Isabel's responsibility.

'How lovely,' Serena trilled, assuming the role of grand hostess. 'You must come to our party.' She was extending her hand and Andrew wondered if he was supposed to kiss it. 'Do sit down, won't you? I think it's time for tea.'

'I think it's time for brandy,' said Isabel. 'Hallo, Andrew. You haven't changed a bit. You remember Andrew Cornell, Mother, don't you?'

It was a pointless question, but Andrew remembered Serena as a gracious, welcoming mother, smiling the extra-wide smile he saw now and which Isabel was coming to recognize as reserved purely for men. They were all smiling at each other. Except George.

'What's all this about furniture?' Isabel asked, breaking up the tableau. George shuffled. He took a clean handkerchief out of his pocket, wandered to the sink, ran it under cold water and took it back to where Serena had retreated to a chair. He placed it lovingly against the lump on her forehead, pressing the cool handkerchief to her skin, keeping her head steady by a gentle touch on the back of her neck. The action was practical, a reminder to those present of their priorities. It was also curiously intimate. It made Andrew shiver. Serena moaned. Isabel sighed. Andrew realized he had not yet opened his mouth to either of them.

'Your brother Robert,' he began. 'Worried about the insurance. I can come back another time.'

'Trust Robert,' Isabel said. 'Full of long-distance ideas. Come into the living room. We all spend far too much time in this kitchen.'

You need help, he told himself, following the graceful curve of her back down the dark corridor towards the fading light of the living room. You need help in the way I have needed help. You have lost your pride. Somehow that reflection neutralized everything and made him calm again.

'George does the fires,' she was saying chattily, rallying herself into some pretence of an ordinary social animal, albeit one who would never have her mother's grace. The fire was laid with old-fashioned skill, he noticed. Newspapers, kindling wood, firelighters, arranged in order with coal on top. He now observed with horror that the marble surround of the fireplace had been painted white. The paper crackled in the hearth at the touch of a match. He wanted to laugh at the sight, wondered if she remembered other times in this room by the light of the dying fire, with everyone else in bed.

'So what have you done for the last few years?' he asked, over-heartily.

'Oh, don't ask. This and that.' Spending that inheritance of hers, he thought with a shade of jealousy. He leant forward, curiosity overcoming shyness.

'And why are you doing this now?'

'Because someone must. She needs me. I need her. I mustn't give up. I've never done anything else worthwhile, you see. So I mustn't fail either. I'm sure I can make her better. Anyway, what does that brother of mine want?'

'He probably wants to make sure that the furniture remains intact, or at least properly recorded and insured. Photographed, perhaps. Your mother won't be able to stay here for ever,' Andrew said carefully. What did she mean she needed her mother? How the hell could something as stunning as this still need her mother?

Isabel looked round and frowned, suddenly determined.

'I don't see why not. It's her home. Moving her would be incredibly cruel and besides, how can it be done? She would never see the necessity. As for the furniture, Robert's welcome to it in the end, but it has to stay put for now. She finds her way around because of the furniture. Like a series of signposts, you see. The furniture orientates her in time and space, somehow. Do you know, I've never really noticed it?'

Ah, he thought, relieved, we are still poles apart. Not notice furniture? Remain immune to things chosen with loving taste in the days when they were affordable? She was what he had half hoped she would be, a silly woman.

'Tell me about it,' she said suddenly, leaning forward towards the light of the fire, depersonalizing the conversation, one ear cocked towards the kitchen. 'You know about these things. What makes all this old wood so special?'

'Age,' he said pompously. 'Age makes everything special.'

She looked at him, amused by his intensity. 'I'll show you upstairs,' she said.

Later he was in his own small house, mercifully free of envy, taking refuge in the things he liked to touch, making an inventory of his friends. Visualizing mother and daughter sitting by that fire, the beautiful and the damned. You cannot be a good daughter, Isabel. You are not the stuff of which good daughters are made. You cannot be a good daughter because you cannot make your mother better.

He remembered how his father's dependence had distorted everything, and he hoped that mother and daughter would be happier.

The kitchen was a cocoon; the house in a time warp; and Isabel was not happy. What had she done to earn such disapproval? Food spat out at supper, the façade of manners gone. Isabel had done nothing to deserve this. Yes, she had left George with Mother, which pleased them both, raced back to the dismal supermarket on the outskirts of town, loaded a poor selection of supplies into the smart car with the crumpled fender, raced home, careful over the fields. Telling herself, I must make this work, I must forget about everything else in order to make this work. Why did Andrew Cornell, and everyone else, drop me so abruptly all those years ago? Too busy to wonder if it still hurt, quickly deciding it did not. Andrew, and James Reilly, and John Eliot. One after another. Damn them all.

Stopping at the gates of the house, Isabel tried to see it the way George might see it, visualizing instead the picture of her mother, rocked in his burly arms. Trying to perceive the elegance of the carefully collected contents of this house in the way Andrew might see them, failing there too. Doubting everyone, herself most of all. Feeling alien, stupid, weepy, even before Mother spat out the food. Then there was a phone call from Robert. Mother answered, with that articulacy of hers which came with evening. No one could see the harridan of the market stalls. Isabel did not want people to see that. She did not really want anyone to know what her mother could be like. She listened to her mother complaining to Robert about the bump on her head, poor darling. Found herself too listless to respond to his scolding: how could she be so careless? Come and see, she told him with her new mildness; come and see for yourself. Was she such a failure that she had grown to this age purely to be so comprehensively blamed?

Bedtime. Peace for the wicked. Go first, Mother. Please go first and leave me alone. Shouting at her, none of this cooing nonsense for a nasty, naughty, wilful little girl, the brat that she was.

'Go away, you silly old woman! Go to bed!'

Simply orders. And then the final act in the day's drama. Going upstairs past her mother's door, with no desire to kiss and make friends, hearing the sound of hopeless sobbing. It rose and fell, this muffled sound of grief, a cadence of sublime misery like the cat at half throttle stuck somewhere inside a cupboard, screaming for release. The sound paused, coughed into silence, continued quavering and helpless.

The heavy door of her mother's room was shut, yielded to a shove. The tester bed which Andrew Cornell had valued with his eyes and admired with well-disguised soul, stood rumpled and unoccupied. Serena resented any interference with her room: she kept it clean herself. The draught slammed the door shut behind her daughter: the sound continued, deafening to the conscience, in reality subdued. There was a row of dolls and teddy bears over the bed, which Isabel would swear she had never seen before until she recognized some of them as her own.

Serena stood by the open window, plump, forlorn, clad in her embroidered nightdress, curlers in her hair, sobbing as if the world had ended. Her body beneath Isabel's spontaneous embrace glowed like a furnace; only the extremities were cold.

The words were blurred at first, then clear. 'I want to die, Issy. I want to die. I don't want to be like this. I want to die. I want to die and set everyone free.'

'Of course you don't. Shhh. You'll get cold.'

'Cold, dead. What does it matter? I should be dead.'

'I never left you, Mumsy. I shan't leave you now. Don't fret. Come to bed.'

'I'm sorry, love. I'm sorry. I can't help what I do. I go crazy when I'm frightened. So frightened . . .'

'I know, I know.'

She did not know, but she understood grief. Serena succumbed, put her thumb in her mouth and allowed herself to be rocked to sleep. The lump on her forehead was pale and shiny. Her size seemed unutterably pathetic: so did the curlers in her hair. Her face was still slack with tears: her daughter's, puffed with love.

My mother loves me. Everything is worthwhile. She keeps my old teddy bears in her room. We truly love each other.

Isabel went downstairs again, carrying the cat dragged from under the bed. You go outside, cat, she told it, feeling slightly cheerful in an odd kind of way. She had made her mother better: there was no anger any more, only sorrow; there was nothing to forgive, simply love in buckets . She shook the cat. I thought you were out already, I put the milk out for you, I remember now. Isabel was feeling capable, fiercely protective, wise, even peaceful. There was no such thing as perfect peace. Peace was for the brave. Neither she nor the cat had done enough to deserve an easy life. They had to reconcile themselves to difficulties.

She could not tell at first what the thing outside the door was. It was russet in colour, lighter than her own hair and she saw it through the opaque glass of the back door, lapping at the saucer of milk she had left. Isabel did not begrudge the milk: nor was she all that partial to the cat which littered the kitchen almost daily with signs of savagery, but she was suddenly enraged at the impertinence of the alien usurper, all sinuous arrogance blurred by the glass in the frosted pane before she opened the door and shouted at it. Shouted into the dark emptiness of the middle of the night.

'Go away!' Then, less self-consciously, 'Piss *off*!'

How long had it taken her to realize that shouting was permissible here, even encouraged by the fact there was no one to be disturbed? Two weeks? Time was already immaterial.

She was too much a townswoman to know the difference between stoat and ferret, or to know the nature of either. If she had, she would not have startled it into such spitting and hissing, its low snarl at odds with its sinister beauty, little white teeth bared, eyes huge. The ferret advanced towards her: she slammed the door shut, watching through the glass as it shook itself delicately and then returned to the milk.

'Coward!' Isabel said loudly, addressing herself. If she left it the victor this fastidious thing would return every night. Seizing the broom she opened the door again, shoved it towards the milk saucer, hitting the thief with energy, wanting to watch it run, yelling at it until, with spitting fury and a snarl, the creature launched itself at the bristles, biting and scratching in a whirl of teeth and fur. Isabel crashed the door closed again, stood trembling on the safe side of the glass, unable to move. The creature hurled itself at the door, then settled back to wash.

There was a sensation of acute loneliness in watching that elegant little beast preen with such nonchalance. Isabel could feel teeth snapping at her face. She was unscathed and unscarred, simply feeling foolish, but if that creature had leapt towards her eyes or fastened on her wrist, no one would have heard the screams. She was the one with the fear, it had none, while upstairs there slept a human being who would never provide help in an emergency.

This was the way she had committed herself to live, for as long as it took. The protector, never the protected. She was numbingly, blindingly, tired.

She was going to be brave. Resolute, indispensable. She was loved.

CHAPTER FOUR

'She's been there a month. What do they do all day?' John Cornell asked his son. 'I mean, what does a lovely young lady do every day with only an old woman for company?'

'I don't know. How should I know? What does anyone do all day? What did we do all day when I was locked in with you?'

'You had a job of work, that's the difference. Somewhere else to go. What does it take to look after one old granny? They don't eat much.'

'I think it's more like looking after a child.'

'Was I like a child?' Father was teasing. Andrew looked at him and saw a grin of monkey cunning. He had a long memory.

'Just like a child,' Andrew said smoothly. 'But you also had a working brain and you couldn't move half the time. That had distinct advantages.'

'Good old days, son. You should have left me to it.'

The auction room was ready to go. People filtered through the porch, paid for the catalogues Andrew had copied that afternoon, wandered between the rows of beds, chairs, tables, speaking to each other in hushed tones, as if this place were still a church. Ah, the reverence of buyers without the refuge of shops. Andrew tried to count how many of them would buy because they loved an object, or because they thought it was a bargain which might turn into an investment, or because it was useful, and how many simply adored the business of poking around among dead people's things. He was never ashamed of his own propensity to do just that: it was only sensible where objects endured beyond lives. He respected auction-house customers: even the collectors, looking for one cup or figurine, crowing with delight over a teapot without a lid; he did not mind the weirdos who simply came in from the cold; he liked young couples with optimistic faces, tentative buyers, to whom bidding would mean a pounding of the heart and terrible suspense. Lesser in his affections were the dealers who waited for the best and squabbled with one another. How much his father might have aided and abetted these foxy men Andrew did not know. His father was too bent to stand up in the pulpit. Andrew was the auctioneer. And he was exceptionally good at it.

'Right. Let's get going. Six o'clock. Where's Derek?'

'Just come in, little bugger. He likes to cut it fine.'

Andrew felt he could smell Derek. Derek, waif and stray of the parish, was the kind of general helper his father would always find in his limping travels round bar counters. He could spot the man in need of cash payment, who would lift furniture, obey orders and not ask questions. Bright, personable and sly; that was Derek, a foil for the other porter, big, thick, reliable Harry. Andrew felt a twinge of guilt. Harry's cousin Bob had been laid off with a bad back. Soon Harry would have a bad back, too.

Two hundred and three lots: Andrew, rising to full height, all shyness, all painful awkwardness, gone, speaking with a voice some called handsome, clear and authoritative. Shy Andrew Cornell, who could not have told a joke to a girl at a party, even when she wasn't listening, told them easily to an audience of dozens.

'. . . Lot number five, ladies and gentlemen. A large framed print of a woman with blue skin in an ornate plastic frame, provenance, Boots, 1956. The telephone bids have been rolling in from Japan . . . Who'll start me at one pound?'

Isabel sidled in at the back. She did not know what she wanted, company perhaps. There had also been the reluctant thought that maybe she ought to persuade her mother to use a commode. Perish the thought of such a prospect, but the weather grew colder while the distance between bedroom and bathroom remained just as long. She hated the creaking of floorboards in the night, imagined an old-fashioned commode made of mahogany, so that it could sit at ease in her mother's room, like any other chair, looking as good as a seat with a potty inside it could look. A poo chair. Isabel's long hair hung down her back, glistening with rain. A commode seemed to be a disgraceful thing to buy so publicly: she was beginning to change her mind about the whole thing.

The figure of Andrew on the rostrum, his lean frame enhanced with the elegance of authority, caught her attention and filled her with amazement. He had never been a talker, but a man who yearned to talk. The audience laughed with him: she laughed too at his comic descriptions, and found her own laughter an unfamiliar sound. Maybe she could wait until the end, ask him about better commodes. No, maybe she would not wait. Not even to listen to that pleasant, persuasive voice. Minimum of sixty lots per hour, the man on the door had told her; bidding open for lot thirty, now. More than an hour to go and the place so swollen, so gummed with people and things, so quiet between the laughter and the sound of the gavel, she did not want to explore. There were people here who might have known her from a long time ago, school friends with babies, people like that. An hour was the maximum to be away from Mother and, with Robert and his family coming tomorrow, she had her tasks. Preparing herself for the question he would ask and she had taken to asking herself, never getting an answer: what did she do all day?

Andrew watched her arrive and watched her go. He registered every face in this room, caught each imperceptible nod, remembered each name: that was his skill, and there was room in between to feel grateful that she had at least seen him, once, at his best. What would he bid for Isabel Burley?

She went home distracted by food for a family. Little Isabel, Serena had mocked, busy as a bee. Solid food, home-made pork pie, a joint of ham, a dish of potatoes sliced and baked with onions and cheese. Isabel trying to show her contemptuous brother how well she could do when she did not take her mother shopping and encouraged her to sleep in the afternoon. It was all laid out in the larder, more in the fridge, except the trifle and the cream, which were in the cellar for lack of other cool space.

Alone, Serena gazed at the display. She had locked the cat

into the cellar to serve it right for being so frightened and so plaintive about going outdoors. She broke off pieces of the pork pie and enjoyed the sticky sensation of pastry crumbling between her fingers; saw the gelatine uncovered and went 'Ughh!' There was a dim memory of eating the best food in the world and never liking wholesome fare like this: she was doing someone a favour by trying it first and finding it lacking. She hacked at the glazed joint of ham with the new breadknife Isabel had bought to replace those that went missing in the weeding expeditions Serena made in the garden. She tasted a clove and removed it carefully from her tongue, dug it into the surface of the spuds. She knew they were spuds: spuds had a lovely sound.

The larder was so spick and span, unrecognizably clean and reorganized, that Serena could not imagine what it had been, only that it was logical to suppose that anything edible in here was for herself, since Isabel was always telling her to eat. Eat, eat, nag, nag. Isabel did not make food, she made mountains: she would make some poor man a good wife. There were lights from the car. Serena opened the cellar door, scooped the fleeing cat into her arms and scuttled down the corridor into the living room. She had a vague sense of being righteous, but also of being naughty. The cat curled on the sofa and began to wash, assiduously. Serena resumed the writing of letters, equally concentrated.

Food. It was the first time George could bring himself to admit even the most grudging respect for Isabel Burley. If anyone had asked, which no one would, he would have said in his abrupt fashion that they did not get on, although he minded his manners and did not think she noticed the way he winked at Serena and she winked back at him to signal their conspiracy against this silly little girl who kept on changing round things that were perfectly all right as they were. But when it came to cooking, there she was, all afternoon, creating the same sort of things as his own dead mother, making his mouth water. He was fascinated by the sight of another person cooking. He sneaked a look at cooking programmes on the telly: he liked to see food taking shape from lumps into edible things. Oh, she was extravagant: she bought apples, for God Almighty's sake, when there were apples for the picking, though admittedly past their best. She had to look at a book to do half of what she did, but she was doing fine. Then he remembered he could not afford to like Isabel or court any improvement in the atmosphere.

George had been able to manage Janice, who kept her hours and went home without ever entering into Serena's affections, but Isabel was different. There was less loud music, fewer furious questions, and the end of that closeness he shared with Mrs Burley and no one else knew about. Such as sitting on her bed in the morning, telling her what to wear today, coming back in the evening sometimes, after Janice had gone, sitting by the fire so that he could postpone going home. Since the advent of Isabel, he had pottered in the kitchen and garden, taken Petal for longer and longer walks, kept his distance. Isabel had poured him coffee when he came back today to witness the cooking. Different coffee, he noticed, disliking the bitter taste of it.

'I think she's so much better, don't you? I hope my brother thinks she's better.'

'Your mother? Oh, yes.' He had thought for a moment Isabel was talking about the dog. He did not think Serena was better. She was having a quiet spell, that was all. There was nothing wrong with her in the first place: she was fine as she was.

'George, you've done so much for her, I don't know what we'd do without you. She says you won't take any money for all the time you spend here. Can't we put it on an hourly rate? It wouldn't be much. Cash, though.'

George thought of the things Serena had pressed upon him. The vase, the teapot, the ornaments, all sold under Derek's direction. No great profit; enough for the purpose he had in mind, which was a good purpose, but not good enough to stop him half knowing it was, in some way, corrupt: the extra money was not for himself.

'I never did want paying,' he said, hideously embarrassed. 'I've got a place to live, unemployment. If I get any money, that'll stop and I'll be worse off.'

He could not have begun to explain to her why he did not want the money. He had no real use for the stuff: money got him into trouble, had him hanging round women, made him feel he could drink. He felt safe when he was here: he had enough to keep the old car going and that was all he needed. Besides, payment for his presence would inexorably alter the whole status of it, and he supposed that was what Isabel wanted. Serena always made him feel a dear and exclusive friend who could arrive when he wanted and stay as long as he wanted. Money would change him into the hired help.

'Something towards the running of the car?' she suggested tactfully. He was tempted, but he shook his head.

'Well, think about it. Perhaps we could settle on what time you get here and what time you leave?'

Bile rose in his throat. He had made his own routine: now she wanted him tied down to hours. She'd soon have him clocking on and off, like in a factory.

'Can't do that,' he said. 'I've got other commitments, see?'

Like now, hiding. Shivering with remembered guilt.

Derek had come into his room about eight o'clock. Flourished those letters about which he had almost forgotten, a shade pissed, the way Derek usually was when someone, somewhere, had given him cash and he wanted company. He sat on the bed and looked at George owlishly.

'Hallo, gorgeous. Why aren't you talking to me these past weeks? I've got something of yours. Picked 'em up by mistake. Sorry about that. Are you coming for a drink?'

'Not tonight, Derek, I'm tired. Another time.'

'Another time? You're always saying that.' He sighed like a beauty queen deprived of the prize. 'Come out for a drink, George. Meet people, have fun. I want to talk to you.'

'What about?'

An evil grin appeared on Derek's dark features. He looked like a wizened jockey, magnificent eyelashes flattering the lined face of a man much older than his thirty years. Something ate Derek from within. George did not think it was disease, merely a hungry tapeworm thrashing around in constant discontent. In the days when George had given half his food to Derek, the lad could have eaten a horse.

'I want to talk about the place you go every day, where you won't take me. It's not fair, George. You told me about a beautiful woman, a princess, you said, and you never let me see her.'

'You've not got a lot of use for women, Derek. Never did have.'

'Not like you, George. Six years for rape. You must have liked it once. I don't know what makes you so fussy now. You're over fifty.'

Age was everything. It was supposed to bring a scintilla of

73

wisdom. Why had he departed from the habits of half a life-time and opened his mouth to this boy? George smiled, one man to another, waiting for worse.

Derek waved the crumpled letters. They were all disor-ganized: they could not have told anyone a story. Especially Serena's, which consisted of lists of words, like a child's vocabulary book. Hope flared and then died in George's slow imagination.

'I'm telling you, George, there's one here with a lot of really hot stuff. I bet it's your princess, writing to a bloke. She's telling him she loves him and she's sorry she bit! That's what they do, women. Bite people. You're better off without them. But it turned me on, it did.'

George lunged for the letters. Derek was only on the cusp of drunkenness and drew back in time, playfully. The letters disappeared into the top pocket of his bomber jacket. He smiled coyly, fluttering the magnificent lashes.

'Naughty,' he admonished. 'Very naughty. Come out for a drink, George. I got money. I miss you.'

George had gone for the drink he did not want, in the hope of getting back his letters. Two halves of bitter to Derek's three Carlsberg Specials made his head spin and left his senses raw, sending up thanks for the food he had eaten and Derek had not. He tried to be polite to Derek's other friends, Bob and Dick, but he did not like them either and it showed. Big, silent men who kept themselves apart. Dick smelled of sweat and his eyes moved incessantly, his gaze lingering on the women at the bar. Thus much George had understood by the time he took the letters from Derek's jacket pocket when the others went to the lavatory. Derek had made the connection between his own daily destination and the address on the letter which begged for a reply: the one about biting someone and being sorry about it. George cursed Isabel, not for whatever she had done, or the contents of the letter which clearly gave Derek such unholy glee, but for the clarity of her writing when she wrote her home address. Where is it, George? Where is it, this big house full of old things and the princess you told me about? Where is it? Derek now knew where it was. He would not need the letters to refresh his memory.

George bought the fourth round, resenting the money. There was a disturbance by the door. Bob, touching up a woman who screamed abuse at him; the beginnings of a fight. Under cover of the noise, Derek leant forward and kissed him. George could feel blood ready to explode from the pores of his forehead. He wanted to hit the man, the way he had once wanted to hit a woman. If he could have borne the proximity, he would have undone Derek's dirty, tight jeans, seized his prick, twisted it, torn it off and thrown it away. That was what queers made him feel like. Even if he had once been convicted of rape, they were worse, coming on strong like this. Derek went back to the bar, the kiss unreciprocated, the thirst unslaked and the cash still sufficient. George fled.

Nowhere to go and no way to cope. He could not go back to his room with the useless warden off-duty and Derek knowing exactly where he was. Nor could he get in his car at a time of night when the police were busy enough to notice the rust on the side and the smell on his breath. Wait in the dark, until sleep overtook them all? He opted for that.

End of October: mist beginning to settle on the so-called old end of town. One mile walk from the suburban end, where the hostel nestled in anonymous ugliness among the rest, next to the brand new Methodist church. Now he was crouched against the wall of the alleyway between a row of shops and the old chapel furniture exchange where he had sold Serena's things. His feet had crunched on rubbish and there was no light. Wariness of Derek and his friends had grown into a terror of revulsion. They wanted something and Derek wanted most.

The alleys of the old town stretched either side. George was shivering cold, dressed in clothes that were fit only for the warm room he had left. The warmest things about him were the letters scrunched up to his heart beneath his sweat-shirt and the desire to dance in the dark with Serena Burley, whom he knew he had already betrayed. Someone else now knew where she was, in possession of all those old, damaged things which someone would want. It was not the immediate prospect that troubled him now, but living long enough to cope with it, what with the voice of Derek in the near distance, wandering the streets in the fog, shouting. He could not face Derek: he would strike him.

'Come out, George. I know where you are: I'll find you, promise.'

George closed his mouth, willed his shivering limbs to stay still. He crossed his arms over his chest and squeezed his eyes closed, bracing himself against the wall.

'Come out, George. I loves ya, George.'

He stuck his thumbs inside his ears; he placed his little fingers into his eyes and, ignoring the dirt where he crouched, he rolled himself into a ball with his back facing the glow of the street lamp.

'I loves ya, George. Where are you?'

The voice began to falter; then it faded. 'I loves ya, George' died away into the night. The effort needed to take his hands out of his ears was enormous: the energy required to move his limbs from curled to straight seemed greater. He writhed in an agony of cramp, of unsound mind unhinged by confrontation. He would stay there for ever to avoid a fight.

He thought of December, when he might freeze as he lay, parcelled up for the dramatic discovery of rubbish men in January. Serena would miss him. She needed him. At two in the morning he unscrewed his arms and walked back to a silent dwelling.

Robert Burley was teased about his name because it matched his physique. Big, tending to fat because of a liking for solid food – cake, real ale and potatoes. He was the kind of solicitor who studiously avoided making real money on account of his principles: knowledge should be placed at the disposal of the community. Conspicuous wealth brought out the Trotsky in him. All property was theft, unless it had a huge mortgage on it, like his terraced house in Manchester. His moral crusades, which were born out of an inability to compete, were never quite as sincerely felt as he imagined. He simply wanted to be worthy. The end result was a wretched practice and a life of endless complication. Envy ate at him like a worm, without making him thin. Only in his own house was he a king.

'Joan! You ready yet, woman?'

'Nope. Take the baby. Look, Robbie, are you sure we have to stay the night? So much easier if we just go there and back.'

'I've said we'd stay, so we're staying. C'mon, love, give me that girl.'

A soft, enormously fat fifteen-month-old lump of baby,

made in his own image and liking. He could not have ordered up anything better: his daughter, his one and only. The four-year-old son, a thin child of quietly precocious habits, was beaten into second place by his sister and did not seem to mind. He had the undiluted love of his mother: he preferred women.

'Don't hold her so tight, Robbie. She'll suffocate.'

'No, she won't. She's all right, aren't you, Cathie?' The child grinned and squirmed. Robert put his finger in her mouth and let her suck. Joan accused him of spoiling her. He strapped the baby in the front seat beside him, even though it was supposed to be safer in the back, a fact he ignored because he wanted to go on sneaking glances at her and because he believed implicitly that his own superior skill as a driver was all it took to avoid accidents.

'My God, this car's like a travelling circus,' Joan complained. 'Why do we have to take so much?'

'Because we aren't going to a place equipped for kids, as you well know.'

Joan sighed. 'I wish we didn't have to go at all.'

Joan was a placid wife, but a shrewd one. They made a duty visit to his mother every few weeks, purely to satisfy conscience. This time they were going because Robert had received a valuation on his mother's goods and he also wanted to make sure Isabel was not colluding with the help. He wasn't worried about the house. There were only a few years left on the lease, which made it worth little to any inheritor. The only hope of getting anything out of Mother was keeping the contents intact and keeping her in it. So much for principles. The prospect of a third child was eroding them fast.

Oh, be fair to him Joan told herself, handing the boy a

carton of orange juice with instructions not to spill it. He does care for his mother: he cares for everyone. He's beaten himself to death caring.

'Is she asleep?'

'Not yet.'

You could not spoil a child by adoration alone, he told himself. Surely not. It took love of a particular kind to do that. Like the love his father had had for Isabel, who could do no wrong, Father's little piece of perfection. He could remember rushing towards his father on Father's return from a foreign trip and being literally pushed to one side, to stand with his arms outstretched and nothing to hold, because Isabel had been behind him. He might as well have been invisible: so might his mother. It made him burn with humiliation, even now. It was one thing to prefer one child to another, he reflected with the wisdom of parenthood, but you had to pretend to be even-handed. Father had not dissembled. And it was not just Father who preferred Isabel so outrageously: there was also Aunt Mab, who signalled it by leaving her everything. One way and another, Robert Burley felt his sister owed him a lot. He owed her nothing.

The afternoon was pleasant, the drive in the past-its-sell-by-date Ford Sierra uneventful. The boy in the back expressed no curiosity whatever about their destination. When they arrived he got out carefully and ran indoors.

They went to the back door, as family should. The front door was for the parties Robert remembered before his father died. Gross over-consumption, where Dad danced with his daughter and Mother flirted with the men. Men who were mostly dead now, he supposed. Perhaps Serena's sexy partiality for men might explain the dearth of women friends now. Widows have long memories. Robert doubted if Isabel had thought of that. He contemplated his own life with satisfaction. A serious man was better off with a plain wife.

'Hallo, Isabel. You look terrific.'

His voice boomed over the garden. Out of the corner of his eye he saw that odd little man, George, sidling away in the direction of the fields. If Robert was startled, not to say faintly satisfied by the change in the sister he had last seen three months before, he did not show it. The slenderness of her was even more extreme: it was pinched. She was breathless and anxious to please. Serena was magnificent. In his bitterness, Robert always chose to forget whose favourite he had been.

'Darlings, wonderful!'

A flurry of warm, scented kisses, smothering him, arms round him like steel, face nuzzling his hair, her mouth finding his ears and his nose, like a puppy. She would never have shoved him aside.

Sun streamed through the dining-room windows reflecting in the table, which Robert was relieved to see had not been chopped up for firewood. More than a thousand pounds, the valuer had said. They went straight in to eat, Joan telling Isabel she should not have bothered: they could have gone out and, anyway, they'd bought sandwiches. It was a strange meal: cooked ham in a kind of casserole that tasted of tinned soup, a bit gluey, baked potatoes. Serena fed hers to the dog. The boy, Jack, attached himself to Isabel like a limpet, refusing to eat anything unless she gave her approval to each mouthful. It was almost normal.

Isabel watched her mother, who seemed transfixed by Robert's face. Serena smiled and nodded, apparently following every word: the sight made Isabel choke with sadness.

She knew by now that words reached Serena through a fog. She was merely mistress of a splendid, deceptive social façade which knew the value of keeping silent, fooling most of the people, most of the time.

'What do you do all day?' Robert boomed. Serena laughed, imagining he had said something funny.

'Nothing,' Isabel said.

What a stupid, unobservant man he was, to produce this brilliant little son, the possession of whom Isabel craved with a passion of need. She had seen the boy as a baby, twice a year since, and each time the sight of his little bird bones melted her own. He knew it, rewarded it with his unblinking stare.

'You know what you do?' Isabel said to him as they wandered in the orchard, taking in the last of the light, giggling as they mashed dead apples underfoot. 'You make me broody. Broody as an old hen.'

'You look like a hen,' he volunteered. The maggots in the apples fascinated him. He looked at everything gravely. 'Are we staying here tonight?'

'Yes, I hope so.'

'I'll come in bed with you, then.'

'Only if your mother says.'

Suddenly she liked the idea of her family. Blood was thicker than water. Robert and she would become friends. They would work out something for Mother. They would have civilized conversations about it, beginning now, this evening, when she would tell them Mother was mad, worsening fast, should not be living thus. She would ask Jack to stay. She would tell Robert what Mother had done to the food. It was simple: she would demand help and receive it. Not cover up any more.

'Have you got a daddy, Bella?'

'A daddy or a sugar daddy?' she teased.

He spread his thin arms. There was a blue vein on one wrist she always wanted to stroke. 'A big man,' he said, as if that explained everything.

'No, I haven't.' She thought of Joe whom she loved with such passion and who had not replied to her letters, and thought, no, he is a little man. So are they all, little men.

The orchard was a satisfying distance from the house. No sound reached it until Joan came out to join them. There was about her a smug, conspiratorial air that boded trouble. But Isabel decided she did not dislike her sister-in-law. There was not enough there: doors open, lights on, no one definite at home. A big 'Halloo!' yelled into the peaceful air made her squirm but caused no reaction whatever in Jack. He was collecting maggots into a matchbox.

'I say, Issy, there's a rather nice man, Andrew he said it was, called to see you. Brought some flowers for your mother. Said I'd come and find you. What have you got there, Jack, darling? Put them down.'

'Andrew? Oh, yes.'

Joan propelled them back towards the house. It was dusk and the sandstone walls had taken on a life of their own, glowing like a soft beacon. Isabel faltered in her step, arrested by a shock of affection and appreciation, punctured when Joan took her arm like a jolly school friend on the way back from hockey, a gesture of the camaraderie Isabel had never found in the days when her mother wrote to her and Joan was captain of netball somewhere else.

'He seems awfully keen, Isabel dear. He might have brought the flowers for you, but Serena took them, so I suppose they're hers, now.'

It seemed somehow obscene to explain in front of the boy that his granny had lost her love of plants and wanted her blooms to be *replicas*, unable to distinguish between the two except for the fact that one sort needed water and were a nuisance. Equally useless to explain to Robert that Granny would have limited interest in his baby; she preferred the durability of dolls. Joan squeezed Isabel's elbow.

'Is this an old flame or a new one, Issy dear? Robbie says you had a lot of chaps around before you left home. I mean, this one looks a bit old for you, I would have said, but very respectable.'

A lot of old flames, Isabel thought, even after I left with my inheritance. They all doused themselves, even the ones I brought home afterwards. First they were there, then they were gone. Have you got a big man, Issy? No, they all disappeared like smoke: I lived on my own. The sweet smell of rot in the orchard and the unwanted touch on her arm made memory part of a cycle. One in the dying phase, while fecund Joan was longing to impart the news of rebirth. The elbow was squeezed again, roguishly. The grin given with the squeeze was supposed to say, Come on, sister, you can tell me, while the school-prefect voice went on.

'Well done, Issy, I say. Must be a bit lonely for you out here on your own. Glad you've got yourself sorted out so quickly. Got to get a man on board. Never at a loss in that direction are you?'

Issy, Bella. Each vision of her shortened name made her smaller, unless it was done with permission and affection. Patience in the face of unintended insult was something she was learning fast, so she kept her voice mild, mindful of the boy who was holding her hand.

'That'll be Andrew Cornell. He's a valuer. I'm sure he's come to see Robert.'

Joan giggled girlishly. 'I don't believe you,' she said.

They had traversed the lawn at the front quickly in response to the onset of darkness over dusk, no one noticing how weedy it was. Jack had his matchbox safely in his pocket. He sniffed the air like a dog.

'Nice,' he announced. 'Ever so nice here. Mum, why is Cathie screaming?'

'What?'

'Cathie. Screaming like that.'

Joan broke into a run.

When George came back with the dog the kitchen was a nightmare of suppressed screams, the adults frozen in terror. There were dirty dishes in the sink and the overhead light illuminated a series of harsh faces. For a moment he could have been back in his hostel, waiting for a fight to happen. Only Serena's expression was blessed with contentment as she crooned to the baby in her arms, rocking it with rhythmic violence, squeezing it hard. Peripheral to this embrace was Robert, who was trying to unhinge her arms from round the baby's chest while Cathie bawled for redemption. They were the screams of distress from a child beyond pique and discomfort and well into the realms of hysteria, face flushed, choking on tears.

'Let go!' Robert yelled at his mother. She grinned, squeezed harder, raising bruises, hummed louder and moved her burden in the direction of the corridor. He had visions of the child's ribs popping out through her ample flesh, her cries dying away into a series of gurgles, then silence. Two doll-like arms beat at Serena's face; the thick, frail neck wobbled dangerously; the china-blue eyes formed slits and the two fat legs hung out of the bundle like helpless sausages with feet. The little boy laughed to see such fun: Jack was beside himself, yelping. Robert was desperate. Tears had formed in his eyes. He balled his right hand into a fist.

'Dance for your daddy . . .' Serena crooned.

'Put her down! I'll kill you!' Joan's voice was hoarse with threat.

Serena took no notice. The baby's screams descended to a steady howl of pain.

Andrew appeared from nowhere, the last visible person, pushed Robert to one side.

'You look lovely today, Mrs Burley. Where did you get that hat? Isn't it noisy? Shall I carry this for you? It is very, very heavy, isn't it?' He spoke loudly and firmly, kissed her on the left wrist, held out his arms beneath the child.

Jack's laughter fell into silence as his mother slapped him. The fridge hummed. They all watched. Mrs Burley smiled more widely than ever. Her arms opened with such abruptness that Andrew's thin back bowed under the weight of Robert Burley's daughter. George was behind him. Andrew passed on the bundle of flesh, bones and shawls with practised tenderness. George hoisted Cathie over his shoulder, holding her under the nappy, letting her fingers claw at his eyes, bending back so she lay on a curve, free as a bird. Murmuring, My aren't you a beauty? Aren't you just a little beauty? The crying descended into a series of hiccups. The women recovered from paralysis. Robert moved.

'I should let her stop here a minute if I were you,' George said amiably. 'She's just filled her nappy. That's what all that fuss was about. What a treasure. Is she yours? What's her name?'

*

They packed the Ford Sierra and had left within the hour. George had gone before them. Robert said he was not staying in a house where his child was not safe; he would not believe that his mother had simply forgotten how to hold a baby. Enough was enough. Serena was Isabel's responsibility. He would be consultant.

Serena had no idea what she had done. How silly people were. She cried when Robert left, but he could not bear to touch her. She turned on Isabel a face of puzzled desolation.

'Why doesn't he love me?' she asked.

'He does, Mum. He does, of course he does. We all do.'

Later, when all the dishes were done and the place restored to tidiness, Isabel saw the ferret, waiting outside the door.

'IT IS NICE AND WARM TONIGHT,' Serena wrote in block capitals. Writing in capitals took up so much time she began to scribble. 'Someone stole my doll. Someone stole my man. I can't remember which was worse.' Sitting on the big carver chair watching the moon from the window reminded her how these clearer spells were becoming briefer, since she had obviously been en route to another place entirely in order to do something different and useful. She sat upright and considered the problem.

She had been looking for snow to fall, snow being an easier option than a knife, but it was too early for that. Or she might have been looking for a book to read. Or, more likely, she had realized that Isabel had heard her tiptoeing downstairs, and that was enough to suspend all movement. It was awful to be followed, terrible to be captive in her own house, and purgatory to have some other woman dancing attendance. Any female with sense, Serena announced with her breath reaching the table, hates the dominance of her mother, but not nearly as much as the other way round.

There was fucking dust on this buggering table, which was nicer than paper, and the light of the moon was preferable to bursting lightbulbs, which blew up in her face out of sheer spite. She watched her own finger waver, hesitant to commit. Something was important. Nothing she could remember. Serena got up and made her regular parade of touching things, as if she loved them. She had never had much time for things, only people. Edward, her husband, had loved things like trophies. She had loved him first as long as he loved her first; she had loved other men second. There was about as much time left for women as there was for God. Neither had ever saved her from anything.

She looked at her fingers. Still five of them. What a relief. Nothing really changed, then. She did not change. Bits of her died was all, like gangrenous toes on bodies in frost. All those lovely manners, which had covered her like a coat. It was not the same as being mad, Serena told the table: she could still dance, still march to a different tune. As for being good, she was not good, never had been.

She added an extra 's' to the word in the dust, so that the sound of it would end in a hiss. Lonelinessssss was a fact of life sometimes cured by illusion, mitigated by the love of a man. For some women, she wrote, being alone on the planet is cured by the love they have for their children. She had loved hers, but never to death and never as a replacement. Mab had loved them as if they were her own.

Serena stopped, shaking her head until her eyes rattled like marbles. Why should it be so difficult for children to accept they were not the centre of the world? Why on earth impose such expectation? Serena put her mind to the task of communication. A game of noughts and crosses which must not be wiped away in the morning. In case somebody won.

She was playing a game with Isabel. First she kept winning when Isabel was small, but then when Is grew into a girl, she wiped the board, stole her father's heart and got row after row of kisses until her mother had nothing left. Not that Edward ever did anything: he hadn't the faintest idea, but that was not the point. The point was the row of Xs. The memory of being insanely jealous. And now this same child was demanding love. 'Give us a break,' Serena scrawled. She could not remember what she had done the day before. Something bad. Her eyes widened.

Look at that! The cat was on the table, smearing the writing. All because she had opened the window on account of hating anything to be locked. The bastard cat had brought her a mouse without a head. That was what lack of inhibition was all about.

Balls.

CHAPTER FIVE

Andrew was dreaming.

'Hush,' someone told him. 'Hush. Whisper who dares. Christopher Robin has fallen downstairs.'

He and Isabel were sitting at either end of that big Knole sofa (worth a few hundred, bad condition), avoiding the springs and talking to each other. They were both a little drunk, which eased the talk and made it slip and slide between things that mattered a lot and things that had no importance whatever.

Listen to me. Listen. It is no person's duty to look after a parent. I should know.

My mother loves me.

Yes. Like a fungus loves its culture.

No. I want to be like her.

At that point Serena crashed through the door, wearing nothing but curlers and demanding a car.

Tell me, Miss Burley, were you in love with what she was?

Why did you leave me? Why did you write me that filthy letter?

When Andrew woke, he was on his own bed, fully dressed, with everything crumpled and uncomfortable. He could feel the weight of a baby in his arms.

Dr Reilly puffed towards the back door. For country calls he wore boots, which gave a certain edge to the challenge of controlling the pedals of the Volvo. At midday the air was fresh with rain, the temperature mild with only a hint of winter warning. Bonfire night: he could smell the smoke in advance, knew he would need his energy and his sobriety for later alarms.

He took off his boots at the door, revealing fisherman's socks of odd colours. Those made Isabel trust him, although she knew he was a wily old bird: Aunt Mab had said so, and what Mab said was always right, although none of her observations meant that the Doc was anything less than an excellent practitioner. He seemed to be the same age now as he had always been, which was old enough to treat as a reliable uncle.

'Anything in particular wrong, m'dear? You said on the phone you wanted me to take a look at your mother. I'd been popping out every week to see her, y'know. George would have called me if there was anything wrong. Anyway, after you took charge I've waited to be asked.'

Looking at the girl he wondered which of the two female occupants needed treatment. She was a funny grey colour: those great deep eyes of hers seemed to take up as much of her head as a bush baby's, but her smile still went straight from ear to ear. A mouth like Brigitte Bardot; no wonder his son had suffered such a bad dose of calf love once. In his eyes Isabel had improved with age: most women did. His son had two daughters of his own now: the photographs were in the doctor's pocket, ready to be shown.

'It's just a check-up. I don't know. Just to give me some idea of how she really is.'

'Surely,' he said kindly. 'Does she still smoke?'

'Yes. Not very often. She seems to forget how to hold it.'

'Well, there's a mercy. No need to come with me. I know the way if she's still in bed. And then we'll have a chat.'

Half an hour later, on her way to the bathroom, Isabel heard the sound of laughter from Mother's room and felt a spurt of envy for Doc Reilly. She had never had it in herself to make her mother laugh, she wanted to snap at him when he sat himself down so solidly at the kitchen table in front of a cup of coffee, but then he smiled and patted her shoulder.

'You've chosen a lonely path to furrow, miss. Don't worry about your mum chortling. Your mother never did mind being examined. She says it makes her tickle. The stethoscope, I mean. She likes it.'

Isabel felt ashamed. 'Can I tell you something?'

'Course. Anything.'

She hesitated. 'Sometimes I want to hit her. My fingers itch to hit her.'

'I don't blame you. I'm amazed more people don't succumb. I don't even know why it's considered worse to hit an old child than a child.' He laughed. It was not the laugh she had heard from the bedroom: that had been Serena's.

Isabel placed her palms flat down on the table. He noticed the prominent bones at the wrists. Then she clasped her hands between her knees, as if wanting to hide the evidence of temptation.

'I could do with some help, I suppose,' she added, lamely.

He frowned. 'Well, to be honest, there's not much of that to be had unless you hire it and I doubt they'd come out this far. You've got two options. You can carry on, or you can abandon ship and leave her to it.'

He gulped the coffee as if his mouth had forgotten the difference between cold and hot.

'Once there's another fire, or the place gets infested, but not before, the Social Services will step in. They'll pretend they have a budget for so-called care in the community, people coming in every day for an hour, you know, but it wouldn't work. They can't afford people staying overnight. It would stagger on for a bit, and then, provided you kept your distance, they'd take her away. There's a nice home in—'

'No,' said Isabel. 'I couldn't consign her to that. She'd lose whatever it is she has left.'

'She won't go any other way than in a straitjacket,' he said roughly. 'And she'll be what they call difficult to place. I don't want to point out to you that there would be a lot more help available if you simply didn't exist. Didn't she tell you about the home helps she sent away? No, she wouldn't, would she? Janice was the only one she could stand, perhaps because she paid Janice herself. You could perhaps get her back.'

'She won't.'

The Doc shook a grizzly head. He hated this kind of problem, couldn't believe the contrast between fact and expectation. Nor could he believe any planner could have imagined care in the community was any kind of cheap option. Speaking for himself, he had no plans to quit drinking or smoking. Once he retired, he would look for other, carcinogenic things to do.

'The only thing I can tell you, if you don't already know, is that Social Services have a legal duty to your mother. They have. You do not. Odd though that may seem. But they won't do a single thing about that duty as long as someone else is exercising it, see? You *do* have a choice.'

She nodded.

The Doc drained his cup and rose. 'Shout for me any time you want,' he said. 'Good coffee. Get out and about more, I would. Now, will you do me a favour? Show me that living room of yours. I used to love that room, had some good times in there. They were great party-givers, your mum and dad.'

'Would she be able to cope if we had a party now?'

Doc Reilly broke his stride across the kitchen floor. 'I doubt it.'

He did not add that he knew of no one who would come voluntarily, and that you couldn't dragoon people to a party. Not even his sainted wife, who had visited longer than most and whom Serena had called a pig, would come. You had to have a big heart to let an old lady get her rocks off by insulting you.

He strode to the west-facing window, looked into the rain-streaked garden, wanting to get his hands on it. Shrubs needed pruning, lawn was like a shrinking hayfield. A movement caught his eye: two sets of twinkling training shoes disappearing round the side of the house. In the distance he heard a door bang shut.

'Do you get many kids coming up here?' he asked sharply.

'Yes, sometimes, asking for water, apples, that kind of thing.'

The doctor moved swiftly. Back in the kitchen Isabel's

93

handbag was open on the table, undisturbed. Outside the door of his car stood open.

'They don't want water,' he snorted. 'They want cash.'

All his loose change, in the glove compartment for parking, was gone. No sign of them down the road. Too cunning by far to let themselves be framed in the lights of the Volvo over the field; too swift for someone who had to pull on his boots. The Doc turned on to the road at the end of the track, purple with irritation. Could have been Serena's purse they robbed, had probably done already, sodding little truants. He could hear them now, explaining it all: 'We didn't take it, Mister. She gave it to us, honest.' He would take a bet that Serena Burley's house was not as well stocked with small objects as it had been a year ago. These were sparrows, gathering to lead in the birds of prey.

There was a white van parked in the place by the graveyard, with windows slightly steamed up and two men inside, drinking their lunchtime tea. The Doc did not notice them. Thought instead of buzzards, hovering in a bleak sky and the way Serena's body had moved in the days when they had danced.

George manoeuvred his old car between the holes in the waterlogged track, spirits lifting in direct proportion to his distance from the town. Beginning as it did at rock bottom today, his mood had a long way to go before it reached buoyancy. He called at Sal's house, just to say hallo, received from her a piece of cake and the day's letters. The mere sight of letters made George squirm: he had never again acted as postman for the Burley household's outgoing letters: let Isabel take those. But the postman still left the incoming post with the neighbours. Nice, willing people they were, but the letters which he dropped on the sideboard at the house as if they were so much nuclear waste, burned a hole in his pocket. Letters should be for ever outside his remit. He was never going to write one.

'Tell that girl to pop in and see us when she's passing,' Sal had urged him several times. 'I don't know why she doesn't, really I don't.'

George had never relayed the message. He had hinted to Isabel that the neighbours were private people who had never forgiven the débâcle of their wrecked car. Frankly, Sal was someone else he did not particularly want to share: George was anxious to keep his acquaintances in different pockets, in case they got together, pooled information and found out where he came from.

He heaved a sigh of relief when he got to the gates of the house. A trail of smoke emerged from a chimney. Back at the hostel, Derek had gone quiet, possibly ashamed. No repercussions for last week's rejection. What a fuss over nothing.

Not quite nothing. Trying to avoid the shameful memory of fear, George could see what Derek meant about the unposted letter from Isabel Burley to her lover. 'I'm sorry if I drew blood,' she had written. 'Sometimes I want you so much it makes me claw at you . . .' The sentence had been reread dozens of times and made him hot. They were all like that, however they disguised it, bitches in heat. George could not catch Isabel's eye, but after the business with the brother, when she had been so helpless, and after his slow absorbing of a letter containing more nonsense than sense, he found he did not mind her quite as much. It was a dull, sullen dislike he carried now; no longer acute. His mind would not stay still but skittered around like the dog when shown her lead: he wanted to chastise it.

Two skinny boys who should have been at school skulked by the gates and scattered as he drove through. Little kids, more down at heel than he had ever been and even less safe. He pitied them for having nowhere to go. George trusted small children and people far older. It was the swathe of humanity in between which made problems.

Everything was as he liked it. Quiet. He put down the letters (two bills, one personal) with care. Serena was dressed and waiting for the kiss to be given behind her daughter's back. It seemed a long time since he had been free to intrude in her bedroom. Sit on the bed and listen to her telling stories, before he told his own. He still had the silver teapot in his car, but he already had enough. Nearer Christmas he would buy the princess her present. Something to help with the problem of words.

Darling Issy,
 Yeah, I did get your second letter, also no. 3, but no, not the first, I'm afraid. Please don't send any more to the office . . . even if you mark them private, they can get read. I'm not the managing director!!! As for apologies, well I don't know if I deserve any of those. I probably deserved what you did. Even when I had to pass it off as a kind of mugging!!! One thing you do, Issy, is make a man think and you have made me think a bit. I've got to sort myself out, haven't I? I hope you've got used to country life and I hope you come home soon, 'cos I miss you.
 Can't stop. Must catch post!!
 Joe

In the privacy of her room Isabel read this missive with something like distaste, trying to embrace the idea that it was wrong to judge a person by the style of letters he wrote, especially if letter-writing had never been part of the arrangement. A letter from Joe, although yearned for, had a strange effect. It was a revelation of limitations, rather like a very large and handsome man opening his mouth to speak and a high treble coming out. Isabel knew that she was not very bright, but even with the awkwardness imposed on them by her violence and sudden departure she knew she had written far better, more honest, letters than this.

Passed off a bite as a mugging, did he? How odd to be able to tell lies with such inventive ease, when she herself was congenitally incapable of telling them at all. And how passionless his prose. She had a funny sense of superiority, born of her personal, illogical and deep-rooted loathing for exclamation marks. They were like someone coming up behind you and making you jump for no reason.

Nor could she understand how she had acquired this aversion. There were so many books in this house, carried from the other houses. Books Mab had made her read and then describe to make sure she had understood. The habit of reading had not persisted into adulthood, although there had been book-worm phases, usually at times when all else failed. And the height of literary thrills in the remoteness of school had been Ma's letters, which always flowed and told stories without ever resorting to using punctuation like cudgels.

Perhaps she would read aloud to her mother. The idea had a quaint, spinsterish charm: Isabel enjoyed thinking of herself as the kind of lady's companion/governess found in the Jane Austen she had once adored. Readings by the fire. How genteel. If Joe could see her now.

There were books lining the walls up the stairs. Books in shelves in the spare rooms, on the old presumption that a guest might need to read. Books in the dining room, floor to ceiling, flanking the fire. Books simply hanging around, acquired on a weekly basis by Serena until only twelve months before. Books she still claimed to read in bed and at her desk. Books Isabel tidied away, noticing without a great deal of interest how the reading had never actually progressed beyond a favourite page, chosen by number; Serena was stuck at page twenty-five of anything.

'George is just off, darling. Don't you think you should say goodbye?' said Serena.

It was one of those uncanny days. Sanity and mildness ruled the house. Water dripped through the bathroom ceiling upstairs and it did not matter. George had taken Serena out in his car to the horrible supermarket and peace had reigned.

'No, there's no need to say goodbye. Goodbye never meant anything, did it?' Serena was yawning. 'I shouldn't look in there, if I were you,' she added. 'I really, really wouldn't.'

Isabel was selecting books from those middle shelves in the dining room which were the easiest to reach, without stretching or bending. Book after book, hardbacked, soft-backed, stored at random, fell to the floor with pages torn.

'Coffee time,' said Serena. 'Or is it tea?'

'Did you do this, Mother?' Isabel held aloft a book from which the torn middle pages waved as she shook it.

Serena nodded vaguely. She seemed to be struggling with the temptation to lie.

'Yes, I did. They . . .' She struggled for expression. 'Insulted me, I suppose.' She went on in a sudden articulate rush, so rare now that Isabel thought wildly that the Doc must have given her a magic pill from his old bag. 'You won't know. You dust tables, you don't read. I couldn't read, you see. All of a sudden, I could not read. It broke my heart. Put them back, dear. It was a bad thing to do.'

Isabel gazed at her. Honesty made a person so endearing. So did the absence of exclamation marks. The times when she wanted to hit her mother were equal to those when she wanted to enfold her. Say, Yes, I do not read, but if I were told I could not do so again, if the books would not do what I wanted, I would scratch the pages in the way I would want to scratch a face. She bent to pick up fragments of paper containing all those elusive, tormenting words. Pages fluttered to the floor.

'Silly old books, Mum. Time for tea.'

What did they do all day?

When Andrew left the town, past the park, straight through the roundabout, he saw the municipal bonfire, built to discourage the amateur from constructing some dangerous inferno in his own backyard. He passed his father's house in the old part, near the church on the one-way system, where his car always wanted to stop, and stalled if he did not, from the transference of guilt from his head to the clutch cable. There was a white van on his tail as he hung left on to the road that led to the hamlet that led to Isabel, the lights of it in his eyes until he slowed down. The van dropped back and he turned up the track, so carelessly that rain from the puddles hit the screen in a great, muddy splash. He felt as if this were the middle of the night and he the bearer of contraband. Fireworks. The rain had stopped. If you wanted to court the daughter, which he did, court the mother first.

Bonfire parties had been favourite occasions in his adolescence. They were a convenient cover of darkness for uncertain fumblings. First put your arms round the girl's waist, light the blue touch paper and wait for protest. That was the way he had been in his romantic, irresponsible years. All the girls, excluding Isabel, had said no. Not in so many words, but with plenty of shuffling excuses: I've got to go somewhere; wash my hair; meet a friend – and find someone better than you. Except Isabel, who did not say no, simply said where? Andrew did not envisage a repeat performance of Isabel's uncomplicated acceptance of sexual overture, but after all this time, he saw a kindness in her generous obliging of a gauche young man which was quite inconsistent with her later unkindness. He had only to look at Isabel now to see that she was incapable of spite and always had been. And what had he done about it? Visited, briefly and awkwardly in the last month, brought flowers, and thought about her all the time.

This spontaneity and determination to beat down his own shyness came at the end of a dreadful day. Moving furniture in and out of the auction room, three valuations with garrulous housewives – two of whom considered their disgusting imitation Welsh dressers to be worth a fortune – and all that with the additional hazard of young Derek in tow, because his father had decided 'the lad had a brain which deserved encouragement'. Derek was ignorant, but he got inside cupboards, shone a silly little pencil torch on things and made loud remarks. His own native dislike apart, Andrew had to confess that Derek was good company. His incessant questions about the value of things, his apparent fascination with their texture, made Andrew wax lyrical and lengthy in reply. Explaining, with his own residual excitement, how it was one piece of wood was worth money, another not; how some pieces of furniture would achieve value in a future generation because they had style, others not. Things did not need to be a hundred years old to acquire status: they only had to be good, built on pure lines and made with pride.

Neither of the Welsh dressers had been made with pride, unless there was any sense of achievement in knocking out a copy of a piece of furniture for shipment to a country you had never seen. Derek liked that. His own remarks on Mrs Brown, with her bouffant hair and best dress to greet the valuer of her goods, as if she was for sale herself, had been funny, but for all his enjoyment of a keen and caustic companion, Andrew did not feel easy introducing the man into the trusting heart of so many homes. Derek had eyes on springs: they seemed to leap out from his head and touch things, leaving a drop of moisture.

Wide eyes greeted Andrew now in the kitchen. When Serena smiled in that fashion, it made him think of Prospero's daughter opening lovely virginal eyes to her first view of young mankind, and it made him feel a prince. Most males, in his experience, did not deserve the accolade of poetry.

'I bought fireworks,' he said. 'In case you didn't have any.' Serena understood: the smile grew wider.

Isabel's smile was graver, equally warm. 'That was kind of you, Andrew. She used to love them. I didn't dare . . .'

He understood: he would not have relished sole charge of Serena around a box of explosives, doubted if she was safe with matches.

'Shall we?' he asked.

'Oh yes, yes, yes.'

They began with sparklers. Andrew planted three of them into a raw potato and put it in the middle of the table; then he encouraged Serena to hold one in her fist, waving it wildly to make ribbons of yellow. She was unafraid of the sparks which stung her wrist, but awkward at first, then fluent, brandishing the sparkler like a conductor's baton.

'I can write in the air! Look! Read it!'

The dog whimpered and shivered: the air was fuggy. They progressed to the damp outdoors, where Andrew's long-distant and loathed boy-scout training came to the fore. He pinned Catherine wheels to a broken fence, stood the rockets upright in empty bottles, moved quickly to keep the display almost continuous. The first Catherine wheel was a blinding, whirring, furious thing, turning madly as if wanting to escape or kill in the process. The third one would not move at all, only spat at them.

'Will someone worry that we're on fire again?' Isabel asked.

'No. Too much distraction.' He pointed. The sky in the direction of the town seemed to glow pink and black.

'More,' Serena begged. 'More.'

Rockets, the biggest and best he could find, while wondering at the time if the expense was ludicrous, then failing to care. Andrew was a careful man only on his own behalf; for others, there was no limit. He steadied the rockets, lit the first. It rose heavenwards with a magnificent rush, like Concorde, he thought proudly. There was a second's pause while it hung in the firmament, and Serena cried out in disappointment. Then a pop; a cascade of blue and purple stars; three more explosions as soft as polite burping; a shower of emeralds, rubies and pearls; then slow, red, hot, plummeting to earth. He lit the next and the next, all three of them breathing *aahh* as the rockets popped, a longer, more lingering *aaaahhhh* as they descended. There was magic in the sighing, pure magic.

Serena actually danced with joy. The lumbering body swayed in an ecstasy of delight. She put her hands over her ears, made little whoops of amazement at the Roman candles, whirled her arms and laughed. The laughter and the happiness were as clean as rain; looking at her face, innocent in such intense enjoyment, Andrew could see the point of caring for her. Witnessing such complete absorption made him glad to be alive. If that was Isabel's reward for her labours, he could suddenly understand the sacrifice.

'Soup? Sausages?' Practical Isabel, captivated but, unlike Serena, still rooted to earth. One of us has to be, he supposed. Serena protested sadly, then accepted the show was over. Back inside Andrew persuaded the trembling dog out of her basket and fussed her into calmness.

In the harsh electric light which made them all blink Serena's face turned a sudden and ghastly pale. 'I wanted to dance,' she gasped and was sick into her handbag. All very tidily done, as if she was in practice.

Isabel swept into action like a seasoned nurse.

'Too much soap,' she said cheerfully, increasing Andrew's shock.

'Soap,' Isabel repeated. 'My wretched sister-in-law brought her a present of pretty soap, shaped like apples and pears, highly coloured. I put it away but she was nibbling it this afternoon. Don't know why. I can never persuade her to eat the real thing.'

Serena tottered to her feet, colour returning, looking for her handbag.

'I'll keep that safe, Ma. Are you going to bed?'

A slow, unsmiling nod for her daughter and an enormous wan grin for Andrew. Nausea made the old lady bewildered and tired.

'It's not fair,' Isabel said fiercely. 'Being sick is so confusing for her because she never knows *why*.' She blew her nose on a piece of kitchen roll. 'Will you follow her, Andrew? Make sure she gets to the top of the stairs, but don't interfere. She wouldn't like that, even from you.'

Andrew walked softly down the corridor, watching Serena's progress. Into the dining room, touching each chair one by one, trailing her fingers along the surface of the table. Moving slightly faster into the living room, opening her desk, looking inside it, closing it again, giving her armchair a pat, as if reassuring a friend. Nodding to the sofa and the piano, moving at a fixed rate between them all, so that even stumbling over the edge of the Indian carpet seemed part of a ritual. Up the stairs, waving good-night to the pictures on the uneven walls. She did not hear his footfall behind her, moved like a ghost, retreating with gratitude and grace into her own world.

'I should like,' Isabel announced when Andrew returned to the kitchen to find her sorting items from the handbag, some already washed, some amazingly dry, 'to get extremely drunk.'

Andrew stood next to her, reaching for the paper towel and automatically wiping dry a powder compact, a lipstick case and a plastic purse. His eye fell on a medley of stained envelopes, covered in neat writing, next to a chequebook.

'Are those yours or hers?' he asked.

'Hers. We write in the same way, almost exactly. I can forge her signature, which is proving useful when it comes to paying the bills. I tried to copy her writing when I was at school. I wanted mine to be just the same.'

The lining of the handbag hung into the sink, saturated, old, worn and torn. Isabel washed her hands as thoroughly as a surgeon, far longer than necessary, in water so hot it made Andrew wince.

'Do you suppose that means I shall be like her one day? Like she is now? With half a mind? Incapable of forming my own words? Waiting in vain for everyone else to translate?'

He turned her from the water and put his arms round her. Holding her wet hands free, she wept into his shoulder.

'I wanted to be like her,' she mumbled. 'Not like Mab.'

He did not know what she meant. There was no romance in this embrace, he concluded miserably. There were things he wanted to say, questions he wanted to ask, but he could not find the words.

Chapter Six

Isabel had wanted to tell Andrew why she did not want to be like Aunt Mab, but she did not because she could not. 'Those with power,' Mab explained, 'cannot bear to lose it. Face it, child, life's a bitch. It's easier for mere observers like me to relinquish hold. I was the war artist, you see, painting camouflage, hiding behind it. Never a front-line hero. So I don't want a hero's farewell.'

Bonfires and Christmas, the occasions of colour which made memory eclipse into clarity. Good old Mab had died in grey November. She had been gifted in the giving of solace: receiving it was never her style.

'Heroine, Mab. The female of hero is heroine. You ought to get it right.'

'Don't be pedantic. Heroines are entirely different animals. They have trembling chins. I'm dying: indulge me.'

Her big, spatulate hands were clawing at the blankets in order to make them tidy, while Isabel looked on. As Mab pointed out in plain words not then understood, life at twenty-one and death at seventy did not suit. Mr Burley and his sister-in-law died within months of one another: cancer for her, industrial accident for him. He therefore remained handsome until the end, losing nothing with age, gaining a certain asceticism to his features. She remained as plain as ever; even her terminal gauntness quite anonymous. Mab was Mab, like a slab of rock.

'How are you, dear? How kind of you to come and see me. Tell me news.'

Always these manners, this ability to welcome, make the visitor feel special. Fascinated by the hideous conundrum of what it must be like to have no future, Isabel could not discuss the present. Or believe Mab's interest in her own, youthful life.

Mab smiled comfortingly. 'Look, poor child, you've got plenty to endure and I don't want fuss at nearly three score years and ten, do I?' she stated from her tidy bed. 'I've had enough of the commas. This is just a full stop. I don't want any of your exclamation marks.'

So that was where the aversion originated. Isabel shot up in bed. Lay down again, aching for the selfless common sense of Mab. Three in the morning, thinking of all those suppressed dreams that were not really dreams but episodes. Listening in the meantime to the creaking of floorboards as someone passed the door on tiptoe. Ghosts. Not Aunt Mab's ghost, far too silent, and besides, Mab's ghost belonged in another house.

When Mab had walked, she rattled. She carried about her person innumerable bits and pieces. She was a spinster, the keeper of other people's keys, carrier of enormous handbags and more secrets than a handbag could ever contain. Sublime in her kindness, embarrassing in her excess. Pulsating with unheard wisdom, booming with her big voice. Don't cry, said Mab, please don't cry. Big girls don't.

Isabel woke into a morning of sweet light, hazy with mist, the kind of day when she could imagine she was on the edge of the sea. There was a fireplace in each of the bedrooms, chimneys long since blocked off, leaving the mantelpieces for decoration. For a moment she thought she was back in Mab's cottage, expected to see the rows of Mab's ornaments. Cups, figurines, bottles and shells, things gleaned from beaches and junk shops for pence, ugly things, curios and objects of beauty all mixed in together. Mab liked Bristol blue: there were vases and jugs in that pure colour all over her house, the only things which Serena did not scorn. They had come to Serena when Mab died, but Isabel could not remember where they were or if they still existed. It was a minor puzzle for a fine and silent morning, something to be attended to later. In the distance, carried on the stillness, there was the rare sound of church bells, tolling for life with doleful joy.

Sundays had little significance, but Isabel had a sudden sentimental longing for the sort of church Mab had favoured along with a token belief in Christian doctrine as a sort of insurance policy. 'You never know, my dear . . . it *might* be true. Even if it does make good people better and bad people worse. Try it: you can always spit it out later.' Mab's true belief had been of the pantheistic kind; ashes to ashes, she said, with the laughing rider that when she died she might become what she had never been in life, a flower.

Downstairs Isabel passed the telephone that never rang, and the dining room, where the window had been flung open. She pulled on a jacket and stepped out into the milk of morning, disorientated by the diffuse light which made her vow to clean the windows. How far she had come to accept this solitude, even while fearing it and filling it with tasks. Halfway down the track towards church, she began humming. Hymn tunes remain stuck inside the head like a virus in the body, Mab maintained; always ready to reinfect with enthusiasm. Towards the end of the track Isabel thought of Mab's grave, detoured into the cemetery out of curiosity rather than guilt. Years since she had been here; so many she could hardly remember where it was; years since Serena had mentioned either her sister or her husband, buried next door to each other for no other reason than the existence of a space.

Was that all? Isabel wondered. Father and sister-in-law were firm friends. Or did her handsome father merely owe Mab a debt of gratitude for all the care she had taken of his children while he and Serena swanned abroad and Mab scooped up little Isabel and stout Robert from their various school gates at the end of term, embarrassing them in the process because her car was always so old and her voice so loud? What a snobby little bitch I must have been, Isabel thought, but I learned a certain lack of inhibition from Mab. She was the one who told me sex was not that important, only what it produced. Get on with it, if I were you, Mab advised, proffering contraceptive prescriptions: get rid of the mystery.

Edward Burley's grave was pristine, the plinth filled with weeded gravel and the headstone free of mud. There was a miniature shrub at each end and the whole thing looked as if it had been dusted. Mab's grave was a mess by contrast, a flat piece of dew-damp hayfield with the parameters of the grave itself scarcely defined, and some shocking dandelions crowding the stonemason's record of when she had lived and died. The disparity between the graves made Isabel feel Mab had been insulted.

Cleaning things had become automatic in her life. Becoming a housekeeper made Isabel mop and polish with a certain relish, as one of few activities which gave her any sense of achievement, gave framework to the day. It was natural to kneel and tackle Mab's grave with bare, cold hands, scratching at the weeds like a hen, pulling up the grass, patting the soil until at last the thing looked gravelike, identifiable as a small and decent monument. The church bells had ceased while Isabel worked, immune to the sound of cars which heralded the arrival of the congregation and the silence that followed as the church swallowed them up. Finally Isabel regarded the grave critically. She doubted if unsentimental Mab would have ever demanded this task of her. She would have touched her niece on the shoulder and reminded her that the spirit had fled.

Mabel, mentor, teacher and useful person, long dead, would have wanted her to go to church instead of wasting time, simply because it was more helpful to belong to a community than not, and because, once in a while, it was perfectly splendid to belt out a hymn without having to worry about the fact you really couldn't sing at all. Mab would have marched in there while Isabel, approaching the kind of edifice she had always taken for granted as offering something to others, felt a certain shyness. It was not the presence of God that deterred her, only the presence of people.

The porch was warm sandstone with a stone seat set into the walls on either side. The door was heavy oak, with a round, iron handle, cold to the touch and clumsy to work. The ring operated a noisy latch which rose and fell with a resounding clatter, announcing the latecomer like a pistol shot. Isabel stumbled towards the smell of humanity. The congregation were at the stage of prayer, bent forward with knees on tapestry footstools made by people like Mab, all of them following the invitation of the vicar to examine their consciences before the next hymn. They were open to distraction. Two dozen heads, some with hats, swivelled in her direction and in one second she saw herself as she imagined they would see her. Stuck in a shaft of sunlight, wearing jeans, boots, black jacket streaked with dirt like her face and hands. At best, a dreamer, at worst, the madwoman's daughter. Half of the faces turned back: the other half continued to stare in shuffling silence. Someone coughed, a prayer book was dropped, then silence resumed. Isabel ran.

They reminded her of something, these eyes staring out of darkness: resurrected the most abiding of all adolescent memories, which had nothing to do with church, and everything to do with rejection. The association was only warmth, dim light and all those eyes. She could see herself, those years before, frequenting the disco she had held semi-sacred in her teens, far more sacred than church had ever been. Rolling into town, feeling blue because Andrew Cornell never phoned back and he was the last of an impressive succession of boys and men who seemed to dump her. Well, three at least in the last year alone. What did it take to hold on to one? Brains? A better job than her unambitious role of secretary? Should she have been what Mab called a bluestocking? She had not known. Mother was distant, Mab on her downward spiral, the house in mourning and all she had to cling to was her own selfish energy and what she had assumed was considerable popularity. A gaggle of local friends, daughters and sons from the better end of town, home from university, drifting as she drifted, liking her, greeting her with whoops of welcome in the normal run of events, but not on that day. The disco was somewhere to go for the unemancipated young. Isabel, dressed up in defiance of gloom, the way Mab encouraged, standing at the door in clothes that sparkled, meeting first the darkness and then the hostile silence, seen by them all, unable to see herself.

Until Doc Reilly's son swaggered to the front and the music stopped. 'Get lost, Isabel Burley. We don't want you here.'

He was childish, pompous, and his words stung. Girlfriends, busy with drinks, hiding their expressions with curtains of hair; other faces either pitying or enjoying scorn. Isabel grinning, sticking one hip forward, striking a pose in her tight skirt, making a joke of it.

'What's the matter? I got the plague, or something?'

'Fuck off, Isabel. Just fuck off.'

No one had ever given a reason for this banishment. The defection of friends had been more hurtful than the death of near relatives, more corrosive to adolescent vanity. People dying was not her fault, but the public loathing of her contemporaries was the petty indictment which sent her out into the wider world soon after, with Serena's fervent blessing and Mab's money. And she still did not know why.

So what? A long time ago. Perhaps one of her boyfriends had been jealous; she was free with favours. Perhaps one of the girls had spread rumours with all the moral outrage of the young. From the distance of a dozen years, she could see how old-fashioned and parochial they had been, how insignificant her own offence might have been, although the wound felt mortal at the time and still ached when she probed it. Too late to wonder now. The road leading to the house was dry underfoot: lonely in a friendly way, receptive to her own voice repeating, I must not be silly, I must not be silly, although it was far from silly to be wary of the scrutiny of crowds. People and piranha fish have much in common, said Mab.

A white van approached her from the direction of the house, moving slowly to avoid the potholes, as if the van were brand new instead of old, dented and dirty. She stood back into the field to let it pass, unalarmed by its presence. Walkers with dogs used this road, people took wrong turnings. The man behind the wheel acknowledged her presence with a slight ducking of a grey head, a smile and a wave. They bowed to one another with Sunday-morning courtesy, which Isabel, fresh from an abortive visit to church, felt she deserved as an alternative form of blessing.

'Tea?' Serena suggested in a voice like a stage butler, a voice straining above the sound of music from her radio. 'Coffee? Whisky? Brandy?' She beamed with self-approval. There were a dozen cups and saucers on the kitchen table, a trail of crumbs from the biscuit tin. Serena looked thoroughly stimulated by the morning's events. Best china from the dining room. Two cups broken. There was a smell of cigarette smoke.

'Been entertaining?' Isabel asked. 'Who was here, sweetheart? Children?'

She was alarmed, but not dismayed, thought of the courtesy of the man in the van. Serena smirked. She was oddly dressed, a regular phenomenon which seemed especially strange in a woman once so particular about clothes, but, like the preference for plastic flowers, not without a logic. Clothing in layers, as if she intended to cope with any eventuality the day might offer by shedding and re-arranging an array of garments that could take her from Arctic to fireside. Lace-up shoes with little heels over thick, turquoise stockings, a petticoat hanging slightly below a russet corduroy skirt, a T-shirt evident below a black silk blouse, a scarf round her head, a maroon blazer and the whole ensemble finished by a light cape slung round her shoulders. Isabel had grown used to it in the same way she had grown used to a number of habits, learning as she went along to discern the difference between what was important and what was not. Clothes were not; love was.

'Who was here?' she repeated, wondering who would want to be here. Andrew perhaps. Wondering at the same time if her complete acclimatization to solitude and half conversation meant she would become unfit for anything else. Serena's skittering across the floor in a pretence of being busy exaggerated a certain shifty demeanour.

'Very nice men,' she volunteered, distinctly. 'They were lost. I showed them round. Made coffee. Couldn't find the brandy.'

'What men? What did they want?'

A saucer crashed to the floor. Isabel gazed at it without interest. Little shivers of blue, red, gold leaf, ready to be crunched on the cold floor. What had happened to Mab's Bristol blue? Robert would roar with outrage to see any form of destruction, even the careless kind, and the thought was not unpleasant. Two weeks and not a word: she could phone him this evening and tell him Mother was playing hoopla with antique crockery, tearing up first editions, playing

Houdini with the silver . . . but then, what silver? Kings silver laid out in rows in a dining-room drawer once. Not any more. Who cared? She didn't, much, except about Mab's Bristol blue.

'Were they nice men, Mummy?'

She bent to pick up the saucer as if indeed it did not matter. What else was missing?

'None of your business,' Serena growled. 'They were friends of mine. Friends of George.'

'George doesn't have any friends.'

'Oh, yes he does. They've got a van.' Serena's face took on a wistful look.

'Such nice, big men,' she said. 'They danced with me.'

'Mother!' Isabel shouted over the din of music. 'Mother! What did you do with all those blue things that Mab gave you?'

'What things? What, what, what?' Then she leaned forward, bent over the table until her pale eyes, lit with concern, wavered within inches of Isabel's own. She raised a hand as if to stroke, let it fall, shook her head.

'Why are you so silly, darling? So silly.'

There was no such thing as absolution.

Do you love me, Mother? Mab did. And I often thought she was silly too.

'God rest ye, merry gentlemen . . .' His fingers drummed out the tune on the steering wheel.

'Aw, shut up, Dick, will you? It's nowhere near Christmas.'

'Look at them all. Cunts. Don't fancy any of them.'

Dick was the driver of the van. They sat three abreast, with Derek squashed in the middle and Bob on the passenger side, each looking through the dirty windscreen while they waited for the cars blocking the end of the drive to disperse. The congregation was slow to move.

'I never could fancy anything wearing a hat,' Bob grumbled. He was grateful that Derek blocked him from proximity to Dick, because Dick smelled slightly. Bodily fluids shown insufficient water: dead meat. 'And all those mothers are the same shape.'

So they were, like tulip bulbs in coats, chatting by car doors in cheerful voices, full of virtue. A good congregation for the day, drawn by the age of the church building. The service had more meaning if they had to make a special expedition to reach it: the modern churches in town, with their lack of adornment and tradition, were less popular despite access from so many more doorsteps. The vicar here had a nice way of reminding his parishioners that God was still on their side whatever the evils of their society. The church had style and a noisy choir. Also the prettiest graveyard where all the agnostics wanted to be buried and the vicar did not mind that either.

'Do you suppose he gets a bonus for every person he pulls inside on Sundays?' Dick queried, looking at a portly figure in a cassock scurrying towards a Ford Fiesta. 'Like Dan does at the bingo place?' Dan was another itinerant from the hostel, not party to this enterprise.

'I doubt it,' said Dick. 'His wife looks like a baked potato.' Then he began to giggle. The giggle smothered itself into a series of snorts as Dick put the van into gear and moved off sharply, making all three bump back against the hard seats. Bob winced.

'Didn't we do well, though?' Derek crowed through his laughter. 'I can't believe it. She invites us in, shows us round, turns on the music. Makes tea in the best china . . .'

'China's not worth much,' Bob grunted, 'unless it's really special and you get a whole set of it.'

'Gives us the guided tour! All you have to do is play with her.'

'Whose car is in the garage, is what I want to know,' said Bob. 'And who was that girl in the drive?'

'George never mentioned anyone else. Only his old princess.'

'Look, Derek, we've seen other people going up there. She ain't all alone all the time.'

'No one permanent. Stands to reason the old dear has some help, doesn't it?'

'Of course. So she should.'

There was muttered agreement, as if it were abhorrent she should not. Moral outrage at the thought of her being on her own. Disgraceful. Derek lied with fluent ease, not wanting to put them off. He had been persuading them into this for weeks.

'Nothing we can't cope with. So? When?'

Silence. A grunting of gears as the van whined uphill, protesting an unhealthy engine. Dick it was with the cash-paying job of driving vans for the abattoir. He had access by night to bigger, better wagons than this.

'What's it all worth then, Bob?'

Bob, with his bent back and uncertain future, knew values better than anyone after years in the trade hanging around John Cornell. Derek was learning fast.

'Depends on where we take it. Coupla blokes in Leicester would give us twelve thou.'

'It's worth much more than that!' Derek yelped.

' 'Course it is. But you have to sell cheap.' The contempt in his voice was apparent. What a pair of wankers. Bob had done this kind of thing before often enough, and had never been less sure of his companions. Derek giggled again: he was a petty thief and a queer, despicable on both counts. Dick had plenty of muscle, access to vehicles and those were his only virtues, Bob thought uneasily.

This was a rum way to augment dole payments, but then John Cornell wasn't going to give him a pension and would not pay him when he was sick, although his son had been round with money out of his own pocket, called each week. That made Bob uncomfortable, but the discomfort was like the pain in his lumbar region, intermittent, variable, better than it had been the day before. Dulled by contempt for his companions, who acted like cinematic villains planning a farcical murder. Pain also dulled the planning stage. It could not compete with the fact that the contents of the living rooms of that house would fetch three times what he had quoted, although two-thirds of that would belong to middlemen. Four thousand each if they were lucky, not a fortune but already organized and relatively risk free. Bit of a scam, taking stuff from someone who would never be able to describe you. If they did not rob her someone worse would, and the gypsy in him did not distinguish between a lot and a little. The big time was for others.

'Why did you tell her we were George's friends?'

'There's no harm getting George in trouble. I wonder what she sees in him? His body, I expect. She made us extra welcome, didn't she?'

'She might remember what you said,' Dick said.

'No, she won't. She won't remember fuck all. She talks jumbo. Get a move on, Dick: he passes this way about now. Got eyes in the back of his head, Derek says.'

'You've got a big mouth. Don't know how you feed it.'

Dick put the van into high gear. Bob shook his head. The way they went on, you would think they were bank robbers planning a heist, not a bunch of men down on their luck. Such a palaver, and far too much chat.

'Soon,' he said. 'Before the competition arrives.'

Which it would. He could scent houses like that, marked for plunder.

George had always considered that men talked too much, as if there was anything worth saying. He adored the sensation of silence so profound it became a buzzing in the ears, filling out the vacuum of the skull until becoming deliciously oppressive. He did not use silence to dream or fantasize: he simply dwelt in it and could not remember afterwards what he had thought in his soundless cave with nothing but the hum, or why he had enjoyed the interlude. Silence of that kind was rare: churches with open doors and dim interiors, offering this kind of reward, were rarer still. George had found the church at the bottom of Serena's track on his earlier wanderings. The door had been shut.

He compromised. The countryside was not as quiet as the grave; there was a motorway at the bottom of the valley, things moving in the undergrowth, the panting of the dog and the rasp of his breath in his own ears, eugh, eugh, as he marched uphill with his arms swinging so as not to break step and slow down into a stroll, which did nothing for his muscle tone at all. Sometimes the glory of the day was such he accelerated into a run, but he ran without grace and it was better to march. Enjoy the semi-silence, knowing that this contentment was the plateau from which he could be propelled, once in a while, into a thirty-second moment of being happy. He coughed. His chest hurt.

George kept his own timetable. Which they, meaning the rest of the hostel, knew about vaguely in the restless fashion of a place where people talked and shouted and screamed and whispered and conspired all the time, as if making up for the noise in the outside world from which they were alienated. We are not wicked men, he had once told Derek, simply lost.

He stepped inside the kitchen, awkwardly aware that he did so at more or less the same time every day, although refusing to admit it, his face glowing with perspiration. Today, silence had been evasive. Too many other people out walking with a cacophony of dogs and greetings. Serena welcomed him when he collected Petal by screaming at him about fireworks and where had he been, he should have been there. George had felt supplanted. Four p.m., as usual, and he hated his own predictability, his readiness to tend the fires, mop the quarry-tiled floor if it were not already done, sit and chatter to Serena if Isabel was not around. Which she was. Sorting out the top cupboards in the kitchen – the ones that almost met the high ceiling and could not be reached without standing on a chair – reorganizing, cleaning, what she did every day to make her useless improvements, irritating and pointless. Looking at her stretched on tiptoe, George felt a pang of envy which was oddly like desire. She had no bum on her: the black-clad legs went on for ever and he realized for the first time why men would find this almost childlike womanhood compelling. He told himself he was admiring the strength of those legs and the way she could twist and bend while his own solid trunk could never manage such a variety of movement. He had endurance: his body could move mountains, while hers could twist like a snake.

'George, can you grab these before I drop them?'

She could turn right round on herself, so her feet pointed one way and her head another, handing down to him a red vase and an old condiment set covered in dust, the sort of thing cupboards tended to contain. Items too good to discard but without current use, hidden from view and ready to be retrieved in a spring clean, exclaimed over and finally put back into obscurity. A little like some of the items Serena had given him and he had sold. Derek had guided his hand and knew about those things. George refused to think about that.

'Thanks.'

The kitchen table was half covered with similar detritus. Isabel jumped lightly off the chair and brushed her hands down her legs. George decided he quite liked women to look like this, slightly dirty and dishevelled and doing something useful: dressed in their best was another matter. His own determined reaction against liking Isabel was becoming definitely rearguard, until she opened her mouth.

'Some men who said they were friends of yours called on Ma this morning. Or so she says. Do you know who they were?'

His heart plummeted like a stone into water, ripples of ice-cold alarm extending to the fingertips that clutched the vase and then put it down with exaggerated care. He turned his back on her question, unable for once to sustain a split-second silence, moving away and turning on both taps at the sink to wash his hands aggressively.

'Oh, I don't think so, Miss.'

The sound of Serena's radio came from somewhere, echoing. George looked into the garden, longing for interruption.

'Well, that's what she said they said. Where do you live, George?'

'In town,' he babbled. 'Got a bedsit. Used to look after my mother, see? Used to work at the factory, got laid off. Don't know many people, don't want to. I like my own company, see?'

'Have you got a phone number there, George? Just in case?'

'No, I haven't. Just in case of what?'

'In case your friends come back.'

'They weren't friends of mine, I told you.'

There was not a word of a lie in that. She was looking at him curiously, debating how far to push. Serena could not live without George. They needed George. She could not afford to irritate him.

'I saw them on the track. Three men in a white van,' she added conversationally. 'Very dirty. I could have written my name on it.'

George laughed. It came out like a yelp. The dog nuzzled his hip and he wondered if she had bothered to bark at the strangers. Probably not.

'I certainly don't know anyone with a dirty van,' he stated more clearly. 'I wonder what they wanted?'

'They were lost.'

'Oh. Well, you can't leave her alone for long, I suppose. She'll always let people in, you know, always did. Comes from being so friendly. There's no telling her; I've tried that many times I can't count. Tell them to come back at four, when I'm here, I've said to her, but she won't. She's cunning, you know.'

He could hardly believe his own words. Here he was, on the brink of criticizing his princess, entering into a kind of conspiracy with Isabel and all because he could not say these men are not friends of mine, but they may well be your enemies and I have led them here. Could not say, look, there's a simple explanation: I live alongside cons in a hostel for ex-cons, being a con myself, and you would banish me from this place if you had any inkling.

Isabel sighed and smiled. He almost smiled back.

'Don't I know she's cunning? Did she tell you she ate the soap?'

The sound of Serena's radio, swinging from her hand, moved nearer the kitchen and George knew the meaning of reprieve. He forced back into being all the former detestation for Isabel Burley. Nothing had been quite right since she arrived. He had not let intruders in here, she had. Her letters. Her presence. Her bloody stupid kindness. And all those surplus words.

Here we are again, Serena Burley said to the frayed and frantic patterns on her drawing-room sofa. Wouldn't I just respect God if only he would concede he was an idiot. Like I am.

She was in love with those firework flames. Things, spitting into the air with all that sound and fury, raining down blessings and hidden messages. She had loved them to pieces, willed them to go on and on delighting her. And she knew that the witching hours grew briefer and less sure, because only an old mad fool would stand here in the dark and cold, craning her neck upwards in the hope that the fires would all start again, or leave a permanent imprint of themselves on the sky. They had blinded her. She wanted them back, missed them and hated them for what they did to her. Reminded her of what it was like to feel transfixed with wonder, taken her eye away from the main chance. Made her want to live. She should have swallowed one of those rockets and have done with it. Eating soap did not work.

Serena hit her shin and recognized the possibility of a bruise. The kitchen was a detestable place and she resented the fact that she seemed destined to spend so much time in here. Mab was the person for kitchens, making jam and other disgusting concoctions. Madame Burley, sometimes known as memsahib, preferred to be a lily of the field: they sowed not, neither did they spin, and they never fucking cooked.

Serena made her words in the stainless-steel draining board, presently filmed with cleaning fluid. *I have changed my mind about Isabel*, she wrote. *She is secretive and devious. Without quite knowing the whys and wherefores of what she does, she has sanitized this place. That's what she does all day, removing implements like knives and scissors to the nether regions of shelves where I cannot reach.*

Serena could not work out if Isabel behaved thus on account of reading all her own messages about wanting to die. She doubted it. The clearest of messages left on windows and tables and paper were cleaned away with daily savagery. Serena stamped her foot. She could not kill herself with a fork; she had not got the strength. She would never die of normal cold. She was far too hardy.

She put her head under the cold tap and found it a nasty experience. The darling daughter lacked insight. She was supposed to give purpose, not take it away. She had the means. Once or twice, the child had flown at her father, flown at Mab and knocked a tooth out. Mab was patient, gloating about what the child had in her. Isabel flies at people and impales herself on them, Serena told the dog. Like a moth with a light.

The draining board was splashed and the words were gone again. Supposing darling Isabel could be made to detest her mother as much as her mother loathed herself? There was always the chance she would indulge in a sort of lethal lashing-out. Then she would have to go, leaving Serena with darling George and a wider range of choices, unless Serena was dead already. This was all too complicated for mere words. Serena decided she preferred the idea of being able to orchestrate her own demise.

There were grazes on her knees from where she had fallen over in worship of the Catherine wheels. Time to go back to bed with a saucer of milk and a nice strong man. Fading away like the wallpaper.

Moving slowly, swearing softly, kissing the unloved things goodbye.

CHAPTER SEVEN

Seven weeks. Home, sweet home and no one watching.

'Dear Joe,' Isabel wrote in a letter that would not contain a single exclamation mark, covering a few sheets of paper she would probably never send. The fire spluttered safely behind a guard. Serena liked to sit close in the evening, crowding it, resentfully, otherwise quiet and preoccupied. The television in the corner muttered, creating a kind of absent conversation. A man ran across the screen waving a gun, his mouth yelling an order.

'I think this was my vision of home,' Isabel continued. 'A fireside in winter and the thought of not having to leave it and go out in the cold. Sitting by the side of someone comfortable. She's being very good . . .' Isabel paused. Joe would not want to know this. His notion of home would be warm bed, food, and bugger the fires. Never mind what he might want to know: she was uncomfortably aware that he would have no curiosity about her life at all. She wrote to put things into words, making a letter out of the words was merely an excuse for writing them and it seemed timely to write. To make something of the time.

'We are strange here, Joe, and yes, sometimes comfortable, but not often. I can hear people asking, what do they do all day, the way I used to wonder what mothers did when their babies slept all the time. They don't, Joe, not old babies either, and you can't have conversations with them or expect reasonable conduct . . . You can't even tell them about the dangers they face. (I wish she was not so secretive about the post, hiding the bills.) And the difference with an old baby is that you can't shout or slap, either. I learned the basic rules about don't run in the road from my Aunty Mab, because I was afraid of her. I can't make my mother afraid; I should hate it. And I wasn't ever afraid of her; it was more complicated than that. I was so proud of her. She made everyone else's mother look so drab and fat while she was exotic, did exotic things, lived in exotic places, married an exotic kind of man . . . which may be why I'm almost content to hole up with her like this, because I don't quite like the idea of anyone else seeing her in a state which is neither proud nor anything like the way she was. Does that make sense?'

Serena coughed loudly, a stagey kind of cough, not exactly a plea for attention, but a preliminary. Isabel had the vision, coming from nowhere, of Mother removing the fireguard and sitting on the coal, squatting on the flames without any sensation of pleasure or pain. Serena's glasses remained dirty, despite a daily wash. She preferred them that way.

'I only say strange,' Isabel scribbled, 'because it is strange to be around someone all the time and not really talk in anything but a kind of baby language. It alters my vision on everything. Did I tell you about taking her to the pub? She

127

wanted chips again, but when she got them, she put half in the top pocket of the man at the next table and smeared him with gravy. Affection, of course, but we won't be welcome back. But I won't let go, Joe, because she loves me, and I need to be loved.'

That sounded pathetic, so she crossed it out. There was another cough. Serena was transfixed by the TV. She raised her hand, pointed two level fingers at the man still running across the urban landscape with his gun and wide open mouth, and shot him, twice.

'Then there's George, who comes and goes. I don't know who he is, where he comes from, I don't know anything except for the fact he turns up. We've never questioned George, you know: not even Robert demanded his credentials, because he is so useful. Too late now. Even though Robert does nothing, I'm afraid to ask. Two reasons, I suppose. I want to make her better all by myself, with no one else getting the credit. I want to be able to endure it, and be proud of what I've done. And I don't want people seeing in the windows. Looking at her like something from the zoo.'

Serena sat back in her chair, obviously satisfied. She knitted her fingers together and nodded at the screen. The dirty spectacles dropped to the end of her nose.

'He's dead,' she yelled. 'That one there. Dead. Shot himself. What a good thing.'

Doc Reilly had given Isabel sleeping pills. He had not specified who should take them.

'As long as she loves me,' Isabel wrote, 'as long as she loves me, I can do this. Only I'm beginning to see things which are not here. Perhaps they never were. Perhaps I need glasses.'

★

Robert Burley was not without conscience. That was the way he would have stated his ambivalent state of mind apropos his mother, although no one asked him to state anything except a case. Part of the relative ease of his conscience came first from the fact that his mother had tried to crush his daughter, and although he did not believe this was anything other than clumsiness, the lack of malice afore-thought did not quite mitigate the crime. Second was the fact that Isabel deserved the burden of looking after her mother because she had led such a feckless life to date. The third factor was that he knew, by comparison with some of his clients, how lucky Serena Burley really was. She had a house to live in, didn't she? A pension and a modicum of health, which was a damn sight more than a lot of other little old ladies.

At the same time he could not quite leave things as they were. He blustered by phone to social workers, without real-izing that this long-distance intervention, not discussed with Isabel, created an animus against her for instigating a nui-sance and against himself for hectoring. Discussions were not helped by the fact that Robert no longer really knew what he wanted for his mother. An element of control with-out effort, a salve to his conscience, one social worker surmised. They quite understood why his mother could not stay with him, nor he with his mother. Indeed they were astonished that he should go to such lengths to explain it when no explanation had been requested. Alzheimer's and the distance between parents and children were both dis-eases of contemporary life, unlikely to go away. The psychiatric social worker could call upon Mrs Burley and assess the situation, certainly: so could the consultant psychi-atrist: indeed, one had done so, at his behest, both before the

129

fire and immediately afterwards, did he not remember? Verdict: she suffered from an affliction of the mind, but could still maintain an independent life with existing support. Now there was a voluntary daughter in residence, there was even less reason to act and besides, what could they do?

'Mental health orders are for extreme cases of danger. Is she still able to pay her bills? Does she eat and wash? Is she incontinent?'

'Yes, with help. Yes, yes and no, I don't think so.'

'You could try and persuade her to come and live in a home nearer yourself . . .'

'Get her off your patch, you mean!' he yelled, furious at the dulcet patience of the tones.

'Mr Burley, I've got a call coming through on the other line.'

Activity was better than inactivity, so Robert was standing in the foyer of a residential home three miles from where he lived, unaccountably nervous. It was all very well to fear death, that was as logical as a dread of pain, but fear of old age had never occurred to him before. Insofar as he considered his own, which was not often, he had envisaged himself as a senior statesman with pipe and slippers, adviser to the neighbourhood, heeded by the young and accorded respect for his wisdom, dying conveniently, as his father had done, before serious infirmity began, his death the object of grief and obeisance to his memory. Indignity did not feature in any of these visions.

'And this is the lounge, Mr Burley. We have bingo on Wednesdays, the chiropodist once a week, a hairdresser Tuesdays and karaoke on Saturdays. Plenty to do.'

He wanted to say he could not foresee the day when the biggest dose of memory loss would make his mother enjoy bingo or the company of the other women who sat in their chairs lining the walls of the lounge like so many puppets paying disinterested homage to the huge television in the corner. These were images familiar enough to save him from showing his shock, but the view was still dispiriting. These were the sentient beings who watched the screen in the way his baby would watch a moving, glistening object. The thought of karaoke was appalling.

'And these are the rooms. Some people like to share . . .'

Dens with single beds and the overpowering presence of the floral. Rose-flavoured air-freshener, chintz bedspreads, everything Serena had despised. Just as she would the antiseptic corridors of polished linoleum, the open doors to bathrooms with pulleys, lavatories with handles set into the walls and, in the distance, the sound of someone howling.

The mentally infirm, the lady told him, live at the back.

She had a face shining with kindness, free of hypocrisy. The proximity of a good heart made him realize that he had not got one.

The overpowering presence of wickedness in the world was not what oppressed him on his way home, but the existence of such reservoirs of kindness with which he could not compete. Saints were so much more irritating than sinners. Especially when they informed him that as long as his mother's wounds were bloodless, the state would bleed her dry. Parents of his mother's generation owed it to their inheritors to die young. And who would look after him when he was old?

The sight of Aunt Mab's Bristol blue glassware, safe inside the cabinet which housed it along with Serena's silverware and her pieces of porcelain which he did not really like, hardly filled him with satisfaction, but not with guilt either. Isabel had not noticed, which was her own fault. Pragmatism had dictated the removal of various items on past visits. One day he would give to his daughter those objects Serena no longer knew she possessed, and the love of daughter for parent was surely more enduring than that of son. After more introspection, self-justification and righteous anger, Robert decided to leave things as they were.

'You were very kind to bring the fireworks,' Isabel said. 'Very kind. I haven't seen her so happy in ages.'

Andrew had a good telephone voice, echoing the authority of the auctioneer, deep, calm, reassuring. She had liked the smell of his tweedy shoulder when she had cried into it, even though she had withdrawn, wiped her eyes, become a hostess. Whatever it was her mother had told her, with varying degrees of emphasis, about never being a nuisance to men, the dictate had remained as solid as an undeniable memory, like the imprint of men's bodies. They existed to be pleased, but in Isabel's present role the necessity of being pleasant all the time had faded away and she did not have either the energy or the inclination to flatter Andrew Cornell. She owed him nothing. He was not her kind of man, since Isabel's kind of men were rarely so undemanding, and he was not a priority. Besides, after weeks of isolation with her mother and taciturn George, she felt she had lost her knack with men, whatever the knack had been.

'I thought you might like to go out for a meal,' he was suggesting. The sound of the phone was so unfamiliar during the day, it had startled her. Serena hovered near, alive with curiosity.

'Where is there to go?' Isabel realized she sounded ungracious.

He chuckled. 'You're out of date with local sophistications. Chinese, Italian, you name it, we do it.'

'I'm not sure about leaving Mother.' The longing must have sounded in her voice, replete with memory of Serena's capacity for sabotage. Broken crockery. Cat's pawmarks in the trifle. Soap down the gullet. Torn books and frantic letters. That was what she did all day: she repaired wreckage and found it impossible to explain.

He hesitated. 'Batten down the hatches. She'll be all right. Promise her next time we'll take her too. You've got to get out, Isabel.'

'Yes I have.'

'Where would you like to go? What would you like to do?'

Deferential questions of this kind always irritated her. If a man issues an invitation, he should also make the plan.

'Wherever you like. I don't know. Somewhere nice.' Nice: another word despised by Mab. Pleasant then, a break, a change.

Andrew put down the phone in the auction-room office feeling slightly deflated. He weaved his way across to where his father sat with Doc Reilly, occupying adjacent corners of a large table of scrubbed pine, each nursing a cup of coffee in front of a shared ashtray.

'Anyway,' Doc Reilly was saying. 'I've told the police it's only a matter of time before she gets burgled, so would they take the patrol out there at night? He says resources are stretched, old son, what with Christmas round the corner. Anyway, most of the young lads, including his own, don't even know where that house is. Safety in obscurity. There ought to be a Latin phrase for it.'

'Who?' said Andrew.

'Old mother Burley. The same old sweetheart you were asking after earlier on. There's been kids up there, pinching things. Kids have grown-up brothers with bigger eyes. That dog of hers is as much use as a wet blanket. Scarcely wags its tail without wondering if it's still attached.'

John Cornell nodded sagely, plucked a cigarette out of a packet and held it to the light, as if looking for a hallmark to prove that this one, at least, was good for his health.

'There's a man up there half the day, though. What's he called? George?'

'For what that's worth. Mustn't judge a man by his history.'

'What's that supposed to mean?' Andrew asked sharply.

Doc turned a cunning eye on him. Andrew could detect the guarded glance of cynical compassion.

'It means he was in my surgery two weeks ago. Being brave about what looked to me like bronchitis. Gives the address of the hostel on the estate. You know it. Oh no, you probably don't, they won't be asking you in to value furniture, miserable dump. Sort of closet institution, where they put ex-convicts. To rehabilitate. What a joke. No wonder he likes going up Mrs Burley's. Does all of us good to get out of the house, but it surely applies to some more than others.'

'Where is this bloody place?' John Cornell lit the health-giving cigarette, shifted in his seat. The doctor recited an address. John Cornell nodded slowly, scratched his rump. Doc Reilly wagged his finger at Andrew.

'Don't you let on I told you that, will you? George loves dogs, so he must be all right. And the old lady loves George, even if society hasn't much time for him. Whatever else there is about him is none of our business, is it?'

'Unless he was a burglar himself.'

Doc Reilly patted Andrew's shoulder with heavy-handed condescension. 'Not as far as I know.'

'You going courting, Andrew?' his father asked, still absorbed in his cigarette. 'The fair Isabel again?'

'Chance would be a fine thing,' Andrew smiled. He had learned never to rise to the bait with his father. Or keep secrets that could be held in evidence against himself later. 'Thought I'd get her out of the house. Good for us all, like the Doc said. You should know.'

'She's a nice young woman, that,' said the doctor, watching Andrew walking away whistling, trailing his fingers over the dusty furniture. 'But what was she thinking of when she was eighteen, nineteen and twenty, John? Men. Nothing but men. We aren't worth it. They give us what we want and we call them tarts. Did you ever hear about those letters her aunty sent to her boyfriends? Or maybe it was her mother. I've never been sure.'

John Cornell scratched his rump again, an irritating habit.

'Hostel for ex-cons on Acacia Drive? Do you know, I think when young Derek comes in this afternoon I might just tell him we don't need him any more. I don't believe in rehabilitation. Or leopards changing spots.'

'Now, that isn't fair, John.'

'Nothing's fair, Eamon. Look at it outside. Night already. That isn't fair, either.'

The gang came across the fields about ten o'clock at night in a big three-ton truck, which Dick informed them, too late, he had never driven before. He was really the butcher's boy in disguise, used to delivering small parcels. He was also as high as a kite, nerves, grass or what, Bob neither knew nor cared, as long as he did not let go of the wheel when smiling as constantly as he did. The sniggering unnerved Bob, but there was no smell of alcohol and the back of the lorry was clean, hosed down every day, Dick said. Bob had supplied a mattress from his back shed, which made the others laugh in unison from the moment they pulled away. What was so funny about a mattress? His other contributions were ropes, old sheets of the kind his incurious wife despised, blankets and other forms of protection for what they were about to steal. May the Lord have mercy on it, the way Dick drove and Derek, with his wicked little elbows extended like chicken wings, digging into their ribs, snorting with laughter although there was no joke except a wagon that behaved like a bucking mule resentful of the saddle. This was all going to go wrong: Bob knew it in his bones, jolted by the van, jarred by the company. He felt like a bride *en route* for a wedding ceremony she already regretted; all dressed up and nowhere to go. The back of this thing, still sweatily damp on account of the lack of warmth needed to make it dry, resembled a shambolic travelling bordello, equipped for a cheap sex maniac. It was only later he realized what had made the others laugh. The mattress was already stained; the bars against the side were designed for the safe carriage of meat. All it lacked was confetti for the takeaway bride of Dracula.

Halfway up the track from the church to the house, coming through a puddle of water, the engine stalled. That was the second time they should have turned back, but they did not. Within half an hour, the engine had dried out and on they went, still exactly like a wedding procession: slow, sure, late.

A clear night with a kindly moon and the promise of frost.

There was another chance to turn by the gates of the house and leave. The near side of the van hit the lefthand pillar with a noise as loud as a scream. Dick reversed away, turned off the engine, waited. All conversation died. Then they went on.

I could get six years for a few hundred pounds, Bob muttered to himself: it don't compute. They coasted slowly down the slight incline to the back door, stopping far short of it. The house glared at them. The passenger door opened with a creak that felt like an injection straight into his spine, making him choke back a groan. They could have been a team of clowns waiting in the wings to perform to an audience already inclined to jeer. They moved towards the back door, one sniffing loudly, the other one hands in pockets, each hanging back, Dick swinging a hammer from the end of his torn sleeve. Then Derek, taller than usual in the cuban-heeled boots that gave him an extra inch height, overtook the other two and reached the door, tripped over something, swore softly, moved to the window on his right. They could see the mist of his breath against the glass in the light of his silly little pencil torch. Two things happened in quick succession. The outside light above the kitchen door sparked into life, as if it had been waiting for something to jolt a loose connection. It illuminated a ferret astride a bowl half filled with milk; the ferret turned and hissed. Next to it, spread over the step, lay a ginger cat, limbs extended in a parody of sinuous fireside stretching, frozen for all time. Definitely dead: you could tell from its peculiar immobility, the angle of the throat and the awful spread of the jaws.

Then the other lights, inside the house, came on. Derek at the window, standing lower than room height in a flower bed, found himself chest level with a naked woman. She had an arm outstretched, doing something with the curtain, which she yanked so it half covered her form and also made her impatient. One large bosom, as big as a melon, exaggerated by proximity and condensation, waggled with the effort. A half-drawn blind behind the curtain obscured her face. The pen torch dropped behind a clump of ragged dahlias. Derek staggered back, hypnotized by flesh so close he could have pressed his nose into her belly-button. When he turned, he saw Bob and Dick moving back towards the van. They were retreating uncertainly, away from the cat. The ferret followed, spitting. In terror Dick grunted and farted, flinging the hammer. It hit the ribs of the ferret with a tiny thud; there was a shriek of pain.

Derek threw himself against the bonnet, pushed like fury. The wagon was moving as he clambered through the open door, remembering, foolishly, not to slam it, as if the noise of the engine were not already loud as they coasted back through the gates with accidental ease and a whining noise. Halfway across the road the brute stopped again and again Dick kicked it into life. The travelling bordello accelerated back in the same direction from which it had arrived, all of them shamed into silence as they lurched over holes in the track until they reached the main road. Turned left past the church; you could swear the dead in the churchyard winked, stuck two fingers out of their fucking gravestones, but that was what Bob said later. For the moment he was speechless.

Dick spoke first. 'Who was it? Her with the curtain?'

'I dunno. Must've been someone.'

'You're fucking right, someone. Old or young?' Bob had found his voice.

Derek faltered. 'I dunno. Big on top. Big. She had a fork . . .'

The giggling began again, relieving them. Great snorts of giggles, hands between knees, nearly wetting themselves, so infectious the sound that Derek joined in.

'In her hand,' he added. They were hysterical by now, utterly helpless. Dick, hugging the central white line, swerved to avoid a saloon car coming up fast on the deserted road. He had got the hang of the wagon, even felt grateful to it. Everything was outrageously funny. Bob roared, Derek giggled, Dick insisted they stop for a pee. In this camaraderie, against the backdrop of failure, suddenly brave again, they pretended that this had been the dummy run and planned the second attempt.

Maybe this was a second attempt. Maybe Andrew was treating her as man does woman, flirting without being obvious. Maybe he was simply as kind an individual as he seemed and was being nice to her. Whatever the reason for his actions, Isabel forgot to question, and since there was no reason to impress, failed to try, found herself relaxing. She was also starving for the kind of food she no longer saw: tagliatelle, green salad, the sort of meal it was a balm to eat, a million miles away from Mother's favourite fish and chips. Serena liked the food she had liked as a child: porridge, bread and butter, jelly and custard. Isabel tried to tell Andrew this, joking and gesturing between mouthfuls, gulping wine. He listened in a way men rarely listened, teased her about the sheer amount she consumed. It wasn't flirting, she decided; it was talking, about something and nothing, while on the other side of the small table his smile grew more attractive, his eyes browner and the grin she had remembered more endearing. On top of that, as well as zabaglione, she could see him persuading

Serena to release her baby grandchild and watch fireworks. OK, he was a nice, unpretentious man with the dress sense of a grandad.

He saw something else. A beautiful, insecure woman with a comic propensity to pull faces and mimic voices. One who defied her intelligence, pushed it down like rubbish in a sack. Acted as she was expected to act until no one was watching, unsure of her authority or talent to amuse. Ready to trip over her feet and let someone ride roughshod over her too-thin body and too-unsatisfying life. All because of the chasm within. He did not know if his observations were right, but since he had done more observing of women than touching of them, watching them dance attendance on furniture, husbands, himself, he hoped his perceptions were accurate and despised himself for the sense of distance that encouraged him to make them. Before grace, after grace, eating food, digesting it, driving along in his car, he was always looking at people like a mild, uncritical voyeur. As if passion were something he had eradicated with the help of an inoculation. He ordered more coffee. Half a bottle out of two shared hardly counted in the drink-driving stakes: and she was steady as a rock as she moved through the place on the way to and from the ladies' loo, not a tremor. He was ashamed of observing that, too. He had a head for the stuff as good as this girl sitting opposite, laughing one minute, then looking at her watch.

'Cinderella time,' she said. 'Gotta go. My mother will turn me into a pumpkin.'

'You give life, you take it away,' he murmured, finding her coat.

She paused in the act of shrugging into it. 'What do you mean?'

'That's what your mother will have done. If this goes on and on, that's exactly what she will have done. Taken your life in exchange for the preservation of hers.'

'It doesn't matter.' She was agitated, to the extent of pressing one arm into the wrong sleeve. Cold outside, winter, instead of autumn. She did not want to go home. Thought of breath on windows, a house where heating demanded labour and preparation, like all the tasks from slow dawn to early dusk. The constant watching, of her mother and herself. The hard-won patience, the constant reiteration to herself of how much, at last, her mother loved her.

'As long as you know,' he said cheerfully. 'I looked after Dad for years. I wish I'd done more with the time, that's all.'

'Does he love you?'

Andrew considered the question with some surprise. 'Yes, I suppose he does, after his fashion. Doesn't like me, though.'

They had reached the car, clambered inside quickly because of the sudden cold and sat, waiting for the heater to melt the pattern of a delicate frost on the windscreen.

'Seems a pity to ruin it,' Isabel said, watching moisture form out of crazy flowers. 'Do you like me?'

'Yes, very much.'

'Which is more important?' she demanded. 'Liking or loving?' The car engine was quiet as the ice trickled away.

'Liking, in the long run. It means respect. Love doesn't always mean that.'

'Oh.'

The silence was not uncomfortable as they cruised away from the lights of the centre, through a suburb and then on to a road lit only by their headlights. He did not play music

141

as they drove, for which Isabel was grateful. Serena's constant music had begun to eat at her nerves.

'I wonder if I've ever been liked, in that case,' Isabel said thoughtfully. She thought in this warm car of Joe, and his heated demands, and his habit of never listening to a word she said.

'You may not have noticed being liked,' Andrew suggested. 'It isn't always easy to detect.'

She had never counted the miles from town; six or seven; ten, fifteen minutes, longer with Mother, but always a journey from one extreme to another, a passage between alien lives. Joe would probably have refused to drive his fancy car up this track and be careless of damage the way Andrew was. Yes, she liked Andrew, even though she disliked making comparisons.

'I don't suppose I was very likeable at twenty, was I?'

He laughed, uncomfortably. 'Does it matter? You were, as a matter of fact, and also entirely lovable. Until you took to writing obscene letters.'

'What?'

They had turned through the gates, stopped by the back door.

'*What?*' she repeated. 'Me?' There was less outrage in her voice than puzzlement, but she no longer wanted to sit beside him. She fumbled with the seat belt and slammed the door behind her. He followed, cursing himself.

Drawn curtains in the kitchen, porch light winking over the corpse of the ginger cat. Isabel thought it was sleeping. Even while knowing that no cat slept thus, still she bent to pick it up, then recoiled. There was a wound in the throat, spots of blood on the paving of the yard, a hammer lying a few feet away. She backed away, colliding with Andrew. He put his hand on the nape of her neck, where the hackles rose. She avoided his touch, sidestepped the cat with a shudder, put her own hand on the kitchen doorknob, turned it, watched the door yield.

'I locked the cat out,' Isabel whispered, her face stricken with guilt. 'And I locked Mother in.'

CHAPTER EIGHT

You do not, should not, lock your mother indoors so that you can go out and play. Upstairs, listening for the stroke of midnight from the grandfather clock, Serena sat in the armchair in her room, conducting the orchestra in the overture to *My Fair Lady*. Her slippers were an unmatched pair: she extended one slim ankle and admired it. The bundle of post, which she carried around like a talisman, waiting for the miracle that would make it meaningful instead of merely important, sat at her feet, free from Isabel's interference. She made one foot join the other, turned both inwards so the toes met, and gazed at them with considerable satisfaction.

There was someone knocking at something somewhere. The music rose to a climax announcing the imminence of Act One.

Such a nice young man, standing in the doorway, dressed so unnecessarily in a winter coat. The music had reminded her obscurely of another form of dress, which bore no resemblance to his. He seemed to be looking for something; eyes everywhere, speaking pleasantly, half of him there and half of him not. A spasm of disappointment crossed her features since the man was not George, but he was still, quite definitely, male, so she smiled.

'Hallo, Mrs Burley. Remember me? I've come to see if you're all right.'

His was a face she had seen before, although not one of those villainous ones with gun in hand which she shot with such regularity on the TV screen downstairs; this one was one of the nice guys she had applauded. A sort of prince, apart from his dull clothes. Far too many clothes on his frail frame. What a waste, when he needed no embellishment other than his boyish grin.

'Fireworks?' Andrew suggested, thinking she might remember him if given a reminder.

'Not at the moment,' she said, wondering what it was he wanted. Her back felt stiff. All that reaching up over the kitchen curtain pole, where Isabel left the spare keys (what a silly place to leave anything), hoiking them out with the aid of a fork, getting down off the chair to open the door, had been activities that reminded her body of the existence of ribs. But it was imperative to resist being locked in, however kindly that had been done. The instinct to remedy such an unpardonable situation had occurred halfway through preparations for a bath. Windows and doors had no business being barred: no one could walk through walls, although this man had. He smiled as she smiled back.

'Mind if I look around?'

That, too, reminded her of a familiar phrase from

somewhere else, and, in response to almost any set of words framed in familiar patterns and delivered quietly, Serena could usually dredge up some formulaic response. Her replies were often way off beam and, equally often, uncannily correct. She had what Doc Reilly called an excellent social armour. She could pass for a wise and articulate old crow, capable of appreciation, even while half of what she said was inspired guesswork.

She inclined her head graciously; winked. 'You're welcome. Go ahead, son, why doncha?'

He opened her wardrobe door, appeared to admire the contents, looked behind the curtains. Looking for a stiff, she told herself. Stiff or stuff; Raymond Chandler on the page or a drugs raid on TV, same difference, same response.

'Are you looking for Stinker?' Serena asked.

'Stinker?'

'The rat.' She laughed gaily. 'He sometimes hides under the bed. He's a very naughty rat.'

'I didn't know you had rats, Mrs Burley.'

' 'Course not. Stinker eats them.' Nice, this young man, but slow on the uptake. She was enjoying herself.

Andrew looked under the bed. There were signs of spasmodic dusting from each edge in, not quite reaching the centre space. Something was hanging down below the headboard at the pillow end. He shifted the whole mattress while she watched him in the way she might have watched a maid sent into a hotel room to arrange a complimentary bowl of flowers, giving him her full and indulgent attention. When he raised one end of the thing on her bed, she indulged that too, as an activity which seemed without purpose but nevertheless was conducted by someone who knew what he was doing. Even if she did not.

'Quite a collection of hardware, Mrs Burley. What's all this doing here?'

All this? All what? Her spectacles were in another place: she felt around for them. Two carving knives, a small saw and a twelve-inch length of barbed wire were displayed on the end of the bed. Serena's smile wavered.

'Mine,' she said, falteringly. 'I think.'

Of course the bed was hers: why did he doubt it? She had no recollection of the things he held aloft, only a sense of sorrow that he might take them away.

He bent over by her chair, bringing his face level with her forehead, and took her hand inside his own calloused palm, a sensation she liked so much she tried to imprint it on her memory, along with other dreams of being touched and held by someone who was not waiting to let go, even though this man's hands were colder than hers. Fresh-air hands, whereas hers were ready for bed, made of paper and full of fragile warmth from sitting in the chair in nightie, slippers and winter coat while the bath water in the bath, long since forgotten, cooled. There was strong, wiry hair on the backs of his hands; he was more like a dog than a cat.

'Puss, puss,' said Serena, stroking. 'Where is the Stinker?'

'Did anyone else come in and see you this evening?'

She looked at him, eyebrows raised, as if the question were impertinent. Pausing in this fashion was guaranteed to make people repeat what they had said several times in quick succession, for as long as the inquisitory look demanded. Sometimes it triggered understanding; not always. Andrew followed the cue.

'Any more visitors, Mrs Burley?' he said, louder, and then repeated himself.

'People? You mean people?'

'Yes, people.'

'No.' She leaned forward, about to impart a secret. 'They can't. People can't get in. Isabel. My girl Isabel. She scares them away. She won't even let me have my cat. She locks it out.' Nodding wisely now. 'She locks everything out.' Her voice descended into a whisper. 'I should look out if I were you. Isabel eats people.'

For a moment Andrew wondered if that were true. The conversation, such as it was, had begun to exhaust him. It was similar to the effect of talking over a din, shouting to make oneself heard, receiving a coded response which demanded he shout louder. Perhaps Isabel was in the habit of scaring people away, for whatever purpose. The motives of others were ever mysterious, even if usually reducible to greed or fear. Or perhaps the erstwhile friends of this grande dame simply no longer had the stamina for little chats such as these. He was surprised to find he minded not being recognized as the provider of fireworks.

'I'll let you get to bed. Thanks for asking me in.' She beamed in benediction, maintaining hold of his hand.

'Don't leave me with her,' she said with sudden distinctness. 'Kiss me good-night?'

He bestowed a kiss on her cheek, felt the hand that relinquished his own move round his neck, drawing him down, murmuring in his ear with sounds he associated with someone enjoying food: yummyummyum. Then, without quite believing the sensation at first, imagining some ghost, he felt her other hand creep between his legs, touching his corduroy-clad thigh, lightly at first, as if feeling the cloth. Then kneading and patting it, in a manner less suggestive of sexual invitation than of someone tickling and pulling the ears of a dog, which, in his case, had no idea how to respond. He

148

stood upright, slowly, detached her hand with a smile and put it back into her lap. The music from her tape deck swelled into the First Act, and the plaintive voice of a street singer.

'Bollocks,' she said, still smiling with wide-eyed innocence. 'Fucking bollocks, is that it?'

He had finally released himself. Close, like that, she had smelled both sweet and sour and on his way downstairs, he wondered if the smell lingered on his coat.

The grandfather clock on the upstairs landing struck a gentle midnight, sweetly and hurriedly, as if getting through the duty while making apologies at the same time. Norwich-made, eighteenth-century, fairly valuable, Andrew noted on the way down. The knives and the saw were tucked under one arm, the barbed wire carried gingerly between finger and thumb. He wondered where she had found it. There was something particularly cruel about barbed wire: it had no value; it existed for nothing but the potential to harm.

When he and Isabel had come into the kitchen, they had known the non-existence of intruders from the sheer quality of the silence. The clock ticking with no need to turn its face to the wall, the dog lazy and docile, the drip of the tap, all clues to the lack of trespass and the sensation that the danger lay within. He and Isabel had looked through the downstairs rooms before he, at his own insistence, went alone to the upper landings. There was no real bravery in a search that could serve no purpose other than the confirmation of innocence. Isabel had resented him for it. By the time he came back, the cat lay outside where Isabel had left it for burial in the morning, with the respectful addition of a shroud fashioned from a tablecloth.

'Nothing,' Andrew said, 'but these.'

She gazed, stupidly, at Serena's armoury, laid out next to

the hammer. Then she glanced at Andrew's face. A sense of guilt made her skin glow pink. Serena purloined things all the time – scissors, forks, screwdrivers – they turned up on window ledges, in the fridge, in the bathroom, and in due course Isabel returned them to their own corners, pretending they had never gone. But she had never imagined there was a theme to this harmless kleptomania, other than a simple feature of her mother, busying herself ineffectually and then forgetting whatever it was she had been going to do. Sew a button on something; change a plug; everyday tasks with everyday reminders and no memory to achieve them. In better days Mother's contempt of domestic chores had not excluded pride in a level of self-sufficiency. She had needed to do everything for herself.

'Do you think she could have hurt the cat?'

Isabel thought of the ferret with the white teeth, then the hammer, shook her head. There was not enough coordination between hand and eye in her mother's slow movements to do such frightful damage, although there was still plenty of strength.

'Might she want to hurt herself?' Andrew asked, inexorably. Isabel felt the undertone of accusation in his voice, hinting at her own inefficiency; it made her clam up in defensive fury.

'I don't think so. But then I rarely know what she thinks. Do you want some coffee?' Without waiting for an answer, she began moving about the business of preparation, like a child sent out of a classroom, walking like a marionette. Andrew came close to her, touched her shoulder lightly.

'Stop it, Isabel. I'm not blaming you.'

'Yes, you are.'

'I wouldn't know how. Look, do you want me to stay? I

think I should, even if it was a false alarm. Nobody's been in here, I'm sure of it. She must have found the keys to open the back door. Why she threw a hammer in the backyard, God only knows. Perhaps she's contemplating a new career in joinery and found the thing surplus to requirements?'

Isabel laughed. She looked a little like her mother when she laughed. Any sexual frisson between them engendered by the evening had disappeared. He could still feel Serena's hand, patting the warmth of his thigh, killing desire more effectively than any dead cat or full stomach. Andrew yawned, half naturally, half contrived.

'Get me some blankets for the sofa, would you? I'll freeze in there otherwise.'

That was neatly done, she thought later. A considerate man. The kind who was gone before breakfast and so diplomatic he could assess the furniture of your soul and not show he found it lacking, the kind who could dispel fear with pragmatism and who always seemed to know better. Which did not mean that he could begin to understand the pressures and realities of her kind of existence: you had to live it to know it. Before Isabel had started this chapter of her life, she had been sick of other people always knowing better. She still was.

She brought him a duvet, glad of his presence in the house but not wanting him closer. Thanked him with grave politeness not designed to wound, and having exactly that effect.

'Oh, by the way,' she said at the door, 'Mother might wander during the night. She does, a bit. I never try to stop her.'

Such a beautiful room. Estate agent's dream for the family with everything, including money. A house, which should have rumbled with laughter, rows, warmth and the presence of children, settled into silence so complete it made Andrew listen to the sound of his own breathing. An hour passed in sleepless contemplation that owed less to the effect of weak coffee than to the slow ebb of adrenalin. Words paraded through his mind like soldiers marching on display, up and down, down and up. Surely there was more than madness in this house: there was jealousy and hatred.

When he heard the echo of the grandfather clock announcing the second hour after midnight he got up and turned on lights for the sake of sanity, beat his arms across his chest for warmth, and sat at Serena's desk, which he opened without a tremor of guilt and no anticipation but to indulge his own curiosity.

It was tidy inside, pigeonholes stuffed with paper in apparent order, leaving a clear surface. 'Dear Andrew,' he recited in his mind. 'Don't you know that Isabel Burley has sucked more cocks than you have had hot dinners, as well as doing it with her father? If you go on doing it with her you'll catch something nasty. Your balls will drop off into her mouth and she likes holding them, doesn't she?' Two paragraphs of this puerile prose had made him recoil in horror a dozen years before, as much for the recognition of Isabel's own fair hand in the construction of the writing as for the content. She had never been particularly clever with words: the letter had been a boast of achievements. You and who else, it said. John Reilly, Rick Murray, David Mason, Jim Partridge, a whole fucking football team. It might have been a child writing in the third person. It was as if she were not writing about herself, sticking in the rude words for effect, but it was more than enough to insult his own manhood, even though the description bore no real reflection of the somewhat shy nature of their own coupling. The shyness and inhibition were more his own than Isabel's, he had to admit, and that alone lent some veracity to the written word. Isabel had become, in his imagination, the writer of poison-pen letters, an unstable and unstoppable sexual fantasist who was not even articulate beyond four-letter words, a neurotic motivated by malice. He had never wanted to see her again.

The desk was commodious, containing correspondence that Andrew supposed predated his own birth, let alone adolescence. The pigeonholes to the right were full of scraps of paper less yellowed by age, folded neatly in halves and then in quarters, reminding him of childish games played with paper, aeroplanes constructed on winter afternoons. Serena's pages were densely covered with words. Bollocks, he read, fucking bollocks. Life is a bitch and God is a cunt. Outpourings of frustrations on to the pages, rude words plastered on to the backs of envelopes, poison-pen messages to self. All in the small but legible hand her daughter had tried to emulate.

Andrew replaced the papers. He considered whether he would ever be able to tell Isabel what her mother had done to that particular fledgeling affair of her younger life, wondered if her Mama had done the same to every hopeful young man Isabel had ever brought home. Written them the kind of letters that would insult vanity, destroy affection and make the recipient either despise her daughter or laugh at her.

He nodded to sleep, debating without much logic the character of a mother motivated by the desire either to destroy or to protect, moved by either jealousy or the kind of love he could not comprehend, glad on the whole that his own mother had died in his own infancy. He thought at the same time how eavesdroppers hear no good of themselves, and how his discovery tonight reflected badly on the self-centred youth he had been. And should he tell Isabel; deciding not. If Isabel lost the illusion that her mother loved her, her life would be untenable.

And then he would lose her too.

He slept through the sound of slow, uncertain footsteps on the stairs and the changing of dark into the beginning of day. Woke to the rumble of the dustbin van, removing two sacks of rubbish and a dead cat before reversing back down the drive in a hurry, covering with their own the marks on the grass left by the big white van.

George had a bedroom window that faced west, dark in the mornings and light in the afternoons. Dark as all hell whenever he was in it. It was a blurred room, featureless. Once inside he felt and behaved like a mouse, nesting tidily inside his own stretch of skirting board, never requiring the prompting of light or noise to wake him. In the last hour of sleep he descended into a deep, dark pit out of which he sailed with the ease of a cork on water.

Into that darkness came a voice, carried on a thick breath.

'Georgie boy, wake up. Wake up, fuck you.'

Stale, sweet smell of alcohol decomposing; sweat crystallized on a cold body, giggle in the voice. George felt his hair being pulled, his ear tweaked, his shoulder shaken, all in a parody of affection. He never locked his bedroom door. The locks were no great deterrent to a shoulder: better to have nothing worth the taking.

'Give us a cuddle, George. Naa, all right then, forget it.'

George had formed his body into a ball, hands over head,

knees to chest. In the manner of a baby waiting to be born and a man who knows what to do when faced with a kicking, it was a pose he adopted by instinct.

'Talk to me, George. That's all, talk to me. Why won't you talk to me?'

The bantamweight of Derek, sitting on the edge of the single mattress, made the bed tilt slightly. George kicked him on the hip, and in one movement sprang upright, hurled the duvet over Derek's head and leapt out of bed. Threw himself at the duvet-covered lump and hit it. Derek yelped; George hit him again, lightly, tightened the duvet over his face and then let go.

Derek lay halfway up the bed, face pink, breathing deeply, legs straddled over the end. He still carried the bottle of double-strength lager, held it to his chest like a religious symbol. George turned on the light, reached for the threadbare sweater on the chair, pulled it on over his pyjamas and stood over Derek with one fist raised.

Derek began to cough.

'S'all right,' he said, raising the bottle feebly. 'Wannad a thingy to take off the thingy. So's I can drink it, see?' He raised himself on one shoulder.

'Sorry about that cat,' he said distinctly.

In an odd kind of way, drunken talk resembled Serena Burley talk. Without any rationale, George knew instinctively where Derek had been. He had known it would happen. Come to think of it, Derek looked like Serena Burley's cat. Big eyes, pink nose, ginger fur poking out where his shirt rode up over his pink belly. George clawed his own hair. He did not look like that. He had dark red hair and was sallow, a different creature entirely.

'What cat?' He asked quietly. He had told Derek about

the cat, and the dog which did not bark. A million years ago. Derek rubbed his eyes, sat up slowly, still clutching the bottle. The big eyes disappeared into slits as he laughed. An unhealthy wheeze that turned into spasmodic coughing that went on and on until Derek's skin turned from pink to purple. Angry though he was, wishing Derek dead as he did, George was alarmed, banged him on the back and watched with concern until the din ceased. When it did Derek sat and shivered. The stupid boy never spent money on a decent sweater for winter, nor on food, and the cloying warmth of the rooms seemed unable to penetrate his bones. George put a jacket round his shoulders, resentful of his own solicitude.

'What have you been up to, you daft bugger?'

The boy was in that state of drunkenness where further inebriation was impossible, although fervently desired to dull the feelings of depression, nausea and general seediness. It was in these maudlin states that Derek came closest to the desire to tell the truth, simply for the sake of it, or simply to pass the time by shocking himself.

'We went to call on your princess. A social visit.'

He wanted to mock and to boast, but the words stuck in his throat. George looked frightening. Ridiculous in sweater and pyjamas, but the big fists bunched by his sides resembled a pair of monkey wrenches. The mist cleared. Derek began to think very clearly indeed.

'And I've been sent to say, why didn't you come with us?' He articulated the words slowly, careful to stress the regret.

George sat down on the bed next to him, keeping his distance, his fists still clenched. Derek sensed an immediate danger had passed, cursed himself for a fool and longed, suddenly, for breakfast. He put a tentative hand on George's arm. George let it remain.

'You could have done, you know,' Derek suggested.

'What? Go and rob an old lady on her own?'

'Is she on her own, George?'

George gave up. The room had the stench of fear. 'No, she's not. You know damn fine she's not. There's this girl . . .' Derek nodded, dropped the bottle and fumbled in his trousers for a fag. 'Yes Georgie Porgie, I do know. And I'm surprised at you, thinking we were calling up there to rob an old dear. What's she got worth having? A lot of old furniture? No market for that, this side of Christmas. No, it's just Bob being curious. He likes girls, does Bob. Dick likes 'em even more.'

'Get out, Derek. Leave me alone. I'm on my way round to the police, tell them all about it. Soon as I'm dressed.'

Derek stood, his groin level with George's face as he tucked his flapping shirt-tail into his trousers.

'Naa, you won't do that, George. 'Cos we didn't do any harm and we decided we wouldn't go back unless you came with us. Think about it, George. Think about it, is all I ask. Bob just wants to take that girl for a ride in his car . . .'

'Get out,' said George.

By the time he got to town it had begun to snow. Flakes twirled like manic dancers, melting on the pavements. Snow without conviction; not the genuine kind which tipped itself out of the sky like a blanket off a rooftop, hushing all protest, but snow designed for the mere creation of misery and nuisance, cold feet and muddy footsteps trailing in shallow brown puddles that had the appearance of gravy. Two weeks into November and the first signs of seasonal paraphernalia marked the beginning of the only time of year when George could properly equate himself with men of violence, on account of a desire to kick out at Christmas decorations and bellow above the saccharine sound of carols. Early days yet: it would only get worse.

He sat in the hideous lights of Littlewoods' cafeteria, watched the early-morning assembly into trays of hot lunches that would congeal before they were eaten, stirring a cup of milky coffee. When he picked it up, he left finger-prints around the rim, the way he must have left fingerprints all over Serena's house. If Bob and Co. did go back to that place, he would probably end up being blamed anyway. He had left traces there, like a spoor. Derek would say he had set it up: Derek had already made him a conspirator. All he could do was stand back and hope. Derek said they would-n't go back. Derek might be telling the truth, although Derek rarely did except by accident. Derek might be right in saying that all Bob wanted was the girl. He clutched at that thought; knew it to be a false hope and allowed himself to massage it into a real one. Let them frighten Isabel Burley half to death, then; just let them. She might take the hint and go home and . . .

George wandered round the shops with the aimlessness of a stranger unsure of the way and too embarrassed to ask. Something for Serena, a single item lurked among all these goods with the sole purpose of helping her with the words and making her happy.

He found the tape recorder he had long since decided to buy. Gazed at it, full of wonder, his heart contracting with love. He could talk to her on this; she could talk back. In the nether regions of the night they could leave messages for one another. Not a lot to say. I miss you, I miss you, I miss

158

you, put coal on my fire and let me be. Love me like your plastic flowers.

If Isabel was chased away, George would get a gun and guard the princess with his life. He stood holding the dictaphone until a stern sales assistant asked if she could help.

She frightened him. He put the display model down and walked away.

CHAPTER NINE

'Shall we get a new cat, Mother? A nice little kitten? What do you think, George?'

'I dunno, don't ask me.'

Isabel turned in appeal to Doc Reilly, who sat at the kitchen table as if he had been born there, feet enclosed in his favourite thick socks of an indeterminate blue. He was known to joke that the state of a man's socks said much about the state of his marriage.

'What do you think?' Isabel asked. 'She's been going round hunting for that cat for two days. Even accused me of killing it, haven't you, Mother?' She spoke in the direction of Serena, who sat smiling at George as George fed the dog. Toying with a mouthful of cereal, Serena seemed able to eat only if he so instructed.

'Eat up, Mrs Burley, there's a dear,' he murmured. She ate, obediently. Doc Reilly watched her surreptitiously. She turned her smile on him, and waved the spoon.

Doc Reilly thought with a touch of horror of Serena's large hands clutching a kitten. He shook his head.

'You'd be better off getting another dog,' he volunteered. 'One that barks.' The retriever, food finished inside thirty seconds, ambled across to him and put a large sticky muzzle on his lap. 'No, Petal,' he said. 'Not instead of you. Alongside you. So, what happened to the cat?'

'George thinks a ferret got it. Don't you, George? I think so too.'

The doctor nodded. 'You'd have to keep a kitten indoors then, wouldn't you? No point raising animals to feed ferrets, is there?'

George echoed his laughter politely. So did Serena, who laughed when it seemed apposite to do so. Isabel did not. The Doc turned to George.

'Well, it's lucky something's guarding this house. Even if it is only a ferret, for God's sake. Do you ever think of stopping over the night, George?'

'No,' said Isabel quickly. 'George has his own home and he does far too much for us already.'

Oh, dear, a bit of an atmosphere. Doc Reilly got the clear impression he was treading on toes, curled his own under his chair and sipped his coffee. No love lost here, he could tell, and he should have kept his mouth shut.

'Anyway,' Isabel continued, 'Mother and I refuse to be scared by silly talk of burglars. Mother's never been burgled yet. Why should it happen now?'

Pride, the Doc could see it. The sort which might come before a fall and would tolerate no interference. He admired it. Ah well, the nights had fully drawn in: burglars needed daylight and they despised the cold. Isabel was probably right. It was long summer evenings and school holidays like the half-term break, which was when he had last seen the kids; those times were the worst threat. In the meantime he had two dozen patients making strenuous efforts to die and he lumbered to his feet in anticipation of poorer houses than this.

'Look after that cough, George, won't you? There's a lot of it about.'

'Aren't you well, George?' Isabel asked with genuine concern. 'I thought you looked a bit pale.'

He winced under her scrutiny, shrugged his shoulders. Sympathy from Isabel was not something he solicited; receiving it sent an arrow into his conscience.

'He's very fine, aren't you, George?' Serena volunteered, nodding in his direction. It might have been a comment on his health or his physique, difficult to tell. Isabel followed Doc Reilly out to his Volvo.

He stood by the door of the car, reluctant to leave. She wanted to ask him something and he wasn't sure he wanted to answer.

'Thanks for coming out,' she began.

'She's doing well,' he said robustly. 'Getting worse, of course, but still much better than most.'

She held the door. 'Doc, you've been around for ever. Longer than me. You listen to things – people, gossip, I mean. You have to. Can you tell me what it was that made me so unpopular before I left? Can you remember that far back?'

Twelve years was nothing; a mere fifth of his sixty. Out of the blue like that, the question took him by surprise. He had thought she was going to ask something equally awkward, but rooted in the present, like the true prognosis of her mother's illness. He decided on a version of the truth, delivered rapidly.

'Nothing, really. You were just the prettiest girl around, and for a couple of years the most precocious. Your Aunt Mab told me she thought you were a bit wild, you know. Someone circulated rumours that you'd given a couple of the young men the clap. Anybody's for a halfpenny.'

She nodded. 'So I heard. Written rumours? Only Andrew mentioned something about letters.'

'Yes. Childishly vulgar. I saw only the one, mind. My son James, remember him? He got one. He was a stuck up little brute then. He's better now, I promise . . .'

'Who wrote them, Doc? Who would do that?'

'I don't know, love. Somebody jealous. Long forgotten now.'

'Somebody must have hated me,' said Isabel. 'And no, things like that are never quite forgotten, are they?'

'Sure they are,' he said reassuringly, although, even to his own ears, his voice was a trifle hypocritical.

Oh God, whatever did you do with human beings except patch them up and send them on their way? She was right. Sometimes he felt he was good for nothing more than tranquillizer prescriptions and sick notes. He could visualize the scene inside the kitchen he had left. Serena, touching George, the way she yearned to touch all men, both of them springing back as soon as the daughter came in, and she herself ignoring the evidence. Evidence of what? Forbidden affection? The occasional malevolence, as well as the occasional clarity and love in her mother's eyes?

Ignorance was a good idea. There were plenty of things it was better not to know.

'Have some lunch, George? A sandwich, at least?'

Isabel had taken to feeding him, whether he would or

not. A ploy, George thought, or preferred to think it, against the other conclusion, disinterested kindness and gratitude for his unpaid labours, something to compensate for their mutual aversion. As long as he could imagine that Isabel gave him food, even of the bread-and-cheese variety, as a means to make Serena copy him in the act of eating, or as a bribe to make him stay longer in order to preserve the peace while she shopped, tidied and did whatever she did all day, he could tolerate the generosity. If it was simply a gift from her to him, he could not.

George was particularly useful less for the heavy tasks, such as getting in coal, and more for the ostensibly light ones, such as persuading Mother to eat cereal and bread in the early afternoon without the deafening sound of the radio she carried with her everywhere, apparently as a means of blotting out other sound, particularly that of her daughter's voice.

George cleared his throat.

'I could come back and sort of babysit in the evenings,' he suggested. 'If you wanted to go out, I mean.'

Serena drew breath audibly. Understanding of the words seemed to come and go like a lighthouse beam. Isabel had long since concluded this had much to do with what Serena wanted to understand, and knew that to be a harsh judgement.

'That's very kind of you, George. I'll think about it. Was there any post today?'

'Nope.'

'I can't get her to give me the bills,' Isabel went on, distracted by the prospect of a dozen minor tasks and Doc Reilly's words. 'She's been hiding them. Do you think you could give any letters straight to me in the future? And I ought to call on the neighbours, thank them for taking in the post, should have done that weeks since . . .'

'She's not well at the moment,' George said quickly. 'Not keen on callers.'

They ate in silence. Sitting across the table from them both, Isabel felt like a guest. She had a sudden urge, horrible in its intensity, to slap both their faces.

As long as she loves me, she told herself with the familiar flush of shame, it does not matter if she does not love me best.

Robert phoned in the evening. Was going to come and visit at the weekend, but things had got on top of him, did Isabel understand what he meant? Life was full, he hinted: the baby was sick and the boy in pain from the dentist. Another time, as soon as possible, certainly before Christmas. Had the doctor called and was everything all right?

'Is it OK to forge her signature on cheques?' Isabel asked. 'Or is it a criminal offence?'

He hesitated, nicely alarmed as Isabel had hoped he would be. Envisaging his sister emptying his mother's account.

'For the electric bill,' Isabel added. 'I've only just found it.'

'Fine, I suppose. How are you, er, off for money?'

'Fine,' she echoed. 'Everything's fine.'

Which it was. There was a bright full moon set high in a sky full of scudding cloud. Mirrored in the windows facing the phone, Isabel could see her mother by the fire, scribbling. TV substituted for music; sound for thought.

She wished Andrew would phone, without quite wanting it. She had a longing for the sound of words formed into sentences, ached for company. A fourth glass of wine seemed a good idea.

This time they came down the track in another van, slightly more deluxe. There was no laughter. Sure they had laughed before, but that was the first time and the denouement rankled still, despite their joking about it. Derek was wondering how long he would have to keep the auction-house job after this – for the sake of appearances, couple of weeks he supposed – as he chewed a fingernail and thought about money. Bob had a dull pain in his back and thought about money. Dick's jaw was slack: his trousers were dirty and he fiddled with coins in his pocket. The equipment in the back of the van was the same as before. Derek was not wearing enough clothes and he shivered.

Three in the morning and the night dead. The sky was clear enough for snow and the track was like a grey ribbon. There was not a single light in the cottage at the end.

'What do we do if she wakes up?' Derek said, still gnawing the fingernail. Now was the time his lies might find him out.

'I told, you,' Bob said, his voice thick with impatience. 'How many times? You know where the phone is. Unplug it, put it somewhere else and if the old dear disturbs us, we shut her in a bedroom and get on with it. For Christ's sake . . .'

'OK, OK . . . No lights?'

'No lights.'

'Gloves. Don't forget gloves.'

Yellow gloves. Dick had got them from work. Very decorative.

They reversed up to the back door. Bob muttered how

this was sensible, get in as close as possible, save on labour and have the thing ready in case of anything which necessitated a quick getaway. A giant in the kitchen with a machine gun, Derek suggested under his breath, stifling the whistle he needed for courage. He looked uneasily towards the window where he had seen the fleshy figure last time, turned and winked at Dick. Dick's jaw still hung open. The memory had surfaced in his brain: the flash of skin had drawn him on, it was the cat that frightened him off. Derek had lost his pencil torch and brought another identical to it. He tried the back door, expecting it to be locked, ready to fiddle with it, because it was he who was best with locks, but it was open. That worried him a little: it was almost as if they were being invited in. There was always something sinister in other people's stupid naïveté.

The moon lit the kitchen through the big windows. It lit the sitting room where he went to unplug the phone, take it back down the corridor and stick it in the van. His training shoes were soundless, he was pleased with that; the yellow gloves twinkled like fireflies. Dick followed with the blankets and, without the aid of any electric light, began a skilful packing of the contents of a credenza. Bob it was who crept upstairs, checked that the bedroom doors were all firmly shut. One was ajar: he did not look inside, but closed it softly. There was within the gentle sound of snoring.

Bob had the list written on the back of his hand; Dick had the list off by heart; Derek too could recite it like a parrot. A sort of shopping list of what was going to be moved and in which order. Get the noisier business done first, get the stuff down that awful corridor either into the kitchen or the backyard, because of the bedrooms being at the front; load the light stuff as you go along and the heavy stuff last. They weren't such a bad team after all, Bob decided as the pain in his back subsided and he watched them work in unison. Dick carried bookcases with the ease he carried carcasses, as if he had done nothing else since he was five; he stacked the dining chairs, got them out of the house and into the van without much of a sound. Then he set about the task of dismantling the table with the aid of ingenuity and Derek's little torch. Derek was good at this too, stacked up drawers from a chest, cantered out with them, never carrying too much or too little, never taking the risk of dropping anything. Ground floor only, Bob had dictated. Pity: he didn't half like the look of the grandfather clock on the landing. Maybe . . . As they worked, all communication was by whisper and signals. Thank God for the moon, which seemed to inspire them. Made them sweat. After an hour they were huddled in the kitchen. They had dismantled half a house. The bloody dog had not moved a muscle and they already felt like kings.

'Fancy a cup of tea?' Derek hissed.

'Fuck off, I found the brandy.' That was Dick.

'Where?'

'Back of that rolltop desk.'

'Give it here, you arse.'

Come to think of it, the fool had been weaving a bit, losing the knack of tidiness, spreading paper from that vast desk all over the floor. Dick must have given himself an extra turn of speed and a stagger from half a bottle of spirits, glugged from the neck. His eyes were glistening, just at that point when they needed a last burst of energy, plus precision, in order to load the heavy stuff. Bob had been cruising on confidence, ready to laugh out loud and shake his fist, but, Jesus Christ. He'd better stuff something else in

Dick's mouth before he fell over. Or take something out. Dick in drink was a dangerous beast.

'Make him sick it up,' he commanded Derek. 'We got a long way to go yet.'

They dragged him to the kitchen sink. He smiled at them until Derek held him over it, making encouraging noises and holding his neck. He snorted like a bull and shrugged them off, snarling.

'Gimme,' he hissed at Bob. Bob spread his empty hands. 'Give you what?'

'Gimme!' Dick roared. Bob put a hand over his mouth, a big, meaty palm. Derek pinched his nose. He thrashed around, knocking over a chair. Just as they lowered him to the floor, footsteps sounded from the stairs. Quiet, determined, implacable, coming towards them. They froze.

The figure of an old lady appeared in the doorway. She fumbled for the light switch, bathed them all in ghastly neon which found them in a huddled trio and herself fully in command of the situation. Her hands fluttered, as if there was something she had forgotten; she beamed. Her eyes moved away to the furniture piled in the doorway. She shivered with pleasure, like a confident child on the brink of a party. Moved smartly to the drawer in the table, pulled it out, extracted three candles and handed them to Bob.

'Light these and stick them somewhere, I would. I knew I should have paid that bill, I *knew* it. Light them from this one, stick 'em on the table, it won't hurt. How *nice* to see you all again.'

Candlesticks. Somewhere in this wonderful heap of goods awaiting removal there were candlesticks. Sitting in a clutch on the draining board, beautiful silver, fresh off the dining table. Bob placed the candles offered from Serena's steady fingers and, with movements less steady, struck a match from his pocket and lit them. Serena sighed, an exclamation of joy as she switched the light off again. The three men remained immobile as she marched forwards with the tape deck she had left by the door and placed it in the centre of the table with care. There was an immediate blast of sound, then the room reverberated to the music of a full-bellied waltz.

'How absolutely lovely to see you, and how good of you to come,' she said, curtsying to each. 'Let's dance. *She* keeps the booze, top cupboard, on the right. Let's all have fun!'

They were mesmerized. Obedience was automatic and seemed entirely appropriate. Bob went to the cupboard. Somehow he produced glasses as well as sherry, a bottle of whisky and one of gin. Derek stepped forward, awkward with politeness. Offered a yellow-gloved hand, which seemed to add to the sense of crazy formality. He noticed her hat, her nightdress, her coat, the little heels to her shoes, sweet. He nodded at Bob and Bob nodded back.

'We thought some of your stuff needed mending, lady. Not the best of times to move it, but . . .'

Serena paused, then took him in her arms.

'Heavens!' she trilled. 'Take it all away, why don't you? Let's dance.'

'Take it away, George,' Derek said gravely. 'Just take it away, man, take it away.'

Come on. If this was going to be the worst of their problems, it was not so bad. Bob could feel laughter gurgling in his chest: the pain in his back had entirely gone. They had all the time in the world. To the tune of a waltz, then a polka, they continued the loading, while the princess, oblivious to the draught from the door, conducted her own orchestra and maintained a flow of commentary.

Isabel dreamed of being with Joe in a nightclub, surrounded by pulsing music. Glamorous darkness and spangly lights on the floor. A body pressed against her own, wanting to go home. She was waking slowly from the slurred sleep induced by wine. A reluctant awakening that did not involve opening of the eyes, but a wish for more sleep and the hope that turning her face into the pillow would send her back into oblivion. She often woke this time of night, aware of Serena's wanderings, and squeezed her eyes closed, determined not to interfere, but checking over in her mind the pitfalls downstairs. There was a sensation of having been half awake for a long time, as if her sleep had been punctuated not by dreams, but by sound.

Alien sound. Music in the distance, coming from the other side of the world, penetrating into consciousness slowly. Once she had established that it was not a dream she could feel only acute annoyance. For heaven's sake, Mother played that dreadful music all day, couldn't she leave off at night? If this was going to go on, then she, Isabel, would have to do something about the wandering, she couldn't cope, not without sleep. Mother, please do not be an inconsiderate old bitch. The phrase, fully formed, popped into her mind, anger getting her out of bed with such speed she made herself dizzy, and angered herself more. She would throw that tape deck and radio out of the house, she would, too. Start wearing earplugs, scream.

It was cold: she could not find her slippers, stood shivering in indecision. Leave it for tonight, deal with it in daylight? No. Dressing-gown, where? Here. Bare feet would do.

Downstairs, past the clock with the moonlit face telling her it was four-thirty, a ridiculous, ludicrous time to be awake, damn, damn, damn. Noticing from her feet up how cold the floor was in the hall. Without rugs on the stones. Without rugs. She looked down at her feet in consternation. The cold burned. She could hear her mother in the kitchen, singing loudly. Turned the corner, saw the candlelight, thought for a moment as she ran towards it that what she had seen was flames and Mother was trapped in there, roasting and chanting.

There was a blast of air from the open back door, the kitchen a mess. Two rolled up rugs from the hall impeded progress. A large man coming in from the yard stopped and stared at her with bloodshot eyes then, slowly, smiled. A smaller man appeared at his shoulder.

'Oh, shit,' said Derek.

Bob turned from the sink where he had been washing his arms free of the oil from the base of the dining table, now neatly installed inside the van. Nearly finished, all of them infected by the old lady's party spirit, full of devil-may-care, give-me-hell any day, and it did not matter any longer that Dick was dangerous drunk. Isabel flew to her mother, clutched her tight, protectively. Serena dug an elbow into her ribs, shrugged her off.

'Go away,' she said crossly. 'You're always spoiling things. Go away.'

'Yes,' said Bob softly. 'Go away, girl. I would. Quickly.'

'I didn't know,' Derek bleated. 'I didn't know.'

'You haven't danced with me,' Serena said, pointing at him.

'Oh yes,' Dick crooned, squinting through the candle-light. 'Oh yes, oh yes.'

Bob moved towards her. Isabel sidestepped him, picking a bottle off the table, holding it in front of her, spilling the dregs. There was a piercing, whisky smell.

'Tutt tutttt,' Serena admonished.

It was so easy to disarm her. Bob simply hit her a glancing, almost apologetic, blow on the side of the head and plucked the bottle out of her hand. She whimpered. 'Look,' he said to her reasonably, 'if you just sit down quietly, no one gets hurt. This your mother or what?'

Isabel nodded.

'Well, she doesn't mind us, so why should you?'

'Get out,' she whispered. 'Leave us alone.'

Dick elbowed Bob out of the way. 'Oh, it can talk, can it? What's a lovely girl like you doing in a place like this, then? She is lovely, isn't she, Bob? Very lovely.'

Which she was in the candlelight, all pale skin, huge eyes, breathless, a dressing-gown patterned with roses, hanging open over a low-necked nightdress that showed the curve of full bosom. Like her mother's had been. Lovely was an understatement. Ripe for the picking: he could have sunk his teeth into that flesh. Isabel felt the dressing-gown removed from her shoulders, felt the cold draught raise goosepimples on her arms, while an acrid, warm mouth grazed her neck.

'Put her down, Dick. You don't know where she's been.' Bob spoke in the tones of sweet and cheerful reason that worked better with Dick than orders.

'I could put her down the cellar, but it seems a waste,' Dick leered.

'Put her in that chair by the fire. Get some rope. Tie her up – loosely, mind. Just the hands. C'mon, man, we're nearly done.'

To Bob's relief, Dick obeyed like a man in a daze, but not

quite with implicit obedience. He manoeuvred Isabel across the floor in imitation of a dance, holding her from behind so his groin pressed into her buttocks, his hands splayed across her breasts, lowered her into the nursery chair which always stood by the stove, his hands sliding down her body, lingering. She sat, blood pounding, the sound of her own heart deafening. She would have scratched and screamed; wanted to scratch and scream, but another instinct prevailed. Be good, sweet maid, don't provoke anything: then they won't hurt Mother and they won't hurt you. Through a haze of fear she made herself smile at Serena as her own hands were tied behind the chair. Smile, to prove everything was going to be all right. The most revolting moment of all was when Serena smiled back, sketched the equivalent of a royal wave, and laughed explosively.

'Nice daughter you've got,' Dick slurred at her.

'Oh yes, she likes you too, I can tell,' Serena trilled.

Someone had turned down the music. Mother turned it up. Bob and Derek began to move with urgent speed, almost running in and out of the open door, laden. Dick was slower, reluctant to move from the stove. Isabel heard the sound of an engine, closed her eyes. The moments were endless; the sounds distant. Minutes passed. Emblazoned on the inside of her eyes was the image of Serena, laughing.

Dick was straddling the chair, his flies undone, holding his penis in his hand, thrusting it against her mouth. Flaccid, purple, grimy, nuzzling her cheek as she twisted her head away. He pinched her jaw in one huge, gloved hand, forcing her lips apart, stuck his penis in, his belly ballooning round her face. Vomit rose in her throat. He thrust, lazily, almost absent-mindedly. Then he looked at his member in dim surprise at its lack of compliance, did not persist. The smell of him was overpowering. He grunted, zipped up his trousers furtively, looked over his shoulder as the engine revved outside. As one final action to appease his disappointment he caught hold of her cotton nightdress, ripped it to the waist, pinched one nipple between thumb and forefinger, painfully hard. She screamed.

In the background, throughout it all, there were shouted instructions, and, over the sound of the music, the noise of her mother, clapping her hands, like a child at a pantomime, her voice rising into a high shriek of utter hilarity. Saliva dribbled down Isabel's chin. The laughter continued.

A different smell now, cleaner. Bob, leaning over the chair designed for the nursing of children, fumbling with the bonds. Speaking. 'Sorry about that,' he was muttering.

Perhaps she fainted for a minute, perhaps oblivion mercifully arrived on demand, but it seemed to her later that she had remained where she was for a long time. Enough for the first shock to recede, the spittle to dribble on to her chest and a self-protective anger to follow in a great white-hot surge which had her screaming over that bloody music, wrenching her hands free. The kitchen swam into focus, candles still burning. Someone had trodden on her bare toes. The pain brought life. Her eyes sought out her mother.

There she was, standing by the door, one arm across her chest, the other waving goodbye into the darkness like a wistful child. As she waved, her body swayed in tune with some long-remembered dance.

Isabel's fingers and toes were as cold as snow, her head wet with perspiration. She could not coordinate her movements; nothing worked to order. Yet she limped over to where the ancient one stood, grabbed hold of the neck of her coat and slapped her face. Once, twice, four times before she lost count. The knuckle of her right index finger caught the outcrop of eyebrow: she could feel that, sensed damage being done, skin torn, and then she stopped. It was impossible to imagine that her hands had done that. Serena's face swam before hers as something hideous, requiring destruction. Isabel was not horrified for the moment, merely temporarily satisfied.

Serena staggered, fell against the door frame, then righted herself. Her hands came up to embrace her purpled face: she closed her eyes as she felt the left one, gingerly. Tears formed. Her head wobbled dangerously on her neck.

'What did I do?' she asked, clearly bewildered. 'What did I do?'

The room was still blurred. Serena's ability to speak worked on Isabel's mind like one more insult, enraging her. Her own tongue felt like an obstruction inside her mouth, preventing words.

'It's what you – didn't do – you filthy-minded old cow!' Isabel yelled and then found herself shaking so hard she could not speak at all. She leaned on the table to keep her balance, looked around, shaking her head unsteadily, trying to suppress the panic and find some clue as to what to do next. Something, before she shook to pieces. She wanted to lie down on the floor, but the floor, she noticed, was filthy. Someone had to tell her what to do. She could not think of it herself.

Serena turned on the light, moved uncertainly towards the candles on the table, blew them out, one by one. With enormous difficulty and greater reluctance. Three, four puffs each. Smoke idled in the air. The tape came to an end.

'They forgot these,' she said sadly, gesturing to the silver candlesticks.

Isabel burst into uncontrollable laughter. Spasms of it shook her naked breasts. Loud, hysterical giggles rising to screams, descending into barks and yelps, on and on, choking her. She staggered against the stove, recoiled from the warmth, collided with the chair on which she had sat, leaped out of it and cracked her knee against the table.

'Take a deep breath, I would.' Serena's disinterested instruction had an effect.

The room settled into its familiar contours, reminding Isabel of duties, obligations and the panacea of little, familiar tasks. It was imperative not to stay still. Without any conscious thought she knew that in movement she would find sanity of a kind. If she did not move, she would freeze in this attitude. She would simply freeze.

With slow steps, she went to the sink and doused her face with water. Put on the kettle, found her dressing-gown and buttoned it, making her fingers work. While the kettle made reassuring noises she found a hot-water bottle with a fleecy cover, gave it to her mother to hold while she herself made tea. The water splashed everywhere; the finding of milk and sugar was an almost insurmountable task. There was a sense of triumph in achieving it. The cup made a loud noise against her teeth. Somewhere in the course of all this, with the deliberate steps of a puppet, she looked for the telephone: it must have gone with the van. She made Serena sip the tea and escorted her to bed with another hot-water bottle. She found witch hazel in the bathroom, soaked a pad of cotton wool and applied it to the injured face where one eye was puffed like a purple balloon. Her touch was trembling, full of revulsion. She marvelled at herself, encouraged herself, muttered under her breath; good girl, good girl.

Serena took all remarks as being addressed to herself. She was utterly cooperative, consented to the wearing of bedsocks and snuggled down sweetly.

'They danced with me,' she said, over and over again. 'They danced with me.'

Her eyes closed.

Isabel's could not. She dressed in the dark, piling on three layers of sweaters with the same studied efficiency that had governed all her movements for the last hour. She went downstairs and lit the drawing-room fire. Her movements were steady now: they had become faster and faster. Her mind was slow; it functioned painfully. The blur of shock was preferable.

Such a lovely room, but the firelight was less kind than the moonlight. Empty, save for a single chair with a damaged seat. They had not bothered with that and the omission, the judgement on it, was oddly offensive. Items removed from drawers and bookcases were littered against the walls to facilitate removal of the carpet. Paper from Mother's desk drifted round her feet. In desultory fashion, like a person hypnotized, Isabel began to tidy them up. She was her mother's housekeeper; housekeepers tidy up. Words hit her eyes. Letters to strangers. Fuck, cunt, damn. Mother's form of communication.

Isabel began to cry. Every ounce of her hurt, as if she had been pummelled. The words were appropriate expletives for the sense of filth and failure that paralysed all but automatic action, and the automatic movements did not quite keep realization at bay. Here was a writer of indecent missives. Here was her daughter. What had the silly daughter done?

Nothing of any merit, ever. Excelled herself. Allowed her mother's property to be removed from under her nose. Gone to sleep drunk, woken too late. Failed to stop them even then. Let herself be violated. Hit an old lady who knew no better. Had she done that too? Of course she had and of course Serena, who did know better, would remember her daughter leaving a mark which she would never want anyone else to see. Serena would remember who had done that, wouldn't she ever? She would shout it from the rooftops. Burglars are nice men in comparison to my daughter: they didn't hit me, they danced. My daughter was already filth before they started.

Isabel stopped sobbing. All the hysteria had fled, leaving a terrible and deceptive clarity.

The neighbourhood thinks you're a kind of whore, anyway. They're not going to believe in you as victim, oh no. What's the difference between a tart and someone who hits her mother? Not much. One kind of poisoned butterfly or another. She'd have to tell the police, of course, but not all of it, only some of it. Perhaps that should come first. Maybe it could wait.

She wouldn't be telling them or anyone else about the vital discovery, of how much her mother hated her. And how she would have to go on with the pair of them rattling round this great house, waiting for the men to come back and dance. Go on into the blue yonder, a happy couple who hated one another and no choice about it, because there was nothing much left in life to do right, nothing to hold dear and absolutely nowhere else to go. And it was all her fault.

She sat, dry-eyed in the emptiness of the room, willing herself to weep again. Mother had unlocked the door.

Invited them in. Would have cheered them on if they had raped her daughter, one by one. Laughed herself sick.

So that now there were the two of them: one mad, one defiled.

CHAPTER TEN

It was so cold, so very cold, that her blood formed itself into crystals. The movement of a kneecap or an elbow seemed to grate. The fire in the hearth had gone out, also her own: she moved with the precision of the waking dead, tidying as she went. Picking things up, putting them down. Then the dog, that stupid, redundant old brute, came wagging towards her, paws clipping the bare wooden floor, a waddling unit of warmth wanting to be let out. She gazed into brown eyes, docile with stupidity, and at that point Isabel realized she was, still, inescapably alive.

She paused in front of a modern mirror the burglars had also left, breathed over the glass and watched the mist form. Not dead yet. Not beautiful, either. Scrubbing herself in the bathroom did not improve anything.

She could not find the car keys and would not look, walked down the road to the church, limping slightly. Imagining herself running away, slowing down to resist the impulse. When in doubt, turn tail. But then, running away was a practice she had adopted too often and it always involved coming back. Isabel made herself think, rooted her thoughts in memories.

What was it Mab had said so sadly? You only know your own strength when you learn to keep on loving someone who does not love you. There was a frost, dampening slowly in the face of the winter sun which swelled behind cloud, more a presence than a reality. Her mouth felt dry and, at the back of her throat, a lingering taste of wine. One step proceeded in front of another, towards a telephone.

She could not remember the neighbours' names; she could scarcely recall her own. It was a miracle that Andrew's card was in her purse. Isabel steeled herself to tell lies.

In the town-centre branch of Dixon's, as soon as it opened its doors, George carefully avoided the sales assistant who had been so dismissive of him last time, although there would have been a certain sense of triumph had he encountered her and proved he could pay for the dictaphone. It was a matter of pride for him to have brought with him in a separate paper bag exactly the right sum, down to the last 99p. The woman behind the counter took the cash without any sign of being impressed by the nonchalant ease with which he presented it. She must have mistaken him for some executive. He was shaken by sudden irritation that she did not want to engage him in conversation: why did he want to buy it, who it was for, how thrilled the recipient would be and how amazing it was for anyone to spend all this money at once. Then he looked around at cameras, computers and ritzy telephones coloured pink and green, and felt himself shrink. He was glad there was no one else in the shop to negate the effect of his own purchase by buying something far larger, and, in the end, was so anxious to leave he almost forgot his parcel.

Where to put this possession, to save it from prying eyes? A problem, that. He walked around town, aware of carrying the equivalent of contraband, wondering about it. The exercise of spending money made him curious and confident. He stepped boldy in and out of the shops, no longer intimidated, looking at sweaters, socks, radios, shoes, items he would only ever consider buying in the charity shops where he was more at home. He felt, in a strange way, content, superior, relieved to be free of the kind of indecision which must surely accompany the buying of goods at such prices. There was a moment of unhappiness when he paused outside a jeweller's and wished against every other wish he could have bought her something pretty, but then he felt the shape of the recorder against his chest, solid and safe, felt, yes, he had done the right thing after all.

Strange, when he was enjoying himself the presence of people receded into the background: even the noise was forgiven.

He felt rich. A big spender. A fully paid-up member of the human race.

By the time George had finished dreaming and failed to discover anything better to do with Serena's gift than carry it round with him, probably until Christmas when he would present her with it, he was late, way outside the normal routine of arrival, and he even felt satisfaction in that. He sat inside the car, making sure he could work it. He said hallo to it twice, then said goodbye and erased it, delighted.

Perhaps by Christmas Isabel would have gone. Gone and long forgotten. Fed up and out of the way. He had an enormous capacity for self-deception: it came from being a dreamer. He could put things out of his mind and on to a different planet by a sheer effort of will, had made himself suspend belief about Derek's plans, just by blotting them out. The refusal to think could be made to last for days: it was a cue to survival, but when he got to the house, he knew. He could almost hear the sensation of his dreams exploding around him like the sound of tinkling glass.

George saw from the gates the signs of the posse of the sheriff's men. One police car, Doc Reilly's Volvo, Robert Burley's Ford still hot from two hours' drive, Andrew Cornell's car which he recognized from his own careful habit of noting vehicles, Uncle Tom Cobbley and all. Not a posse, a jury, waiting to find him guilty. Instead of going into the house, which he knew he would have to do sometime, but not just yet, he reversed the car down the road, left it and walked away across the fields.

If there had been an ambulance he would have faced up right away. As it was he wanted to preserve the residue of hope for an hour, paced into the valley, counting his steps, breathing with deliberate regularity. He stopped beneath a tree and tried the recorder again. 'I didn't do it,' he repeated, his teeth chattering. 'I didn't do it.'

John Cornell looked at the auction room and wished his son could love him with half the intensity with which he loved his son. No method of loving could be identical: any way would do, as long as it carried acceptance and fair judgement. Such as son recognizing that father was not entirely without heart. Or seeing at some point that he admired a boy with such high and naïve principles of honour, even if it meant a dearth of bloody common sense sometimes. It was just as well that one of them had been a cynical opportunist for most of his life: but hardly the same thing as the crudity of theft that Andrew suspected. Andrew had far too much fine taste for his own good. Antique furniture was not worthy of veneration: it existed to be acquired and no commodity was worth that much respect. Business was business: buy cheap and sell dear. Looking after a dog was more important.

The telephone he held in his hand was cold to the touch. He supposed it was efficient of the police to phone anyone in the business as soon as ever to tell them to look out for anyone flogging large items the day after they were nicked. Routine procedure, but it was this assumption that all thieves were congenital idiots which led to so many of them getting away with it. For Christ's sake, that stuff was long gone. No one would deposit it on their own doorstep. What troubled him most was the idea that his son might suspect he had something to do with it. Perfidious he might be. Pragmatic to the point of brutality. But dishonesty on such a scale was self-defeating.

'Tell them,' he said to the disembodied voice at the other end, 'that if they want to borrow stuff, I got plenty in store they can have. Really.'

Borrow it, keep it, what was the difference? It was only money.

He wanted a word with that son of his. About the young woman; about her mother and her aunt.

'How is she?'

'She keeps asking about the cat . . .'

Serena sat on the single chair, close to the fire, with her handbag over her arm, smiling politely. She reminded him of the queen, posing for a photograph to put on a stamp. Privately, and with difficulty in keeping his estimation from becoming obvious, Andrew Cornell found Robert Burley quite ridiculous. There had been a conspiracy of efficiency and quiet voices before he arrived, a decent aura of shock and respect between the time when the faint voice of Isabel had caught him unawares and he had told her to wait where she was and he would come and collect her, bringing a phone. Then he arranged the arrival of Doc Reilly, whom Andrew considered she needed, along with that of the police, all huddling together, pooling God alone knows what theories and information, murmuring names and instructions while someone else arrived to add to the mess with fingerprint powder. And yet R. Burley acted like a conductor. The sort, Andrew thought, who would reduce an orchestra to anarchy before the end of Act One.

'I don't understand how this could have happened,' he was saying for the tenth time, looking at his sister with an expression supposed to be sorrowful, but, in reality, merely full of sorrowful recrimination. The look given to a destructive idiot one is bound to forgive. Andrew wondered how many people in the world considered Isabel to be a fool. He did not; Doc Reilly did not; only her brother knew better. I must ask him, Andrew thought, if his father was also a bully.

'It must have been someone who knows the house,' Robert stated with all the authority of an expert. 'I can't believe you didn't hear a thing.'

'Not at first, no.' Isabel was mild. 'But I did, finally.'

Robert did not appear to register that her passivity was brittle and artificial, too calm to be genuine. 'And you saw them but you can't even remember what they looked like? Amazing. Even the one who tied you up?'

She winced. 'Not very well. Faces get distorted in candle-light . . .'

'Colours, too,' Andrew added.

'One with a big nose,' Isabel said, deliberately vague. 'One with a big beard. One with . . . Oh, never mind.' She stopped and stared at her feet. Slipper socks; most unbecoming. Whatever else had been seen in the kitchen was not going to be mentioned. She was confused, speaking like a person with retarded intelligence, but some things she could force herself to forget.

'Which one hit Mother?'

She was even vaguer about that, her voice lower. 'I don't think any of them did. I think she fell.'

The voices echoed in the room. It was a fat little police-man, without uniform, who was doing the fingerprinting. He had taken to making his reports to Robert, obviously sensing a natural leader, Andrew thought ironically. What a clean house this was, the fat one remarked now; very few sets of prints, and probably none from the burglars.

'Of course it's clean,' Isabel volunteered. 'I've cleaned it top to bottom.' She looked at Robert, a hint of mockery in a voice that was otherwise toneless. 'That's what I do all day.'

Your prints, said the man, chattily, Mrs Burley's, of course, and those of a third party. All prevalent in most rooms; all three in Mrs Burley's bedroom. Would the third party be the gentleman called George whom all of them had mentioned?

'George?' Robert demanded. 'George? He walks the dog. What would his prints be doing in her bedroom?'

'A word about George,' Doc Reilly began, apologetically. Needs must, he supposed, hardly a breach of confidence, and hardly any choice either, other than to communicate to his inspector friend in the corner what little he knew about George. The inspector, thin and sallow, stood apart from them all, listening.

'He could only have gone into her bedroom to pry,' Robert burst out, desperate to cast blame. 'And where is he now? Hours late.'

'I need this man George to get his prints for elimination,' the fat man said, fussily. 'Where is he?'

'And I need tea,' said Doc Reilly, irritated beyond his belief.

On cue with that observation, George appeared on the threshold, flanked by that damned dog. He seemed to have shrunk and he looked on the verge of tears, regarding the emptiness with dismay.

'Hallo,' he said, eyes on Serena. The rest of them need not have existed.

She crowed with delight. 'George, darling!'

'She's OK, George,' Isabel said sharply. 'She's probably the only one who is.'

He shook his head from side to side, the only part of him he seemed able to move, confused and slow.

'You'll be needing some more coal for that fire,' he remarked finally. They all seemed to expect him to say something: it was the best he could do.

The shadowy, thin policeman stepped forward. 'George Craske, is it?'

'That's right.'

'And what do you know about all of this, George?'

'All what?'

'Twenty thousand quid's worth of burglary is what, what did you think I meant?' The voice seemed to gloat.

'Leave him alone,' said Isabel.

George shrank further. It seemed to Isabel, from the outside, as if the fat and thin officers closed ranks on George, ready to surround him, with Robert on the flank waiting to move in and kick. There was fear in his eyes, along with unshed tears. It would be like this watching a gang forming, she thought. Assessing their chances, lowering, ready to charge.

'Not exactly new to you is it?' the thin one said unpleasantly 'Got form, haven't you, George? One for rape, three or four for theft from an employer. That's right, isn't it?'

'Jesus Christ!' Robert shouted. 'And you've been in *my* mother's bedroom. Christ almighty, Isabel, did you know about this?'

She shook her head, oddly unsurprised by the information, which did not seem to her to be of the greatest relevance. They had all known there was something odd about George: why be amazed now? She shook herself, desperately trying to gather energy for something that was more important than her own fuzzy exhaustion.

'Look,' she said levelly, 'I can tell you one thing for sure. George would never have anything to do with this, never in a million years.' The earnestness of her announcement created a momentary pause. She was surprised to find such certainty, such animation in herself.

George moved slowly and knelt by Serena's chair. The isolation of it in a room otherwise unfurnished added to her air of a royal presence, with him the courtier.

'Are you all right, Mrs Burley?'

She nodded, emphatically.

'Are you sure now? Who hit you? Did they hit you?'

She looked at him with adoration. Touched her own forehead, and then touched his brow, as if the action of so doing would transfer the contusion from her own to his and it was an injury he would willingly accept. It was a little like a blessing. The sight of the contact made Robert squirm. Doc Reilly coughed. The thin policeman did not care for it either.

'Who do you mean "they", George? Do we know how many you mean by "they"? I mean, how many you showed around in the first place? Your friends, she said they were. From the first time. She can't say much else, can she? Which you must have known, if anyone did, I suppose. She can't say what your friends looked like either. Very useful.'

It was a quiet, taunting voice, grating on the ears, each word a fresh graze. Robert came closer, swearing under his breath, ready to pull George away from the vicinity of the regal chair. It was too much for George. He punched him in the soft part of the gut and, in the same moment, all the men were on him in a pack. It was a decorous and swift manhandling, as if rehearsed in deference to the women. No further blows struck, simply a restraint against which George struggled briefly before he stopped and stood limply, with his hands pinned behind him. He allowed himself to be patted down by the fat copper, who seemed to be out of breath, jerky with excitement. Those precise, rather feminine hands, which seemed designed for powder, prints and other unpleasant minutiae of life, found the dictaphone. That was all there was. He held it to his ear, shook it, turned it over, and then depressed the switch. They all listened to the sound of George's voice, speaking uncertainly at first, then louder, repeating himself over and over.

'I didn't do it,' said the voice. 'I didn't do it.'

Silence fell upon them like a stone into water, the ripples going wide.

Serena's harsh shout of laughter jarred. 'Lovely, George,'

she cried. 'How clever you are! You clever, clever thing! Just what I need!' Then, in a lower, more confidential voice, 'I liked your friends, George. When are they coming back?'

'Give it to her,' George muttered. 'It's hers.'

The thin one almost purred with satisfaction, dying to state the obvious. 'If you didn't know about this burglary till you got here this afternoon, Mr Craske, how did you know you didn't do it?' He nodded at Robert. 'We'll take him with us, sir.' He spoke like a man offering to remove the rubbish.

'Stop it!' Isabel shouted. 'Stop it now! Listen to me, this is crap.' She moved to put her hand on George's shoulder. 'George would never be involved . . . You can't possibly believe a word she says. Friends? What friends?'

It was the first time she had ever touched him. Beneath the sweater his skin was boiling hot, his eyes, for once meeting hers in a way he normally avoided, looked at her as if he had never seen her before.

'George,' she began, shaking him. George, she wanted to say, I don't like you, but I know you better than them.

Robert elbowed her aside.

'Do you know something, Miss Isabel?' George said over his shoulder. 'She always seems to hurt herself with you around, and she never did before. At least you haven't bitten her. Yet.'

No one heard but Isabel. A blush covered her face from chin to scalp, her mouth opened and closed in a resurgence of her so far suppressed shock, and, in that moment, she lost all pity for him. The pity was for herself.

He was ushered away. A slow shuffle beyond the door, the procession continuing down the corridor, three bodies in reluctant embrace.

'See you tomorrow!' Isabel yelled.

Another door slammed.

Serena struggled to her feet, sat back. She began to cry. A low pitched, keening noise at first, which rose into a howl of despair. Isabel could not bring herself to touch her. It was Andrew who hugged her and tried in vain to stem the flow. Isabel watched them with complete detachment.

Then, choosing the moment, the lights went out.

The sobbing died and Serena gazed at the light of the fire as if it were a new discovery. Then turned her gaze to the dying light outside. 'Electricity,' she said. 'Must pay it.'

The winter of this discontent was depressing. A different, shivering kind of darkness by ten at night. The light of a summer evening seemed remote.

'Do me a favour, boy. Stay awhile.'

It was not like John Cornell to plead. He made it sound so gruff that the request seemed not really to matter, but it was still a plea.

'What's the matter, Pop? Feeling my age?'

'I'm not as old as that Serena Burley. She must have had her kids late on, mustn't she? Not good for a woman, that. They've got too independent by then. Start young, that's the answer.'

Andrew smiled. To be honest, the cluttered comfort of his father's small living room was welcome relief. Being concerned for Isabel, which he was, did not make any difference to the fact he had been glad to get out of the house and leave her with her brother. He had been rather too helpful, he gathered, becoming *de trop* in the face of blood being thicker than water; found himself dismissed. A sense of loneliness had driven him to his father's and he was more than content to stay. At least this old boy had a tongue in his head and was not a hypocrite. Andrew found himself driven into approval of his dad by the sheer effect of contrast with another man. He poured them both generous measures of whisky.

'If I drink this and then another, which is what I feel like doing,' he said, 'I might have to stay the night.'

'That'd be nice,' his father said.

They sipped companionably.

'Pity about what happened up there,' John said. 'I should have liked the chance to buy that furniture. Sometime, when no one else had any further use for it.'

'I know. So would I. I feel personally insulted by someone stealing stuff and then wasting it. Don't worry, Dad. I know you wouldn't have jumped the gun.'

John grunted, obscurely pleased. 'You know who chose most of it, don't you?' he said. 'It wasn't Serena who had the eye for a bargain in the seventies. It was her sister, the lovely Mabel. She was the one with the eye, and never did seem to resent the fact that she was buying the stuff for her richer, well married sister. Well, anyway, she and her brother-in-law, they were the ones with taste. He found stuff wherever he was, but Mab had a gift for knowing what was good. Plain as a pikestaff, clever as a monkey, mad as a hatter. I had a fling with her, once.'

'Did you?' Andrew was amused. He restrained his avid curiosity. Despite the mellow mood, Papa was quite capable of refusing to tell a story just to keep him in suspense. 'What was she like?'

'Straight up the wicket when it came to sex, but quite impossibly possessive. Seething cauldron, that woman. When I told her it was no go she wrote me a filthy letter.'

'Significant letter writers, these women?' Andrew remarked drily.

'The habits of childhood,' his father said. 'We all wrote let-ters. Telephones never quite became second nature. What's going to happen up at that house?'

'I don't know.'

'Alzheimer's,' his father said dreamily. 'We used to call it senility. Your grandmother had it, did I tell you? In the days when there was no question of sending anyone away. Probably poisoned my attitude to women. Made me guilty as hell when you stayed put to look after me. You know what it does? It makes the person who's got it an absolute monster. Not a sweet little old thing, except in appearance, but a bundle of harm. Completely selfish. Completely irre-sponsible and quite incapable of love. If I ever get like that, boy, do us both a favour and shoot me. I'm not a good man, but I don't want to be as bad as that. Not without enjoy-ing it.'

He paused, extended his glass for a refill, chuckled grimly. 'Old granny wrecked us. You'll have heard tales of sweet eccentricity. Not tales of a wilful bitch who used the last remnants of her brain to manipulate. Fixed on survival. No one mattered.'

'That bad?' said Andrew, lightly.

'Oh yes, make no mistake about it. It's the form of insan-ity that drives other people mad. It'll do that to your Isabel.'

'She's not my Isabel. She's her brother's sister and her mother's daughter.'

'God help her, then. God help her brother too. He was a nice little boy once. Adored his mother, but she was never there. Mab didn't like him much. There's nothing so destructive as duty. I don't want duty from you, never did.'

'What do you want, then?' Andrew was grinning.

John pretended to consider, also grinning. 'You aren't that

194

bad a business partner, I suppose. Otherwise, a bit of grudging admiration would do. The mutual kind.'

Andrew nodded, as if sealing a deal. They were going to get drunk. His father got up and went in search of cheese and biscuits. A long time since lunch.

'By the way,' he said. 'Something I forgot to tell you. That little runt Derek, the one you never liked. Doc tells me he lives at the same address as that George you both told me about. Handy, isn't it?'

'Shit,' said Andrew.

It reminded him of something else. In his pocket, was a pencil torch he had found in the Burleys' backyard.

How fickle you are, you dreadful old bitch, Isabel thought, and how nice it is to indulge the disgust. There she sat, head of the table, Serena the queen, face decorated by a crazy black eye about which her daughter could not even feel shame. Laughing as Robert cut up her fish and encouraged her to feed scraps to the dog. And there she was, regardless of the betrayal of her lovely friend George, lapping up the attention Robert saw fit to give her. She did not even notice that he was acting like a politician, paying exaggerated tribute to someone's very important baby.

Isabel detested sitting in the kitchen. She congratulated herself on the amazing job she was doing in blotting out what had happened in it. The effort was debilitating, but survival depended on making it.

'Nice,' Serena was saying. 'Very nice, but too hot.'

'Blow on it, then.'

'She can be very sweet? can't she?' Robert said. Oh God, when could he go home?

Isabel could see his mind whirring, evading conclusions.

He had regaled Isabel with recent experiences of typical old folks' homes, working himself into a lather. It was still out of the question, wasn't it, he pleaded? Look at her now, happy as a sandboy, and what a shame it would be to deliver all that insurance money over to the state. She felt monstrously tired, almost beyond fatigue and into a light-headed state in which the only thing that would weight her to earth was the effort of pretence and the food she did not want to eat.

'We've got to decide what to do,' Robert stated portentously.

'There isn't much to decide, is there? Apart from the fact that you'll go home tomorrow. You must. All your responsibilities.' The irony was lost on him.

'Yes, but we'll have to get someone in to help. Stay overnight. The police think these men might come back. That's quite common, I gather.'

'Robert, exactly who do you think would be prepared to stay overnight in a deserted old barn like this? Nurses from a nursing agency? Then we would have two and a half women guarding the place as opposed to one and a half.'

'I take it you're prepared to go on? With a better security system, of course. Good girl!' He could scarcely keep the relief from spreading into his voice like sugar dissolving in tea.

That was not quite what she had said, but she could not think coherently. She could only think of sleep; not having to move or make any decisions whatever. The lethargy would have made her agreeable to suicide; she was aware of it and powerless. Words happened of their own accord.

'Oh, yes,' she said. 'The worst has happened already. It can only get better. Besides,' she added, without looking at her mother, 'we probably deserve one another.'

Robert had been good at practicalities. Such as getting the lights turned back on by dint of a combination of telephonic persuasion and cash. He had also sorted out the post. Got Serena to sign her cheques like a lamb. So useful to have a man round the place.

Robert had a dim memory of bedrooms in boarding schools, a memory he resented. The one allocated to him here was scarcely different. Cold sheets, so chilly he remained curled for half an hour, gradually easing his toes further and further down until he lay almost straight. Thinking of his daughter. George in his mother's room, no, not thinking about that. Fretting his head with thoughts of money and rage at burglars, not quite as keen on the desperation of the underprivileged as he might have been. Wondering if Isabel was having an affair with that Andrew Cornell bloke and that was why she was so biddable. Could be the answer to a lot of problems if they got together. And then, a man who dealt in antiques, now was that coincidence or not? Surely it was; his sister was not clever enough to conspire.

Somewhere way beyond the middle of the night he decided it was perfectly proper for a real man such as himself to have a real hot-water bottle. Fuzzy from the half sleep which is all that was possible with icy-cold feet, he fumbled downstairs. Poor Isabel, he thought for the first time, she must have done this. Halfway down he paused, wondering what it must have been like to hear ghostly music in the distance.

He saw her at the bottom of the stairs. His mother, standing by the front door, wearing all her night apparel and a pair of white gloves. Her pose was ambiguous; she could have been beckoning someone in or waving them away.

She drooped in disappointment, like a sad flower. Such a nice party. He regarded her with longing, then with despair. Thought of all the times when he had been favourite, and she loved him with such intensity and then left him to those playground boys. He could not bear to watch. He backed away, lay in bed listening for her until he slept and, with the advent of morning, told himself that he, too, had been dreaming.

This time Serena sat on the black-and-white tiles by the front door and looked out through the glass, in case they came back. Such a disgrace to have let people in through the kitchen. The kitchen was for the sort of painful person who volunteered to do the washing-up at the end of a party, like Mab. Everyone else pissed as a parrot, and her at the sink, smiling up from the suds like a sainted martyr. For all Serena knew, she was still there. Last night's lot seemed to leave a hell of a mess and have taken half the food with them when they went. In a coach.

The truth was, she was not at all sure of what had happened, although she did remember being put to bed with half her clothes on, tsk, tsk, drunk again, she supposed The people from the party had stayed on, including her own son, which was surprising, because she could not recall him being much of a party animal. Poor little boy, the one she had missed most of all. Other boys hurt him at school, and she had not looked after him. Mab said playgrounds should be fun. Her son, big boy now, had told her they were hell.

It was sad for him to be afraid of playing.

It all made her contemplate the strange and charming magic exerted by a convivial crowd of people. She drew a smiling face in the air, too lazy and tired to leave her miserable daughter a message to that effect. She wanted to say that they should do this kind of thing more often and, if the child really wanted to persist in the lunacy of wanting to preserve her mother's miserable life, all she had to do was arrange for similar injections of spirit at regular intervals. Rooms should be cleared to make room for lots of men, without their boring wives. They could have parties for the fire brigade.

Of course once she got hold of that fucking recording thingy darling George had brought it would make life so much easier. It would save her from writing down her daily list of words, in the same way she had done in a small vocabulary notebook in school in order to learn at least twenty new words a week. But the words she remembered best were the ones that were forbidden, also the shortest: fuck, cunt, bugger, shit and damn. Words that sounded like exclamations, easy to expel in a series of gasps.

She had worked out on paper various permutations that did not sound as good. Tunc, rebugg, tish and nadm, to say nothing of raft for fart and palc for clap, not as satisfying at all. They lacked a certain resonance. There were no replacement words.

Serena sighed impatiently. So many tasks, so little time. Her room sailed over the house and she doubted if it was still attached after all this junketing. She had to go and unlock the door in case it snowed. Duty was a terrible thing.

She followed her usual route, hands outstretched, ready to touch the pictures and the chairs, the sofa, the clock, the table, the candlesticks. The dark was not really dark when it was occupied. There was a kind of light dancing around things.

Once she got away from the glass it was blacker than the inside of an oven. She felt, all of a sudden, as if someone had cut off the last joint of every finger, leaving little stubby knuckles waving at air, nothing to touch at all.

Nothing to direct her feet.

She clung to the door and waved at her own reflection. Beckoning for someone to come and show her the way back to bed. Footsteps came and went and she could not move for terror.

CHAPTER ELEVEN

An old lady with a worn-out mind was a mixture of animal, vegetable and mineral. She had to be made to ingest all those things. That was all there was to it.

She's significantly worse than when I last saw her, the psychiatric nurse told Isabel.

'Quite some time ago, wasn't it?'

'Three months. You could have called us before,' she said defensively. 'There are far more critical cases than this.'

'I'm sure. What do you mean by worse?'

'Memory loss, worse. Lack of social awareness, worse. She bothers less with the façade. No greeting today.'

'You aren't a man, you see.'

The woman ignored her. 'Lessened ability to perform ordinary domestic tasks, rather more eccentric about appearance, less physical coordination. Suffers slightly from persecution mania, which I don't remember noting before. Claims to have been bludgeoned by the cat.'

Isabel was silent.

'But still compos mentis in flashes. Busies herself, fairly careful in her movements. Conspicuously clean.'

'Early toilet training never forgotten,' Isabel quipped. 'And yes, she loves a bath. Absolutely independent about that. It's the only time I'm grateful for the fact she can't bear a locked door. She plays with toys in there, floods the place. Great fun.' Stop burbling.

'The burglary must have upset her,' the woman suggested with grave professional concern.

Isabel tried to prevent herself snapping. In another situation, she told herself, I might like your cheerful countenance and pity you for your impossible job, but at the moment I loathe the sight of you. Mother is not upset about the burglary. I am. It is me in pain, not her.

'The local authority can provide various aids. Rails, handles for the bath. Day Centre, twice a week?'

They can also piss in the wind. Isabel accepted the Day Centre suggestion and the offer of home help as occasional babysitter, both designed to give her a respite. All problems can be cured by tinkering. She lied to Robert on the phone, said there was more. New locks, a security system loaned by the police. There was. Mother had watched the installation of it, carefully. Hidden in the hall cupboard, once turned on it would detect movement beyond the kitchen. But as long as Serena wandered at night it was impossible to leave it on. The police had been called out and cancelled in time twice already.

'She's sort of on the cusp,' the nurse said, not without admiration. 'Extraordinary case. She seems to keep the worst at bay by sheer effort of will. Tells me she writes everything down.'

'On the cusp of what?'

'I don't quite know. Complete change, or breakdown? She swore at me, you know.'

'That's nothing different. She has a penchant for rude words.'

'Funny, isn't it, what we retain? Admirable, really.'

'Fucking disgusting, really.'

Isabel had the feeling that while Mother had passed a test, she herself had not. She no longer exuded that air of compassion; nor was she gentle; not actively unkind, but not particularly patient either. She was like someone who, resigned to a sentence of imprisonment, has decided to play by the rules, albeit resentfully. The home help appeared the next day, equally resentful, easily intimidated by both of them. Isabel used her presence as an escape route. Looked over the promised Day Centre, where there was not a single male person in sight among the crocks lined up against the wall, and left in a hurry, despair, failure and revulsion dogging her heels. Stocked up with animal, vegetable and mineral, came home and locked them both in. She bought a tapestry to keep her hands busy and stop them itching to slap. She bought soap, shampoo, gel and facial scrubs, scoured herself nightly, trying to eradicate the lingering odour of shame.

The Day Centre would not work. Without quite defining why, Isabel was sure of it and took no steps to warn or prevent disaster. Allowed them to take Mother, resplendent in hat, skirt, with three cardigans adding to her breadth, plus ghetto blaster under one arm and handbag carried like a cudgel under the other. Watched, without much sympathy, when the car came back three hours later, the woman driver resembling a person who had endured three rounds inside a boxing ring with unfair opposition. Ghost-coloured, she was. Mrs Burley had caused mayhem. Loud music, blaring. Telling them all they were a load of old farts, or was it tarts, and why didn't they get up and dance. Tried to haul them out of wheelchairs. Fought all the way home, wanting to drive the car back. Had them all over the road.

'Perhaps she got a bit overheated,' Isabel suggested, smiling sweetly.

'It was nice,' Serena announced, refusing to get out of the passenger seat. 'Very nice.'

'Nice for you,' Isabel said, pulling her out without any attempt at persuasion. 'Not so nice for them.' She scowled at the driver, challenging. 'Same time on Thursday, then?'

'I'll have to check . . .'

'Of course you will.'

Perhaps, Isabel reflected, four days after the emptying of her mother's house, it is me who has made her worse. Why on earth did I ever think I could make her better? I offered comprehensive care to someone I loved, thus taking away what little responsibility there was left in her; maybe the downhill path would not have been as swift without me. I am silly. Silly and sullied. There were times when a jumbling of words seemed a useful saving of any kind of analysis. She did not speak to her mother; she hissed at her.

And then there was George. Sitting on her conscience like a heavy toad, his absence filling the house, even though it was a relief. In the early afternoons Serena set out a tray for tea. It took a full half hour, all her movements indecisive, looking at cups and saucers, moving in and out of awareness of what they were for. Then sitting beside them with her gaze fixed on the back door, waiting with the dog. Waiting.

Isabel could scarcely bear to touch Serena. She did not want to touch anyone, or to be touched. Not on the hand. Not anywhere on the skin. Especially when the van came up to the back door. Andrew and another greeted by Serena like honoured guests, while Isabel quailed, heart in mouth. Impossible to imagine the dancing men would come back, not in daylight, not so soon. How easy it was to terrify with an act of kindness. By the time she had stopped shaking, Andrew had explained himself. A spare sofa and a couple of armchairs, he said. My father thought you could do without a dining-room table for a while, didn't use it much anyhow, did you? But the living room, that nice room with the fire, well, pity to waste it.

They were not the family of sofa, chairs and rugs that anyone present would have chosen, but they were clean and they were adequate. They sat in the vastness of the drawing room like forlorn creatures seeking warmth, comic caricatures of the real thing, refugees from an alien culture, speaking to no one. Isabel was aware that gratitude was in order, spoke it, but could not feel it.

'What's happened about George, Andrew? Do you know?'

Of course he would know, sooner than she. Via the all-male network that was morally obliged to tell her last, in case she got upset.

'They had to let him go. On bail to return in a couple of days. Pending further inquiries. Condition of bail not to come here.'

He watched her closely, wondering why exactly she had become so brittle and what it was such news might provoke in her. Anger? Amazement? Relief? Robert Burley was reported to have expressed the first two, while she seemed indifferent. He wished she would open her arms instead of hugging them to her chest, let him melt some of this fierce and secretive resentment.

'Oh, I collected the post,' he said. Three letters.

'Mine,' said Serena, grabbing them with the speed the dog took a titbit.

Andrew watched. He felt as if his fingers had been bitten.

'Mine,' said Isabel, seizing Serena's wrist, squeezing hard until Mother's fingers succumbed and she gave a sharp shriek of pain. Her protest was not coupled with surprise. It was as if such treatment had become commonplace. Andrew did not like what he saw, Isabel hugging rage and fear against her ribs, her face as sharp as a beak.

You can go home now, George Craske, for a day or two, and bad luck to you. Don't shake my hand, will you? Come back the day after tomorrow, or we'll come looking.

What have we done to you? Nothing, in any obvious sense. Oh, they could have been violent, but then George's own experience of the police, admittedly not recent by any manner of means, had never included rough stuff. Persistence to the point of tears, yes, violence as such, no; he had never even feared it. All they had done before giving up in disgust was to use a kind of malevolent chumminess to turn his life inside out and leave the raw nerves of it exposed. About those previous convictions, Georgie Boy? You were a cook, weren't you? Yes, for a works canteen. Could do with you in ours, Georgie. Three works canteens, wasn't it? Two arrests for thieving from your employers. Then there was that girl in the third, amazing you could get another job, wasn't it, but I suppose way up north they might not be fussy about someone who can actually cook what real men eat during the night shift. Is that right, George?

He could feel himself beginning to weep. Felt grateful for that little hostel room where anything of value was already gone and there was never any point in saving things, not like his other rooms in olden, golden days, stuffed with items he might just need later: packet soup, tins, foil containers, napkins, towels; things which even he could see no logical reason to steal. I had a hungry childhood, he said. Not much of an explanation to the supervisor in the last set of kitchens. He'd taken a shine to her and been ignored, ain't that right, George? Like Isabel Burley, is it, George? Like the teapot in your car? We know you're a thief. The question is, how much of one?

'No!' he shouted. Although, perversely, it calmed him. At least they had got something totally wrong. Reassuring, that. Don't touch me.

So why did you rape her, George? Why do that to the poor girl? He could still hold on to the way they had not got their facts quite right, because it had not been a girl, not as such. A mature woman who'd given him the wink, put him on the day shift to be under her eye, although the crowds and the noise drove him witless. He couldn't talk to her, couldn't explain. Whichever God allocated vocabulary had been unkind to him. Can't talk, George, that's your problem. Haven't got the words.

You told her a lot, George. Actions speak louder than words, don't they? She came and found me after dark. A pound of bacon in my bag. There'd been an argument, end of shift. Waiting in line to be checked out, leaving me last. They had music on in there all day. Wasn't a man worked there didn't shout and scream. Pay was awful too, we were expected to steal things. See? She did see. She was a nice woman. I hit her with something and found myself giving her one. Last time I ever gave anyone one, if you take my meaning. Never again, I swear, and never on a kitchen floor. Although, God knows, my life's been spent in kitchens. Poor cow. She was going to shop me and I thought she liked me. Thought it would put things right, and it went too far.

Women are a bit difficult, George, aren't they? You did hit her quite hard. I mean, no one could have said she was consenting. Not what with being unconscious at the material time. I suppose she moaned in appreciation, did she, George? Brutal rape, it says here. You even pleaded guilty. Your sort of bastard stops at nothing.

Don't know what you mean, George said. He didn't. The translation of ethics from one offence to another made no sense to him. Couldn't they see? A petty thief and a haunted, limited man did not automatically meld into other forms of dishonour. They did see. They believed him, literal men that they were. Questions about friends were met with the same confusion. Questions at the hostel, indifferently conducted since everyone was bored by now, seemed to reveal a welcome, if friendless, inmate who cooked. Not a skill common with burglars.

So that was what he was. A harmless little rapist with a connection to a burgled house. The sort of face and boyish hair for whom some mad old lady might invent the friends which a sweet motherly woman like that might wish him to have.

Not the violent, claustrophobic man who walked into the ice-cold air in search of Derek. Derek, who would survive any questions, the reformer's dream, because he was never short of the words. Derek would hit a princess and walk away with an explanation about a cupboard door attacking him on the way out. Derek made shit smell of roses. He had no scars. Mr Milk Froth. Pimply, purply rat-haired fuck of a cunt, was he.

The one thing they had done was give him back his dictaphone.

The warden looked at him with sorrowful opprobrium, told him his room had been searched. He knew, did he not, that his tenure in it was temporary, dependent on him not being charged with another criminal offence. Sod off, George told him, I've not been charged and I won't be either. Have you seen Derek? The man looked at his watch. Oh, he'll be away at his work, now. They brought back your car and he borrowed it. That's what I want to see him about, George said, neutrally. The warden was proud of Derek. Kept himself smart. He did not know that he was facing in George the only criminal he might ever meet who had accepted what he had done and was sorry for it.

George was hungry. He supposed, quite irrelevantly, that the only bonus of a couple of days in police cells was not spending money on food. Not that this kind of hunger was the same as the desire to eat; he did not want to give himself that kind of comfort, slow himself down, stop him jogging past the neat little houses into town.

Fog was wreathing around the old church hall near what used to be the railway station. It added anonymity to the innocence of daylight. George knew he would find Derek there, because a sense of justice informed him that that was the way it should be, simply on account of the fact it was his turn for something to go right. He had told himself that all he wanted to do was ask Derek why? Why steal the furniture and drop him in it? Why pick that particular house and not another?

Fate was kind enough to deliver him Derek without allies. Everyone else gone, and him left in charge of the shop. The boss at home, nursing stiff legs and business was slack, anyway, the way it was as soon as people got a sniff of Christmas. Seeing Derek, whistling at the back, ignoring the creak of the door, George paused for a moment to wonder what anyone would ever want with all this stuff. To live in such confusion: a warehouse full of furniture was something disgusting when he considered how futile it was and how empty that room of Serena's had been. Furniture with numbers on, waiting to be possessed, made no sense.

Derek, still whistling, pushed his bantamweight against a table, getting it lined up with the next thing. Gave it a wipe with a cloth, totally absorbed when George hit him. So much for questions and conversation.

It could not end there: Derek was too quick, too strong, to be stunned by a blow on the back of his head. He pretended was all, falling across his table until George tried to drag him off, then whirling round and pushing a foul-smelling rag into George's face. Hitting him below the belt, encountering rock, opening his mouth to speak, his wet, red lips forming an O. George smacked him in it, followed through to the ribs. Trust Derek to raise his hands to protect his pretty face, serve him right. He was soft in the stomach; all his power was in his head, that filthy little brain of his.

He butted George, catching his forehead with agonizing accuracy, so that George saw redder than ever. Kicked away at Derek's shins, so that he fell among a pile of chairs, screaming. One of the chairs seemed to explode into a series of legs. George took one and hit Derek in the lower part of his face. He used the wood like a hammer. More than once. He was not counting.

Something crashed in the corner of the room. The furniture was closely and unsteadily stacked, the floor uneven. The shiver of breaking glass from a capsized wardrobe door stopped all other movement, so shocking was the sound. Without thinking, George dragged Derek in that direction. There was blood on his hands. There was the dim thought that if he placed Derek and wardrobe together, the damage might appear accidental, provided no one looked closely. Derek's jaw hung crooked, broken, teeth smashed. There would not be much by way of words coming out of that gob for a while.

Or ever? George listened for the sound of breathing, heard the rattling. He had his heel poised to stamp on the jaw, hesitated, stopped. Didn't particularly want him dead.

Someone would be in soon. No one left junk like this unguarded for long. He took his car keys from Derek, which felt, oddly, like some kind of theft, taking something out of someone's pocket, and it was then he began to see the enormity of what he had done, the sheer, bloody-minded stupidity of it. It was not even as satisfying as he had imagined, this transitory sweetness of revenge. Five minutes ago he could have defended himself against the world. Now he could not. Ten minutes since he could have said he was still a free man. Now he could not. There was a set of overalls hanging on a hook in the back office. Huge, made for a bigger man than he, covered the blood nicely.

Then he was out of there, remembering the car but wanting to run. Back to the hostel. Looking at the wreckage of the room. Took his spare sweaters and the old boots that no one else had wanted, stuffed into a polythene bag. Left an old

211

envelope from the hall on his bed, bearing the legend, 'Gone to relatives'. Chance would be a fine thing. If his relatives existed George did not know them. The message seemed sadly dishonest, so he changed it. 'Gone home.' People could impute whatever meaning they liked to that. He felt uncharacteristically clever as he walked out into the darkness, a clever fool with the mark of Cain branded on his forehead.

Into a car which smelt of Derek and the sense of nowhere to go.

The trouble with kindness was that it had to be first earned and then repaid. Isabel did not like these kind of debts. It was death to self-respect to begin and go on owing someone something. She could not accept that as her due. There was a nagging feeling which made her feel that she owed Andrew something, just as she owed the world, as if she still had to explain herself, justify her existence. Muddled it was, but she could not accept generosity with grace, even on behalf of someone else. She did not want victim support, either: it made her feel like a victim. She wanted the whole lot of them out of her hair, but tea must be made, biscuits produced, the situation talked about, as if the theft of belongings had been the most important thing about the invasion. She shivered. She was always cold. She made all the right, hospitable moves and would not let anyone around her settle.

And when they were gone she looked at the letters. A formulaic, citizens' charter type letter for Ma from the Electricity Board, an inventory of things stolen from Robert, and a letter from Joe. Mother waved from her new chair by the fire, struggled to get up. The sight of paper coming out of envelopes seemed to enrage her.

'Darling!' she yelled.

'Don't darling me.' Isabel plonked into her lap three of the largest books with torn pages, sufficient to weigh her down into her seat without doing damage. Enough to get several minutes' respite while the poor old sweetheart worked out a way to get them off her knees and on to the floor while darling daughter retired to the kitchen. Perhaps a letter from Joe would change the universe. Give the greyness a tinge of pink, if that could be imagined. Lift the afternoon fog. Stop everything from being animal, vegetable and mineral.

Sweetheart,

No word from you and I do miss you! What do you do all day? Life here is busy, busy, busy! But there is a window coming up soon, a whole free weekend, so do you think you could get away, just before Xmas? Or I could come nearer you! There must be hotels in your neck of the woods! I don't suppose you'd want to bother your mother, and I wouldn't want to bother her, of course, but on the 16th, 17th (or thereabouts, depending on you), I'm all yours!

Issy, I know I'm slow about a lot of things, but I have been thinking about you . . .

A series of pictures rose into her mind in a rising tide of panic. What would he think of this place, the patrician grandeur of it, the lack of any kind of amenity he held dear? The second image was Aunt Mab saying out loud, this one is not worth his salt, my niece is worth far better, my niece is the price of rubies. She shoved that image away along with the first. Thought instead of Joe climbing all over her like a man faced with the Matterhorn, protesting allegiance to no other cliff face. The shivering of cold began again. All those bloody exclamation marks. Shallow, Mab was shouting: men are as shallow as puddles. Isabel finally felt nothing but a lethargic sadness. A fog of melancholia which mirrored the garden outside. Until she heard her mother shouting. Torn books had a use after all. They were fuel for the fire, which sparked and caught the edge of Serena's long corduroy skirt. The hem was smouldering into a half-hearted flame.

Isabel seized her under the shoulders, hauled her upright where she stood uncertainly, grabbing the mantelpiece while her daughter stripped the skirt from round her middle. Plumped her gasping mother back down in the damn chair, chucked the skirt on the fire, knelt at her feet and checked her legs for damage. Nothing. She could have used that big, heavy skirt as a fire screen, or blackout curtains. Sitting in suspenders and heavy stockings beneath faded silk drawers, Serena looked ludicrous. She spoke urgently, reached out her hand. The shock was not going to kill her. The screams were more rage than fear.

'I need to talk to you,' she said. 'Tell you things. Like I didn't ever. Got to tell you things.'

'There, my sweetie,' Isabel crooned, looking with something like pleasure at the image of her mother, knees apart, thighs pressing against suspenders, old-lady knickers, all of it resembling some dreadful parody of glamour. 'You just sit still. It's so good to see you without your dignity,' Isabel crooned. 'Get some idea how it feels, do you? I hate you: do you know that? I hate you.'

*

Andrew found his father's little helper. There was a sharp smell of blood, urine, faeces, marking the spot where Derek had begun to crawl in a circle. Whichever way he looked, there was a view of wooden panels, legs, a forest of inanimate things offering nothing but impediment. Derek could not pull himself up with his hands: if he took his hands from his face, his face would drop apart. Andrew stared at the face. It recalled a previous fascination with surrealist paintings.

Andrew had nursed an invalid, was no stranger to the stench of human excrement. He knew how to control revulsion. Ambulance, yes. Turn the man on his side and clear the airways to ensure he did not choke, yes. He knew that his footsteps going away to the phone would create desperation. He did not hurry.

He had always disliked Derek with peculiar intensity. Compassion for him now did not mean the same thing as liking; nor did it defy his instinctive conclusions. It was a small town, after all.

'In a minute, Derek, in a minute. Going to be all right in a minute. The ambulance is on its way.'

Derek had such sweet blue eyes. His nails, spread in a fan across his blood-streaked cheeks, looked dirty and pale. A film of varnish clung to them.

'You fell into the chairs,' Andrew said evenly. 'And then, half dazed, you staggered into the wardrobe. Raise one of your little pinkies if you understand.' The fingers remained still, the look desperate.

'This piece of wood,' Andrew continued, holding it up, then throwing it away, so that it clattered and echoed, 'has nothing to do with anything. Just as George has nothing to do with anything. If it was George, you get tied in with a burglary, or why would he hit you? Not that he did. Of course. Not George's style, is it? And you had nothing to do with any burglary, of course. It would never cross your mind.'

This time the index finger raised itself in a kind of salute, which Andrew acknowledged. There was the comforting sound of the phone ringing.

'You'll be all right, Derek. Dad's got an insurance policy against accidents on the premises. Only accidents, mind. Not assault.'

Derek closed his eyes and attempted to nod. The effort was alarming, an audible movement of bone and the granular sound of torn cartilege.

'One last thing,' Andrew mentioned evenly, standing up so his feet were level with Derek's head. 'Did any of you buggers touch Isabel?'

The tortured face, swollen to twice its size, looked at him in blank denial. Enough, Andrew thought. Enough. I have implicated myself in sufficient violence for today. First Isabel's, then my own.

It was not Isabel's house. Her house was in another place, another time zone, almost another climate. Circling round her mother, who had taken that evening to following her like a shadow, behaving like a hungry cat rubbing round calves in an orgy of cupboard love, Isabel made herself feel homesick. For the metropolis, for useless Joe and the sound of sirens, alarms and other punctuation marks which made her life seem crowded. Knowing that the rereading of his letter to her might implode this self-induced longing, she consigned that to the fire. Along with Mother's damaged petticoat. There was no protest from the owner, only a cry of admiration, reminiscent of fireworks, as the remnants of it burst into flames and flew up the chimney. When Isabel traversed the dark corridor to the kitchen, Mother was her shadow, talking aimlessly. When Isabel went upstairs to the lavatory, Mother went too, hanging about until she had finished, like a person lost. Chatter, chatter, chatter. Worse than the deafening sound of the music machine she had confiscated.

What was she talking about with the stream of words she produced in response to enforced silence? Things, Serena said. Things. There were snippets of ancient grievances Isabel recognized from previous tellings hitherto ignored. About darling Aunt Mab always washing up. About parties. Each room visited created a pause, a change of subject. She was suddenly affectionate, wanting to touch. She stroked the living-room walls as she might have stroked a cat. Patience wore thin.

'Got to tell you things, darling. Where are my letters? I need my letters.'

Isabel doused the fire. 'You didn't write letters, Ma. You used to. Oh yes, you used to do that a lot. Then you wrote letters to people abusing them, didn't you Ma? I found some of the drafts on the floor. Some you sent, I suppose, others you forgot, left in the desk. You wouldn't want Doc Reilly or George to see those, would you, Ma?'

She kicked the coal. 'You probably got this wonderful idea writing letters to my lovers. Jealous cow,' Isabel continued, talking to herself. 'Probably just as well they got posted.'

'What letters?' Serena asked, head on one side. The bruise above her eye was rainbow-coloured, could have been the result of an extreme application of cosmetics. 'Letters,' she repeated with wonder. 'A, B, C. See?'

'And all you write now is a list of favourite words. I saw those too.'

Serena tapped her forehead. 'Words, darling. I need them to tell me things.' She looked slowly about herself, as if expecting to find them littered all over the floor. Words she wrote but never said out loud, because they were rude.

They were back in the kitchen. The security system was so simple a child could work it, the man said. Serena had watched with avid curiosity while it was put in place, enjoying her view of the broad back of the man who installed it. She had examined the keys for the new locks with apparent indifference; she examined them again now. Let her get out, then, if she wanted, Isabel thought. I don't give a shit what happens to me. She felt as if she was being followed by a cloud of flies. Tomorrow Serena could have back her music.

'Isabel, darling?'

'Yes? What?' Cross to the point of fury.

Big eyes, hooded lids ready to burst in that lined face. 'Why do you hate me? What have I done?'

Fucking nothing. Bitch.

'Isabel? Can you take me down?'

'Down where?'

'Down into the snow. I don't know. I don't know the way.'

'What snow? What way? Say what you mean. Follow the lights.'

'Oh, yes. Good-night then, my lovely cat. Good-night.'

CHAPTER TWELVE

Serena had a certain step, slow, quick, quick, slow. She could do it in a kind of dance, as if she measured indecision with every set of steps. The music acted as a design for movement. Slow, over the difficult stairs; fast down the smoother corridors, like a waltz, or a polka needing a partner at every turn.

Without George she was rootless. She went round the house, slow, slow, quick, quick, slow, looking for him. Looking for someone. It was a big house; the empty ground floor echoed to the sound of footsteps. When they stopped Isabel wondered where they were: when they began again she wanted to scream. Poor soul. No cat to trail round after her, no man to mouth kisses, poor Mummy, who had to make do with her daughter and a daft dog.

Serena liked the sound of her own steps: she put on her boots and stamped; she made as much noise as an army on the march, except at night, when she tiptoed. She wanted to talk all the time. Isabel stayed silent, wanting to punish. She took refuge, in her bedroom, in the corridors – so that she would know which way to run when the footsteps came towards her – and, finally, in the bathroom. The floor littered with towels. The place smelled of Mother.

Can your mother wash unaided, she mouthed to herself? Oh, yes, all but the teeth. She likes to wash, morning and night, but in here, and everywhere, she leaves a trail of mess.

A week after the burglary, Isabel squinted at her steamy reflection The face was not her own. An alien cast of features, set into a skull wrongly shaped for too long a neck, blurred back at her. Get into your car and go, she told it. Why not? Pride? A lack of confidence about that outside world, as if she were as incompetent in it as this old cow with her marching? She gave herself a wan smile. The distortions in the mirror were not entirely the premature ageing and brutalizing of a face. The glass was smeared with fingerprints. It could almost have been writing, someone writing in the steam. I DIDN'T DO IT, on one corner. She looked closely.

There was a banging on the door.

'Can I come in?'

'No.'

'Yes! Yes! Yes!'

Isabel was mesmerized now, less by her own reflection than by the writing and the thought of fingerprints. George's fingerprints in Mother's bedroom. A fact forgotten. Cunning replaced impatience. Curiosity replaced a sense of futility.

The thin policeman had been back, keeping an eye on the house. Isabel felt oddly brave about the prospect of the burglars returning. There was safety in the possession of a mobile phone and the simple alarm. Burglars with big pricks were not as intimidating as an animal, vegetable, mineral old woman who had come to behave like a malevolent ghost. And nothing was as frightening to Isabel as herself.

'Come down to the kitchen, Mother.'

Isabel got pen and paper, squashed Serena into a chair facing her writing implements. As a version of *Playschool*, this sometimes worked, although daylight and writing did not always go together in Serena's mind. Writing was for after dark.

'Write it down, Mummy. Go on, write. You haven't done your letters.'

The therapy was not going to distract this time. Oh, how she detested her, pitied her, failed to recognize her. She wanted to guide that large hand, fuelled by that deficient mind, across the paper. Make her mother write once, and once only: I am sorry for what I have done to you.

'I don't want to do this.'

'Yes, you do. Get on with it.'

One hour to go until the social worker arrived to take her to the Day Centre, probably the last time they could manage. It had never been a long-term project. The waiting between respites seemed interminable. Isabel had a sullen ambition to get inside Serena's room and Serena's bloody-minded mind. There was no privacy left to violate in this house. She had begun by vowing to respect her mother's desire for that precious commodity. Left her desk alone, left her room alone.

Serena cocked her head. 'I heard my cat,' she announced. 'I did, I heard her.'

'Where?'

'Down the cellar.'

221

Isabel was seized with malice. 'Go and find it, then. I won't stop you.'

Serena could fall down all those steps, those damp and listing steps, fatal to old limbs. The door could be locked against her resurrection. If she were to choose her fate, it was surely better than burning to death.

'I shall, but only if you come with me.'

Serena spoke with a calm deliberation that sent a chill through Isabel's spine. She was not mad, merely a stranger. A stranger with a terrible instinct for truth, bent to the task of forming words on a page with the slow patience of an industrious, dull-witted child. She seemed to guess how much Isabel loathed her, relished it. Don't do it, said the words. Don't.

In an all too brief Day Centre respite, Isabel drove to the shops for food and bits and pieces, and, on impulse, stopped by the church on the way back. Maybe Mab's grave would provide some inspiration. She would tidy it up again at least, a sop to conscience for the fact that the increasing untidiness of the house was becoming a matter of indifference. The days were so grey, the ration of light so mean, the barren lack of order seemed less accusing and Isabel remained constantly tired. The ghost of Mab might lift the resolve with earthy advice, remind her of duty and honour, and postpone the business of going home.

The graveyard was like a stage set of what a graveyard should be before dark: damp, lifeless, peculiarly verdant, even in winter. The black slate of memorial stones shone with the perspiration of damp. Isabel changed direction to amble down avenues of graves, fascinated by the grim tranquillity of this car park of the dead and the manner in which they were commemorated. No Mums and Dads here; all inscriptions conventional and respectful, but small control over violent pink granite, a headstone shaped like an aeroplane, a weeping angel holding a guitar. Something in the hedge caught her eye. Lurking beneath the holly was a phone. At first she thought it was a deliberate joke, part of the mementoes, a piece of wit left in case Grandad in the adjacent plot should wish to phone home when he was feeling better. Then she recognized the phone from the living room of their own ravaged house. Stuck with a label, an old phone, nothing newfangled about it, thrown into the hedge by a passing thief and looking forlorn. Isabel touched it, gingerly, left it where it was. Moved on to the graves of Mab and her father, quickly looking over her shoulder. Nothing; an innocent afternoon in the middle of the week when no one but she was visiting the avenues of the deceased.

Someone had improved on the tidiness of her father's grave. Sprigs of holly from the hedge sat in a tin on the neatened gravel, giving the thing a festive air; the letters of his name were free of the misty cobwebs that adorned Mab's less fulsome inscription. Isabel stared at the holly leaves, waxy and shiny, sharp. The holly bears a berry . . . as red as any blood . . . The lines of the Christmas carol stirring in her mind, making her want to hum the rest of the words she could never remember. Her father had a fine singing voice, she could recall the sound. He would sing at parties; once he had serenaded her on her eighteenth birthday in front of fifty guests and all she had felt was embarrassment. A strict and loving man, resented, ignored, adored; far too demonstrative for a teenager obsessed by masculinity of the more youthful kind, hellbent still on them and the approval of that distant, amused mother. Isabel had never credited him with his own personality: he was provider, ruler, more absent than present, loved madly on the first day he came home before his attempts to exert control made him irritating. Darling, distinguished Dad, a slippy kind of memory, perhaps because his wife never discussed him.

Isabel was saddened by her ignorance of him, puzzled and alarmed by the recent attentions to his grave. Someone had tended it before; she had known that and had failed to question it when she had given the same attention to Mab's miserable patch. There could be a sort of contract cleaning service for graves, as far as she knew, although it seemed a strange service to be provided by strangers. She no longer remembered what she had thought about the disparity before, other than it creating another notch on the guilt scale for not thinking about it at all.

Grazed nerves made for vivid imagery. Kneeling on the edge of Father's plinth, she could imagine a disembodied arm extending from Mab's grave, sticking up out of the earth, twisting and busily plucking at the weeds. Tidy, organized Mab, unable to tolerate mess for long. It was, after all, Mab who had rooted the family here; she may even have found them the house, or maybe they had dumped themselves so close because she had been vital to the arrangements. Isabel was surprised by how little she knew of any of this. How little she would ever know now. How strange and sad it was that it was her mother whom she had sought to emulate when, all the time, Mab was the one worth copying.

She stood up in sudden disgust. Maudlin, macabre and escapist. The dead were dead: they did not mutter in their graves. Nor talk to themselves, as she did, nor suffer the chattering teeth that afflicted her as she ran back to her car, flung herself inside for the flimsy protection it afforded, pitched the thing back up the track as if it were a jeep and the holes in the road did not matter.

A light appeared in the window of the neighbours who lived next to the church and faced the parking space. A curtain twitched. Look at the way she had parked her car, that girl; look at the way she drove it. She was just like her mother, both of them nutty as fruitcakes.

'What does she think she's doing?' Sal said to George. 'She took off like all hell was behind her. Seen a ghost or something? Only for a minute I thought she was about to come through the window. Like her mother nearly did the other year.'

'She wouldn't do that. Not normally.'

'You all right, George? Sure you don't want another bit of cake?'

She half wanted him to go, half to stay. Her old man had never been keen on George. It was a trifle embarrassing to have him stay so long, sit about talking as if he were waiting for something. He was nice enough, always had been, but awkward company. Sal was puzzled, but since he seemed so ignorant of the burglary that had brought Isabel to the door, and then the police with questions about what she had not seen, he was less than rewarding.

'No thanks, Missus. It was lovely.'

'Look, there she is, Mrs Burley, being brought back home. That's three afternoons this week someone's taken her out and brought her back. Gets shorter each time, though. I'm glad someone does that. I don't think her daughter looks fit to look after her.'

225

'No,' said George. 'I'm not sure about that either.'

Sal was a mixture of window-hopping curiosity and a curious lack of observation, aided by hardness of hearing and the constant companionship of her television set. George often wondered why people who lived in the middle of woods and fields still found their greatest acquaintance with nature in wildlife programmes. As long as he had visited here, for post and cake, Sal had always been indoors, wore the pallor of a woman who never went for a walk.

'Don't you want to take the letters, George?'

'No, leave 'em. Nothing important, I'll be bound.'

She didn't question why he hid his car round the back instead of parking on the road. George was grateful for that.

'Going to snow,' said Sal, affecting a country wisdom learned from the weather forecast. 'You can tell by the sky.'

'I hope not,' George remarked.

Indeed he hoped not. He was becoming afraid of the cold.

Passing the church Andrew Cornell realized that he still had the habit of prayer, learned by rote early on and preserved entirely for addressing an amorphous and anonymous God on the subject of the weather. Such as, why are you allowing it to snow? Please don't. Offering some form of atonement to the deity if he would listen. Perhaps the deity realized that, although the blossoming skies and first flakes of white might curtail his errand of mercy as he made his way to Serena Burley's house with a television in the back of his car, the errand was not actually done from the purest of motives. What motivates a man to feel concern for a woman unless it be lust of a kind? No, it was not disinterested kindness. He simply did not like a day to pass without seeing Isabel's face. Even though she sent him away, denying his attempts to lighten the load, even though that face was as pinched as a shrivelled berry, the rest of her as spare as a winter twig, and what she exuded was a bitter sap. He wanted to help because he wanted at least a sight of the girl he thought he could perceive beyond the smothering blanket of her responsibilities. No, he conceded, it was not selfless; otherwise he would not also want her to look back and see him.

The snow was light and damp, uncertain snow, the same as the last week of purgatorial English weather, teasing with bitter cold, daring a citizen to go about his business. The solace of these days for children was the prospect of Christmas; for Andrew, long conversations with his father. What that man knew astounded and sometimes disturbed him. Made him realize that his own habit of secrecy was an inherited feature. We should have been spies, his father said. The things we have in common, son, are a matter of blood and cannot be avoided. Father was wise, in his way; a man to be trusted, enjoyed, but not always liked for his perspicacity.

There was the same form of greeting from Serena, ecstatic, fluttering, but fading into a fixed smile and a constant patting of his arm, as if to ensure he was solid flesh. A contrast to Isabel's greeting, friendly enough, relieved even, but not sufficient to make him feel his presence had been sorely missed. The television was produced, with magnetic effect on Serena. Andrew fixed it in the living room: cops and robbers blared from the screen, loud, dramatic music. He noticed a new fireguard around the fire, ash spreading on the replacement rug, dust on the mantelpiece. Serena sat, apparently content, blinking at the screen through unwashed glasses.

'Why didn't I think of replacing the telly?' Isabel asked, wrong-footed again. 'Should have done that first, shouldn't I? Why am I so stupid?'

Don't think about it, he murmured: I had one spare.

They took up independent residence in the kitchen. There had been a nursing chair by the fire he had admired before, now relegated to a corner. Crumbs on the table, dishes in the sink, the dog restive for attention. Isabel watched Andrew taking in the details, felt herself afflicted by a sense of inadequacy.

'It was my mother wrote those letters, you know,' she told him, not wasting time. She was beyond making polite conversation and this was the first thing she could think of, however irrelevant, to offer as an oblique excuse for the sloppiness that was evident all around her.

He shook his head. 'I don't think so.'

He no longer did. It no longer mattered. He wanted to tell her about Derek, ask her if this little man, last seen sweetly silent with a wired-up jaw in a hospital ward, resembled one of the burglars; wondered if the hint of revenge for the theft of objects to which she had been so clearly indifferent would make any difference to her desperate malaise. He decided not.

'I hate her,' Isabel said. 'That's what's making all this so difficult. I would be brave enough, competent enough, if I didn't have that at my back.'

He reached over the table and took her hand in his. There was a perceptible flinching, but she did not pull away, smiled at him briefly and apologetically.

'You could go,' he said. 'Just go. Someone would pick up the pieces; someone always does.'

'No. It may seem mad, but I can't just go.'

'Look,' he said, 'I can't help you if you won't let me.'

'You help a lot, Andrew. I don't know what we would have done . . .'

'Only it occurred to me that if you could perhaps see the woman she was, the one she used to be – and I don't mean a woman who might have written malicious letters when her mind was unhinged by the menopause – well, you might find it easier.' He was flustered.

She let her hand remain as was. 'What do you mean?'

'Discover what she was like. Go through her things. Try and remember what it was you loved about her. Look at her all over again. She was magnificent: my father says so, everyone says so, I knew so, so did you. If you're so determined to stay, you need . . . justification. If you haven't got a vocation, you either look after someone out of love, or a relic of that love. You can't do it without respecting her for something. Seeing something. Does that make sense?'

Not really, he could tell by her face, and even to his own ears his words were pretentious and silly. What could he know?

'Explore this house. I would,' he said softly. 'How closely have you really looked? Look for clues. Attics?'

She shook her head. 'Small. Empty.'

'Cellars?'

'Cold and cluttered. Things get shoved down there because it's easy.'

Something stirred in her even as she shrugged. The same curiosity that had stirred earlier in the day. The challenge of a task. Finding something more in the mother who had betrayed her, spat on her devotion, then and now. Looking for something that would justify the veneration for Mother which she had carried around for a lifetime. Looking for redemption for them both.

Andrew looked out of the window uneasily. The snow was falling thick and fast, hectic globs of white, fighting each other. Tomorrow was auction day: he could not afford to be marooned out here, although the thought was in other ways far from unpleasant. There were duties, as well as hopeless causes. She caught the direction of the glance, translated the anxiety.

'Oh damn. Is it settling? Look, you'd better go. Don't worry about us. We've got enough of everything.'

She wanted to say, come back soon. Talk to me about something else. Tell me about your father and the way we were, alleviate my inward-looking life by allowing me to listen to more than these footsteps. She liked him; inside the barrier which had erected itself, she liked him plenty, but there was no room for such a suggestion, because she could not feel herself worth liking. Silly and sullied; his attention made her less excited than afraid of what he saw and what he might find. A body which had currently lost possession of whatever it had been that passed for a purpose in life, or a soul. Not a lot to offer anyone. Which made it a mixture of sadness and relief to see him go.

The snow brought warmth, acted as a draught-excluder. She could feel the weight of it grow on the roof and gather round the windows, a shroud for her own abandonment. It lent a peculiar sense of safety; no burglars would begin to traverse this. The house would become anonymous beneath this blanket, so would she. Snow calmed the nerves, took away choices. It was easier to be this kind of prisoner when the snow fell with such gentle finality. Closing them in with greater inevitability than they did themselves, blurring everything except resolve.

Mother complied, snoozing in front of the fire, paper round her feet, head dropped on her chest, the television set chirping news of snow drifts before going on to drama of a less believable kind. Good.

Isabel went upstairs into the realm of her mother's bedroom, where she had rarely been except to check for excessive mess and lack of hygiene. On the whole Serena managed it well, changed her bed sheets with great ceremony and sufficient regularity, brought back down from there cups and ashtrays and most of the detritus she had taken in. Apart from barbed wire and such, Isabel reflected, but there had been nothing else beneath the mattress: one sly visit had ensured it. One must allow as much privacy as possible; the Alzheimer's leaflet said so. She was the guardian of the manor, not the owner of her mother's life, and she followed the advice.

There was a huge Victorian wardrobe, walnut-veneered, a piece of furniture successive generations had found invaluable, unfortunate, grotesque, useful, arrogantly space-wasting – large enough to house a small car – and finally magnificent but not yet a work of expensive art. Andrew's auction would sell it for more than it cost and less than it was worth, Isabel reflected with a smile of congratulation for new-found wisdom. But she was interested in the contents rather than the design. He would look at it from the opposite viewpoint. He thought she did not listen, but she did.

Inside, the level of organization was astounding. Isabel began at the lowest drawer. The first two revealed silk underwear, vests, chemises, nightdresses of uncertain age, folded

231

into creases that had become permanent. They were all scented with lavender bags, sprinkled with pot pourri which exploded against her nostrils with a stale, sweet smell. She remembered her mother's clothes, the finest kind, simple to the point of being stark, deep navy blue, cream, camel, black, enlivened with crimson, white, searing pink. No patterns, no flowers, no glitzy buttons, but a love of stripes to offset the effect of long, lean lines. Suits, tailored in Singapore, worn to perfection on that statuesque figure which went in and out in all the right places, legs reaching waist via dimply knees, the line from then on leading to a fine set of shoulders and a face of laughing splendour beneath a hat.

Hats were another thing. Hats for country and town. Hats of velour with crooked feathers. Delicious hats of yellow straw, trimmed with navy ribbon, fit for a garden party or a colonial lawn. A turban for a 1940s gown. In the hanging compartment of the friendly compactum were three evening dresses, shimmering, while on the other side there were three suits, suitable for all occasions. Heather tweed with pleated skirt, still fresh, smelling of mothballs, a swanky number in white and one in brilliant red, which Isabel recalled her wearing. The bottom compartment held shoes. There were labels on the drawers, such as 'Keep for further use', or, 'Coloured stockings to go with particular outfits' and, by the shoes, a reminder, 'More shoes in chest in cellar. Also his'.

Most of these clothes, and even the shoes, would not fit Serena now. She had thickened round the middle; her feet had broadened. She wore, on a regular basis, a medley of the same few things in various combinations. The daily decision about what to put on first took longer and longer, as if she were persuading these remaining serviceable clothes to aspire to the elegance of another age.

The dressing table revealed costume jewellery, again never worn now, but not extravagant. Large lapel pins, a dozen sets of earrings, diamanté, pearl – all paste. Plus another notice in smaller writing, 'The rest of this in chest in cellar'.

The cupboard by the bed contained a carrier bag full of old diaries and letters. The letters Isabel did not examine: the sight of letters made her shiver. The diaries she decided she must approach with caution. The pages were closely covered. A glance at one, fifteen years old, revealed nothing more than pages of reminders, businesslike records of obligations and appointments and that alone relieved the daughter who was beginning to feel like an intruder, although she had begun from the standpoint of considering her mother deserved no better.

Isabel sat on the floor and allowed herself the long delayed luxury of tears, which she had forbidden herself in the last few days, afraid that tears would be the beginning of falling apart. It was not the reminders of former glory that affected her so much, but the painstaking way in which it was categorized. There were salient reminders of another life more varied than any Isabel herself had known, but what was more impressive was the effort to keep it in order. Serena's memory must have been fading when she wrote these painstaking labels, trying to make an inventory of personal possessions before they, too, escaped into the fog. And for all that the tally was spartan. Serena was not a hoarder. She could have kept far more than this, written a dozen more labels, given more evidence of the spoiled life Isabel was convinced had been hers.

Isabel went downstairs to the cellar, led by Mother's writing. She did not check to see if Serena still dozed: the television sound was a reassuring murmur. Snow had began to gather outside the back door.

Her forays into the cellar had been minimal so far; the gloom of it had not attracted the spring-cleaning fervour that had so polished and improved the house. There were the stone shelves she had used to store food before Robert's visit with his family: that, as far as she was concerned, was the major use to which the cellar had been put in party-giving days. It had been the anteroom of parties, beer and wine kept in there, boxes for glasses, large dishes that had no use except when feeding a multitude. Serena's liking for cooking extended to highly decorated mass catering where attention to detail in the cooking was less important than the finished look of a buffet where food would only be snatched by chattering guests. In the first room, where a cobweb-clad bulb illuminated brick walls, there was nothing but junk: two boxes of Christmas decorations, the cheese press, empty bottles, curtains and old blankets otherwise used as floor covers for painters and decorators. Broken chairs. There was a door from the front cellar to a further room at the back. Not a secret place: the door was always open on account of being impossible to shut, but she had never ventured there where the light scarcely reached. Not for the sake of finding more rubbish.

The hinge creaked in protest. There was a small window, set into the base of the house, source of a sudden blast of air and giving a surprising and comforting illumination from the whitening world outside. Not enough to see much more than the dim outline of more broken objects. There was nothing that announced itself as a chest of belongings that would reveal either treasures or answers to God knows what. Isabel shoved a hand through her long, lank hair. It was corny being down in a cellar looking for something which those thorough burglars were unlikely to have missed.

She moved back to the relative familiarity of the first room, stirred the old painting clothes with her foot. Strange, she seemed to remember there had been more of these once, and they had been neatly folded. She had looked, in the early days, to see if there was anything worth retrieving. Some impulse of automatic tidiness made her pick one up and begin to fold it. The blanket smelled of turpentine. She halfway liked it down here. The cellar was not a sinister place: it was an extra pantry, no more nor less, full of clean, cold air, as if the damp that made the steps shine penetrated no further. The silence was soothing.

Something dropped from the blanket. Oblong, shiny, black. Familiar. A dictaphone. She bent to pick it up at the same moment that the door above her slammed shut. She froze. There was no preliminary to this sudden sound, no footsteps. Then only a slight hesitation before, one by one, the bolts went home and the light went out. Isabel raced up the slippery steps, skidded, fell, clawing at the walls, landed on her hip halfway up. Staring upwards, all she could see was the frame of the door outlined by the light from the kitchen. She scrambled up again, carefully this time, until she was behind the door, kicking it with one foot after another until both feet were sore. There was no sound whatever from the other side. Isabel felt an absurd desire to hit the wood with her head, instead pounded it with the heels of her hands. Silence. Not even a whisper of breath. Then the presence of the dog, snuffling round the doorframe, whimpering in protest, until, in a burst of sound so close it was shocking, there was music. Loud music, fit to drive away devils, big-band sound, inviting someone to dance.

'Mummy!' Isabel screamed. The scream became a wail. 'Mummy, Mummy, Mummy!'

George envied the warmth he could see through the windows. It was no fun camping in a car, sheltered and hidden in the furthest outhouse, but at least it was quiet. Couldn't go on indefinitely, though, not with this snow. The belfry of the church was better, so easily accessible it made him wonder why others did not use it all the time. It was where he would have retired later tonight, but the road was dangerous now.

There were many reasons he had given himself for watching as he did, none of them complete. Underlying them all was the pull of the place, like a hawser to a ship which strained to escape a harbour wall in uneasy seas. Then there was the fact that he must hide somewhere. Indifference to whether or not he had killed Derek did not stop him being terrified of the possible consequences, nor was the terror equal to the shame. Prison walls, crowds – he would rather die of cold first. Then there was her, the mistress of his celibate heart, whom he could not leave. Impossible to try, impossible to consider. She was in danger, poor lamb, far worse than his own. She was imprisoned by a girl who would hit her, abuse her, had done so already, the author of all her misfortunes, and his own.

Even George knew, as he painted lurid pictures of his own muddled motives, that there was something slightly wrong with the scenario: it was Isabel, after all, who had made some attempt to defend him and he was grudgingly grateful for that, but it was also she who blacked her mother's eye, looked at her with that weary contempt, pushed her about the house and threw her clothes in the fire. People were always locking their doors against the world when the danger really came from within. Serena looked so tranquil, asleep in her chair, so innocent.

But now what was she doing? Suddenly nimble, radio in one hand, appearing in the kitchen where he had seen Isabel descend the cellar steps, purposeful. Shifting the dog away from its station by the open cellar door by kicking it roughly, shutting the door, taking a breath, fastening the bolts. He could not hear, but he could feel the bolts, imagine the sound heard from below. Look, Mrs Burley, my lovely, he found himself saying, this is not quite fair. Very cold down that cellar. You might not like that child of yours, but it strikes me she's all you've got, and if you hurt her they'll take you away. She isn't so bad, is she? He heard himself pose the question about the hated Isabel and it shocked him. Perhaps it had been lurking there all the time, perhaps the cold had got into his bones, perhaps it was a sudden and complete empathy with someone, anyone, under lock and key. That was a terrible sensation: terrible.

The snow was gentler now, a steady fall of delicate flakes as he moved round the side of the house and stood a few feet distant from the site of the little cellar window, almost obscured even without snow. He willed Isabel to think of it. If he had managed to crawl in there, then she, lithe, agile thing she was, could manage to get out; he remembered the way her body could twist and turn. He stood, oblivious to the cold and his icy feet, which he had tried to keep dry, concentrating his mind, trying to influence hers. Lift the window towards you, he said, pull it out; it's rotted away from the wall. If you were a thief, you would know exactly what to do. There's a way out, silly girl, find it. Furtively, he ran there. Moved the snow, tugged, ran back.

The music faded away, along with shuffling, triumphant foot-steps, moving in time with a waltz. The dog remained against the door. Isabel could hear the animal breathe, fancied she might even feel the warmth of her if she sat with her back pressed against the wood. She tried, but the step was cold. The dog whimpered, and that was a comfort. Isabel put her head between her knees and wept for the mummy who was not there. She could have been ten years old all over again.

Mummy had left the frame of light around the door. Kind of her, so kind. For a minute Isabel almost succumbed to the same hysteria she recalled following the departure of the burglars, felt again that revolting sensation in the mouth, the helpless humiliation. She could sit in this cellar and laugh herself warm. No, this was incarceration, not violation. Survivors choose survival, Mab had said, until they have no choice.

She was standing now, with her arms across her chest. She could feel her knuckles supporting her bosom. She took her pulse; too fast but getting slower. A sign of recovery. But I am a damaged bird, trapped in a cage. Not bird as in bimbo, bird as in dark-feathered crow, with wings, and beak, capable of survival. Why does she do this to me?

Only the curious survive, said Mab. Isabel touched the wall surrounding the door. At this level, it felt dusty, but not chill. Perhaps it was here George had spent a night, or more, whispering to the dog once he had slipped through the kitchen. The dog would stay there all night. She had never been kind enough to the dog, who had been her idea in the first place. Dogs took a long time to die, bitches longer.

How long would she take, in the absence of any surplus flesh? Why does she do this to me? It is nothing as simple as hatred.

There was greater warmth by the door, but it was still cold, with the whole weight of the house pressing down on top of her. No one would arrive in the morning. She would have to preserve enough energy to shout in the afternoon, or the evening, unless Mother relented. Which she would not. Isabel tried to talk to the dog; the response was anxious snuffling. Keep warm, then. Terror feeds on paralysis. Move.

The echo of the fading music remained in her mind; along with school dancing lessons – not the balletic kind but the enforced tuition in how to do the waltz, the quick-step and two Scottish dances, redundant now for most social occasions. Isabel descended the steps again. She put the dictaphone on a stone shelf, safely, and she could feel to pick up one of the decorating sheets and fling it round her shoulders like a stole. She remembered her mother's garments, silk stockings and all, as she moved across the cellar floor like a person on a very small, uneven dance floor, controlling a reluctant partner. Slow, slow, quick, slow, that was it; move aside, please. I am the most beautiful girl in the room. Isabel could remember an eightsome reel, the Gay Gordons and the Viennese waltz. Her mother would have danced them better, in better clothes. The air was cold against the skin. Why should she, generous soul as once was, do this to me? Amazing, she must have been, in her evening gowns.

The dancing grew more hectic, then slowed when the sweat hit her eyes. Blinking it away, Isabel realized that the darkness had been an illusion. The detritus stored was all dimly visible. Dancing was comfort; it had the effect of blocking thought and provoking it. There was light in this darkness. There was the window and George, not a man of stealth, might have used that rather than the door. Thought had acquired her mother's rhythms. Slow. quick, quick, quick.

Took her time, she did. Ages and ages until he saw her slithering out, black against the white, clutching at the ivy on the base of the wall, hands pink, her face a pale blur. George wanted to cheer, restrained himself, followed her as she stumbled back across the route he had already followed, her arms hugging herself. At that point he would not even have minded if she had seen him, but she was hellbent, noticing nothing, not even the footsteps already partially obscured but still visible. She was a brave brute, really.

He was several yards behind when she reached the kitchen door, peered though the window. Serena had gone to bed: the dog pawed at the inside of the door, for once barking madly. No good waiting there, my girl, neither of them can let you in. Isabel moved down the contours of the house, first invisible, then visible, punching the glass on the french windows with her fist wrapped inside her sweater; she was going to hurt herself getting through there. Big panes of glass, tinkling. He winced.

George had seen the burglar-alarm box on the wall and suddenly remembered it. The house might suddenly reverberate with sound, but it did not. She was, in a manner of speaking, safe inside, probably, if she had a thought left in her head, turning it off. He felt in an odd sense almost triumphant for her. That was a cruel thing to do, Mrs Burley, darling: you mustn't do it again.

Perhaps Isabel would go upstairs and hit the old dear. No,

he did not really think that, could not, somehow, imagine it. Hitting people came from heat; it was not something done by a body shivering with cold. There were lights in the kitchen now. She might let the dog out, and the dog might run towards him.

George went back to the car. The snow sighed into drifts and ceased to fall. The silence was the way he had once liked it.

CHAPTER THIRTEEN

It was the action of climbing back into the house, standing still in the sudden warmth and listening to her own heart-beat, which told Isabel the truth of the situation. The panic, the cathartic sound of breaking glass, the onset of pain which came with the heat from the dying fire, the contrast between life out there and life in here, the futility of scream-ing into silence, all revealed to her what she was in this house. In her mother's eyes she was, quite simply, an intruder, with no more business on the premises than any burglar. A burglar was preferable; a burglar had discernible, even admirable, motives. He simply wanted surplus things, things which were going begging. His needs were simple: it was the demands and expectations of a daughter that were outrageous. There was no particular dislike involved. Serena did not have love left for anyone who carried all those obli-gations of blood. She was not rationing it; it was not there to be rationed. There was no malice, simply a vacuum. Isabel had the utter calmness of the survivor, coupled with a crazy desire to laugh. If it were me apprehending an intruder, she thought, I might lock them out of the way, let them grow cold or hot, deal with the problem in the morning. If I remembered. But then, if I were mad, I might not remember; even less would I care who they were. I would not pity anyone who destroyed my peace and privacy.

My mother might have been locking out the nuisancy ghost of the cat.

It had been, in a fierce kind of way, sweet out there in the snow, which had sunk into her indoor clothes. Fear created its own perspective; the release of it brought a dizzying clarity of vision and the opposite of fear. When Isabel opened the back door for the dog, she nearly envied her brief, lazy, leg-raising interlude in the snow. Petal hesitated in the yard, sniffing, reluctant to return, but, as always, followed the stronger instinct: to obey shouted orders. A little like myself, Isabel told her, touching with still-cold fingers the warm ruffle at the back of her neck. Bum life for a bitch.

Finding herself on the brink of understanding was fine, but it made no difference to the next step. A reluctance to catch the train in the morning in order to get to a job she did not like did not alter the necessity of stepping aboard the carriage. Isabel the burglar went upstairs, as she was obliged to do, whatever Serena had done to her. Because it was necessary.

Do you love me, Mummy? No, of course not. Why on earth should you? But I loved you. I just didn't realize you had become the child, that's all. I was asking for the moon and no one owns that.

Serena slept, her profile lit by the bedside lamp with its

paper shade so browned and frayed by clumsy handling, the survival of it was miraculous. And how long was it since she had stopped using the right bulb, unable to differentiate between one hundred watt and sixty? The curved lines of the lampshade beams stood out like the veins in a wrist, the parchment was as pock-marked as Serena's brown-spotted skin; the two could have married into a colour scheme. White sheets, a face furrowed against the pillow, all of it sloping into the pristine cover, leaving on the one side a profile like a skull, under it the bulk of facial flesh. One hand was under the pillow, the other arm held the blanket close to her chest. In repose she was as beautiful as living daylight, the hair abundant curls of luxuriant grey. No rollers tonight. Her eyes were wet, blinked open and then closed again, the moisture making the pouched skin beneath shine like dusty leaves in rain. If there was any idea in her mind that she might have killed, humiliated, terrified this daughter of her flesh, there was no sign in this innocent sleep. There might have been no knowledge either. Isabel could not love this lump of body and skin, but neither could she hate it.

Her position looked less than comfortable, twisted somehow in slumber so that she sprawled all over the bed at an awkward angle which Isabel wanted to straighten up. She stopped herself. Mother, Serena, whatever this stranger was named, could sleep in whatever position she pleased until she met the undertaker. Or whatever God it was she may have worshipped. I do not know you, Ma, I do not know the first thing about you, not even the way you sleep.

Her right palm was extended over Serena's neck, fingers flexing, twitching. There was an instinct to strangle her mother, as well as to stroke. Place long, thin fingers on that fatty neck, feel free to slice into the folds over the larynx, end that life. She could have killed Serena for her single crime of not knowing how to love her.

Blood fell on to the pillow. Isabel's numb fingers were webbed with blood which hung in icicles from tiny lacerations not yet discovered, pumping indoors, frozen outside. For a whole minute, she let the blood drop on to her mother's forehead, where it lay like bright red pebbles before shifting into rivulets along the deep-set lines of her brow. Isabel regarded the blood with disinterested fascination. She sat by the side of the bed until some sense of survival made her raise her arms, reverse this flow. It was a strange way to pray, arms straining out of sockets like this. She linked her fingers, stretched; drops of blood fell on to her hair, mess, more mess.

Serena opened her eyes again, sightless blue. 'Please,' she murmured. 'Please. Let me go.'

The eyes closed slowly. Isabel sighed.

'Don't worry, darling. Love where you love. I know it isn't me. It isn't your fault you are what you are.' She leaned closer. 'And, by the way, George is here somewhere. He left you a message. Lots of love, get your rest.'

Her mother lay sleeping, bloodied. They did this, Isabel remembered, to the huntsman who has caught his first stag.

In the bathroom, treating the cuts to her hands and arms with shaky efficiency, Isabel could only feel enormous relief that the blood on her mother's forehead was not blood she had drawn. She trembled in the aftermath of that temptation.

In the morning, long before Serena awoke, Isabel found the chest in the cellar. Inside, there were two large teddy bears, plus three small parcels, tied in polythene with a dozen elastic bands each, making them difficult to open.

One contained earrings, the second her father's cufflinks and the third a ring from a cracker. Otherwise, there was nothing inside but paper.

'Thank God the snow's melted,' Andrew observed to his father. 'Fickle stuff.'

'It's just getting ready for the real thing, shouldn't wonder. Been playing about for a week. Wish I was God. In command of the weather.'

Doc Reilly nodded. On a morning like this they allowed themselves a little sherry, poured into smeared glasses taken from the display cabinet that flanked the rostrum in the chapel. An electric fire alleviated the cold of that part of the room. The rest of it was fairly empty. Buyers had collected their goods; compensation offered and accepted for breakages. There was little left except a few rugs: the place almost homely. In the town centre, Christmas decorations had appeared on lamp posts. The lights did not extend as far as this, although John had entered into the spirit of the thing by pinning tinsel round the rostrum. For the last auction before Christmas he might wear a Santa Claus hat, if they did not have to cancel, which seemed likely.

'How are you going to manage, John? You've got no one to hump the stuff.'

'Nope. Bob's worse than ever, I doubt he'll come back at all, his brother's pretty useless and Derek had that . . . accident. There's only my son and heir, and although he's wonderboy, he can't carry a wardrobe all on his own. Besides, he's got other things on his mind, haven't you, Andrew? Still, it's not the end of the world. We never take much, this time of year. They're all out there buying in crap as if there were no tomorrow.'

'Derek getting better, is he?' Doc Reilly asked.

'Far as I know. He isn't getting worse and he isn't dead, so he must be. Not saying much at the moment. That won't last. Silly bugger.'

'Very apposite, I must say, calling him that.' Doc Reilly's shoulders heaved with gentle mirth. Yes, they are a pair of conspirators, Andrew thought with affection. The liking was tinged with a healthy suspicion. They have a common cynicism: they know exactly what they're talking about, so much so that they keep what they know from one another and admit it at the same time. The best form of communication was hints, winks and silences. Canny rather than crooked.

'Well,' said Doc Reilly, heaving himself upright and looking at Andrew expectantly, 'as the elder statesmen of this parish, what are we going to do about it? I mean, do you want us to tell Isabel?'

'Tell her what?'

'Oh Christ, she don't know the half of it. I bet she doesn't know whose act to follow now. She's got her aunty's common sense, her mother's looks and her father's sensitivity. They all loved her, after their fashion, but it was Mab who was the control-freak. Ruled that bloody household whether she was in it or not. I don't know what happened before they came to live here, I can't guess, but she'd already done a good job undermining Serena's authority. Edward Burley would always listen to her first. She even dictated where everything went. No wonder Serena enjoyed having the place to herself these last years.'

'Is that so?' Andrew murmured. He felt vaguely uncomfortable talking about it, although he wanted them to go on.

'I can see Mabel, now,' his father said, dreamily. 'She knew she was dying a long time before she let on to anyone

247

else. You told me that, didn't you, Doc? She knew for more than a year. She was well capable of doing a bit of dividing and conquering before she went. A great letter-writer. She could have made sure her niece didn't marry too young, she always disapproved of that. Also made sure she got out from under by giving her money. Mab was good at arranging lives she couldn't own. Only she would never do it by a direct route.'

'This could be nonsense,' Andrew said.

'Of course it could be. It's nothing more than pure, bloody-minded speculation,' Doc Reilly replied. 'It comes from me, John here, my wife and a couple of patients. But that's the best we've got.'

'None of this helps the present,' Andrew remarked.

'Nope,' the doctor agreed. 'Nothing does.'

'What's happened to that poor bastard George?' John Cornell asked.

'No one knows. He didn't return to the nick as ordered. They're looking for him.'

'And will those burglars really go back?' Andrew wondered.

'There's no telling.' John was looking at his feet. 'Well, two of them might. Not in this weather. And if they do, they'll trip over an alarm.'

They would not trip over an alarm. Not even a man trap. The alarm was an exercise in uselessness, unless the house was empty. Robert's promise of security, augmented by the mobile phone in Isabel's room. There was no point turning it on at night unless Serena was locked in her room, and that was impossible to contemplate. Because there was a connection between switching the switch and the arrival of two policemen after ten minutes, she was, intermittently, fascinated by it, although it was something which faded in and out.

'Come away from there, Mummy. See what I've got.'

Isabel was sure that what she had would please, she was learning fast. The teddy bears had been greeted with pleasure, the Christmas decorations seemed to have the effect of making Serena imagine there was going to be another party. They spilled out on the kitchen table, dusty and dated and varied, the nicer rubbish from the cellar. Would there were more of them, since Serena clearly found them both curious and delightful. Dust did not bother her. Tinsel could furnish a room. The decorations made her tranquil and had taken hours out of the day since their discovery. Serena chose one golden foil device to hang against a window frame, took it to the living room, placed it with enormous care, changed her mind, tried another, with all the consultative care of an interior designer. Isabel was similarly tranquil; it could even be said they were cheerful together: there was an element of both resignation and courtesy about them both. Isabel had taken her behaviour right back to the beginning. Or near the beginning, when she had first begun to comprehend the need for alternative language. She cooed at Mother as she might at any frustrated child. She cajoled rather than ordered. She reversed the flow of Serena's chatter by chattering herself, not incessantly, but frequently. Serena kept touching her arm.

'Now look, Mummy. I did tell you about that switch, didn't I? Naughty switch. I know it brings out the fellas, but they won't be pleased to see you. And there's another reason. I've got the feeling Georgie is out there looking for you. If he wants to come in, even though those nice policemen say he mustn't, that's OK by you, isn't it? We don't want to set bells ringing, do we now?'

She must have repeated the words a dozen times. Some of them might sink in, especially in this mood; most of the words were true. Mother could somehow tell when she was being told a lie. Whatever she received by way of wisdom was filtered through an imperceptible net. The whole difference in approach came from the release of the need to be loved by this childlike lady who only happened to be her mother. If she treated her like a robust but delicate stranger who needed care, it was all so much easier. She was not a daughter any more: she was simply someone with a fierce sense of responsibility for someone who was helpless. There were two of them in need, after all. Who loves you, darling, if not me? One needed to give, the other to take. It was a neat, workable equation.

Isabel was not entirely sure how this conclusion had come into mind. It had percolated for a while, she supposed. Solidified when she remembered herself standing in the chill of the cellar fumbling round in the dark with that dictaphone. George knew about love and how simple it should be: he had even recorded it.

'I love you, Serena B. Whatever happens to me, I'll always be that way. I hope you find this. It's for remembering words with.'

A few weeks before Isabel would have been insanely jealous of George, indeed had been. For knowing her mother better than she ever would and meaning so much more. It did not matter where he came from and what he might have done. He had the password to her mother's affection and that was all that mattered. He was a good man in his own way, capable of mistakes, possibly violence. That gave him and Isabel something in common, she thought wryly. And if Mother was going to screw up her life, had done, would continue to, she did not see why George should be put on the same bonfire.

'I like this green tinsel best, don't you, Mummy? But I like the glass balls best of all.'

'Balls! Oh very funny,' Serena giggled like a girl who has just discovered how funny the word bottom is.

'Not those kind of balls, Mummy. Honestly not.'

Glass baubles, light as air, turquoise, silver and blue, to be dusted and handled with care. Isabel's mind went blank at the prospect of Christmas, apart from a calm conviction that she would still be here, but not for much longer afterwards. She would do what she could, but nothing was definite.

'What did you do with these, Mummy darling? Hang them on a tree?'

Serena was not able to tell her how the house had once been decorated. Isabel, who had avoided Christmas like the plague, could scarcely remember. The day itself had always featured Mab, she recalled; Mab had also starred in the preparations, doing the boring bits Mother loathed.

The radio played softly, not bothering either of them. Twigs painted white, that was what Mab did, she had whitened or silvered winter twigs, fixed them in chicken-wire inside a huge silver vase, hung the turquoise, silver and blue baubles from them and placed them above the fireplace. Serena had always wanted more colour than this conservative arrangement, but Mab's taste prevailed. The thought filled Isabel with curious unease, and yet the idea appealed. Mother's preference now was a series of fat little Santa Clauses, highly coloured plastic, suspended on frayed

251

scarlet ribbon. Things from the market, plastic flowers, bright and artificial. Who cared about taste?

The sky was the pink of optimism when she went out into the garden on one of the most peaceful afternoons of her life. She was not a daughter any more, she had no allegiances, no rights, but there were aspects of the place she loved. The colours of it, the determined grandeur that stood proud over the desecrations of time and neglect. There were ghosts on the tennis court, cavorting among the moss. The lumpy lawns, which she had earlier regarded as a shame, retained the right to be a lawn, but only just, while the kitchen garden had long since relinquished identity. The orchard where she had walked with her nephew. She was not really out here to collect twigs; she was walking in a widening circle with open eyes. Wondering where poor, daft George was and how cold he must be. He might have lived for her mother; she did not want him to die for her. The dog went ahead, found the car in the last outhouse, scarce big enough for a car and certainly not designed for anything better than pigs. He must have pulled the rotten door across, leaving enough space to enter and exit. There was a residual warmth about the place, a smell of exhaust fumes, but of himself no sign. Isabel found a clean tissue in her pocket along with a Biro, and wrote, 'Come in the house, G, Serena needs you. Love, Petal.'

Words were everything, they were all a person needed to get on in life. He might not come because he was cold: he would come if he were needed. He must have watched them long enough to know all other visitors were temporary. He might be watching now. Watching her usher the dog away home, the dog taking two steps forward and one back, yelping the way it did so rarely and only then for those worth affection. The pink sky had turned grey. No red sky at night, to be shepherds' delight. There had been red in the morning, shepherds' warning. The day had begun as it died, ominously cheerful.

She wanted to tell Andrew all this, because her clarity of vision now cast him on the side of the allies, and, even if he were not, then in all likelihood he would do as she asked. It was not much to ask. Since he was likely to arrive anyway, on one of those carefully contrived errands that so often coincided with early evening, Isabel felt she did not have much choice. Depending on which of them arrived first. There was no master plan about any of this: she was not a planner. It seemed important to follow instinct, like the dog did a scent. That was the only thing the dog was good for.

Inside, it was warm again. Colourful with the tinsel, while Serena tinkered and one of them waited.

Do what you like with my life for now, Ma, Isabel said. Not with George. She was hanging more tinsel over the drawing-room window where the snow had drifted in and Isabel had done her best with damaged hands and cardboard. They were somehow, waiting on those damn fish and chips.

Isabel noted, with some satisfaction, the dog nuzzling round the cellar door. Seven o'clock, dark as midnight, and the snow had begun to fall again. Serena came back into the kitchen, took up a knife, looked at it quizzically, and began to peel a potato.

'Too cold,' she said. Isabel laughed. 'Yes, and when it's cooked it'll be too hot.'

'Who else is coming? People?'

'I don't know.'

Serena's face puckered.

'Now, now, sweetheart. No feet stamping, please. Be a good girl.'

Serena wandered away into the pantry, looking for something more interesting than the potato. It had all been sweetness and light and now she was bored. Isabel's thoughts drifted, hung between anxiety and a strange contentment. She hardly noticed her mother sidling out of the kitchen, back to her fireside, did not mind. Serena in the vicinity of the kitchen sink was more hindrance than help. The dog at the cellar door grew more agitated, looked at Isabel in dumb appeal, pacing around her legs, telling her something.

'Yes,' she said. 'I know, yes. In a minute. These things take time.'

She went to the pantry for the frozen fish, wishing there was more than frozen vegetables. Maybe a cheese sauce would do something for tasteless cauliflower.

Serena appeared at her elbow, giggling. She had moved so quietly all day, the result of slippers rather than boots.

'You know what I've done?'

'Stabbed a spud?'

'No. I turned on that thing. People coming. Soon, I think.' Serena grinned with enormous satisfaction. For a moment Isabel was back to wanting to hit her, then she shook her head in furious amazement at what this wandering, wavering, determined intelligence could achieve. Serena was in search of a party, therefore switch the alarm on and call the police, simple. It took ten minutes, driving at speed. They were already looking for George; they would be here any time now. She opened the back door and heard, sure enough, the distant whine of an engine.

254

'Mother, you're an idiot. Go and put your hat on.'

If there had not been the question of that poor simple-minded fugitive down in the cellar, Isabel might have seen how farcical it was. There was time to wonder if the coal-house fire, which had been the spur for her coming here, had been merely the result of Mother's desire to attract large men to the premises. Lights appeared in the backyard. Serena was tidying her hair with busy fingers, watching though the window.

Isabel stepped quickly to the cellar door, the dog getting in the way. She called down urgently. 'George! Stay where you are, for God's sake. Don't go out. They'll go round the side. Stay where you are.'

As the first burly officer blinked in the light of the kitchen, Isabel was in the act of closing the cellar door behind her.

'Good heavens,' she said gaily. 'What are you doing here?'

Andrew appeared behind the third officer. He saw her raised eyebrows and shrugged.

'Coincidence,' he said. 'They overtook me. What goes on?'

They might have been less patient about the whole débâcle and their wasted time and the hazard to their vehicles bumping up this track if Isabel had not been such a pretty sight. Hand over mouth, fluttering eyelashes, enormous eyes wide with worry to have caused so much trouble.

Andrew watched what he could see was a performance. He wondered why it was she would not step away from the cellar door. Amazing to see a police officer simper. They searched the house anyway, just to be obliging. One walked around the outside of the building quickly, hugging himself against the snow which began again in earnest. They might have stayed longer but for the twittering of Serena as she followed them about, the obvious, delicately protested mistake and the fact there was, by now, a man in the house with a proprietorial gleam in his eye. They lingered in the kitchen long enough to warn the young lady that if George Craske should by any remote chance appear, she was not to let him in on any account.

She said, of course not. Wicked George Craske. Sorry about my mother's busy fingers.

George sat shrouded in the painting clothes, conscious of the smell cutting across the more unpleasant smell of his own body, bathed in the hot flush of sweat that had turned to ice on his skin. This was prison without the crowds; this was humiliation and despair; he had never felt weaker, or more profoundly ashamed. Tears dripped down his face; no sobbing, simply tears, turning to icicles on his chin. He could hear the reverberations of noise in the house: the sound of many feet, voices which he could not distinguish. He waited in misery for the light to shine on him, to discover him like a rat in a trap. Men to bundle him upstairs, banging his head against the crusted walls as they went, himself unable to fight, limp like a corpse.

When the silence fell, it covered him. There was nothing to do but wait and hope.

'What was all that about, Isabel?' Andrew asked.

She turned to him, put her arms around his waist and buried her head in his neck. Was this a performance too? Let it not be. He squeezed her gently; it was the body of a greyhound, slender and deceptively strong, the flesh warm. If she kissed him, he would know she was acting, but he would let himself be fooled. He was disappointed as well as relieved when she did not, simply remained closed against him until she sighed an enormous sigh into his shoulder.

'Go and keep Mother company, would you?' she asked, withdrawing from him, no longer the flirt. 'I've got to get George out of the cellar.'

He held her at arms' length, looked at her questioningly. It was a look which said, 'Do you know what you are doing?' but he did not accompany it with words. It was a satisfying thing to have her judgement unquestioned, a novel experience.

Serena was trying to attract Andrew's attention, pulling at his sleeve. The departure of all those lovely men had left her at a loose end. Andrew was the only one left.

'Come and see my decorations,' she demanded coyly.

'Of course,' Andrew said gravely. 'Delighted.'

Isabel opened the cellar door, put on the light and got on with peeling potatoes. After counting she added several more and put on the radio, loud. She could see the snow falling outside the window, and wished she was making a more ambitious meal. Never mind, they could have candles. Give the place that party air Serena craved. No one would be going anywhere tonight.

George emerged into the warmth of the kitchen blinking like a mole. Shrivelled with cold and the more corrosive effect of anxiety, he stumbled in and smiled at her. A proper smile.

He was dirty and the smell of him overcame all other odours in the kitchen. Isabel considered the immediate offer of a bath, then decided that this was the kind of implied insult that would offend him. It could wait.

'Could you lift in that coal for the fire, George? Just outside the door. Thanks ever so.'

As if nothing had happened. She was the Janice, he the friend. Each to his proper place.

'Can't let the fire go out,' he said.

'Oh no. Never do that.'

He stood awkwardly, looking round the kitchen as if he had never seen it before, nodding with satisfaction. The dog stuck her nose into his crotch: he fondled her big head absently. Order had been restored in here. Isabel continued peeling potatoes.

'Is she all right then?'

'Yes, George, she's fine. Oh, you know. I lose my temper with her from time to time, but I've got better at it. The dog's been missing you as well.'

He nodded, easing slightly. He was not in a position to judge someone for loss of temper. Then his legs seemed to buckle and he sat abruptly on the edge of the table, arms folded across his chest, like a drunk pretending to be sober.

'Oh dear, George, take a chair. I don't think you're look-ing after yourself properly. Have some tea.'

She thrust it in front of him, along with biscuits, contin-ued with the supper so that she would not watch him eat chocolate-chip cookies with the same speed the dog ate dinner. He was temporarily restored, his complexion turning from yellow-white to pink. There were the dark marks of exhaustion beneath his eyes. The health was fair, she decided. George would last a long time out in the cold. Far longer than she would have done herself.

'Thanks,' he said.

'No bother, George. Sorry about all that row, earlier. Ma set the alarm off. Why are the police looking for you, George?'

He grunted. 'I beat up one of the burglars. May be that.'

'Oh, I see. You'd better stay here, then. They won't be back for a while.'

There was a comfortable silence.

'Do you know what, George, I think I'll poach this fish rather than fry it. What do you think?'

'Fry it.'

The dog's head on his knees was like a hot-water bottle.

'And I think I'll put some masking tape over that bloody alarm switch.'

'Good idea.'

Another pause. The sound of waltz music drifted down the corridor.

George cleared his throat. 'I used to come back and read to her at night, you know,' he volunteered. 'Sit on the bed and read to her. Nothing more than that. I wouldn't, you know. I mean, I couldn't.'

'Shame,' said Isabel.

'What do you mean, shame?'

'Shame you had to go home, you silly bugger. Shame about people talking. There's five bedrooms.'

'She'd tell me things. About her husband loving you and that sister of hers best. About places they'd been. Wonderful places. She didn't want to come back.' He looked down at the big-eyed dog, communicating with it. Isabel waited, heart aching with a dull remnant of the old, sad jealousy.

'Talking and dancing stopped her wanting to kill herself,' George added. 'She hated it, you know. Hated it like poison. Losing the words. I kept on taking away the knives and things. Perhaps I shouldn't have done. People should die, if they want.'

The fish sizzled in the pan. The smell of frying food made him salivate.

'You did everything for the best, George. That's what we all try to do, isn't it? Don't let her break your heart.'

She began to set the table. Four knives, four forks; he counted them slowly and audibly, suspicion dawning.

'There's Andrew as well, George. Don't worry about him. Now, will you go and tell them supper's nearly ready? You'll just have time for a wash. Trust me, OK?'

He did. It filled him with wonder.

CHAPTER FOURTEEN

Trust me.

Bob said it was utterly mad and Dick agreed, but the one was in pain, the other halfway loco, and both had taken the appropriate anaesthetic after going to see Derek in hospital.

There had not been any significant sympathy for Derek. Neither of them liked him all that much, at least not enough to feel desire for revenge on his behalf, but he was a horrible sight. Bob was the family man, so he took the grapes, a touching tribute for a fellow human being who was required to take sustenance through a straw. Dick remarked on the sensitivity of the gesture. Both of them looked the souls of concern as they crept towards his bed. A couple of concerned drinking companions. Nothing very much was said: they were merely inquiring after his health. From Derek's supine position they loomed over him, looking by turns avuncular, sinister and, finally, dangerous. In the sterility of the ward the blood and sweat smell of Dick, exaggerated by the heat, wafted towards Derek's busted nose like a lethal perfume. They promised to come back. He put up two fingers.

Purpose achieved, they were still shocked. Shocked into the fourth round of Carlsberg, which deadened pain nicely. This is the last chance, Dick said.

Last chance for what? Well, we aren't going to get as much as we should for the big lot, and I reckon that old bird must have some jewellery somewhere, stands to reason, doesn't it? And you want that clock. Doncha? And she's got a cellar. We never looked in the cellar. Booze for Christmas. We forgot those candlesticks.

He was right. Bob had dreamed of that grandfather clock in his waking hours, wanting something to measure the reaches of the night.

That was all, Dick said. Jewellery and the clock, nothing else heavy.

Why now? Bob asked, thinking how he might never work again.

Because Dick had a van that night, and if they waited until Derek was better he would not have a van, on account of a couple of days before Christmas he would be laid off, you bet.

You want the girl, Bob said, admiring the nerve.

No, I don't, plenty of girls and that one's too thin, believe me. Dick's jowled face was turned in the direction of the plump bums lining the bar.

Bob jeered. After a week, they'll have that house on a trigger. Bristling with alarms.

Na. They'll be feeling safe again. We could go anyway. Just to have a look.

What about the snow?

What about it?

*

It was a real party. Andrew remembered Serena and the fireworks, the way the sight of them had transformed her face with joy. Sensation was what she wanted, to wallow in it and forget her constant puzzlement. Lights, music, the distraction of sound and visual stimulation. Around the kitchen table, by candlelight, there was one interruption for the telephone. Robert Burley calling: was everything under control? In the background, he could hear jazz, male laughter, Serena's high-pitched giggle. In the foreground his sister sounding breathless.

'Who's there?' he wanted to know. Isabel almost mentioned George, bit her tongue in time and sounded carefree enough to worry Robert profoundly.

'Oh, just a couple of people. Mother's having a lovely time.' Mother, centre stage, not worrying about words, pulling faces towards the phone, making them laugh at her, enjoying it.

'Don't forget the alarm system.' Robert's answer to everything. Lock the trouble out.

'Never. Wouldn't dream of it.'

For a moment, she was sorry for him.

There was nothing to be kept at bay but the snow, which stopped and started, started and stopped. George decided he would regard this as his Christmas. Isabel, his friend Isabel, had already told him he could have Robert Burley's room for as long as he wanted. He had one task, she told him, one only. He must teach the dog to bark. She said this gravely. He was slow to see the joke, but when he did his laughter was cataclysmic. His face was shiny after a bath and his giggling was of the infectious kind, a neighing sound that was funny in itself, sparking unconscious mimicry. Isabel no longer minded that she had never made her mother laugh as he now did: that was someone else's privilege. Hers was to provide the fish and chips and pudding with tinned cream as if it was a feast.

It was a feast. Andrew had put coloured paper round the candlesticks; when the candles burned low, it caught alight. Brief flames. Shrieks, like a children's party. Food consumed with nothing left over for the dog.

No one asked George questions, but he told them about where he had lived. Andrew told George that perhaps they could talk about a job, when all the fuss had died down. George took that as a literal assurance that the fuss would die down, and in this semblance of family, holding Serena's hand beneath the table, there was nothing that was not possible. Andrew wondered at himself, offering work to a man with such a record, purely on the basis of his own and Isabel's judgement of a good heart. How spontaneous of him. Perhaps he was losing his respectability, growing to like rogues and act without analysis, like his father.

Then Serena said she wanted to dance. The wine that Andrew had produced along with the sherry had been consumed. George did not like it, took a little, Serena copied him, Isabel and Andrew drank the rest. There was not enough for excess, sufficient to oil the mood of loud relaxation. All of us against the world, and the world cannot get at us tonight. Nor any other night. Why not dance?

'How very old fashioned,' Isabel murmured. 'Like a 1950s film. Waltzing in front of the fire. Andrew, I don't know how to do it.'

'Slow, slow, quick, quick slow . . . Or is that a quick-step? Just shuffle.'

Serena had forgotten how to dance. She could manage a fairly rhythmic movement with energy, with George holding her at arms' length, as if they were dancing the tango. Which, in turn, they tried, like a quartet of clowns, with exaggerated, pouting faces and dramatic gestures. That made them weak with laughter, and they managed better when they moved to rock and roll. Anyone of any age could jig around to that. It was all deeply, gloriously silly. No one in that company was wider than the most foolish.

The hours blurred into bedtime. Serena faded first. George took her to bed. A little later, when she and Andrew went upstairs by common consent, they could hear his voice reading to her, and, later still, his movement from her room into the one that had been Robert's. George was an oddball, but a gentleman.

Andrew sat on the side of Isabel's bed. The rooms were no longer cold: the house seemed to have generated enough heat for an army.

'I haven't an ounce of passion in me,' Isabel said cheerfully.

'I could tell you a story,' he suggested. 'Or I could just lie beside you, quiet as a mouse.'

'That would be nice.' She yawned. 'I'm worried about George. One of these days he might realize that he isn't as important to her as she is to him. No one is.'

'It can wait. Am I important to you?'

'I don't know yet. You have to wait too.' She hesitated, trying to remember something, but she was slightly tipsy, on a range of sensations which included a novel feeling of calm which came from having done something right, entirely by accident.

'Tell me something,' she asked, sleepily, as she lay on the bed and pulled a blanket over her clothes. 'If you were to write a person a letter, would you use exclamation marks?'

He considered the question. 'Whatever for? I thought you only put them in to show that someone was shouting.'

'That's all right, then.'

At about four in the morning Serena left her room and went downstairs. The key for the door was easy to find and the alarm was silent. She looked at the snow, first from one window, then the next, shaking her head at the marvel. It had snowed on and off while they danced; something so comforting about the snow; in the morning it would be different. The living room still held its warmth; she hummed to herself and turned two brief pirouettes, which made her dizzy. She looked at the dictaphone in her hand, puzzled over it and threw it away. No energy, these young things, going to bed when there was so much else to do. Such as get out when the going was good. Quit when you were ahead.

Serena tried to write a message in the condensation on the window. It was going to say, Love you really, darlings, you don't need me, but the phrases were too complicated and her arms were tired. She managed to scrawl 'luck' before she forgot the import of the message or why she was trying to write anything. Did she mean 'lick' or 'fuck'? The snow outside was mesmerizingly white.

She had difficulty opening the back door, because of the unfamiliar key, but the sheer desire to paddle her feet in the white stuff prevailed. She liked the sound of her awkward footsteps over the yard. The fresh snow creaked beneath her feet.

The drive was unrecognizable, a carpet of white. She made for the gates, where the road dipped and the snow was deepest. It was all unutterably perfect, warm and welcoming as cotton wool. Then she lay down and listened to the silence.

She crossed one hand across her bosom and, with the other, conducted the music of the stars.

The van proceeded over the fields because there was no choice. This was an even worse example of insanity than either of the other two expeditions. It was imperative to go on because there was nowhere to turn. It had become an exercise in survival. They would not stop at the house, not for anything. They would simply use the gateway to try and get the vehicle round and then go back. Get out before they were really stuck. The taste in Bob's mouth was sour, stale beer. Regret that he, the leader, should have let himself be led. Dick said nothing about anything. He made muttering noises to the engine, words of encouragement which sounded more like threatening prayers. His breath smelt of anxiety. In between other noises, he whistled between his teeth.

There was less snow through the woods. Dick exhaled a sigh of relief. He turned into the gates and began to reverse back. The wheels spun, encountered an obstruction and the van bumped forward, violently, rocking them in their seats. Bob moaned: it felt as if he had been stabbed in the back. Dick gunned the engine, swearing. The wheels spun again and they bounced back. He wasn't a wimp like Derek; he was a good driver when he was desperate.

The ground floor of the house was illuminated like a Christmas tree. Worse than the town centre at five in the afternoon and far more welcoming, it beckoned all strangers.

Bob could see tinsel at the kitchen window. 'Fuck this for a game of monkeys,' he whispered. 'Get us out of here.'

'All right, all right, all right.'

Halfway through the woods Dick began to shake. Bob did not understand. It was easier going back. In the light of the moon, they could follow their own tracks. Dick shook like a man in the throes of delirium tremens. His teeth chattered as if they would break.

'Whassa matter?' Bob shouted. 'What now?'

'We hit something, Bob. I know we did.'

'Snow, you daft bastard, only snow.'

'No. A fox. Something. I felt it move.

'Fox? Dog? For Jesus' sake, stop crying, Dick. Whatever it was, we probably did them a favour.'

May God have mercy on her soul.

Robert Burley blustered. He had brought his son to the funeral, for the good of the boy's education and so that he himself would have a hand to hold on either side. Also because he feared there would not be enough of them to give the sensation of a crowd. He vowed to include in his will a clause in favour of cremation. That way, he would save his relatives from having to hang around in the cold. The thought of a funeral in summer did not enter his mind. The two did not go together. The old died in the winter.

Or they were murdered by neglect. Nothing much preyed upon his mind other than a dull sense of being thwarted by the lack of something tangible to blame for the whole sorry condition he was in. His mother had somehow out-witted them. Blackmail in death as well as life, a continuous process.

He wished, irreverently and again with a maddening sense of being beaten by a short head, that he had steered his mother's liver-spotted hand into making a will. He could even have done it without her: he could forge her signature well enough. He had always been able to. Anyone could copy her hand, cramped though it had become. Mab had taught her to write: Mab had taught them all.

Ashes to ashes. Half the insurance money, under the rules of intestacy when it should have been all of it, because the whole thing was Isabel's fault. There was not the same right in law to charge a person for negligent management of an adult as existed for a child. You could be imprisoned for being drunk in charge of a vehicle, but not for being drunk in charge of a demented old lady. His thoughts were a medley of angry colours, trying to find an outlet for the channel of molten sadness which filled his gut under his suit. Trying to turn it into rage when he knew there really was no room for anger.

He shoved himself in front of George and stood on Mab's grave without thinking. George had no business here. Robert regretted his action, but still he did it. He could not change. He felt betrayed. Quite a crowd, a respectable number for a funeral, including neighbours and friends he had never seen.

'Where were they,' Robert hissed to Isabel, 'when we needed them?' She did not move. Her imperturbability was another irritant.

'They were trying to manage their lives,' she said. 'Like you. Like I should have done. As people must.'

Isabel listened to the wind that buffeted the graveyard beneath a leaden sky. Whispered her own variation on the prayers. Goodbye, Serena, wish I'd known you and what made you tick. I'm not going to let you wreck me more than you already have. Do you hear me? Robert's son detached himself from his father, uncomfortable with the pressure on his own, small fingers. He moved to Isabel and put his hand in her pocket. She smiled at him and pulled a soon-this-will-be-over kind of face. He found a packet of forbidden bubble-gum nestling against the lining. The coat was not black like everyone else's. It was a brilliant red, Mab's favourite colour.

Mother, Isabel thought, what a monster you were to die in this fashion, simply to tar me with the brush of feckless-ness. You picked us up and dropped us, left us squirming in the mud, George and me. Extracting the last ounce of drama and guilt, the way you always could. You got the house full of men in uniforms again, didn't you? You wonderful old cow.

She winked at the boy to indicate it was OK to chew the gum with such loud concentration, and turned her head. He should not have been here as his father's prop. Weeping was a private business. She thought she would weep for ever and ever, until all the fluid was gone from under her skin. The sense of loss and unfinished business was a bottomless pit, a fountain of endless tears.

It was a short but convoluted route, Andrew said, between wishing someone dead and wishing against all wishes that they were still alive.

Back at the house (back at the ranch, as Robert's wife play-fully labelled it), Joan neglected the supervision of funeral meats. Easy-peasy, sausage rolls and stuff. Not a wicked woman, simply a shrewd one with a life to conduct. She was looking at how Rob and she could really dance the light fantastic here, even with only five years left on the lease. Tennis on the tennis court; chairperson of local committees; devotee of local causes, homeless kids from town staring at Laura Ashley curtains.

She should have been a vicar's wife was Andrew's unspoken verdict. One of those people who believed there was nothing which could not be fixed. But she was right. The house needed children. The nice old punchbag dog was the first part of the furniture. People died so that others might be able to live. In the style to which they wished to become accustomed. Robert said she was cynical; pregnancy always brought about an advanced stage of pragmatism, Isabel said looking through a smeared window pane, good luck, get on with it.

'Where do you live, Isabel?' John Cornell always wanted details. Even when mashing a sausage roll between stubby fingers and carrying a large whisky. Always suss out the opposition when they look weak. He found it difficult to imagine why any youth, his own son included, found this pale and puffy-faced, big-eyed girl such a hot item.

'A flat. In a block.' Isabel seemed to have difficulty in placing it, put a hand to her brow and laughed uncertainly. 'Caretaker and carpets, all that stuff. He's probably installed his relatives by now. You know what families are,' she added.

'It'll only be a bit dusty, I expect,' said Doc Reilly, kindly, kneading the toe of a well-worn shoe against the dustless boards of the drawing room.

'It wasn't pristine before. There was blood on the walls when I left.'

That mystified him.

There was less dust than she would have expected, but then Isabel could scarcely remember how long it was she'd been away and how little she'd thought of her home in the meantime. An apartment, like she told the good doctor, in a block, with a view of the sky and security provided by a caretaker aided by electronics. Autumn when she had left, winter now. Washing lay fusty in the machine, the windows were grimy and the air was stale. She looked with disinterest into the cupboards full of clothes and hung up her bright red funeral coat. Flung her single suitcase to the back and began to clean.

In the life that had preceded the departure, the silence would have unnerved her. She would have left the dirt and flung herself at the telephone, worked her way through every contact in her black book, looking for attention. Now she liked it. The prospect of a quiet phone was not frightening.

Six-thirty in the evening, the ideal time for a man to call upon his mistress, even if she had sent him a letter kissing him goodbye.

Nothing new in that. Isabel enjoyed the occasional tantrum. Joe knew that as well as he knew how she could be twisted into compliance, like any woman without much will of her own. All that fiery passion turning into sweetness, the contrasts he loved, even when they hurt. He stood at the door armed with a bottle of wine and a bunch of roses. Clichéd, he thought, but foolproof. Rang the bell and yodelled her name. The door opened on a long safety chain.

He proffered the roses and the wine in their unromantic carrier bag, puckered his mouth into a kiss. A hand reddened with housework stretched through the doorway, plucked the bag from his fingers and retreated. The door slammed in his face.

'I love you, Isabel!' he shouted.

She could hear the exclamation mark. Tough luck, boy, I'm busy learning how to like myself. Somebody's got to do it.

She looked at the label on the bottle. Not bad.

*

Andrew arrived in the new year. The city streets were covered in slush and the January sales clogged the pavements. It confirmed what had been formulating in his mind. For all his years of discontent he enjoyed the lack of anonymity in small-town life. He would never want to hide away in the wider streets of a metropolis, even if he felt at ease in Isabel's flat with modern furniture he would never have chosen. But he knew he would never persuade her back unless she wanted to go. There was nothing tentative about her greeting or her smile; nothing much of the flirt, either. He looked at her expressive face and her gestures, searching for clues to what she might become. Never a writer of letters.

There was news he could impart and news he could not. No, no burglars found and no clues. Yes, George was as well as could be expected, using muscle to shift furniture, caretaking for Andrew's father, with whom he got on surprisingly well, by the use of very few words. An interim arrangement; something better would turn up. Andrew had corresponded with Robert, without success, about George keeping the dog. Furious letters, in a desperately familiar hand. Andrew did not mention that. There seemed little enough point.

Isabel had taken the silver candlesticks and that was all. They suited a glass table as well as they had suited polished wood. She had found beeswax candles, looking like sticks of honeycomb and smelling sweet. The room was soft with the scent of affection, understated and unmistakable.

If he were the someone to love, it would have to be on her own terms. There would be no dynasty. Let the body howl for that fulfilment. There were a number of things she was going to be and do before she was at risk of losing her mind, but there was one negative. She was brave enough and strong enough to vow it now.

She was never, ever, going to be some child's mother.